# REFLECTION

REFLECTION

# Also By Brad Mathews

**Thousand Branches Series**
The Thousand Branches
The Venom Storm
The Satyr of Fulton Manor
Tomb of the Phoenix

**Era Sinistra Trilogy**
Era Sinistra
Era Sinistra-The Shadow
Era Sinistra-Skyglow

Decay
The Girl from South Track
**Revelation Trilogy**
Revelation (Book 1)
Reflection (Book 2)

# REFLECTION

REVELATION
BOOK 2

BRAD MATHEWS

Unity Star Books

Published by Unity Star Books



ISBN: 978-1-962577-08-3 (Softcover)

ISBN: 978-1-962577-09-0 (Hardcover)

ISBN: 978-1-962577-11-3 (Ebook)

First Edition

Dedicated to all the construction personnel I've worked with, from design, to labor, to managers, and everyone in between. We are united.

Darkness cannot drive out darkness: only light can do that.
Hate cannot drive out hate: only love can do that.

Dr. Martin Luther King, Jr.

# Contents


The Laws of Interdimensional Time Travel XIII

1. Aegean Gods 1
2. Voice of the Swan 7
3. Eidolon City 17
4. Ouroboros Network 29
5. Gorgon Deep 39
6. Here Be Dragons 47
7. Pythagorean Secrets 57
8. Strix Talons 65
9. Aphelion Shadow 75
10. Guardian Sphinxes 83
11. Heiress to Circe 91
12. Ode to the Daemons 101
13. Paradoxos 111
14. The Journey of Orpheus 121

15. Hands of the Hecatoncheires 129
16. Eurydice in Chains 137
17. Shades at the Lethe 145
18. The Asphodel Dead 155
19. Cerberus and the Song 163
20. Dreams Beneath the Elm 173
21. Finding the Minotaur 183
22. Tears of the Heliades 193
23. Algea Metempsychosis 203
24. Phlegethon Desire 211
25. Water for the Danaïdes 221
26. Arachne's Tapestry 231
27. Prison of the Titans 241
28. Cryptid Palace 249
29. The Wrath of Echidna 259
30. Titan Uprising 269
31. Revenge 277
32. Euclidean Sorrow 287
33. Titan vs Titan 293
34. Elysian Fields 305
35. Gaia's Earth 313
Glossary 321
Acknowledgements 323

About the Author 325

# The Laws of Interdimensional Time Travel

(As described in this series)

1. Memory cannot work in reverse. You cannot remember events from a future dimension and your reality belongs only to you.

2. When you travel to another dimension of time, you disappear from your current dimension and replace your future self in the new dimension.

3. If you die in a different dimension of time, you cannot exist in any of them.

# I

# Aegean Gods

The floor vibrates as if Ian were dancing to whatever passes for music these days. Rolling her eyes, Becky flips through the pages of the book she is reading, a nonverbal cue that I should go check on whatever our son is doing. In protest, I cross my arms across my midsection before rising to my feet. My muscles ache and my joints pop.

As I pass the window I see the summer sun beating against the glass, bathing Harrisburg in an orange glow. Our home populates a plot in an average neighborhood near the outskirts of the downtown area, a humble locale dotted with historic houses interspersed with aging buildings from a period of infill several decades ago. Should I have the means and the time, I could upgrade the windows and furnace.

The horizon seems to flash as the window's view passes behind me. I pause in one spot, turn on the balls of my feet, and gaze skyward. High overhead, where the moon cuts a thumbnail-shaped hole in the darker region of the sky, the Big Dipper twinkles. My stomach pangs with an unknown regret, as though ancient history were speaking runes to my very soul. The resultant uptick in my heartbeat rattles my ribcage, causing a knot to press into my abdomen.

My eyes narrow as I near the end of the hallway. Ian normally keeps his door shut when he's playing his video games; the console is one of those virtual movement arrangements that, when paired with a set of virtual reality goggles, can make it feel that the player actually *is* battling an array of mythical prehistoric creatures.

I knock before swinging the door open, and Ian's movement ceases. As if incorrectly locating the door, he spins to face the window and cranes his neck. The way he tries to pay sudden attention while wearing the goggles looks endearingly ridiculous and causes me to smile.

In my line of work, I see VR goggles often. Project Managers don them whilst navigating the three-dimensional building models produced by architects and Building Information Modeling detailers. Customers and architects share their vision with virtual renderings, which they can pan around and zoom into to see any part of the building with perfect, detailed clarity. I have even seen a team of surveyors carrying around a tripod to laser scan interior areas, so that an assistant can then stitch the many images together to map the interior space in real time and virtual space.

Back when I got into the construction trade, VR was still niche, and crews built projects the old-fashioned way—with physical prints rolled up and stacked on a tilted plan table so that the work supervisors could review project requirements and direct their personnel accordingly.

Ian swallows. Without taking off his goggles, he remains facing the window, waiting for me to speak.

"It's time for bed," I say. "Take those off and get into your pajamas."

Hearing my voice, he turns about twenty degrees but faces the bookcase instead of me.

"Mom said I could stay up," he says, clutching at the elastic band holding the goggles to his face.

"Did she? That's not what she just told me."

"Maybe she's lying."

I frown. "Do you really want to tug at that string?"

Frustrated, he pulls off the goggles and dangles them at his side. An outline of red encircles his eyes and crosses his forehead just above the brows, a sign he's been wearing the goggles for what may have been hours. If I were a self-described good parent, I would have confronted him over an hour ago and helped him to read the biggest words in the book he'd chosen from the shelf.

In the moments where he's visibly trying to concoct a good excuse to stay up, I survey his room. Toys big and small have spilled out of the closet, creating a minefield of sharp plastic edges and rubber tires, some hiding behind piles of haplessly strewn clothes. His bedsheets lie knotted into an enormous ball at the corner of the room, above which the shelves display memories and passionate interests.

"I'll just finish this one part," he says, holding up his goggles.

My attention has shifted from him to the mess. I scan it further while a headache builds in my brain. His sketch pad and colored pencils, which he uses to draw whatever interests him, lie dogeared beneath a stack of aging homework sheets bleeding red. Missed homework—that might explain his subpar grades last semester.

I reach down and pick up the entire stack to brandish it at him with disgust. My frown grows deeper when the sketchpad book flops open, allowing a trio of pencils to cascade to the floor. I disregard the fallen pencils and study the drawings that take up the page.

Black wings scour a smoky skyline above a city that resembles Philadelphia, while a sooty fog dominates far away beneath the moon. About a dozen light squares in the high rises glow red and emit flames. He's only ten, but his attention to detail is stunning. His imagination can get out of control; I figure he may have a future in the creative arts.

"What's this?" I ask.

"What does it look like?"

"It looks like you have a wild imagination. If you'd keep practicing, you could go to graphic design school like you've always dreamed about."

He puffs out his chest. "It's not practice. Look, there's even a date."

He points out a series of numbers hidden along the talons of an enormous creature. September 16, 2033—next week.

"Prophecy? Have you been calling nine-hundred numbers?"

He looks confused. "What are nine-hundred numbers?"

I don't have time to explain. Instead, I exhale and close the book.

"That's what happened," he pleads. "You remember it, too, don't you?"

Rolling my eyes, I decide to play along. "Of course I do. Put the game away and get into bed. Don't make your mother come up here."

"She's just going to tell me I can stay up. I'll make you a bet."

"Five dollars." I put my hand in my pocket to reach for my wallet, knowing I haven't carried cash in over a decade. "See you in ten minutes."

Over the years, stretching and foot traffic have torn a rip in the carpet that I often trip over. I carefully sidestep it as I back out of the room. Replacing the carpet is another expensive project I don't have time for, and Becky insists we don't need to call a contractor because I know what I'm doing.

Sighing, I shut his door behind me and tiptoe back through the hallway, pausing at the second-story window. In the several minutes I've spent in Ian's room, the sun has inched lower beyond the horizon and the orange hues have shifted to reds and cooler blues.

I allow myself several moments to gaze out at it.

*Ride the storm.*

It comes as a thundering voice in my head, but quite unlike the wispy remnants of decaying thoughts.

The sea lashes below. We're standing atop a ledge overlooking it all. A pile of boulders breaks the waves, and then night replaces everything. The glow of fires fills an empty cavern, and bones are scattered in all directions. The tide roars within my brain, rising to a chaos so deep that pain shoots through my temples like rivers of flaming acid.

My heart hammers in my chest and my forehead erupts with sweat. I clutch at the windowsill to steady myself as the scene stretches away, farther than my imagination can render. Suddenly I face the landscape alone. Lightning flashes in the sky, and agony pours through my bones. My eyes arch downward and my lips quiver with terror.

The landscape transforms into a ruined city before my eyes: Broken skyscrapers lie in heaps amid the destroyed streets of Philadelphia, and the fog rolls toward embers of flame while the black, winged monster, the dreaded Typhon, rains chaos onto the city.

It disappears in a flash. I prod at my forehead to ease the pain away.

Stumbling down the stairs in disbelief, I shield my face so that Becky cannot see my expression if she looks up from her book.

"Did you tell him to shut off the game?"

I can hear the pain rattling in my voice. "He says you told him he could stay up. Made a bet. Please don't tell me I'm out five bucks."

She sighs. "Relax. It's not like the fires of the underworld are coming to swallow up your life."

"What the hell are you reading?"

She pauses, and I catch a brief glimpse of her expression. No surprise lurks within it. Assuming she doesn't realize he's missed homework, I let it pass and focus on the strange sentence she's just uttered.

But it does something different to me.

I bite my tongue, tiptoe into the kitchen, and wait for Becky to climb the stairs. Perhaps a glass of water will drain away the fanciful visions. Still, they are etched into my mind so firmly that they can't be premonitions or the product of an imagination seeking avenues to release a creative spark.

The pain in my forehead confirms it—the apparitions in the window are memories of events I have never experienced.

*Ride the storm.*

*You know how to find me.*

If Ian 'remembers' it too, or hears the same musings out of the dark, we will have problems. The apocalypse is on our doorstep. I dare not step out into the carnage.

# 2

# Voice of the Swan

"*You know how to find me?* What's that supposed to mean?" Becky folds her arms across her stomach while straining to appear somewhat less agitated.

"No idea." I shrug and glance toward the window.

"What? You're not going to go looking for him, or whoever it is." Her eyes appear as daggers of obsidian, reflecting the diffuse light from the lampshade. At any other time it might have made her appear more affable, but now it just makes me nervous. I don't even realize that my muscles are twitching and my joints are stiff.

"Well—"

"Well? Jesus, Ker. Make up your mind."

"Of course not." I furrow my eyebrows and take a half shuffle-step away from her toward the raised marble bar top that separates our cozy dining area from our generous living room, on whose décor Becky has spent untold sums. All I know is that it's comfortable, at least when Becky isn't bombarding me with questions I don't know how to answer.

"Then maybe we should put on a movie. Do something besides think about it."

I let my eyes appear quizzical and slacken my palms at my side. "I mean, you *saw* the picture Ian drew. What does that tell you?"

"That's he's got more of you in him than me? You're the last one who should be dismissing his creativity."

A sigh escapes my lips. Instead of offering her another word, I tread barefoot over the soft carpet, grasp the remote, and collapse onto the couch. Normally she would take this as a concession, but I can feel her eyes burrowing into me even as I pretend not to notice.

The curse of memory, a term I had once coined, sticks in my head. The longer I relax, and the more I study its nuance, the more it applies. Some say memory is a virtue, and a sign of sharp thinking, but it has proven itself a double-edged sword more times than I can count. Somehow, the darkest images from my past lurk deep in my brain, threatening to dye my entire soul black.

Why should I remember things that have never happened, though? There's only one person in the world I trust to offer insight, and he lives in Philadelphia, where he spends an inordinate amount of time on the streets.

Does he even have a phone number? There's no way to contact him other than forgetting my present obligations and travelling there, just to find out I'm as crazy as ever. Maybe it's just rubbing off on Ian, or it actually is in his genes.

After several minutes scanning through streaming options and deciding nothing looks interesting, I chance a sideways look at Becky. She has picked up her book and started reading again, only her body language suggests she's faking it. Instead of taking in the words, she's fuming. Becky might show her frustration outwardly, but the real trouble comes when she's silent.

"What looks good to you?"

"Whatever you want."

Well, that does it. If I decide to watch my favorite film franchise for the fiftieth time, it might only make the situation worse—or it could somehow soothe her anger. Many men say they don't understand women, but understanding women should be far less complex than understanding Becky. Yet for better or worse, she still surprises me.

"I see."

She plops the book down on her lap.

"Do you, Kerry? Do you really see? Because you've been walking blind for the last six months. I don't know why, and I probably don't want to know, but there's clearly some new adventure you want in on—so go for it. Do whatever you want. It's not like we've committed to spend the rest of forever together or anything."

Ouch. There's pain, and then there's what she's dealing out.

"There's something you've never told me; I know it, you know it. But the only person who can determine when to tell me is you. Whenever you're ready—no pressure."

I don't have a clue what she's alluding to, but somehow the fault slams into my skull with the weight of a cement truck. Harley once described some problems with memory, and even provided a case study whereby he falsely described an accident victim's attire and asked if I agreed with him. If memory is both a blessing and a curse, logic might argue that it is subject both to success and failure.

I try to change the subject. "Maybe something Jane Eyre. You like her."

"Nice try, Ker," she says without peeling her eyes away from the book. "And her name's Charlotte Bronte."

"I meant *Pride and Prejudice* or something similar. You know, 'chick flick.'"

I crack my knuckles. The term 'chick flick' seems a subtle jab at the female persuasion to me, so I tend to avoid it, but Becky uses the term liberally. Sometimes an emotional escape comes best when she can latch onto the feelings of a heroine who knows what it's like to be her.

She rolls her eyes. "That's Jane *Austen.* You're such a man."

When she starts slinging compliments as attacks, I know she's infuriated. Still, as far as I know nothing has set her off, other than me trying to explain that I suddenly remember some things that I have no business remembering, insinuating that Ian is a part of it, and that I have heard a voice in my head exhorting me to find him.

It would be hilarious to any other woman, but not to Becky—because she knows me, inside and out. In fact, she knows me better than I know myself, as frightening as that may seem.

"Does *Pride and Prejudice* sound good, then? We can snuggle."

"You'll have to get me drunk first," she jokes.

"I can do that."

A bottle of chaparral from our first anniversary is gathering dust in the attic. We decided at first to save it for our tenth, but after a year or two the idea dissipated. Like the first anniversary cake topper it sounded romantic, but the way Becky described it, the vomiting didn't feel romantic at all. It turns out that, even frozen, year-old cake tastes like year-old cake, and everyone knows that even week-old cake is disgusting.

She's seen *Pride and Prejudice* at least fifty times, and despite me mentioning my love for classic fiction a time or two, I've never watched it or even read the book.

I select 'Play' on the television screen and she shakes her head, pushes the book onto the armrest, and settles her head on my shoulder.

Thirty minutes in, I could swear it's been hours. I utter a halfhearted joke and expect her to at least offer a half-syllable chuckle. Instead, I get nothing—she has fallen asleep before the real start of the action.

If I turn it off, she'll wake up and hound me for being insensitive. My only choice is to brave it.

By the hour mark, I'm only half-conscious. The movie has taken a dark turn, but then again, it's probably my imagination playing tricks on me.

Thunder claps in a dark, cavernous space, and I'm shuddering in the cold as an icy rain pelts my skin. The sky is a morose shade of dark blue, tinged with earth-toned flecks that rattle overhead.

Beside me stands Vanessa. Suddenly I can remember her; she breathes in deeply, expecting the worst as the tempest builds. The mausoleum extends outward beyond the limits of my perception as fluttering hues of orange batter at the air overhead. When she speaks, my eyes are flung open.

The movie's climax has arrived, and my heart is racing. Vanessa. She was there, in the flesh, and now she's gone. I should not remember her, but she's as much a part of my reality as Becky or the living room in which we are now sitting. My breath has grown short as Becky stirs.

*Bear the gift, Kerry. You've heard me before.*

What gift? I struggle to make sense of it. My mind has gone so far off the map that finding the strength to move or think is difficult, but the voice is familiar to me. I have heard it only once, when Becky and I toured the power plant and I lagged behind the group to admire the electrical work in a particular room.

Cygnus, the Swan.

Legend says that when the swan sings, someone is about to die. How can Cygnus even exist? I can't fathom the reality-stretching involved with such a truth, if indeed it's possible.

I swallow and allow myself a moment of self-pity. Becky will fly off the handle if I tell her about this. Again, Harley is the only man I trust.

When Becky awakens, the credits start to roll and I feel her gently kissing my cheek.

"What did you think of it?"

I don't dare tell her the truth. "It was ... interesting."

She utters a humorless chuckle. "You fell asleep, didn't you?"

"You're one to talk."

"It's okay, Ker. It's not for everyone, but at least you gave it a try. My friend Chelsea's husband literally ran out of the room when she suggested he watch it."

I scoff. "Sure, that happened."

"Whatever. The point isn't the movie, it's the companionship and the intimacy that counts. You scored tonight."

"I wasn't aware of a competition."

She takes a moment to gaze into my eyes, but staring back without the necessary emotion will feel so hollow that I won't even be able to fool myself. And if I can't fool myself, Becky sure as hell won't fall for it.

I toss the words of the Swan back and forth in my mind until they lose all meaning, and formulate a plan while trudging off to the bedroom. Offering Ian a distraction would be the easy part; his friends all live nearby, and they would jump at a day of fun, trampolining from the hand-built treehouse two blocks over, enjoying a water balloon fight, and gorging themselves on pizza. Becky will be so pleased at me doing this that she'll lose herself in overseeing it, at which point I can take Ian's sketch book, drive to Philadelphia, and present it as evidence to a jury of one: Harley.

While I warm myself under the blanket, Becky prepares for bed in the bathroom, which can sometimes take hours. But before long my eyes are drooping, and I begin to drift off. If Becky enters and touches me now, there will be a me-shaped hole in the ceiling before I can come to grips with reality.

Instead of falling asleep, I only groan.

The world is turning itself upside down as the darkness and the air around me ripples like viscous teardrops into a pool of memory. The ceiling appears to bubble at the foot of the bed.

Becky, entering in her satin nightgown, tiptoes upside down in midair, and her face morphs into Vanessa's. She stretches and blurs, and before I can make sense of the inverted bedroom, the walls and the bed dissolve until I am shuddering alone in a sodden field miles away from civilization. My exposed skin swells and turns pale with the cold as a fuzzy moon penetrates the mist overhead.

Panting, I trudge through the mud, with no destination in mind. My brain works overtime trying to make sense of this world of chaos. The mire seeps through my toes as thunder rolls in the distance.

*Find the Shade.*

The Shade?

What is the Shade?

The hypothermic moisture impales me as I scan the horizon for a sign of life. In the distance, the ground slopes downward to a marshy area fronting a swelling stream, and a thick canopy of deciduous trees shades the water, wherein death dwells. This is not Harrisburg, or Philadelphia, or anywhere on the way that I know of.

My first thought is of finding clothing or shelter, but where I should find a barn or other farming structure, I discover nothing but the icy rain.

The road may be a few hundred yards away, or even miles distant. To gather my bearings, I keep an eye out for traffic of any kind. Even an abandoned tractor might provide shelter until morning, if it ever comes.

I shake with frigid terror as the sky opens and the mist parts, allowing a clear view of countless stars. I know most of the constellations now that I have spent years studying the more fascinating aspects of astronomy. The slice of the sky that reveals itself shows only two constellations that should occupy disparate regions of the sky.

Any elementary school kid can identify the first: The Big Dipper. But less than a degree west of its handle lurks the Southern Cross with its wings spread and its tail straight as if to take flight. It seems to stare down at me even as the rain begins to fall.

I trip on a stone and the mist converges again, then I shiver as I try to wash the mud from my bare knees and my chest. Any farmer happening on a boxers-clad man wandering alone in his field might be suspicious enough to open fire, if not call the cops, yet I am surprisingly lucky.

No one comes to my aid, even as I approach the stream. A shadow of a man stalks me from the darkness in the trees. Well over six feet tall, he watches me as every icy step invades my essence.

He seems sardonic but offers no aid.

After at least ten minutes, he stretches out a hand, and I reach for it on instinct.

He pulls me into the disquiet, motions me to sit on a nearly horizontal tree branch above the babbling creek, and says nothing.

"H-h-help m-m-me."

I cannot see his face. Like all those should-be horror moments from suspense movies, he remains shrouded in the dark as if to make light of my struggle and keep me questioning the reality in which I find myself trapped.

"You're—are you a ... farmer? Do you know how to get back to Harrisburg?"

He says nothing.

"Talk to me. It's kind of the rule when it comes to welcoming half-naked strangers in the rain. Even if you intend to mock me."

"Not of this world, are you?" His voice is deep, somber and creepy, yet remains stoic through every syllable, barely rising above a gravelly whisper.

"Of course I am. Earth."

"What is this 'Earth'?" His voice doesn't indicate sarcasm or even a tinge of sadness.

I tremble when a blackened hand points downstream, where the brook meanders into wilder, darker territory.

"Where are you headed, earthman?"

"Harris—No, Philadelphia." I amend my sentence while hoping that in whatever realm I have been transported to, Philadelphia exists and so does Harley. He will set me on the right track, but this stranger has different ideas.

"You got a long way to go, my friend. So maybe you should take it from the top."

"I'm free-ee-eezing," I stammer.

His silhouette seems to nod. "Course you are. There's a house about a mile upstream, can't miss it. Big brick edifice, two-story, with white columns and a hip roof. Colonial style. But first, tell me why you're here."

"I—wait, why can't I remember?" It's as if an invisible veil has erased all traces of earlier interaction from my brain, and I can only remember the voice of the swan.

"You know about Cygnus?"

My sudden clarity doesn't perturb him in the slightest. Instead of reacting in a predictable way, he lets his face droop downward to the muddy soil lining the creek, where tiny seedlings sprout up like wild grasses on the savannah.

"Long time since anyone's mentioned that name. Fascinating creature with a great backstory, which you'll know all about."

"I was expecting a human," I rattle on, aware of how ridiculous it sounds. If this were any normal person, he'd be suppressing laughter, but instead he shows no visible signs of amusement. He gazes downward at the soil for perhaps ten minutes.

"Then again, maybe you could use a refresher. It was a night like this, eons ago. The rain made puddles into ponds, ponds into lakes, creeks into mighty rivers. He came out of the sky, shining like a beacon. Landed on the road, lit up like an oil lamp, and then vanished. Everyone here knew what it meant. He doesn't call out to anyone anymore, but he's still real as you and me."

His way of speaking draws me in. Through it all, his pitch remains unchanged, but instead of droning on and on, the story rises and falls like waves in a storm-tossed ocean. The glimmer in his narrative is terrifying, and worst of all, he seems to know more about me than I can explain.

"What do you call yourself, earthman?"

"It's Kerry."

"Good to meet you, Larry. You ready for the ride of your life?"

I shake my head in the dark; if I don't dress in something more comfortable than my skivvies soon, I'll start hallucinating.

The curse of memory holds everything and nothing. A human cannot run on memory alone—he needs foresight and the moment, too. Without that, he will be little more than a vapor in the wind. My head aches as I begin to long for something that was never mine. My own reality has been severed from me, and if I don't get back to sanity, I will forever roam the lifeless fields as a body with no heart, or a heart with no soul.

# 3

# Eidolon City

The stranger spends the next minute or two studying me, every detail from my bare, muddy feet to the dark expression covering my face in the shade of the trees. The murk makes him appear colder, wiser, and more mysterious. When his eyes flit to my sodden hair, he pauses as if a tiny detail has captured his attention.

"Am I supposed to go, or..." I stammer, without moving. I would go anywhere warm and dry, preferably where new clothes and shoes await me. The mud is soft, but the occasional rock or stick embedded within it jabs painfully at my soles.

"Where do you want to go, Larry?"

I swallow, letting my thoughts linger on Becky and the nightgown she was wearing what feels like moments ago. "Preferably Philadelphia. I know a guy—"

"Just so you get it out of your system early," he interrupts, lingering on the 'early' as if he's about to say something either horrible or bizarre. "There is no Philadelphia."

That simple statement drives a rusted stake through my heart. For a moment, I can only gape at him, hoping it's a figure of speech or a joke.

I fumble over my words. "I used to live there."

He frowns in the dark, pulls his shoulders back to sit up straight, and seems to look menacing.

"Did you now? Construction is at least better than destruction."

"Yeah, but ... wait, how did you know I'm in construction?"

He shrugs. "Same way I know your nickname is Larry."

"You said you didn't know me. Didn't you call me earthman a minute ago?" I don't have time for these mind games, but at the moment I don't have an alternative. Though the rain has dissipated over the last twenty minutes, the chill remains, and the mud is still somehow both slippery and sticky. Going a mile upstream on the riverbank, alone in the dark, would be murder on the feet.

"I was trying to gauge how well you know yourself," he explains. "Which seems to be very poorly."

"If you know I was in construction," I say, subtly relenting, "then you know I lived in Philly, proving once and for all that it *does* exist."

He shakes his head. "And bad on retention. There is no Philadelphia *anymore.* What remains of that great city on the Philadelphia River is twisted mounds of rubble. And before you ask about the million other people who lived there, they're gone. Every single one of them—men, women and children. Less than memories, barely a step above urban legend, if you forgive the double entendre. He does have a knack for vengeance, wouldn't you say?"

Although I'm trying to hide shock and sorrow, my lip quivers as sheets of icy rainwater flow down my bare chest. "Who's *he*?"

"Construction worker. Makes sense a nameless, faceless ... person would garner more attention than the reality that one-point-six million of your *brothers* perished. Some escaped, of course. Some *tried* to escape and were devoured in the process, but it doesn't matter. I'd wager not only do they still exist, at least on some plane of reality, but that they've joined the army."

"Look, I don't know what the hell you're talking about. I'm not in a hurry to stay around here; I need to get home. She's alone in bed, probably, and watched me vanish."

"Or at least that's how it is from your perspective, but you'd be surprised by what others get out of the same experience. Not just different feelings or different memories, but different facts. Shame that humans are made in such a way as to figure out how to build two-thousand-foot towers, or create life on a cellular level, but have to rely so heavily on faulty shared information.

"Everything you see in the news is one interpretation."

"That's why you read multiple sources," I say. "Some people lie."

"*Most* people lie," he counters. "Without even knowing they're lying. Is it still 'bearing false witness' if the witness is perfectly true, but only in your own mind? There are holes in every logic puzzle. That's why they're called puzzles in the first place—"

"You're rambling. Tell me what happened to Philadelphia." By cutting him off, I erase any evidence of his initial thought. He seems taken aback, but reading his facial expression in this shade is difficult.

"Maybe it's best that you get that ... witness. Firsthand. But I could save you the trouble by saying you already have."

"Horseshit."

"You might not have seen most of it; they say you arrived after they'd moved to the suburbs and then vanished into the smoke, never to be seen again. Tragic."

I can see him shaking his head, but his body language doesn't communicate regret—there's something deeper there, something darker, more loathsome. I swallow, taking this information to heart but with the seeds of doubt he's already sown. If the human experience is so fallible, how can I trust his experience? But some of it does ring true.

If I travelled to the remains of Philly, would I be able to find Juaquin's apartment or office? Or is he dead?

"I wasn't there at all," I shoot, swatting away his assumptions. "Were you?"

"You might say I was on the pond in Central Park," he says. "Feasting with the ducks."

"You're from New York?"

He shakes his head. "Italy, actually. Long story, and you probably wouldn't believe a word of it."

"You might be surprised," I wager.

"I would show you, but it's too cloudy now.

"I was a king. It all started when a friend of mine fell into the river and drowned. Best friend I ever had, and it tore me apart. Zeus sent me to the heavens in the shape of a swan to commemorate my late friend. You know what they say when someone's about to die? They're singing their *swan song*. I hold that idiom particularly relevant."

I shake my head and stare at him through narrowed eyes. Mythology is a fun subject, but none of it is real. He is pulling my leg, and I'm beginning to form a story that will put his to shame. "I was an astronaut, headed for the Virgo Cluster, when I was consumed by a black hole. I don't remember anything in there, but the myth that nothing can ever escape is not true. It spat me out and I ended up here in Pennsylvania, where everything is upside down and backwards. That Zeus character."

"Funny," he says, stroking his chin. "You know how the Virgo Cluster got its name? It's a group of galaxies within the Virgo Constellation, which originates from Demeter and her daughter Persephone. Virgo, of course, means—"

"Purity. Innocence."

"See? You're not totally incompetent. Tell me: Did you ever find her? That young woman you sought."

"Becky?"

"I think her name was Sarah."

How could he know about Sarah? She used to come to Philly once a year, and we would have fun together, doing things like going to the movies. But we fell out of contact shortly after I met Becky and moved to Harrisburg. This freak show thinks I was searching for her? What an idiot.

"I guess I did. What do you call it when you're certain you want to be with someone for the rest of your life, but fate intervenes in such a pleasant manner that it proves your earlier desire wrong for all eternity? Serendipity. Or should I call it Sarahndipity?"

"So clever," he scoffs. "And yet, so naïve."

"Maybe you can tell me more about her."

"Can't see how it matters to your current quest, but I'll play along. I never actually met her, but I talk to people, including a woman named Ariadne. You probably wouldn't remember her, but she's the only reason you even exist."

"Sure."

"You see, she gave you something valuable. Powerful. Powerful enough to defeat an army of monsters that would have erased you from existence."

"Cool story," I say, narrowing my eyes and nodding.

He catches on to the expression in the most inopportune time imaginable. The rain begins to fall more heavily, pelting us with enormous drops of water, rolling off the leaves that shelter us. He doesn't react to the downpour in any way that I'd describe as human.

"You'll figure it out soon enough," he says. "Meantime, let's get you to that mansion."

"I'm not going out there in this," I say.

"Well, it's almost over, anyway. Give it five more minutes. You could tell me all about Becky. And your son."

"My son is Ian," I start, not caring to linger on the seemingly impossible odds of him knowing I have a son.

I start describing Becky while Cy pretends to listen. "She is an education administrator, and far smarter than I could ever dream of being. She's into the arts, literature, nature, you name it, and she knows more about classical music than Bach himself.

"I met her at a party a few years ago, where I didn't know a soul. She came and struck up a conversation. She was beautiful, I asked her to dance, and the rest is history. We were proud when Ian was born, and that kid's as smart as his mother. He's got a brilliant future ahead of him."

"How often do you go up to the lake house?"

"What lake house?"

He pauses just long enough to offer a coy grin that shines through the dark and the heavy rain.

The creek is inching higher at every moment. If we're unlucky, a flash flood will sweep us away and I'll never see Becky and Ian again.

"That's right, you haven't bought it yet. That comes next year."

"I've never wanted to own a lake house," I say, counting down the minutes. "Not that it matters—you were just making small talk."

"Small talk often leads to big things, wouldn't you say? At least Becky would agree."

Almost abruptly, the rain diminishes to a drizzle and then fades away entirely. I may not have been keeping track of time, but the stranger's prediction of five minutes is a lucky guess.

We remain silent as we step out from under the canopy into a soupy mud with embedded blades of grass sharing space with expansive brown puddles. Despite the misty air, the man is familiar with the path. To avoid the lowest ground, where the mud is too watery to traverse by foot, he arcs wide up a subtle incline where the rainwater is carving deep canyons in the mud, creating tripping hazards. This doesn't seem to be a safer route considering the weather, but it seems to be affording us better time.

Meandering upstream and never straying more than a few hundred feet from the accompanying tree line, we traverse the soggy farmland until we reach a pocket of hills that causes the rainwater to flow in a network of tiny rills that weave through jumbles of rocks, tangled roots, and thickets of underbrush that blur the boundary from grass to canopy.

Ten minutes into the trip, I decide to pipe up with some nagging questions that don't seem to surprise him.

"You never told me your name."

He hesitates while sneaking between a thick tree trunk and a bush that must house a half-dozen wild animals. As we venture further into this gulch, the canopy darkens overhead with each step.

"You can call me Cy."

"Okay, Cy, how do you know all this? Or should I say, what makes you think any of your assumptions are true?"

"I have made no assumptions."

"What about that naivety comment? Or the assumption that I know nothing about mythology?"

He grunts as he trips on a slippery boulder stuck in a triangle of tree roots. He clearly knows the terrain better than I do, but then again I assume he's lived in this area for a long time, and I can't tell left from right, let alone north from south.

"That was an observation," he muses. "Human beings often judge one another by how they observe their words and behaviors. When one tries to deny what is plainly true about the other's experience, he tends to pass it off as an assumption, which is another form of deception. Even if the concept is accurate to that limited bit of information, a man tries to convince himself he knows more than any other soul ever could, and maybe that's true. Only *you're* in your own body, after all. But sometimes, you don't want to acknowledge dark parts of your personality that plainly manifest in your actions, so you attempt to hide them from others to make them disappear in the mirror."

"I don't do philosophy," I say, my tone rising sharply. "Such a waste of time."

"All men engage in philosophy," Cy whispers. "Even simple things like predicting what might happen on the way home from work, or speculating on what someone else is thinking, you do it daily. You just don't know it. The ancients like Plato were not really better at it or more prominent than anyone else; they were just good at getting many people to listen to them, sometimes to their own detriment, so they became famous.

"Plato observed some things the elite at the time didn't want to hear, so they tried to kill him. Which, as a matter of fact, only made more people seek his counsel, contributing to his fame. Plato, then, wasn't as skilled at thinking as he was at speaking, and that happens to be a common flaw amongst mankind.

"I know what I know by observing and listening to the stories of others. You should really try it sometime."

"What makes you think I haven't?"

He steps over a jumble of roots, makes for a steep hill at the intersection of two swollen streams, and attempts to gauge whether it will be safe to climb the slope. It looks rocky enough to have resisted the rainfall and features roots sturdy enough to hold our weight.

"Your whole presence here suggests it," he answers. "You might be good enough at listening when your life depends on it, but when others share their thoughts, yours become too significant to overcome. That information is available only to you, contributes to that cognitive bias, and helps to shut out contrary opinion."

"Thanks, but I don't think that's entirely accurate." I stumble—trying to tiptoe between that bias he talks about and heeding his actual words is a foreign concept. Contrary to his opinion, I do have a history of listening to others when I deem their information valuable. Often, they demonstrate that value later, so storing the advice while it suits my needs is important to me.

"Maybe I'm right, maybe I'm wrong," Cy meanders on. "The point is, you pay attention when you need to, or you would not have so easily forgotten so much of the truth that Harley offered. You assumed he was a crackpot on the street because you wanted to see him that way, rendering his warnings less than effective.

"If you had listened intently, you'd know exactly why you are here, and more important, how you got here. Did he or did he not warn you not to abuse the concept of time travel? You didn't listen."

"Time travel? I remember Harley. He was a good friend. Never said a word about time travel."

Cy sighs. "Think about it, son—you sought him out. I remember it well. He taught you an interesting lesson about the failure of human memory, do you remember that? You don't remember that it was Sarah that made you want to talk to him? Because you wanted to find her. And he told you to look in the shadows. You looked a little too hard, forgetting that he told you not to do it, because of the numerous problems associated with interdimensional travel. One of them being that memory doesn't transfer between dimensions, making it easier to get lost.

"That's why you don't remember any of what happened to you, because in your home dimension, none of it actually happened."

"Yeah, I sought him out. How do you remember it?"

Cy begins climbing the slope before he utters another word. Waiting until he's made enough distance, I consider ways to direct the conversation in the near term. I grab onto a root and reflect on the frustrating truth that Cy has been directing this conversation, and I have been ignoring some of the things he's said.

The climb proves more arduous than I expect, but once we've made it to a flatter spot where the trees grow less densely, I am ready to engage him with fewer distractions.

"You said you remember it, like you were there or something. Or have you talked to Harley personally?"

He grunts and stares ahead, toward a clearing in the visible distance, which would only equate to a hundred yards in these trees and this weather. "Both."

"I didn't see you."

"You'd never seen me before or heard my name. Tell me, Larry, do you remember what was taking place across the street when you first met Harley? Or the second time?"

"What, you're a street performer?"

"Observer," he corrects me. "And I happen to enjoy good music and good art."

"Still doesn't explain how you know what our conversation entailed," I counter. This idea might be the proverbial ace up my sleeve, because if he was in the crowd across the street, there's no way he could have heard a single word either of us said.

"How much time would you guess Harley used to spend there in that overhang? Two, three hours a day, sometimes more?"

"I think he told me anywhere from three to seven, depending on the weather and how he was feeling."

"So why would it surprise you to know that I knew Harley? After I saw him go into that bakery with you, I had to ask him what the hell it was all about. And you know what he told me? That you were bright, but clumsy. His words."

I shrug. "Sounds like him. How long have you—*had* you known him?"

Leaning his head back, Cy combs his hands through his hair and gazes toward the clearing. "Maybe six months or so. I had migrated to and from New York. Came to know Harley pretty well."

"Which leads me to my last question." I stagger. "You talk about human behavior as if you understand it, yet you are not human."

"I'm perfectly human," Cy assures me. "Reincarnation might be rare, but it's an actual phenomenon. I live in the stars as a swan."

"How old would that make you?"

"In human years, sixty-two." He raises his eyebrows and glances upstream to chart a course through the muck.

"But I'm not the first reincarnated human you've ever come across either, am I? Harley told me you knew a goddess called Callisto."

Shrugging, I shiver against a sudden icy breeze and try to adjust my eyes to the growing light, which may be the coming glow of dawn. "I don't know any Callisto."

"But you did," he corrects me.

"When? I'm pretty sure I'd remember knowing a goddess, my wife excluded."

Cy utters a cynical chuckle and takes a couple of measured steps forward. "Oh, you're so sure? You don't remember her because it hasn't happened yet. You met her in your home dimension. You just didn't know she was Callisto. Harley said her name was Vanessa."

I give him a blank stare.

"Tall, black, with long braids, and a sharp wit."

I continue to stare.

"But I'm going to prove it to you rather than explain it, because I also know why you don't remember any of it."

I utter an exasperated sigh and follow him, trudging through the thickening mud. The sun will rise soon, clearing the mist and drying the mire in this forest, unless it rains again. The terrain levels out ahead, yet we traverse a subtle rise and stay in the shade. When we emerge at what I consider to be the tree line, which is comprised of some undergrowth interspersed with short grass and stubby domestic shrubs against the forest backdrop, I marvel at the estate in front of us.

The house looks massive, a red and white brick monolith with round pillars squaring a vibrant red front door and pie-shaped windows, standing at the end of an acre's worth of well-manicured lawn. From the end of a quaint, compacted gravel road, a path constructed of concrete pavers emerges and meanders through patches of flowers and bushes to the broad, red brick stoop framed by two neat hedges and a pair of poplars.

The home sports a classical rectangular footprint with large, white-mullioned windows set back in white stucco frames, amidst sections of textured red brick. Some of the rainfall still drains from the roof, a wide, hip-style structure supporting asphalt shingles that overhangs the stoop at least four feet over the pillared entryway.

Perhaps a wealthy family known to host lavish parties owns a manor like this, but only a pair of cars sits in the driveway, leading me to believe the house will be quiet today.

Cy nods at it and mutters, “Impressive, isn’t it?”

Its two stories are indeed spectacular in this secluded forest. Judging from the architecture, the house could be at least a hundred years old, but through diligent upkeep it doesn’t look a day over thirty.

“Who lives here?” I wouldn’t know the name, but he shrugs the question off as unimportant.

“The Secretary of Defense,” he breathes. “Harley K. Whitworth, Jr.”

Harley? It couldn’t be the same Harley I knew all those years ago, could it? And a high-ranking government administrator to boot? I try to shake my head at the coincidence, but Cy recognizes something from my reaction and seeks to set me straight.

“Not a coincidence at all, actually,” he explains. “I’m sure Harley will enjoy telling you all about it, if you’re in the mood to listen.”

As we make our way toward the front door, the question Cy would not answer prods me at the front of my mind. Why, now, when I’ve been ripped away from whatever reality I was in just hours ago, would he not reveal the most important information I need to hear?

“You said you’re going to prove it?” I ask. “When?”

He offers me a sharp smile that seems to glow blue with the predawn light. “In the future.”

# 4

# Ouroboros Network

A pair of man-sized decorative urns flank the doorway as we enter, setting the stage for a minimalist, contemporary interior with a half-dozen pieces of nondescript art set at various heights on the wood-paneled walls. The sun streaks through the upper transom windows of the grand living room, a dome-ceilinged entrance way adorned with luxurious sofas and several gold-riveted, felt-upholstered wooden chairs.

Expecting the butler or caretaker to greet us, I stand limp behind one of the urns and try to understand the cookie-cutter shapes on the rim. The recurring pattern takes the shape of a dragon but sports a lion's head. Have Harley's tastes evolved or did someone else decorate? So many questions to ask, so little time.

A wide, curving staircase hugs a far wall, leading up to a white-railed landing lit by a pair of small crystal chandeliers, which reflect the incoming sunlight. A man in a business suit strolls past on the balcony, pauses, and nods at an approaching figure.

Harley appears a moment later, wearing his customary straightedge expression but with a jagged smile. He knows his visitors at first glance.

Folded over his left arm are a pair of jeans, a black T-shirt, and a pair of shoes, which may or may not fit me. One of his assistants must have told him that I'm shivering in my boxers.

He descends the stairs while clutching the curved white railing for support. A natural hunch bends his back, and his salt-and-pepper hair has gone almost white. The wrinkles have carved deep lines in his face, yet he retains the traits that constructed his persona years ago.

"I'll be damned," he utters as he nears the foot of the stairway. "They said I had a visitor. Was expecting another dignitary or department boss looking for some funding, but instead I get an old friend in his underpants."

He is wearing a neat sport jacket with no tie over a clean white shirt with the top button undone, and tasteful business slacks. He waves his hand at a woman in an apron carrying a tray of hot food and invites us to sit.

Harley chooses one of the riveted chairs and taps his fingers while Cy and I settle into a sofa behind a coffee table and a Scientific American magazine resting atop the famous yellow border of the National Geographic.

The reading material of choice for anyone hoping to rub shoulders with the Secretary of Defense.

"You don't look a day over forty," Harley says with a sly grin.

"Thanks, old friend," Cy says, grinning back.

Harley nods and tosses me the clothes. "Referring, of course, to the Titan himself, or as some call him, Larry. How is it you look so young? What's the secret?"

I hesitate. "Uh..."

"Succinct, as usual. I assume you have a cosmic conundrum or two and came to the expert."

Remembering how he once compared himself to Neil DeGrasse Tyson, I swallow and flex my fingers. No such riddle has been twisting my mind of late, so I belt it out. "How did I get here? One minute I'm—oh Jesus! This can't be happening."

Harley looks taken aback. "What would that be, my friend?

"She's fading."

"You're referring to your invisible girlfriend?"

I assume he's referring to Sarah, whom Juaquin ribbed me about because I intended to follow her into the unknown. I have not seen Sarah in years, so I shake my head. "Becky."

A dark expression covers his face as he rests his gray-flecked white hair against the backrest. It makes him look as though he already knows what I'm talking about, which can't be true.

"I assume you're looking for an answer more sophisticated than, 'rode in a town car up the gravel road.' Or would you rather refer to it as the scenic route?"

"I was with Becky an hour or two ago." I struggle, scanning my memory for lost information. "Romantic evening, bottle of wine, chick flick. And then it all turns upside down and I'm slogging through the mud and icy rain to find a stranger." I gesture at Cy. "But it's like it's been decades, and there are only memories. I can't even tell you what she looked like last night, what she was wearing."

"Odd situation," Harley quips. "I'd call it unusual, but with you, there's no such thing as usual."

"Where the hell am I?"

"My home," Harley says, eyeing the high domed ceiling. He drags his feet over the decorative rug, which displays patterns similar to the urns'.

"No.... *Here.*"

I don't intend to sound cryptic, but in this mental state, I don't even know how to define 'concrete' because everything has gone symbolic and fuzzy. All I know is this *here* only differentiates from *there,* my bedroom. Will Becky still be waiting if I go back now?

Harley is wearing flat-bottomed business shoes that strike a delicate balance between glint-in-the-eye, excessive shine, and weathered. Somehow, in this well-appointed mansion, he looks like a fabricated version of his former self. He's left behind the 'street' persona for a casual sense of style that, while not off-putting, only invokes traces of the personality I once knew.

"Place can have a lot of different meanings, based on context, Larry. You ought to know that better than anyone. But you being here suggests otherwise."

I squint in the sunlight, which casts dusty lines through the interior air, making it feel warm and musky.

"Then let's start with you," I wonder. "How did you get here?"

Harley nods, as if he's been expecting the question. "Fascinating story. You can read all about it in my memoir—*Street to Suite: A Journey to Remember*. Bestseller, of course."

"Trying to sell me your book already? Never once imagined you marketing anything."

"Used to do that all the time," he argues. "I primarily sell ideas, and some of them happen to be captured in a book."

Trying to appear engaged, I nod and force a smile. "Give me the footnotes."

"You know the funny thing about watching people on the street? Once in a while, you come across someone really interesting. In this case, Mayor Archimedes, as I call him. Archinson. Handsome guy, great personality. He was surveying the local arts scene one evening for a local news piece on the Philadelphia arts. So, cameras on, he wanders across the street to get perspective from a real-life citizen."

"Talked for hours after the newscast was over. Invited me to his office for tea, and before I know it, we're sharing our vision on politics. Me, the hardcore centrist, Archimedes, the classic liberal, except he doesn't know it all. Sometimes the TV lights don't show the real character within.

"A couple of years later, Archimedes is being tapped for Secretary of the Interior for President Lorenzo K. White, and he still remembers me. Archimedes contacts me about a position on his staff, thinking it sends the right message about the American Dream. Working class with the real-world experience of a non-politician, non-billionaire, which had become an endangered species in American politics.

"A year later, he promotes me. Then promotes me again. The end of President White's term was an interesting affair; he'd been voted out, but Archimedes has gained the attention of the next president-elect. But Archimedes plans to retire, and suggests I take his place. Mind you, the new prez has already tapped someone else, but he interviews me carefully and suggests I might play a key role in Defense.

"Because I'm not like the rest of the elite—I have a knack for watching and listening, and that makes me qualified to anticipate tactical and political moves more quickly than almost anyone, apart from retired generals maybe."

His monologue doesn't bore me. Instead, it tickles a fancy deep in my brain, just out of the reach of rational thought. Rationality may be overrated, but it often hinges on creative inspiration. Something at which Harley has always excelled.

"I guess congratulations are in order," I say with a slight sneer, which Harley could likely see through. I'm not interested in politics, but his story has lit a spark in the back of my mind.

"And now it's your turn, Titan. Tell me what you've been doing the last thirty years."

*Thirty years?*

It can't have been half that since I last saw him. He came to my wedding, after all.

"Advanced to desk rider, project supervisor about two years ago. Been living in Harrisburg with my wife and son. Pretty quiet, otherwise," I say, hoping he doesn't pry into the details.

"Son's still living at home? Would have thought he'd be married and have kids of his own by now."

"He's ten."

"Come on, Larry. You know better than that."

"There's no way you've gone so far in only twelve years," I accuse, quickly doing the math inside my head.

"You're right. It took me thirty."

I decide to change the subject. "Why do you call the mayor Archimedes? Triangle head?"

Harley offers a brief chuckle. "Not really. But he *was* ahead of his time. You know there's an irrigation method over two thousand years old. The brainchild of the mathematician, inventor, and engineer who perfected it. The original design has been modified hundreds of times, of course, but still the same general principle applies, involving a giant screw in an open trough. The operator turns the crank to make the screw spin, and friction draws water up the shaft with no electrical or mechanical power. Some older wells use the technique to this day. It's known as the Archimedes Screw. And the mayor was once a plumber."

"Fascinating."

"Cy might know more about him than me," Harley says, nodding his way.

Cy's inauspicious silence hadn't grabbed my attention until now. I gaze at him, half-expecting him to offer his take, yet he only nods and clasps his hands on his lap.

I peel my eyes away from him before a glint catches my eye. Snapping my attention back to it may be an obvious movement to either of the other observers, but I don't care. Cy is wearing a ring on his left hand. Its finish looks like stainless-steel 316L, a polished finish that reflects any ambient light. I peer at it for a half second before he moves his hands.

The ring has taken the shape of a slithering serpent coiling around his finger and gnawing at its steel tail.

"I know a lot of things," Cy confirms. "You've been through a lot you don't remember. You've been to other dimensions."

"Bullshit."

"You still don't listen," Cy says. "You want to know why your last memory took place eighteen years ago?"

"My last memory was—"

"Because it *was* eighteen years ago. I expect fresh memories will come soon enough, but we have little time if you want to get back there. And we can help you." Cy's voice rasps at the end.

"We?"

"The Secretary and me." He nods.

Harley spends several seconds stroking his beard. "I believe I have a room that should do the trick. But you should get dressed first."

"What are you talking about?"

"You must have wandered through another portal," he says. "May be tricky to find your way back home this way, but we'll have to try."

"There a bus station around here? I was hoping for Philadelphia, to meet you." I hold my breath a moment, thinking back to the last time I saw him. The details are fuzzy and disorganized, occupying a cluttered part of my brain that sees little use.

Harley studies my expression for a moment, and then nods. His eyes narrow the longer his gaze penetrates the darkest parts of my soul. We have been acquaintances ever since that last meeting, keeping in touch mostly through social media. But he apparently knows more about me than I'd realized. A common phenomenon in this room.

"You like the house? It's colonial, you know. Dates all the way back to the Puritans. They used to believe some amazing shit. Such as, one way of treating witchcraft possession was to lock the victim in a dark closet for twenty-four hours, no food, no water. And would you believe it works?

"See, how they thought possession worked, a demonic spirit invades the victim's brain, sets up camp, and makes the person do weird things. Incantations, odd card games. There was always a dark disposition when an evil spirit was present. After twenty-four hours, they usually came out with a brighter outlook on life if a bit confused and disoriented. Because the human mind, when exposed to long periods of darkness, tends to reflect its surroundings. When a yearned-for change is so sudden, it causes disorientation, which others would view as funny. You get where I'm going?"

"No."

"Legend has it there's a closet in this house, and one night the Reverend put a young woman in, and she never came out. You could say she was spirited away in the night, not a trace to her name."

"Uh..."

"You believe me?"

"N—Not exactly," I stammer, trying to fit the pieces together.

"Good, you probably shouldn't."

"Because you're a politician?" I hope my joke lands with a devastating blow, but it has no effect on him. He steams ahead with his train of thought at full speed, threatening to drive me into the ditch.

## MEMORIES:

The veil is white as a pearl, and the sun and intermittent breeze make her hair come to life. She smiles at me with trusting, joyous eyes, her lips parting in the middle to reveal brilliant white teeth. My heart batters at me inside my ribcage, pushing me to the edge of the life I'd spent so long constructing. It all comes down to the "I do."

Years later, she smiles again. The bottle of pills causes me to ask the question: "What are these for?" The label says it all: Pregnancy vitamins. We're having a baby.

After the labor, he is born. Tears of joy pour from her eyes as I stare into them. The moisture reflects a piece of me I've long since forgotten, something I considered to be dormant, now real and bare. I cry, too. Relief. Joy. Transcendence.

We watch our son grow up. The first time he rides a bike, I see the remnant of his mother's smile manifest in his grin. It expresses pride and the thrill of accomplishment.

"Ian, you did it!"

The "I do" echoes in my heart as it pelts me from within. But the sun fades, and the darkness spreads. The reverberating "I dos" become a heart-wrenching throb of "I don't understand."

"YOU ready to take it on?"

"Just one more question," I say.

He waits before standing, and Cy has already pushed himself to the edge of the sofa to stand up.

"You called me Titan twice this morning."

Harley shakes his head. "You said it a long time ago. I thought it meant something, as if you'd experienced something beyond my understanding. Used to laugh at it. But maybe in some ways it's true."

He stands after he finishes his explanation. I have no memory of ever referring to myself as a Titan; I have never been one to boast or say anything prideful. But there it is—Titan. I don't think I'm ever going to internalize that.

Motioning me to a closed, white-paneled door around the corner from the foot of the stairs, Harley turns to Cy. Not listening to them, I take the clothes and walk into the bathroom. A warm sensation tingles my spine as I dress, rendering the teeth-chattering chill a memory. When I emerge from the bathroom, Cy glances my way and Harley grins about something suspicious.

Harley leads Cy and me through the maze of the grand room into a dim hallway painted in a strange shade of pink above the chair rail, a continuous run of polished wood spanning between door frames of the same shade. Three doors along the corridor, about two-thirds of the way to its dead end, Harley pushes open a door, revealing a storage cabinet packed with plain cardboard boxes of various sizes.

Cy leans against a stack of boxes and nods at Harley as I gaze at another door straight ahead. The carpeting in this room is softer and fuller, like a thick gray shag that clashes with the color of the walls, where the pink has weathered to a duller gray.

The door closes behind us as I reach for the knob and inhale deeply. I push it open, and the darkness and close quarters evaporate into an expansive sea of stars that sails past as we tumble through the heavens.

# 5

# Gorgon Deep

The stars spin themselves into a maelstrom of light that erodes my sense of reality. It recedes until there is no dark, light, up, down, left, or right, and the *inside* only exists as an isolated realm where the beasts rule.

When I open my eyes, only the cold, lonely dark invades my soul, penetrating to the very foundation of everything I am. My heart skips as I scan my surroundings for anything real, either a marker I can use to locate myself, or Cy's hulking silhouette. Either the darkness has devoured him, or he watches me from an unseen distance without speaking.

Humidity in the chilly air soaks through my clothes, right to my bones. This world is unlike anything I've ever known.

The darkness emits a shrill scream as splashes of icy rain whip through the wind. My field of vision extends ten feet in front of me, although guessing could have disastrous consequences in the long run. Within that ten feet, only amorphous shapes and shadows blur against the landscape.

"Hello? Cy?"

My voice is dead. The cadence and rhythm of my words shrivel up, stripping the emotion from my voice. They are only echoless words.

"Cy? This isn't funny."

*Cy is not here. You fool.*

The words strike a chord of agony. They build themselves in my brain and then evaporate as quickly as they'd arisen.

During my lonely years, enveloped by darkness, I engaged in intense conversations with myself. It felt as though there was someone listening and responding, but it was always my own thoughts, amplified by my distorted voice.

But this is different. *Cy is not here.*

How did I get here? Putting the pieces together causes my brain to ache. Everything up until this point is disjointed and disorientating, and the worst part is that no memory propels my thoughts. Nothing but the most basic information of who I am and what traits compose my personality. There has to be something.

When I speak, is my voice even audible? A croak escapes my lips, providing an unsatisfying answer. The world around me is a paralyzing nightmare that shreds my very existence.

Images play in my brain without rhyme or reason, and the longer I view them, the less I care to see.

Hands in front of me pluck at the strings of a guitar. The fingers are calloused, but not from hours of musical practice. Soon those same hands hold a collection of shiny cards over a blue tablecloth, thumbing through them as if plotting a next move. When the cards disappear, a notepad with hand-scrawled notes rests next to an open hardback book whose glossy pages flop over to a previous page, revealing an illustration of an elf-warrior wielding a longbow and flaming arrows. A pencil lies idle beside a pair of marbled twenty-sided dice.

And then that disappears, and the same hands lug a long, metal clip with twistable binding screws containing a thick clump of two-foot by three-foot paper. The plans land with a thud on a table, and then the owner of the hands sorts through assorted fasteners and hardware.

The surrounding darkness gradually lifts and adds color to shapes, which begin to assume a solid form. When it becomes concrete enough to discern structure, I see only disarray. Pieces of things lie strewn about a curving path like discarded remnants of broken souvenirs.

The debris stretches to the limits of my perception, perhaps twenty feet. Some of the detritus paints blackened charcoal lines across the veil—or horizon—that limits my vision. Paper, plastic, glass, and splintered wood, all reduced to confetti.

*You see it, don't you?*

A thought arises: *Where am I?*

*Look closely.*

My hands vibrate at my sides as I obey the command. Without a common theme, the detritus is only "stuff." I stare at it as the icy rain pelts my forearms and drips into clouded puddles near my feet. Something floats on a thin film atop the water. A crumpled and torn piece of cardboard washes against my feet and a faded photograph becomes visible. Another yellowed shred of a photograph appears a few yards away, and then another. There are thousands; cards of uniform size and shape intermingling with the rest of the destruction.

I can't make out the details on the cards from this distance, but I don't need to. A horn on one card against a holographic background hints at one of those kiddie collectible card games.

The pieces assemble themselves before my eyes, splinter-by-splinter, and fragment by fragment. Rain-ridden wind whips the pieces into a tornado of garbage as the heap grows higher.

The heap takes the form of ... are those legs or tentacles?

As I watch, the debris collects into another shape. A fist smashes it again into a billion pieces as the darkness floats in and out of view. I croak and back away from the creature that seems to gather out of the colossal storm of discarded material.

Its dozens of unseen eyes watch me as I stagger away. It takes one huge, thunderous step forward as it leers, bellowing in a tortured howl that reflects my most agonized screams. Atop its head, ropes of refuse flop lazily on the breeze. Its chest reveals the figure of a woman, and the ropes upon her head perk up as it moves, all aiming toward me like red-eyed, piercing daggers.

*Jesus Christ, no ... this can't be—*

More words assemble themselves and fall apart.

*You are nowhere. This is you.*

I could do without the riddles. Is some being planting these words in my head? I watch as the monster leers and growls, taking on the sound of my own frustration.

She *is* me. All of it. Me. Pieces of a shredded and destroyed persona constructed out of heavy, sodden air intent on devouring the only thing left.

I shudder as it lunges forward to seduce me.

"You know you want me," it barks. "Just reach out. You can have her again. All of her. Never let her go, just touch me."

"Uh ... I..."

*Touch her, Kerry.*

My arm begins to swing outward of its own accord, reaching toward the head of a snake that coils around her waist. I frown and recoil in disgust, but I cannot control my hand.

The scaly skin of the beast prickles under my finger for a split second before the creature collapses into a violent storm of flying debris that could destroy me.

Now once again in control of my own extremities, I turn to run. Lighting flashes as the storm of my life billows behind me. Having reduced the senses in my arms and legs, the rain forces on a throbbing numbness as I sprint into the darkness that envelops me.

The ground is solid beneath my feet. Cy breathes in my ear as he pulls me up by the arm, dragging me onward into the sea of black. Its frothy waves burst into a wall of mist as we sprint onward through the furious storm.

"Where did you—"

"No time for that," Cy grunts as he dodges a metal projectile. "Grab that lashing!"

"The..."

"The lashing! We've got to get away, and it won't go in the water!"

My heart rumbles. Tied to an oblong, cubic stone via a well-worn groove, a rope rests on the stone landing. Numbness spreads through my fingers as I fumble with the cord but manage to loosen it just enough to allow one end to splash into the water.

The icy mist shatters my consciousness.

Instead of watching me, Cy busies himself untying another rope ten feet away and launching what appears to be a heavy sack into the water-filled hull of a simple sailing vessel.

"Larry! Jump."

I spring upward with enough vigor as my muscles will allow, leaving a splash in my wake. Whatever *it* is slashes at my feet as I go. Letting my eyes adjust to the darkness is of no use. The *it* seems to be darkness itself, billowing and folding in on itself in concert with the wind-whipped mist.

The dark erodes part of my shoelace as I push away. It gnaws at Cy's back as he flails into the boat and pushes us away from the rocky shore into a churning sea. Waves ten feet high slosh over the gunwales as Cy hurries to correct our course for the gale-force winds. The horror unfolds before me as an advancing wave attacks the shore. The dark cloud stands back from the rocks, absorbing the mist as the boat lurches beneath us. The wave lifts us so high that spotting the shore from overhead would be like peering into a neighbor's yard from a treehouse.

"Goddamn it, hold together!"

CRASH!

Water fills my throat as I gasp and flail my arms about in the frothy sea. The wind carries us further away from the shore as more lighting forks across the sky. Does Cy think sailing into a hurricane will offer escape from a cloud of smoke?

If we reach the shore, I'll hit him with a shovel in frustration. Instead, survival is my only interest. A rope swats the foamy surface of the water and instinctively, I grab hold. The next wave brandishes its might just feet away. It swells upward, carrying me right toward the boat as I cling to the rope.

Pain rips through my abdomen as the wave slams me against the hull. Breathing seems impossible; coughing up saltwater confirms that I'm going to drown.

"Get aboard, you shit!" Cy roars through the thunder.

Splashing around in the violent water, I grasp a stainless-steel rod affixed to the rim of the watercraft where the rope is tied. Cy grabs one hand and pulls backward. Soaking wet, I can guess I must weigh at least fifty percent more than when I'm dry. He groans as he staggers back, slipping as he goes.

He loses his footing as the sailboat jostles with the waves. The mast rocks back and forth and clinks with a million wind-tossed drops of rain and mist as the boat lists harder to port.

"Arrgh!" He lands on his butt on the railing, using both hands to prevent himself from flying overboard.

The textured plastic floorboards are still slippery, carrying a swishing puddle two inches deep that gathers around his ankles. The water's weight could capsize the craft, I assume, but I don't have any idea how to react.

I fumble with a flapping rope on the mast, at least to steady myself as the next wave towers overhead and bears down on us.

"This is going to hurt like a sonofabitch!" I howl.

CRASH! The impact shears the mast clean off its bolted attachment plate, allowing the ropes and the sail to flap violently in the wind. Tatters of fabric pelt my skin like an icy dagger as the smell of frothy saltwater fills my nose.

Gasping in horror, I widen my eyes as a monster wave at least fifteen feet high gathers the surf and rolls toward us. The wave will be powerful enough to break the sailboat in half. Instead of taking action, I cower.

Cy sees it coming before I do, grabs the handle with both hands, and pierces my heart with his gaze. The boat tilts as the surge pushes us into the stratosphere and groans with strain as we crest the wave.

Another white cap arrives to crash over us after we drop into the gap.

"KERRY!" a woman screams amidst the winds.

I recognize the sound of her voice and my heart leaps inside me.

The wave smashes onto the boat with enough force to pull us under. Clinging to the ropes on the detached mast, I feel the water submerge me, pulling me downward into the brackish depths. My eyes burst with pain as I wedge them open to reveal a murky blackness that envelops everything.

The saline waters will drown me before I make it to the surface, but a sudden blueish glow grabs my attention as a fierce undercurrent tows me deeper.

Hands materialize out of the water, grab my collar, and drag me upward toward a sea of debris.

The water invades my lungs as I surface. The hands have vanished, taken by the rushing waves towards the smoke cloud hugging the shore.

I flail in the water, trying to determine where I am and how far away from land I have strayed. Cy is nowhere to be seen; the massive swell has destroyed our craft, reducing it to a field of shattered tidewrack that bobs on the fierce waves.

A smaller wave, still carrying enough force to drag me under, rolls toward me. Tugging at the rope to gauge the mast's location does me no good. It has vanished under the waves, leaving me clutching a tattered, soaked rope with nothing to tie it to.

"Kerry!"

Agony flushes my soul. "B—" I gargle saltwater. "Becky!"

She momentarily becomes visible between two gigantic waves. As the next surge pushes me upward, I gasp in horror when I see that the shore has vanished. Yet Becky still calls for me. She stands on a blue platform at the foot of another wave that heaves her upward. When we reach the same eye level, the waves carry me down and her upwards. And then the hands reappear.

"You don't want to go that way, friend," Cy gasps.

"You—no, we ... we gotta save her. The ocean is going to—"

"She's not there," he says.

I pipe up to argue, but the next white cap bludgeons us before I can get a syllable out. Pain roars through my whole body as I tumble through the abyss. I can see her face in my eyes, calm despite the raging storm. Her touch rips through my flesh like a dull, electrified saw. I'm going to die out here. And Cy is going to watch.

The darkness folds as an unseen force pulls us downward at least a hundred feet. I inhale the saltwater as a vortex drags me into a black hole that will offer no escape.

# 6

# Here Be Dragons

MY saturated clothes stick to my body as I lie shivering in a pile of warm sand. I sit up to see where we have landed.

The sun is dipping lower, toward the western horizon where a line of green skirts a sea of dunes at least twenty miles across. Above, stars are sparkling like glittery pearls scattered across a universe of light blue. To the north, a rugged mountain range gnaws away at the darkening sky like saw-teeth at sunset. The orange glow of the setting sun paints the sand with strokes of deeper browns and reds. A lone bird caws from where a loose grove of dying trees pokes at the nightmare with jagged streaks of white.

Cy draws in a breath to get his bearings, narrows his eyes and takes a step toward me.

"Where are we now?"

He huffs. "No idea."

I suppress a sudden urge to punch him. Memory is already beginning to fade in this dead, forgotten environment, tearing away the essence of myself and replacing it with coiled rage. We shouldn't be here. She was screaming my name, and I failed to rescue her from the sea. When I realize that Cy had dragged me under, I step toward him, clench a fist, and bury it in his stubbly cheek.

"Goddammit!"

The sand provides no echo.

Dabbing at his face, Cy growls at me. "Feel better now?"

Not at all.

I'm shaking with that agonizing stream of adrenaline coursing through my veins and feeding my brain with corrosive thoughts manifesting in obscenities. Instead of answering, I'll force him to answer for it right away.

"We left her."

Shaking his head, Cy backs away from me, runs his fingers over his scalp, and breathes something gravelly. "There was no *her*, Larry. You don't understand yet. And I don't blame you, frankly. But you will soon enough."

"She was *drowning,* and we left her to save our own skin. The coward's way out. You put on a tough face because you want me to see you as anything but an equal. Get me to Philly or I'm going to rip your face off."

"Who are you talking about?"

"*Her!*" I scan my memory for her name. Her face slowly vanishes behind a thick black veil. It's a name I should never forget, but I cannot grasp it.

"Those screams were not from a woman," he explains. "It was a siren."

"No such thing."

He frowns. "Of course not. Better get moving."

My hand still vibrating with anger, I press him. "I'm not taking a step until you explain to me what the hell is going on. Spill it."

At first gravelly, his voice becomes smoother as he finds the right words for a first sentence. "Memory has always worked differently for me, partially because I have more experience. I don't know why you came to meet me at the creek; I assumed you were stranded, and unlucky enough to be wearing minimal clothing and no shoes. But no one steps out into the rain in their pajamas. No one sane, anyway.

"You needed some place warm, and I took you there. To see Secretary Harley. We went into the closet, and that's where things got hairy."

"You're insane."

Again, he offers a nod, letting his gaze stretch to the sandy horizon behind my shoulder. "It took us to another dimension, another timeline. Because you are the traveler, I'm subject to your future and your past. Places we end up should be real—I don't understand why they aren't."

"I give it twelve hours until we shrivel up under the sun," I guess. "So think on it. What does it mean?"

He gulps. "It means we're dealing with a force that can literally destroy us, a fate worse than death. Imagine every atom that makes up your body lost into the ether to bond with other elements or fuse into new ones."

"Makes no sense," I stammer.

"I think we're off the edge of the map, and that introduces a new kind of danger."

"Explain it to me like I'm five."

His gaze to the horizon stretches far longer than it should, further infuriating me. "Cartographers used to label unexplored territories with an unusual notation. These places are unknown, so we fear them."

"Every inch of this godforsaken globe has been explored."

"Has it? There are vast areas on this earth no man has gone before. We've sent people into orbit, but not the deepest and darkest portions of our oceans. We don't truly know what's down there, so deep that light can't penetrate. The aphotic depths should be home to creatures we can scarcely imagine based on that fact alone, and Earth is nothing more than a tiny grain of sand in billions of deserts of this size. In the entire history of humanity, we've managed to travel less than a few hundred thousand miles. We can't go farther because we lack the ingenuity and it's dangerous. So far, we only know of one place in the entire universe where life flourishes. That doesn't mean there isn't life elsewhere, it just means we can't imagine what it looks like. Its fundamental makeup may be vastly different than ours."

"You and Harley must have been high when you were talking about this one."

"The Secretary is a smart man. But no one pulls their intelligence out of thin air. I'm guessing you don't remember the power plant anymore, and maybe you shouldn't."

"There are hundreds of power plants," I argue, my voice twitching. Allowing rational thought to cloud my sense of immediacy, I push my shoe through a loose mound of sand and watch a tiny beetle skitter across the surface in search of food or shelter—or to evade a predator.

"Let's just say that I knew about you, then. Because of Harley. I introduced myself to you, even."

The beetle digs itself into the sand and disappears. Ten feet behind Cy, a scorpion rears up to attack. Let it sting the bastard. Within moments, it inches away, having devised an alternate route to its prey in order to avoid its bigger foe.

I don't bother to pretend I understand what the old man is talking about. Instead I nod, frustrated. I could still pummel him, but this desert evokes a dread that drains the emotion out of me one drop of serotonin at a time. The will to fight for my idea of truth fades with my feeling.

Then again, do I know anything to be true? If he's right and we've somehow slipped into another dimension, it violates the laws of physics.

He continues in a monotone, but I have lost the will to listen. Where might civilization be? If we can find a road, we can hitchhike to a city and hop aboard an airplane and fly home. That he doesn't understand where we are is more than a little unnerving.

That orange orb highlights the peaks in swathes of dirty brown and red, rendering it a rocky furnace unsuitable for travel. The mountains should offer a reprieve from desert heat after the sun sets. Even slightly cooler air might at least offer a refuge for food. I study the skyline as Cy explains something I don't want to know.

"And I don't know why we ended up in the storm with that Shade. But where did you go before that? I lost you somewhere in between the mansion and the shore. I was about to escape without you, but then you just had to show up at exactly the wrong moment..."

Then again, the trees at the desert's edge a few miles west will boast a better variety of food, even if some or most of it is poisonous. If we are in Africa, a forest like that might have monkeys. We could eat like them if necessary.

"...You're not even listening, are you?"

"Uh..."

"That's what I thought. We're in some deep shit here, Larry. The sooner we brainstorm our way out of it, the sooner we can get you back to where you should be: at home with your wife."

"My—my *wife?*"

"I see," he says, a look of understanding crawling across his face. "Therefore, we're in the past. Which leads us to the obvious question of why? It must mean something to you. Care to explain it?"

"It's oblivion," I say, disbelief crowding the thoughts in my mind. "Who is she? Is that—who the siren was imitating?"

"Said too much already," he mutters, shaking his head. "We gotta go, otherwise any number of things might happen, and few of them good."

"If you say so," I say, satisfaction towering in my brain. Me, married? It's too good to be true. If Cy tells me in a few hours about a shiny new bridge he's trying to sell, I'm going to wring his neck so forcefully that his saliva will be a boon for all manner of nocturnal life.

Instead of antagonizing him, perhaps I should listen to what he has to say. Even if he doesn't know everything, he's proven he knows more than me, and that might just be enough—at least to get us out of this wasteland into a different peril. Trying to predict what might happen next sparkles with a terror I can't hope to describe. It burrows deeper into my heart than any emotion can possibly fathom, all the way down to that crater containing the remnants of my memory.

The trek across the dunes could be our undoing. My clothing has dried over the last thirty minutes, leaving behind the sour smell of salt. Humidity should dissipate in this environment, but salt won't.

Perhaps landing here at sunset will prove to have been the best possible scenario. Otherwise, with no water, we'd be drying skeletons in the sand in a matter of hours.

The sun has dipped low enough to douse the oranges and yellows into an ocean of blue. Overhead, the stars glitter ever brighter. The darker the sky, the more of them appear. Living in the city never provides such a grand perspective. The urban landscape seems so vast, on a scale almost unimaginable to creatures in a barren wasteland, but the bigger the city, the smaller the universe becomes. Artificial illumination drives away all but the brightest of celestial light. When everything is broken down to that local level, people grow meaner and uglier. Challenging the mind, this perspective offers a reflection of everything that was and will be, a glimpse into eternity. Without it, there is nothing. The soul grows thinner as the rat race intensifies.

"We might be getting close to some ruins," Cy says.

He stalks thirty to forty feet ahead of me, carefully stepping through the sand and keeping our trajectory level. The dunes around us tower higher and higher as the sky burns brighter with the countless stars.

"You know the good thing about life in the desert?" Cy says. "You can see miles ahead so you know what might eat you before you're something's dinner."

"Great. Lions."

"Lions are the least of your concerns; I suspect a sphinx might prowl these lands right about sunset. Everyone thinks they originate from Egypt, but several civilizations have told of them, including the Greeks. You want to know another interesting fact about Egypt, Larry?"

"Not really."

"There's a Philadelphia. They named the city after the Greek ruler Ptolemy II Philadelphus, who became known for marrying his sister. Thus, the nickname 'City of Brotherly Love.' You wouldn't think they would literally name a major American city after incest, but here we are."

"History is interesting," I say, following thirty feet behind and occasionally looking up at the billions of stars. Countless civilizations used to flourish under these very stars long before mankind invented its own light, removing the need for a celestial outlook. Still, I'm not interested in the lesson—if he continues, I could punch him again.

A pile of square shadows looms a quarter mile ahead of Cy. He keeps us headed in a straight line toward it, engaging in small talk that begins to make me drowsy. My eyelids droop lower as we near it. The rocks look more natural than they had fifteen minutes ago, and not the least bit inviting. They could be a haven for snakes and untold other creatures who seek shelter from the oppressive sun.

We enter the rocks and circle until Cy surveys a dark crater. "You first," he says.

Without knowing what I'm committing to, I hunch down, press my hands into the sandy earth, and slide head first into the black. Dark replaces my body as I go, hurtling amongst myriad stars and galaxies. I marvel at the eternity of nature. Many ancient societies believed in an eternal afterlife. Flying amongst the stars, I now understand why. Human nature requires a higher platitude; if humanity is forever doomed to a single dusty rock in the cosmos, it has little aspiration, and without that, the world's greatest thinkers would be nothing but neurons and there would be no reason for any of it.

I close my eyes and let the weightlessness take me.

I land painfully on hard stone, as if I'd traveled mere inches. Squeezing open my eyes, I take in the urban setting, the rocky, green-studded mountains in the distance, and the crumbling columns on a flat-topped hill amidst the chaos. Modern day Greece.

"I don't know about you," Cy says, materializing to my right, "but I could go for a gyro right about now."

"Maybe a sightseeing tour of the Acropolis," I suggest, eyeing the distant monument.

"You don't have any idea why we're here, do you?" he says.

I think it through and shrug. As invigorating as the prospect of travel is, I can't put the pieces together into anything resembling a whole. A mass of moving parts may not be the pieces of an engine; it could cave in my skull trying to put more complexity into a system devoid of reason. Why indeed? Why the storm? Why the desert? And why the *construct* formed from pieces of me?

He keeps his eyes on me for at least thirty seconds. "I guess not."

"Do you recognize it?"

He nods, signifying that he knows what I'm getting at. "A few more people than there used to be. And they've let it go to hell."

"Birthplace of democracy," I mutter, shaking my head. "Inspiration for the American experiment."

"*Demos*," he agrees.

"*We the people*. The first three words of our constitution, which coincidentally, was written in Philadelphia."

"Do you understand why we're in Greece yet?" he asks.

I shake my head.

"It's the birthplace of it all: gods, goddesses, everything. Athens itself is named after a goddess."

I offer a subtle nod and step into the shadow of a shop whose lights have been extinguished for the night.

"Do you know why?"

I have nothing.

Together we creep along the shadows of the buildings, avoiding shortcuts into dark alleys and hurried Greek citizens after sundown. The buildings grow somewhat taller in the densest, oldest parts of the city, and artificial light has nearly wiped out the stars overhead, bathing the sky in a terrible glow of white and yellow like the center of Philadelphia.

A shop door opens and a woman wearing sunglasses and a tight dress darts out, nearly colliding with a man staggering alone across the sidewalk, and glances at us for a split second.

The buildings in this part of town rise to uniform heights, each with a flat roof and molded parapets over several windows. The sidewalk slopes upward to crest a small hill, where a well-lit alley juts off to the right. A few sets of stairs lead up to buildings and other alleys. Some cities are built on top of the land, while others are built into it.

Each structure plunges downward through layers of soil and bedrock, stair-stepping into residential areas much too steep for most roads. Somewhere in the alley, an argument ensues. As it's being conducted in Greek, I can't make out what they're saying, but the emotion is palpable.

Cy pauses at a nearby streetlamp and peers into the alley. A woman totters up the stairs to an adjacent street, carrying a few shopping bags at her side. A man follows her for a moment and disappears into an unmarked entrance twenty feet up from the gently sloping stone pavement we stand on.

"Athena's Marketplace," Cy says, reading a sign on a building face a few feet from the bottom of the stairs. "May be a good starting point."

"Or a good way to get scammed out of our money," I wager.

"You don't have a dime on you, earthman."

He's right: no wallet. Finding myself in a foreign country with no identification and no money would be a disaster in all normal scenarios. Here in this 'dimension' it is absurd. I'm little more than a face.

If Cy and I were to become murder victims, the police would have a legendary mystery on their hands. Many theories would be posited, causing those responsible to glower with arrogance—and, of course, every one of them would be wrong.

Under the streetlamps, Cy guides us to the door marked with the sign. A beige cloth awning shadows a pair of steps with a decorative iron railing bolted into the building's stone veneer. He pushes me in that direction after deciding that the shop is still open. Ten feet from the steps, a man with gray hair accosts us, speaking English.

"Tourists, beware. Some strange people go into that shop, and some don't come out. 'Less you want to be transformed into the ether, I'd steer clear. There are museums telling the *real* truth."

He staggers away and Cy shrugs. "The real truth is what the history books say it is. Leaves no room for exploration or nuance. Just an 'it is what it is' way of thinking. Surely you don't think there's only one authority on the truth."

"God," I say, allowing my mind to wander.

He eyes me for a moment, narrows his focus, and places one foot on the steps. Whatever the sentiment behind his expression, something dark must lurk there or he wouldn't have made it.

"*Deus ex machina*," he mutters. "The Hollywood cop-out for whenever writers have built a situation they can't explain away with natural plot points. It's all too convenient, except when it's done as parody."

"Maybe there really is a God, though," I argue. "You don't think this universe and its mythology comes from nothing, do you? If you ask me, it's all proof positive of God's existence."

He sighs as he pulls open the door. "But which God?"

# 7

# Pythagorean Secrets

Foreboding. That feeling when you enter a dark doorway into an unfamiliar room, the dank air creeping in on your sense of self, and in that moment the world seems to turn itself inside out to appease an intimate, psychological darkness you cannot explain.

The air stabs at me with a million icy needles as my eyes adjust to the scant light.

A candle's flame dances in the distance, illuminating a dusty collection of cloth hardbound books on a wide, floor-to-ceiling bookcase. Handmade trinkets of various styles litter the front edges of the shelves, to foretell what secrets may hide in the voluminous tomes.

The murky corridor, walls stained with splotches of deep browns and dark reds, stretches twenty feet, decorated with framed paintings depicting heroes and legends. The pictures bear no markings, leaving the identities of their subjects to the imagination.

Where the corridor opens into an oblong room, shelves of various sizes and heights signal a museum-like shop. A lone counter next to the bookcase houses an antique cash register that would not be out of place in one of those Americana-themed diners attempting and failing to mimic the innocent flair of the 1950s. A tall, surly man with a graying beard and an unkempt mop of silvery hair putters around behind the counter, crouching low to replace stock or check inventory. He either pretends not to notice us or allows us generous time to peruse his shop's wares unimpeded by a pushy salesclerk, which oddly enough might convince me to make a purchase.

Such as a cushy floor rug hung like a tapestry from a nearby brick wall, similar to those faux-brick veneers home architects specify to invoke a more rustic feel. Except in this case it's the real thing: weathered and chipped spackle, applied in excess, confirms the genuine quality. The rug blends maroon and golden hues in artistic balance, revealing cut-out images of men with swords and shields marching. The mohawked helmet of a Trojan is a prominent decorative choice.

Plexiglass shelves hang beside the rug, clinging to the brick in an irregular pattern. The shelves display various bits of pottery, some cracked, some shattered, and some intact. I study one fragment for longer than I should. Beside it, a small, printed postcard in a plastic sleeve describes the item as a genuine *ostrakon*—a piece of pottery with what amounts to a handwritten vote. Originating from the time of Plato, citizens used these bits of pottery as a democratic way of expelling one citizen from their society for ten years, according to the placard.

A variety of mathematical sketches inscribed on imitation papyrus adorns another shelf. The centuries-old ink bleeds through the pages at certain points, where the artist may have paused and changed direction with the pen. One such sketch is unmistakable as the proof of the Pythagorean theorem, showing a right-angle triangle contained within three squares.

The accompanying postcard describes it as the most famous mathematical concept of a misunderstood man with a deep secret. Pythagoras, it claims, had enjoyed continued success and advancement in the mathematical field, so much so that he had garnered a legion of followers as if he were the head of a cult. The card encourages readers to check out several books about the legend himself, at least one of which may be displayed in this shop.

Cy brushes against a display of a real life-sized urn standing five feet tall. He studies its markings in the transparent glass case illuminated by a pair of LED bulbs.

Stylized flames lick at the feet of a two-dimensional man with arms and legs outstretched like the so-called mathematical depiction of the perfect male form, but without the lines and circles denoting symmetry.

He stares at dozens of figures below him, those unfortunate souls burning in his abyss. I look away before I can allow myself to read the placard.

Overall, the owner has decorated this shop like a museum, and the cool, shadowy air helps to invoke that mystical sensation.

I make my way to the bookshelf and scan the titles for clues on the subject matter. Hippocrates catches my attention at once, but I keep going until I happen upon a book about Pythagoras.

Gently pulling it out of its niche on the shelf, I run my fingers across the delicate fabric stretched over the hard cover and stroke the cool, gilded lettering with my fingers. I flip it open to a random spot and thumb through a dozen pages before falling on a section about his life's legacy.

Reading takes the edge off everything that has happened so far, whisking it away into the vault of memory to be accessed later. Behind me, Cy has taken to a new object of interest, but I pay it no attention.

## MEMORIES:

Becky flips a page in her thick paperback and looks up long enough for me to glimpse moonlight in her eyes. That split-second of interaction holds a lifetime of emotions, everything from gentle love to venomous rage.

How can a woman so gorgeous and warm communicate such frosty anger? I see it in her eyes as I watch.

Moving closer, I slide up next to her on the couch, lift her elbow, and nestle my face against the soft white wool of her sweater. Closing my eyes brings a fleeting moment of peace wherein I can revel until I get old and not miss a thing. She kisses me gently on the forehead and resumes reading the flowery prose she professes to love so much. I don't care for romance or chivalry, which she often describes as an endearing defect. Her heartbeat fills my ears with a sweet rumble as I drift off to sleep.

What must be hours later, she has abandoned the book on the sleek, glass-topped coffee table and kisses my lips until I'm wide awake. Our tender session lasts at least twenty more minutes.

And then I'm kissing something else—a cold, steel washer electrically welded to another. I turn it over in my hands as tears splotch onto my cheeks.

A chill races through my body as my muscles spasm—agony. An ageless, untraceable pain pulses through every pore, blinding my eyes to everything but Becky. I place the object in her outstretched hands and walk away from her one last time.

But I'm not alone. The other woman's dark braids rise and fall beside me as we walk into a misty forest. Who is she? Is she even real?

Cy approaches to my left, carrying what might be a package of playing cards. He dangles them at his side and looks over my shoulders as I read the fascinating history of Pythagoras and his followers in the scientific community and at large.

"You don't want to know how much that costs," Cy says, lowering his voice. "Looks like a first edition. Set you back a good thousand euros. I've got a better idea."

I roll my eyes, which he takes either as a compliment or hilarious insult if I'm gauging his coy grin accurately. "What, poker? I don't suppose the Spartans and Trojans used to engage in tournaments."

"You don't think they had games?"

"Apart from the naked Olympics?"

He grins and raises an eyebrow. "You know that clothing restricted their movement, not to mention the heat. You don't want to imagine the chafing that comes with—"

"I get the picture," I growl.

"I don't suppose you're ready to abandon this silly establishment."

True enough, I'd formed a predisposed opinion before entering, assuming a kitschy tourist-themed assassination of the genuine history behind ancient Greece. Instead, the shop asserts a more nuanced theme, invoking genuine interest rather than some conversational knickknack to entertain houseguests. That conversation wouldn't be about the piece or the shop, but the excursion and appeal of vacation. Running from attraction to attraction long enough to take selfies before ancient monuments just to prove you were there; drinking fine wine at tourist restaurants while examining the GPS map to scope out your next destination, and if the streets confuse you, insisting on speaking English to the Greek citizens and acting dismayed when they can understand at most five words of your incessant questions.

Cy doesn't miss a thing.

He slips the playing cards into his jeans pocket and looks up and down the bookcase. "If I didn't know any better, I'd say there's a back door to this place."

Eying the glass door next to the counter, which lets in the filtered glow of outside streetlamps, I stammer, "Yeah, the one we entered through."

He shakes his head.

"*Another* back door. To an even darker alley. You up for it?"

"You know what? I think I'm done with the whole whatever-the-hell I'm going through. You find the door, write me a letter from where you end up. I'll be in Harrisburg with my wife after I catch a flight."

"Your wife," he scoffs. "So now you remember? Guess that means we're in the right dimension."

"What the hell are you talking about?" I slap the book closed and clutch its binding while waiting for a wide-ranging explanation that I already know will not come, because Cy is annoyingly terse.

"I told you—"

"And what is it with memory? One minute I barely know who I am or how I got there, the next I'm recounting scenes like they just happened yesterday, like location has something do to with it."

He hesitates.

I breathe in. "Oh God. Location does have something to do with it."

"You're onto something now. Let's hear it."

"If we are really in different dimensions—different times—it affects my memory. Because the human mind doesn't do memory backwards."

"Fundamental law of time travel," he says, nodding. "Have you figured it out yet?"

"No."

Chuckling, he says, "You will. But I don't suppose we'll want to hang around here too long. Perhaps I'll tell you what was on that urn another time."

"Maybe on the way out the *back door.*"

Cy disappears from my shoulder and approaches the polished, wood-topped counter. Behind it, the shopkeeper uses his hands to push himself up via an unseen under-shelf. He eyes us and speaks something in Greek.

Nodding, Cy emits a clipped Greek sentence and thumbs through his wallet, or more accurately, what one might describe as a wallet. Little more than a folded ply of burlap covers the scraps of paper within. This ought to be good.

He pauses to comment something in Greek and waves a hand at me in explanation, to which the shopkeeper nods and smiles.

"Twenty euros," the shopkeeper adds to the end of an animated screed about whatever interests him about my appearance.

"What a ripoff," I breathe, post facto hoping he doesn't understand English idioms.

The shopkeeper eyes me with a suspicious gaze while Cy regales him with what must be a story describing how we got here and our intended destination. The man wouldn't understand if his life depended on it, but he listens anyway because he's much more personable than me, and Cy could be trying to milk him for information on something.

"Twenty for a pack of cards?"

"A really important pack of cards," he says in English, glancing at me.

"Great. Let me know when you're done explaining the true nature of the universe, and I'll be over here reading about the *real* Archimedes."

Frustration has always played games with my verbal tone, at least as far as Becky is concerned. Sometimes when it gets too severe, I take it out on whatever is near me, but I'm careful not to break it and feel foolish afterward. Other times, I get snippy. With my old friend Juaquin, that always led to banter; with Becky it provokes a bitter silence, which she fills by reading that damned book, which she promises I would enjoy if I'd just open my mind a centimeter.

To which I'd reply sarcastically, "...or fifty."

Cy rests his 'wallet' on the counter and pulls out a wad of foreign currency as I turn away. Probably counterfeit. At least he isn't trying to pay with plastic or *ostraka.*

The shopkeeper rambles in English about the ills of tourism, without revealing how tourism benefits his business, regardless of how he feels personally. The laws of economics sometimes conflict with the views of those running the shop or wandering among its goods.

Back in Philadelphia, I once conversed with someone who attempted to explain socialism in a positive light and why those ranting about it are wrong—or even worse, hypocritical. His explanation revealed its own form of hypocrisy. As critical as he was of capitalism, his shop depended on it. The hell with the social evils it promotes when unencumbered by law and regulation.

*Hypokrites*. The bookshelf might carry a book on that phenomenon.

I peer at the titles until my eyes fall on a book on an upper shelf about Erebus. For one reason or another, the name rings a bell—something about it tugs at my heart. If the dread it evokes turns out to be false, I won't be better off. Its mystery pulls me in. The candles on a shelf several feet away flicker as I reach up to grasp its spine.

Cy and the shopkeeper chuckle about something in the background as the chilly air pokes at me. Erebus, the god of darkness. It beckons me.

*Grab it. Pull it out.*

My heart skips a beat. What was that? A voice in my head that didn't originate from that confused jumble of space and time inside my skull.

I reach for it.

"What do you think, Larry?"

My hand pauses. I haven't understood a word of the conversation, and now he wants my input? I stammer a nonsensical reply and let my hand waver in space inches away from the book.

"My friend's an avid reader," Cy belts out in English, while glancing at me. "I'm sure there's a cure for that."

"More books, my wife would say," I hazard a guess. Searching my mind, I can't remember a specific time she ever said anything similar, but it sounds like her.

But now Becky is so far away that my current means of communication can never reach her. The thought makes my heart bleed like the wrong kind of ink on delicate parchment. In this time and place, why can I think about her in such vivid clarity? Is this dimension closely related to the one we inhabit together?

Cy stands up straight, bids the shopkeeper goodbye, and steps to my shoulder. "You sure you want to know about Erebus?"

"It speaks to me," I say, again reaching for the spine. *It speaks to me*. Oh, Jesus H. Lord. If I were in the mood to laugh at my disjointed use of language, I would. Awkwardness is an art I have perfected over decades of scurrying about living life yet achieving only measured successes at key intervals.

*Take it.*

The chilly air has adhered to the soft, aged cloth stretched over the spine, and the gilded title and byline have faded into a mottled, chipped yellow over hundreds of years of use. The air bears down on my hand as my fingers curl around the lip of the spine and my muscles wedge it free from the shelf. As it slides, the entire bookshelf moves.

Trying to grasp a feeble understanding of what has just happened, I glance at Cy and pull the tome harder. The bookcase slides away from the wall as I pull it out, flop open its pages, and stare on into a pit of venomous black.

An expanse of stars swirls into a virtual cloud of light as the darkness fades into space. The frigid vacuum locks me in its grasp, akin to the coils of a serpent, unyielding until I give in to its effortless might.

I gasp when I see what remains of the city. The seedier industrial district is rotted beyond recognition, and that slippery cold that so often chills the metropole pushes deeper into my skin. Cy exhales beside me and shrugs.

# 8

# Strix Talons

Buildings lie in ruins everywhere I look. It's Philadelphia, but everything is amiss. The skyscrapers that should be visible from this location remain shrouded in a soup of a particle fog that refuses to settle, limiting our perception. As if it had been sacked years ago, it has fallen silent like no city ever should. And the air reeks of a dank undercurrent of death, as though millions of corpses have decomposed, and their stench still lingers on a chilly, moistened breeze.

My heart trembles. "What the hell happened here?"

Cy only mumbles something I cannot understand.

Adrenaline batters me from all sides, yet his expression amidst the swathe of destruction stays even. Either from a lack of surprise or a lack of concern, his reaction makes me want to punch him in the face.

"I ... I don't understand," I yammer, breathless.

"It's the right place," he mumbles. "But it's wrong. Not unsurprising, but not an easy solution either, unfortunately."

"Really? What gave it away?" I clench my fist at my side and wander a few steps toward a dilapidated industrial building that stands alone among the rubble.

"You want to get home or not?"

"I'm sure you're going to take me there, right after you're done dragging me through trashed distortions of reality and far-flung places that don't concern me in the slightest. Just to educate me. The hell with it all—I don't need you anymore."

"Walking away? Not a simple path from here, my friend. You're never going to get home without me. You'll be lost until you cease to exist."

"Beats all this bullshit with Egypt, and some playing cards at whatever the hell that shop was."

Cy exhales. "You remember the shop. We should talk about that before it disappears from your memory."

"I'm never forgetting it."

He offers a humorless chuckle. "Give it an hour at best."

I scoff, but he has taken a peculiar interest in a demolished shack, which rests atop a flat of cracked concrete where weeds are shooting up from the gaps. A slotted steel bar lies twisted and toppled, its metal sign hanging loose from a single, rusted screw, which has corroded the rest of the faded green with streaks of orange that look like blood. Beneath the bent post, half of a graffitied bench rests under a gauze of dust, insects, and shattered glass.

Cy stalks in that direction and clears away the dirt and glass, causing the ants to scatter in every direction. Chunks of broken concrete are mixed amongst the debris in particles ranging from a single cement-coated pebble to a six-inch thick section of slab outweighing either of us.

I make room for Cy as he fumbles through his pocket for something and sits.

"Used to be a bus stop," I wager.

"Take a seat."

Pushing on the broken slab is of no use. Its grooved bottom side features a torn sheet of corrugated metal decking, which serves as a uniform tray for the concrete. Looking overhead, determining from whence it came proves straightforward. The second story of the nearest standing building still supports the roof with a grid of once-yellow and -orange pipe posts. Sheets of wafer board over the window holes have come loose and lie in heaps of chunky sawdust below. At the edge of the second story deck, a broken-out notch of the slab lies crumbled at the building's foundation. A five-foot long scrap of rusted decking steel dangles in front of a shattered bottom-story window.

I kick a bent piece of rebar away from the bench and sidle onto the seat so that the signpost digs into my back.

Cy has taken to unwrapping his purchase from the shop, removing the deck from the box, and flipping through it. "Looks good."

"You're not suggesting poker now," I say, watching him fan out a choice of cards for me to pick one.

"These aren't face cards—well, there are faces *on* them, but you get the picture."

"Detailed picture." I swipe a card from his hand and lay eyes on a rotten skull with ruby eyes blazing like fire beneath a mane of mottled black hair. The rigid figure poses with its chest puffed forward and its hands in its lap. Its skull supports sagging, rotted skin, and bits of red muscle still cling to the jaw. Trying not to gag, I hold the card to my chest and watch him fan out the hand for me to make another choice.

A waft of sickly odor drifts between us, making me want to retch, but Cy pretends not to have noticed.

Behind him, the mid-rise residential towers four blocks away have been reduced to a cracked and buckled concrete column studded with rows of dirty rebar, but the remainder of the structures have eroded.

"Pick another card." He pushes the hand closer to my face.

I pick it out of his hand and study it. The subject sports crooked, spiraling horns, a dark complexion, and a serpent of fire coiling around its outstretched hand. A black cape flutters beneath his hulking stature and his face seems to bubble like a million black fly larvae eating away at the flesh.

"Gross."

"Give you one guess who that is." He studies my unchanged expression. "A hint: You've met him before."

I fling the cards away in frustration.

"Ah, *that* kind of game."

"I might consider this fellow a king of Spades if these were poker cards. As such, they're similar to what's referred to in these modern times as tarot cards."

"You're going to tell my fortune?"

"What do you see when you put them together?"

I growl and relent to play his game. "I guess a master and an apprentice. Maybe this skull guy is learning to be evil from this ridiculous artwork that is supposed to resemble Satan."

"We Greeks did not believe in Satan."

I shudder. "You're saying this horny guy is Hades?"

He flashes a sardonic expression and pulls the cards closer to his chest. "His cousin. The god of darkness—Erebus. And that is one of his servants. An army of souls, some living, some dead, some halfway in between. They're slaves, but they're loyal."

He shuffles the remaining cards into the deck and picks out several new ones, again fanning them out in front of him. A rattling sigh escapes his lungs as the skeletal city lurks behind him.

How many dead? Millions? My nerves fray at the edges as I consider it, attempting to devise a mathematical equation in my head. With enough warning and time, hundreds of thousands could have escaped the destruction by car, bus, or train. Thousands more, perhaps, by air, not to mention bikes, boats, ferries, and those brave enough to flee on foot. A reasonable estimate might total a third of the city's population, but that still leaves plenty. And yet I see no corpses in the rubble.

"Maybe we can take a look at some more important people later," he says, gathering up the cards and stuffing them into the box. I bend to pick up the cards of Erebus and his slave, plant a hand flat on my back, and groan in pain.

He takes them from me and pushes them into the pack before depositing it back in his pocket.

"Why's this one building left standing?" Asking out loud sounds outlandish, but it manages to perk Cy up.

He stands and brushes residual dust off his trousers, stretches his back, and gazes at the edifice.

The upper portions of its exoskeleton are missing, perhaps either ripped free and burned or never installed in the first place. The building's three stories contain a hungry darkness that promises shelter to those willing to enter. Like us.

Any exploratory excursion will be fraught with danger; if the building had been under construction at the time of the destruction, several obstacles to various degrees of peril could stand in our way.

*Go in.*

That menacing voice again. I try to ignore it, but it returns with enough force to propel my leg muscles in that direction.

Unforced, yet compelled, I consider where the entrance might be while Cy tails me. He kicks a heap of loose gravel, sending a screeching sound of metal on pavement into my ears. A sheared fragment of something made of sheet steel rests near his feet. Its three-foot-long half bar shape folds and creases at the break. Entangling a fluttering strand of cotton or hair, its sharpened edge gleaning in the hazy twilight. Just touching it could be enough to draw blood.

It might be a handy weapon should any villain skulk in the dark. I pick it up by the blunt end, brandish it around me, and begin a more confident stroll around the back side of the building, which fronts a blacktop service road squared with accents of chipped concrete beneath heaps of debris. Discarded steel members, construction materials, glass, nails, concrete, screws, rebar, and flecks of splintered white plastic lie in a heap of ruins at least six feet deep.

In the center of the pile, scraped paint reflects the scant light that illuminates a circle of black belonging to a buried car in the abandoned neighborhood. There may be a skeleton in the car, but it doesn't concern me.

The visible paint was once a deep sparkling blue that would have lost its luster over the years and may have belonged either to a sporty sedan or compact crossover. Not an ideal construction vehicle, but then again, workers drove their own cars, parked in a back-lot staging area, and walked the rest of the way.

A chain-link fence, maybe decorated with poly cloth signs, should ring the job site, but no fencing material remains. Perhaps after construction stopped and the workers abandoned the property for good, city personnel removed the fence, but then again the public safety department would have had protocols mandating it stay until the half-finished building were either completed or razed.

Another possible culprit might be loose bands of survivors and looters hoarding fencing material and arms to ward off any remaining forces of evil.

We tiptoe past the car, where a broken streetlamp, bent from some impact, lies mangled and coated with concrete dust across a smaller pile of debris, which contains crumbled ceiling tiles, twisted T-bar framing, pieces of metal strut, threaded rods, and sections of black iron piping.

Around the corner, a set of double door frames with missing glass panels occupies an inlet shaded by an intact part of a concrete deck. A coil of heavy chain and a giant padlock secure the doors in the metal frame, and glass shards glitter in the scant light as we make our way to the doors, which remain jammed shut.

Climbing in would not prove difficult. I lean over a damaged push bar by bending my stomach, flinging my legs over, and resting my feet on the smooth, dusty floor.

Cobwebs flutter in my wake, allowing strands of silk to drift and stick to my skin. I brush them away and stand back for Cy, who has taken a jogging approach. He lands one foot on the push bar of the opposite door, vaults himself high into the darkness, and lands crouched on both feet. Both dust and silk fall down from overhead as we make our way through the shadows.

The entry area, long devoid of color or decoration, stretches at least fifty feet along a back wall, whose diagonal, grid mesh windows somehow remain intact. The lobby houses a row of metal chairs in disarray; some sit bent or collapsed, while rust and chipping paint mars others. Torn-out stuffing and upholstery, once affixed to each chair, occupies a linear heap of foam and fabric along a far wall, where breezes have deposited it.

Sitting in any of them would be a painful experience for the posterior, as tiny nails and rivets attach a sheet steel seat to a painted tubing rim with a razor-sharp attachment lip.

Beyond the foyer, the darkness lurks deeper. Cy inches forward toward a set of double doors that are graffitied with fading gang colors, and I follow.

The next room is a pitch-black corridor, where the ambient light from outside filters along the walls in dusty orange stripes. Holes in the wall sheathing offer dusty, cobwebbed views into adjacent rooms filled with an array of supplies, boxes of parts, and pieces of discarded plastic ties and metal fragments strewn throughout.

"We should try to find an electrical room," I say, remembering how I'd studied plans in my years as a construction laborer. In most buildings, the electrical room abuts a sparsely trafficked back corridor, and codes prohibit any penetrations through its walls unless those services directly supply the electrical room.

I gaze into the darkness overhead and spot a hazy maze of piping and supports. Either to save on cost or to offer utility access to the racks of piping and ductwork, the lack of a ceiling implies industrial use. Finding the main trunk of a shiny, insulated duct in the darkness is easy. Even over a hundred feet from the double doors, the insulation glistens with patches of reflected light, which bend and scatter just enough for me to see dark bulbs of piping, hanging chains, and the one item I look for in particular.

A rack of metal conduits chases through the shadow of the duct, beneath a wire basket raceway filled with dozens of wires with dead-end legs shooting into every light fixture and every room. More conduits join the rack as we pace into the dark, culminating in a heavy-multi-tiered electrical rack carrying dozens of metallic tubes.

Sooty strands of spider silk are draped over grated transfer grilles above various doors. Branches off the main supply duct serve rectangular boxes, supplied with a pair of hose-braid water connections coupled to insulated copper tubing. The ductwork branches join a separate rack of pipes in the center of the corridor.

Following the electrical rack to a terminus, we reach an ell bend in the hallway and enter a world of near total blackness.

The electrical gear in the power room should house a master on-off power switch in a transformer box, before supplying power through a spaghetti of conduit to various control panels. If we can find the correct switch, the light can only help.

Then again, our purpose for entering the building is something I have not considered. The building's interior could lead to a way out of this destroyed hellhole of a city. Such a portal may serve as a route to the *real* Philadelphia—the one thriving with millions of lively citizens instead of broken structures, deserted streets, and obliterated architecture.

The room in question awaits us twenty feet along the enjoined corridor, after a left turn. The dozens of conduits punch through the wall via an insulated isolation panel embedded within the wall sheathing. Only a single duct penetrates the wall high above the conduit chase, and its uninsulated, tarnished-steel surface might well be an exhaust or return duct.

The door will be locked, I guess. But after one pull on the bent-plate handle, I spy a set of keys dangling from the lock. Twisting the key loosens the door and lets us into a dark, oblong room whose dusty flooring is charred by something black, and a dried pool of sticky liquid.

The dark allows a circle of vision no more than three feet in diameter within the room. Propping the door open may provide a little more light to work with, and a lone box of metal parts, bent conduit tubes, and fastening bolts will do the trick.

Cy flips the light switch at the doorway to no avail, while I study the electrical gear mounted on the walls.

One large steel box, labeled as a UPS panel, occupies an otherwise blank section of wall a foot away from a squattier box four feet high, and above that, an identical, unlabeled box terminates two feet above eye level. Mounted to the surface of the wall above the gear, large conduits swap positions overhead. The bulk of them lead from the transformers to the UPS panel, while smaller runs three or four abreast feed the six panels on the opposite wall.

I shimmy the box toward the door and wedge it into the door frame. Although the door's weight compresses its sides, the box retains just enough structural integrity to keep the door open. Even though the light in the adjoining corridor is scant, it provides somewhat better vision.

Beneath the transformers, thick tubing penetrates the ground-level slab and serves as the primary power supply to the building. The power meter must occupy an underground vault outside the building, supplying the transformers with a set of large-diameter conduits. I tug at the doors of both panels, and they refuse to budge, but a solution presents itself within seconds.

In the gap between the gear, a discarded tubing run with a flattened end tilts against the wall like a sword. I discard my weapon and let it clank to the floor as I reach for the tube.

The conduit is lightweight but rigid enough to not fold much under the pressure of prying the transformer doors open. The flattened part of the tubing is not thin enough to jimmy behind the lock, so I place it on the floor and stomp on it until the end gives way beneath my foot.

Visible only as a black silhouette in the dark, Cy stands motionless, gaping at something in the dark.

Returning the tube to my hands, I insert the flattened end in the narrow slot between the locked access door and the sheet metal frame, and push with all my might. The conduit flexes in my grip.

After at least a full minute of prying, the sound of straining metal reaches my eardrums. The conduit bends more and more as I increase my pressure. In no time it will buckle, rendering it useless, but not before a metal-on metal pop echoes through the room.

I gasp with delight as I issue an exhalation, which Cy ignores. He is still staring at whatever he has found, while I swing open the cabinet door with my trembling fingers.

Cold sweat beads on my forehead as my heart leaps through my stomach all the way to the top of my throat. A dry, raspy screech escapes my lips as a bony rat scurries out of the open door and skitters off into the darkness.

Gathering my frayed nerves once again, I reopen my eyes and horror fills every nook in my veins with venomous adrenaline. My heart pours blood relentlessly through my veins, attacking my arteries with a surge of pressure. The horror before me elicits a harsh scream, which still doesn't wrestle away Cy's attention.

Inside the transformer, amidst various components, thick, dusty webs, and gnawed wires rests a dusty, red-tinged skull. Rotted flesh clings to its jaw and eye sockets along with strands of long, curled hair gathered into a sickly, clotted-blood knot where the scalp once rested.

My heart batters inside my chest as I emit a dry, raspy sound and try to calm my jittery senses.

Behind me and to my right, Cy croaks.

I peel my eyes away from the skull and follow dried blood trails from the jaw to a hardened red-black pool that gathers at a low point in the sheet metal box.

"God!" I shout, still horrified.

Turning to approach Cy on the balls of my feet, I twitch with the streams of agony-inducing blood coursing through my veins.

He is staring at a row of bones, a femur, a full ribcage, and a pelvis. Metatarsals become visible as Cy shifts his weight.

At least three bodies, with rearranged bones, lie in a chaotic heap in my field of vision. Examining them further reveals that one of the victims is female, sporting a curvy spine and broader pelvis. A metal ring bands around one of her carpals, and a fragment of another metal rests on the concrete near the end of her fingers.

Struggling to corral my nerves, I bend down to study it.

Agony rends my heart, tearing my emotions to shreds as I pass the two electrically welded washers between my fingers.

"God, no—no, it's not..."

"Kerry?"

I whisper her name as tears splash onto my cheeks and my muscles spasm. "Becky. It can't be."

"How do you—"

"YOU SON OF A BITCH. *YOU* DID THIS! I'M GOING TO KILL YOU!"

Cy breathes as I scream and kick a ribcage to listen to the bones scatter on the floor.

"There's—"

My sobs become uncontrollable as the poison of adrenaline clings to the inside of my veins to tear me apart from within. Tears drip onto the floor as I curl into a fetal position next to her. *Why? Why her? Why now?*

The only sound I can hear amidst my own labored breathing is merciless laughter bouncing off the insides of my skull.

# 9

# Aphelion Shadow

My soul lies in tatters, hidden in a surreal darkness that plunges so low that not even sorrow can thrive. A groan slithers down my throat and settles into my abdomen while Cy peers at the skeletons as if in confusion.

"We gotta get out of here," he mutters.

His tone implies an understanding of my suffering, emphasizing that speaking in any voice other than a low, mournful one can only intensify the pain.

The chilled concrete floor warms beneath my body. Turning the welded washers over in my fingers, I allow anger to filter through my heart. "Go without me. Bastard."

"Larry—"

"Unless you want to be decapitated with your head in a transformer, too."

He nods and shuffles his feet in the thick gauze of dust that has accumulated over however many years it has been since the city was abandoned.

"You have to understand something."

"There's no one else to blame. I don't care who did it—you're responsible. And I can't escape now. Returning home ... seeing my son ... without her ... I'd rather be dead."

"Stay here too long and your wish may be granted."

"What do *you* know?"

"Do you want to save her or not? We can do that if you just trust me." His voice seems to echo in the room amidst the dust at the last syllable of every sentence.

An unexpected knot of understanding rises within me, scouring my brain with a perpetual darkness that I cannot defeat. Where it came from I can't decide, yet it rings true deep within.

"If you die in another dimension, you can't exist in any of them."

"She may not be in another dimension." *Un, un.* He exhales a frigid breath and waits for my reply, yet his posture suggests an unnatural patience that only darkens my mood.

"We share them," I whisper. "Always."

"Then how would she get here?"

"Erebus."

Again, he breathes in slowly and shakes his head as if none of it makes sense. A sudden desire to strangle him crashes into my brain.

"Theres only one entity capable of such evil."

He reaches into his pocket with his free hand, opens the pack of tarot cards, and flips through them with the pictures so near his face that the colors can only bleed into an amorphous blur.

Pulling out one particular card, he brandishes it at me, expecting me to take it. Even if I could reach his outstretched hand, I couldn't care less about his cards.

Instead, he lets it flutter to the floor, shuffles away towards the transformer box, and mutters something under his breath. As I lie prone, curled up in an infantile position that might evoke laughter, the darkness settles.

The card lands face up and skitters to a stop on the dusty concrete, inches from my face. From my angle, the dim light entering from the corridor paints the image with oblique shapes that smash together into a dense knot of blackened twine.

*Thwack, Thwack!*

Cy grunts as my fingers caress the corner of the card.

*Thwack, Thwack!*

Still no light.

*Thwack!*

Perhaps supposing that all light switches are in the off position, Cy scoots away from me through the dust, his footsteps scraping with every muffled pace.

Spying the image with Cy's shadow blocking most of the light, I cannot make anything out. He flips the switch multiple times and then shuffles back to the transformer as if to inspect the wiring.

With no one left to turn the power back on, permanent darkness might grip the city for centuries. Then again, the chances of that are slim. The militias in the suburbs and the farther flung cities will have restored power and routed it to their population centers by now.

Troubleshooting it might reveal many problems preventing the power from coming on. Either the utility company has disabled the meter and shut off service after years of neglect, or rats have gnawed at the wiring to make any circuit closure impossible. If we didn't have so much time on our hands, tinkering with it would be pointless.

When he steps away from the door, the dusky light reappears. I pinch the card between my thumb and index finger, holding it high enough to examine the deity it depicts.

The picture bleeds red, as flame devours a twisted tower of serpents upon which a blackened figure stands with ruby-shard eyes, long, mangy hair, and ibex horns that coil upward to a pair of glittering pinnacles.

Legions of followers writhe naked before him as fire dances around their flesh.

"Are you saying this is the work of ... Hades?"

He growls. "A theory."

The building shakes, and the subtle vibrations kick up puffs of dust and rotting corpse even as the energy transfers to my bones. My knee pops as I peel myself up off the floor.

Power crackles within me. I can almost feel my fingers sparking with energy, yet my body emits no glow.

Cy groans as the vibrations die and then reassert themselves, stronger.

Passing the transformer and leaving the skeletons in the room presses measures of guilt into my stomach, but Cy takes the lead and exits into the corridor. Clutching the washers in my other hand, I mash the card of Hades into a peeling clump of cardboard and follow.

The shaking grows stronger and accompanies a sudden rush of howling wind. Outside, a storm of debris could shred us to bloody bits within seconds. The howling sucks the life out of the corridor.

*Boom!*

*SLAM*

*Crackle.*

If we stay much longer, the building could crumble on top of us. My heart burns into overdrive as Cy sprints around the corner to confront a swirling blackness that has eaten away the front half of the building and is tearing the rest of it to shreds.

The noise increases in pitch as ear-splitting howls accompany falling beams, clanging pipes, and crumbling architecture. The wall sheathing reduces itself to dust as we skid to a halt, and the metal partition studs twist under the crushing weight of the slab overhead.

As if it has seen us, the oil-stain shadow undulates as the concrete cracks and fine-grained dust filters through.

A series of hefty *clanks* join the din, and soon the racks of conduit, pipe and ducts may flatten us. Another side room might provide more safety should the utility supports fail, but then again, the second-floor slab could crush us if the shadow doesn't erase us first.

I screech as I jump through a gap in the failing wall studs. Metal creaks a moment later as Cy joins me in the next room.

The Shade simply evaporates the building and its debris as it advances toward us, and then a second later, a loud shriek indicates that the deck inserts have failed. The pipe and ductwork crash down in segments along the length of the corridor. Metal and bits of concrete uproot themselves from the ruins, and rotate as though hurled by a violent tornado.

Every particle vanishes into the cloud as it eats its way toward us. Cy hurries toward what appears to be a closet tucked into the corner of the room, and I run behind him, twirling the washers in my fingers.

Air horns and crackling fires spark fury into the maelstrom as the shadow tears the building apart piece by piece. The concrete begins to fail and huge sections of it reduce the metallic ruins beneath it to shrapnel. Seconds tick by as the shadow devours the closet walls and the concrete tumbles.

We hurtle through a swirl of darkness that has gathered itself into a vortex. The shadow has eaten us alive, but as the maelstrom abates, the confetti of debris settle into weightlessness. Together we tumble among the stars while looking back on the building, which collapses into one rumbling cloud of dust and smoke like a spectacular tower demolition video.

The sound reduces to a low grumble and the stars twinkle as the debris tumbles in space.

Suddenly, it all vanishes.

And there's dark.

## MEMORIES:

Becky tiptoes into the room, draped in a black robe, and her hair is wet and tangled from the shower. She lays her amorous eyes on me as I approach, wrap my arm around her back, and kiss her gently on the lips.

She leans in, pushes me backward, and collapses on top of me in the bed. The kissing intensifies as my clothing slithers off my body.

In a breath of excitement, it is over. She snuggles with me in the dark as my hands caress her bare skin.

Ian stands in the doorway, as if stirred by nightmares. Instinctively, I grab at the covers and pull them over our bodies so that only our feet stick out.

"Mom?"

I frown and kiss Becky's lips as he quivers, tiptoes into the room, and crawls over the covers between us.

Becky gives in, pulls the covers down to expose her shoulders, and wraps a free arm around him.

He emits a harrowing sigh and issues a single tear. “I’m scared.”

The city glitters in the night as we make our way through crowded streets. Live music beats away any feelings of sadness as the drums liven up the atmosphere. Couples skitter away from tables under shade tents on the sidewalk, and together they waltz to the rhythm.

Overhead, the buildings skewer the star-scape with a million shining windows stacked like yellow diamonds a thousand feet high.

A bus idles near a street corner where a throng awaits, as an illuminated red hand keeps them at bay. Along the intersecting street, a trio of cars interrupts the music and the street dining. A festive atmosphere is building around us.

One car pulls to a stop on the next street and the back door opens. A woman with black heels and a loose, knee-length skirt steps out of the car, flings her arms around her lover, and plants a gentle kiss on his lips.

Farther along the street, the music’s tempo increases as it drowns away the night with sonic color. More couples arise to dance in the streets, hindering our path through the masses.

Overhead, the stars twinkle as a group of birds squawks and flutters skyward. I narrow my eyes as I turn sideways to allow a gentleman in a gray suit to lead his lady onto the street. He gives me an awkward glance as I weave through a sea of tables. A few couples remain seated, chew on scrumptious meals, and engage in clipped conversation between rockabye songs that dazzle the crowds.

“Where are we?” I demand. “You said Philly didn’t exist anymore.”

“Cities are different from people,” he shouts. “We have come out in the past, where the city is alive and well.”

*Very* well.

A couple presses their lips together in the dark as the musical energy vibrates in the street.

“I don’t understand. This can’t be the past, because I remember…”

I *do* remember. This can only be the past for him. My heart flutters in my chest upon realization. Finding Becky and getting her to safety is crucial, but it's impossible without transportation or money for a ride to Harrisburg.

Before I understand what is happening, the horizon folds in on itself, and the stars wrap themselves up like a Christmas gift. The dancing couples transform into twirling bits of plastic, and the skyline shimmers like an animated dream.

Moments later we are floating amongst it all as it fades into miniature beneath our feet. We're being dragged upward as if gravity has ceased to exist, and my heart nearly falls out of my chest as pain envelops me.

The stars begin to spin, and I close my eyes to take in the weightlessness.

When I wedge them open, Cy is no longer with me.

Floating through the nothingness like a feather on a restless breeze, I spin further into the abyss, where pain is whittled away to be replaced by a somber feeling of peace.

The hurt vibrates in my heart and then disappears. When I open my eyes again, a woman is floating toward me in the ether.

Smiling, her face framed in amber hair, and her white dress fluttering behind her, Sarah grasps my hands and pulls me closer. In the distance, a dying star flares. She mouths something that looks like "*I'm glad you've come to join me.*"

But then she, too, vanishes into a hazy cloud of white that drifts into darkness.

Out here nothing stirs, only me. And that dying star.

And my memories.

All of them coalesce into a viscous vat of liquid so deep that individual feelings bleed into one another. My heartbeat ticks up a notch as I watch the stars twinkle out one by one. And that dying star flares one last time before blinking itself out of existence. In an instant, I am nothing but a mass of atoms drifting apart one by one.

# 10

# Guardian Sphinxes

The sky pulls me higher and higher until I'm embraced by a frigid, limitless ether. Sarah's wispy image disappears, and a cosmic dance of a billion stars replaces it. I'm forever alone.

Somehow, I can still hear Cy's voice clanking around inside my head as though my skull is comprised of flimsy aluminum, and the reverberations make his words unintelligible. How did I get here?

The world I've known my entire life exists only in memory now, but those memories are so salty that if I dwell on them, my acidic tears might vaporize in the microgravity vacuum. Thrills, sorrows, joy, and agony populate that world. Out here nothingness stretches far beyond my field of vision. Shimmering a thousand light years away, a tiny red star winks as I approach, but not before the nearer stars gather into the shape of a lion. A thousand tiny dots build the image before a woman's face materializes.

Unable to control my trajectory, I hurtle toward it. As it grows in my perception, it loses definition until the shape eventually vanishes. Frosty space belts at me, but a powerful white light awakens to bathe my skin in warmth.

*"You still have my gift, Kerry."*

The voice echoes as though it had originated from my own brain, but as the gravity of the light draws me in, a shape begins to emerge.

Nearby, clad in a glowing white dress with a shoulder cut-out, stands a woman. She pulls me closer without extending her arms as panic rocks my heart. The heat intensifies as I near her.

*"Use it for good,"* she says.

The good has vanished from my heart, and emptiness reigns. "There is no good in me," I croak, as though I cannot control my own words. "The light has gone out."

*"There is always light."*

*But only if there is always darkness.* Concocted of my own words, but free from thought, that malicious whisper in my head returns. My heart pulses within its void.

Space will swallow me whole, rip me to pieces, and crash my frozen remains into a lifeless asteroid if I stay out here much longer, but for now I cannot control where I roam.

*Dark always wins.*

"You don't know," I rasp at her. "She's gone. All of her, and soon even the memories. I can't go back."

Her image flutters as the icy vacuum sweeps over me, sucking the breath out of my lungs as I ponder. Reaching out for her, I see her disappear. The red star has become a boiling planet. I careen toward it so fast that it makes little sense. I should be able to sense the speed, but with dimensions so stretched, the shrinking distance is only perceptible visually.

*Slave.*

"I serve no master," I shriek. But the words die in space as the hellacious, burning atmosphere swallows me whole. My body glows as I sink into the furnace of the clouds, which may liquify me or compress me into a lump of stone that will break into a billion pieces.

*There is no escape.*

Soon I feel nothing. No me, no Sarah, no Becky, no mysterious woman with a gift of light. My thoughts erode as I fall through the poisonous clouds.

*My feet fall flat on a cracked pavement of slate that stretches out as far as I can see. No one greets my arrival, but others must exist here. Unless he has sent them elsewhere.*

*I know who he is.* The One. *The one who has saved me from myself, who has freed me from that dank prison of lies, which had forever distorted my perception of truth, dignity, and self. A master who has treated me so well and given me so much that my only required repayment is ultimate loyalty. The sacrifice has already taken place.*

"Larry."

Someone lightly slaps my face, lunging over me as though he is about to remove my soul from my body.

"We're not out of this yet, pal," he breathes.

*"The One,"* I gasp as buildings sprout skyward in the night. The expression on Cy's face tells me something is wrong before I can look around. Urgency tugs at his movement, but his face has gone rigid and stale, as though carved from hardwood. A spot of blood has appeared over his brow like a black knot in dark grain, grown sooty from a storm of dust that must have flashed through the city, rendering it powerless.

The buildings are a series of pitch-black rectangles stacked a thousand feet high and a murky mist has shrouded the moon so that only a soft white glow illuminates the scene.

"You ... you were ... she was ... where the hell am I?"

"City's about to eat it," Cy grumbles, pulling me to a sitting position with his hands curled in my fingers. "We'd better not be around when it does."

"I ... where is he? *The One?*"

He pretends not to hear me, as if my sentences are so diced and misarranged that the message has gone dormant and engenders no meaningful reply.

"Eat it ... as in..."

"Don't know how it happened yet, Larry. It was Philadelphia, alive and well, but then it stretched, the people vanished, and the dark won over. I feel we're in the wrong place at the wrong time."

"What the—"

I have no time to finish an unformed sentence before a towering black form rises out of the buildings, lunging a thousand feet high. Merciless it spins, growing larger and pushing at the tallest building.

The edifice groans with a deafening roar as it teeters and topples. A huge plume of concrete dust blossoms before the shadow, bathing it in grey. But the beast pushes through it, regains its form, and topples yet another building, which crushes a shorter one next door.

Screams might have echoed through the streets if Cy and I were not here alone. He brushes up next to me, grabs my hand, and hurries under a dim overhang. He rattles the door handle, but it won't budge. Furious, he kicks the pane of glass with a surprising jolt of energy, which shatters it. The glass cuts through his pants and bloodies his ankle, but he endures it without complaint.

Darkness spreads as he reaches into the void where the pane once rested, unlatches the door from the inside, and ushers me into the lobby.

A foyer a hundred feet long greets us with graceful, inlaid tile floors set into motion with a meandering river of blue tile, while the steel inlay strips reflect the scant light from outside.

Laid out without reason or form, dozens of leather chairs scatter throughout the lobby in an organic and engaging way. The arrangement contrasts the lifeless parallel rows at the Department of Motor Vehicles, which only allow for friendly conversation if neighbors tune out the ambient sounds and turn their bodies away from the object of their attention.

The deserted lobby emits sterile vibes that creep through the senses as we walk into the abyss.

Why are we always fleeing from demons, which can devour buildings, by hiding *inside* buildings? The irony strikes me but I say nothing.

Cy leads me along a dark corridor until we approach an elevator door. He presses the button as if expecting something to happen. Grunting, he pries with his fingers into the folds of rubber separating the sliding steel doors and pulls them apart until they budge. In the meantime, the building struggles under the weight of the beast as it bears down on our refuge.

I join him in pulling at the elevator door until we have shimmied it open far enough to allow a child to wriggle sideways into the elevator car. Cy wedges himself into the dark slot, grasps my hand, and wedges the doors open further by pressing his back on one door and nudging the other with his foot.

CRASH! ROAR!

Thunder rocks the building as it vibrates, ceiling tiles crumbling to dust and the suspending cables buckling and snapping under the motion. We escape into the darkness as the entire ceiling grid collapses to the floor in a swirling cloud of dust that will cake the chairs and tiles in several inches of debris.

The elevator car disappears. Together we fall, at least eight feet, before it all comes crashing down. The building's upper floors squeeze the lower floors tighter, compressing the entire structure into crumbling slabs of concrete that sandwich furniture, pipes, sheet metal, wires, and paper.

We spin in the nothingness for several seconds before the black overtakes us.

The wind howls as the concrete elevator shaft shields us from the rampant destruction. Cy busies himself, standing up, kicking at what seems to be a pump with a pair of connecting pipes, and looking up into the column of darkness that surrounds us. A rectangle of black frames the door opening. Reaching up, Cy curls his fingers around a metallic ledge. Using the pump head as a foothold, he yanks on a vertical piece of metallic tube that's sturdy enough to hold his weight.

"What are you doing?" I breathe.

"Trying to escape."

He plants his toe on a protruding ledge of wires clipped to the wall with a series of J hooks, pulls himself up using the strip of steel, and reaches for the narrow ledge of concrete at the foot of the door opening. I watch him climb as a mechanical whirr fills the elevator shaft from above.

Cy hears it, too.

"Curses!" he yells.

Shimmying his fingers into the doorjamb, he attempts to pry the doors apart, just as the heavy whirr settles to a sudden clunk ten feet above his head.

He scoots outward, away from the center of the door, and, still clinging to the concrete ledge with his feet perched on the strut piece, reaches for what appears to be a switch.

From my knowledge of building floor plans, every set of elevator shafts usually accompany an elevator mechanical room, which houses the machinery necessary to control the elevator. This room feeds the shaft's interior with wires and a series of heavy metal belts that build tracks onto the wall to keep the elevator steady. The pulley system feeds up the sides of the walls with thick, braided cables attaching to a pinion high overhead, which then suspend the elevator and guide it up and down along the tracks.

That it appears to be in good working order doesn't dawn on me until the elevator lurches to life once again. Cy groans as the elevator slides upward and away.

When he's managed to slide himself to the shaft's far corner, he reaches for a tiny black square embedded in a rectangle of steel.

He flips at it and, as if on command, the elevator door slides open. A *ding* chirps from outside to signal to prospective riders that their car has arrived.

He gazes into the face of a stranger six feet above him, who looks to be wearing a confused expression. The light cascades through the open doors and allows me to gauge the climb ahead of me.

"Make them stop the elevator," Cy yells. "Before it flattens us."

"Us?"

The man peers downward and watches me settle my foot on the grooved pump head.

"Get security!" the man shouts. "Shut it down."

Moments later, the whine of the elevator fades away, and the metal cables click and slacken for a second. The stoppage allows me to climb high enough to grasp the edge of the opening. Strangers reach their hands out to help us.

When we crawl out of the elevator into full daylight and an intact lobby, I manage to get a real taste of its elegant quality.

Fake plants adorn low tables between banks of leather armchairs. Their decorative black pots highlight odd decorations, dog-eared magazines, and clipboards.

White and beige tile lies separate from the flowing streams of pale blue flooring that resemble a river though stone. An adjacent corridor juts off into a romantic dining area, where couples chitchat and servers carry shining plates of hot food to the hungry patrons.

The scent of the food wafts into my nostrils, reminding me I haven't eaten in what feels like days.

"What do you say we grab a bite?" I mumble. "Maybe we can try a different means of getting me back home, if it exists anymore."

"Or discuss what might be out there. I don't like this one bit."

"That, too," I agree.

I eye a cart carrying empty plates next to a stainless-steel counter, behind which chefs and kitchen staff clamor. A cook appears behind the counter, pulls a receipt from a corkboard track, and pushes a plate of food to the edge of the counter. She yells something at someone else, who hurries to put together a side dish. My stomach grumbles.

We enter the dining room and take in the ornate theme of gold-tinted artificial relics. A golden pyramid stands on a far wall beyond a passageway flanked by two sphinxes. The coincidence gnaws at the back of my mind as we settle into a comfortable, yet isolated booth and examine the tile and wood-topped table between us.

Cy reaches for the napkin dispenser as I arrange and neaten the tray of sugar and sweetener packets.

He pulls the pack of cards from his pocket, grunts, and slaps them down between us before a skinny, dark-haired server saunters to the end of the table.

She greets us and slides a pair of menu cards toward us, before hurrying away to help another table.

I pick mine up and begin to scan the delectable offerings while Cy visibly tries to build a stable explanation for everything that has happened.

"Excuse me," he says, looking up at a man leaning toward his date a few tables away.

The man narrows his eyes, perplexed, and studies the two dirty strangers that greet him. He says nothing and attempts to refocus his attention on his date, but she, too, has taken to staring at us.

"Sorry for my interruption," Cy remarks, as if unaware of how we must look.

They may have assumed us to be vagrants by now, who just happened to have found enough money on a sidewalk to afford an enjoyable meal. In truth, that perception wouldn't be far off. After all, we have been wandering, and are somewhat short on luck. But Cy must have money, or he wouldn't have agreed to sit down for a meal.

"I'm wondering if you can tell us the date?"

"Uh. September ... September 12."

Cy nods. "What year?"

The woman gasps as her partner rolls his eyes.

"I've always wanted to do that," Cy adds to me under his breath.

The man nods, as if understanding has suddenly overtaken him. He straightens himself, bows his head, and offers us the one damning piece of evidence we have waited for: "Twenty fifty-nine, of course."

# 11

# Heiress to Circe

I gobble down the appetizer Cy has ordered for us to share without a second thought as to whether he wants a bite. He nibbles at the crispy, cheesy flatbread crust and flips over Tarot cards one by one, as if in search of something important.

The decorative style in this establishment seems an odd choice, based on everything I know about Philadelphia. Yet Cy's explanation of the name's history makes the theme seem fitting if he is telling the truth.

How much had Greek culture influenced Egyptian, anyway? And how had the Pharaohs reacted to Greek occupation before the Ptolemaic dynasty? If I remember any of this when I get home, I will consider reading one or two ancient Egyptian history books.

Will I remember? With all this dimension-hopping Cy and Secretary Harley talked about, I haven't had a chance to sit down and apply logic to the concept of memory. And Cy had the audacity to suggest I've done this before and don't remember. If the food hadn't commanded my attention, I might have found the nerve to reach across the table and strangle him.

For now, my only choice is to go along with everything he says and does. More and more, evidence suggests that Cy has no better idea what's going on than me, which ratchets up the tension with every breath.

"How old is your son in the year 2059? Not that it matters."

I mentally do the math. Becky and I met at that dance party in 2026, married eight months later, and brought Ian into the world less than a year after that. "I guess twenty-two," I mumble, shrugging. "But why would it matter?"

"Becky buys the lake house when he's eight or nine," Cy wagers. "Which means—"

"Lake house? Riiiight."

He shrugs, picks up the last slice of pizza, and eyes it as though he'd just snatched the last morsel of joy from my fingertips. "Fine, don't believe me. It's just that it would have happened about 2045. A couple of years later, you have that battle."

"Which lake?" I guzzle my soda through the straw and sit back while he gathers a pair of cards between his fingers and fans them out before his face. He doesn't bother using the napkin before doing so.

"Doesn't matter. I'm guessing a long way from Harrisburg."

I nearly slam the glass down on the table when I hear it. I could launch myself across the table and punch him out right now, but I choose to restrain myself. "How do you know I live in Harrisburg?"

"Come on, Larry. I thought we'd established that I know more about your life in these dimensions than you do. Nothing wrong with careful planning about where to take you."

"As if you had any control over that."

He takes his turn to launch a glare at me, but lets his muscles slacken after a second or two, even as I seethe. "I concede. But then again, knowing where you've been might inform where you're headed, and if current events foretell, we're about to—how would you say it? See some serious shit?"

"I see a serious shit right now," I garble after swallowing, unaware that I'm raising my voice, which will attract concerned and annoyed stares from the other diners. "I'm going to pummel you, you bastard."

He nods slowly. "You could do that. And I believe you. Then again, you and I share the same destiny right now."

"What do *you* know, you immortal piece of goose turd?"

"Larry."

"I'm sorry sir," a waitress says, appearing beside our table. "Would you please keep it down?"

"I'm not keeping anything down." Disgust overrides my demeanor and Cy deserves what I'm unloading on him. Keeping the meal down is my hope, but anger may disrupt it.

"Please, sir," she snips, "or I'll have to ask you to take it outside."

"I'll take it outside," I shout.

"You want to leave me, Larry?" Cy doesn't act threatened. He sits back and slides the cards across the table face down while surreptitiously nodding at them, as if they hold all the answers. "I'm not a seer, just a stranded traveler like you are. Hell, I don't even have a map, but I at least have a *piece* of a map, which, by my estimation, makes me more informed than you. You can go it alone, but your chances of getting home shrink drastically if you do. Consider an alternative."

"An alternative to kicking your ass or leaving you?"

The couple beside us stares, but I pay no attention. They might think they're witnessing the breakup of a relationship, but I don't care what they think, or even what Cy thinks.

The meals arrive just after he slides the cards to me, but for a moment, I don't bother to glance at them. I prod at my steaming entrée with my fork while pondering what the future might hold. Being in the dark is never a pleasant feeling, but being blinded without a clue as to what the next step holds allows an icy wave of fear to wash over me. Goosebumps erupt on my forearms as I stab the pieces of my food and force them into my mouth.

By the time I'm a third of the way finished eating, Cy diverts his attention from me and starts to eat. The warm darkness of the décor eats away at the mood in unpredictable ways. While designed to keep diners comfortable and thus encourage them to spend more, it evokes shards of blackened rage and adrenaline in me.

Between bites, Cy glances at the two cards and swallows. I drop my fork on the plate with a *clink* and gaze down at them. A dark, swirling vortex of dust and glimmering stars adorns the back surface, invoking awe. Inviting. Charming. Everything a Seer might need if such a person exists.

Relenting, I slide the cards off the end of the table while pinching them between my thumb and index finger. The first depicts a dark-haired woman wearing a brooding expression. She rests in an elaborate throne with gems encrusted in gilded highlights on the carved legs and stretchers. Grasping a twisting wooden staff with a blue stone glued to the end, she wears a see-through tunic that exposes her left breast and ends in light lace just above her ankles.

The other card shows a bright background of a pictogram sun that spreads alternating shades of yellow in every direction and casts oblique shadows of cypress trees to scurry toward deeper shade.

"Interesting combination, isn't it?" Cy gulps down a morsel of food and speaks without bothering to swallow first.

"Not even a little," I lie. The illustrations get my mind churning at a rapid pace, making me almost forget my plan to batter him senseless after we've eaten. Cy can see the wheels turning through my expression, so I slap the cards on the table and devour the rest of my meal before guzzling more of my drink.

"You don't know who they are, and that's fine."

"The cards? I don't buy all this mystic crap."

"Which is weird, to say the least."

In any other setting, his retort might leave me scratching my head or laughing, but here, its nonchalance elicits a careless aura where mysticism should be the order of things, rather than the exception.

"In Ancient Egypt," Cy starts, pointing at the sun card, "they called this one Ra. We know him as Helios, who happens to have had a daughter, among several other offspring.

"Her name is Circe, an enchanting, seductive sorceress with several magical powers."

"Magic? Why should I care about her?"

"I'd say we can use someone like her right about now. I can't say whether she's ever been reincarnated, but her existence at least hints at the possibility that there are other enchanters. Where do you think we should look?"

"Got a portal back to Greece?"

"Well..."

I shrug before finishing my drink, pretending I have a wallet to fish tip money out of, and wait for him to fumble the beginnings of a plan.

"This is Philadelphia," he says. "I wager there might be a mom-and-pop metaphysical store or two in the area."

"Those people are nuts," I dismiss them.

"Which might complement fruits like us. What do you say?"

"Market Street," I affirm. "Tourist mecca. I happen to know a place Harley used to sit outside to watch the streets."

"Exactly."

"Wait, you know about it?"

His dismissal almost makes me want to gag. "Son, I've spent more time with Harley than you have—before the president chose him as Secretary of Defense. I know the shop. Can't say I've ever gone inside."

The Egyptian-tinged ambient music stirs lustrous melodies that only spread reams of frost into my trembling spirit. Wallowing in the decrepit remains of something resembling a life, I allow sorrow to slither through my soul, expunging all pleasure.

## MEMORIES:

Flowers. In thin glass vases, scattered in bunches, gathered into perfect artistic arrangements with sleek greenery, and tied together with tight rubber bands. Apart from florist stores, I'd only seen so many flowers of various types once before. They crop up everywhere, in three-foot-tall urns next to a dark-stained pulpit, the mournful hands of parishioners, and even the closed lid of the ornamental casket.

Torment flows through my body as I gaze on. A twenty-year-old Ian stands next to me with tears in his eyes but remains otherwise motionless. The sun bakes through high stained-glass transom windows, and an opalescent arrangement ties the chapel together in an enriching splendor. Had I never met Becky, I may never have experienced this setting, yet here I sit in agony as I await her company.

Ice floods through my veins as I gaze at the casket. There's nothing there but the numbing pain that replaces loss after death. I cannot stop the tears from streaking through the colorful masterpiece and rendering everything a hazy mosh-pit of clashing colors that swirl in a vat of dystopic evil.

The ooze and haze blinds me from anything resembling real life, where I cower in darkened corners to escape from the tremors of hell that otherwise might destroy all the flesh that clings to my bones.

Smoke filters through the chaos, and when I open my eyes to flush away the confused kaleidoscope, Ian has disappeared. The pews are empty, the pastor is nothing more than a painted statuette, and the floral decorations have given way to a timeless age that has allowed them to wither and crisp, darkening the enchanting colors. No one is here but me and the empty casket.

And the soulful hymn has expanded into a dysrhythmic, minor key ambiance that shreds the scene into a soupy fog that washes away life itself.

Cy breathes deeply as we exit the well-appointed hotel lobby and emerge onto a sunny street where life shoots in every direction. Music of a different type strums from a few blocks away. I first gaze up at the hodgepodge of new and old crystalline towers. The shining spire of the skyline's crown jewel gives it away as Philadelphia at first glance.

A hundred people flood into a crosswalk when the red hand turns white. Cy makes his way in that direction before I stop him. We're going to have it out here and now.

I shove him from behind and he prepares for the moment I have expected for a long time. No fear touches his eyes. Instead, he seems to anticipate it, which somehow increases my ire.

The sun departs into a network of cumulus clouds, which cast gray shadows that flutter over different sections of downtown.

"Never let a good moment go to waste," Cy grits.

I rumble a nonsensical reply.

"I suppose I've had it coming for a long time. What better time than now, huh? With everyone watching. You'll be the big hero you've always wanted to be, and me, the cowering villain who's finally met a companion he can't best. Do it. I'm not armed."

I shove him again, and he staggers backward to the curb.

Again, he reacts in a manner I can't control. He shrugs it off and stares at me as though unconvinced by my aggression.

"You're the reason she's dead!"

"There are lots of reasons for a lot of things. But sometimes there's no reason for anything. The saying 'everything happens for a reason' is a lie."

I tremble and spit out my reply. "*You're* the liar. And I'm going to break your goddamn neck."

He shuffles a half step backward as he turns his back to the sidewalk and then the building storefront, which reflects the back of his head. The glimmer of the sun peeks out from the clouds, and the resultant reflection blinds me.

Together, we dance in a swirling motion, drawing the gaze of too many passersby. The strumming of the guitar in the distance draws nearer as we circle around one another like two bodies orbiting a single, invisible node of gravity.

A car horn honks at a jaywalking pedestrian, which distracts Cy for a moment. A split second before my fist collides with his face, he panics, steps backward, and stumbles. Collapsing in defeat, he rolls onto his back and gazes up at me, a cool grin creasing his face.

I kick his side with the full brunt of every ounce of force I can muster. He groans and rolls over. Allowing him a moment to stagger back to his feet, I prepare to attack again as he puts up his dukes.

A flurry of punches strip that grin right off his face, but I'm not done with him yet. He turns his cheek at just the wrong minute as I see a small spot of blood on his lip.

Hurling one final punch, I listen to the crack as my knuckles smash his nose, which causes blood to pour down his face.

Relenting, I relax my fists at my side and tremble while he dabs at the blood on his lip.

"Feel better now?"

"You might want to have that looked at," I mock him.

Nodding, he tilts his head back, searching the skies for something that may never arrive.

I haven't been in a fight since high school, when a basketball player shoved Juaquin's friend Kel into a locker. I may not have liked Kel much, but I defended him anyway, and it felt good. Kel didn't thank me, and I didn't promise an ongoing alliance, but the exchange was cathartic.

That same emotional sensation resounds now. My nerves settle as we make our way through downtown.

Hoofing it to Market Street this time of day may take over an hour, but Cy has taken to walking instead of hailing for a cab. I don't bother to protest, even as the ebb and flow of anger whirls through my senses. It might take me days or months before I gather the will to fight him for real, and if he puts up a defense then, I'll know for sure we're on different teams.

The swellings of street music rise and fall with the motorized hum of traffic even from four blocks away. The clouds gradually scoot off toward the East Coast, and behind them, a cool mass of Canadian air pushes through the city.

A crowd has gathered on a busy sidewalk around the felt-lined case of a solo saxophonist playing a somber yet elegant jazzy tune, drawing the people nearby to listen to his soulful music. A couple drops a few bills into his case, smiles, and strolls away hand in hand. A dozen people gather around an old man speaking rhythmically into a microphone, while a shorter man in the back starts snapping his fingers, encouraging the rest of the group to cheer on the poet.

I set my eyes on that familiar spot where I'd met Harley all those years ago. I can still remember his frazzled look, but the wisdom that played out on his face comes back even more vividly. The cadence of his voice sounded like something special, worthy of being listened to. How he'd managed to blend his words into such an inspirational tapestry, I may never know.

The metaphysical shop stands idle today; no one hunkers in the shadow of its overhang, and few shoppers show they've noticed its existence. The open sign is a black, felt-backed banner with grooves and the letters arranged in perfectly spaced kerning. It hangs by a narrow, fraying strand of twine around a projecting peg of an obsolete jig that would allow the owner to open the window if the contraption ever worked.

The display table behind the window rests in front of a black partition curtain that might allow only traces of light to exit into the street. It displays handcrafted clay pots and urns of various sizes next to a mismatched array of gemstones featuring a round geode cut in half that allows thousands of alluring violet crystals to spill out onto the table. Behind them, an arrangement of eclectic candles flickers, bathing the entire display in a surreal gauze of yellow light.

I'll never know how I missed the charm when I met Harley here, but the fact that this shop has stayed in business ever since serves as a proud testament to Market Street's tourist allure.

A bell dings when I push open the glass door. A petite woman behind the counter is wearing a thick set of glasses that highlight the silvery curls framing her face. She glances toward us as she explains the various properties of a stone a gentleman is holding, while an old cloth hardcover book rests on the glass countertop next to his outstretched hand.

The customer breaks eye contact with her when we enter, looks flustered, and flits away into an aisle of candles and books.

"How can we heal you fine gentlemen today?" the woman asks in a youthful, yet gravelly voice.

"I—we were wondering if you know anything about ... magic?"

"Magic of what sort?"

"I—well, I don't know exactly."

"My friend here is lost." Cy comes to the rescue. "We were wondering if you know a way to help him find home."

"Not home," I interrupt. "Becky. I can't live without her."

"A woman," she chimes in, wearing a glittery smile. "You want her to fall in love with you? I have some charms to help you with that."

"I'm not buying," I counter. "I'm asking if you can save her life. See, she died. A few—well, I don't know how long ago. For me, here. But I'm supposed to be with her right now, fourteen years ago. I ... I..."

"It will cost you a session," she agrees, "and my rates aren't cheap. Only a powerful spell can do what you desire."

"I ... oh my God." I stare at a felt mat stretched out across a bark-rimmed polished tree trunk coffee table, lingering in a dim, curtained backroom with an array of real candles encircling another mysterious tome.

"Are you familiar with a goddess named Circe?" Cy asks, unwilling to play along.

She offers a suspicious shake of her head and leans forward. "I'm Miriam. Come back at nightfall and I'll tell you a secret. Our session will start at nine. Don't be late."

"A reading?"

She shakes her head and frowns, while scouring me with her narrowed eyes. "A healing."

# 12

# Ode to the Daemons

Instead of exiting the store, we browse the aisles for ten minutes just to examine the diverse array of merchandise. Without knowing the so-called properties of healing crystals, candles, books, or other items, I only allow for color, texture, and style to garner my attention. Cy scrutinizes the shelves as though he knows what he's looking at, thumbing through a book for five minutes before scooting it back into its perch to resume browsing.

"You don't actually believe in this hokum?" I prod him, appearing at his side.

"What's not to believe? Keep an open mind."

The urge to slap him passes through me. "Uh-huh. I'm the most open-minded person you'll ever meet, but even I have my limits."

"Then again," he begins, "in time, there are fewer limits. Setting limits is a good way to constrain yourself."

"Which is not necessarily a bad thing," I argue.

He runs his fingers along the spine of another book, a nonverbal cue that my opinion means nothing to him. Tying my destiny to him may be the biggest constraint I can imagine, yet he continually warns me to stick with him. Is it because he cares where I end up?

The mental insinuation makes me gag on my own tongue. *Sure he does.*

No, he needs *me*. I'll discover for what ends later, I promise myself, but resolve to stay wary of him every step of the way. Thinking of him as an ally is another imaginary constraint, one that promises potential devastation.

"It's good to learn about things," he says, "even if you don't believe in them. One can't make that determination without considering the information, can he?"

"If learning it is valuable to me personally, I'll do it no questions asked. But it isn't. None of it is. It's all a distraction from my real quest."

"You don't know your real quest yet."

"Sure as hell doesn't revolve around you."

He raises his eyebrows. "Regardless of how many times I've had to save your ass? I didn't have to do it."

I allow myself to utter a low growl that even in the quiet store, Cy won't be able to hear. "Then why did you?"

"One doesn't become king by lacking a conscience," he says.

His response makes me scoff. "Haven't you read anything about democracy? *Demos.* The people. Lack of conscience is *exactly* how one becomes king."

He grabs me by the crook of my arm and makes a beeline for the glass door, passing a neat selection of tie-dyed T-shirts, scarves, and other apparel.

"Do you really want to talk about democracy? Here's a little-known fact: It doesn't work. Never once in world history. In Greece, it resulted in a classist system where only twenty percent of the people had any say, and that's if they actually considered slaves as people.

"And the United States? The system isn't even pure, and we see its disastrous effects playing out in real time. Extremism, one-upmanship, an unwillingness to compromise, and the people having the power to sow whatever lies and hate they think appropriate because it's good for democracy. But it's really just a fast-track to totalitarianism."

I'm going to smack him again, but I swallow my rage. "Oh, you're one of *those* people."

"See what I'm talking about?" He raises his voice when we walk out the front door to the establishment, and I rest my back against the stucco and brick veneer between the storefront displays. "'*Those* people' is an attempt to eliminate certain classes you deem unworthy. You clearly don't even believe in true democracy."

We're on a tangent that is making me lose sight of what I'm aiming for, but the mere act of debating is serving as a strange tonic to awaken my passions. I don't care what Cy thinks of democracy, because he's wrong.

I seethe for five minutes while he meanders through an explanation about the divine purpose of humanity, or some other opinionated garble that doesn't interest me in the slightest. Seeing my disinterest, he trails off and gazes at the saxophonist, who is winding through a slow, syncopated melody with effectual pauses interspersed by towering peaks.

"When is nine o'clock, anyway?"

Though he'd previously shown his stylistic preference for asking pointed questions to provoke thought, his body language suggests he doesn't have the slightest clue.

I haven't lived in Philadelphia for years, but the couple in the restaurant said it's September. The weather seems right, and near the equinoxes the sun spreads light through the urban canyons in a peculiar manner. The angle of the sun and its position gives me clues to estimate the time within a half-hour. "In about three hours. Did you miss sundial school?"

I allow myself to smile at my own wit before the words can escape my lips. If Cy were a fan of wordplay, he'd offer a sarcastic remark right now, but his lack of response proves that he doesn't know the first thing about Christianity, and doesn't give a damn what I think about anything. At any rate, it wouldn't prove him worthy of having around, except for the part about him saving my ass, and I've already lost track of how many times he's done that.

Instead of saying something, he watches the saxophonist until the crowds wander on to other attractions on Market Street.

"Maybe I'll just meet you here at nine," I say, spying a bakery a few doors down. On the opposite corner stands an old bookshop, which, if I am lucky, is still open for business. I could use a reprieve from his smarmy attitude, unless I want to fight him again. The throngs might pay good money to watch, but I'm not interested in the confrontation.

Instead, I turn my back on him, stroll past the storefronts, and disappear into the bakery, where the rich aroma hangs in the air like a dense cloud of deliciousness. I'd be keen to sample its offerings, but I don't have a dime in my pocket. I'd have to raid Cy's 'wallet' first, which can only lead to a discussion about the penalty for stealing, and that would make me want to slug him.

Ten minutes in the bakery is more than I can bear. The meal at the Egyptian-themed restaurant is still settling in my stomach, which should be enough sustenance to keep me on my toes for three days of dislocated adventures and convoluted traumas.

It's all *convoluted* as *hell* and Cy isn't even good at explaining what little he knows. This would be enough to drive me insane if I didn't have a single purpose in mind. If the mysticism and witchcraft nonsense proves even half as effective as advertised, I might consider it a measured success in pointing me in the right direction, at least. The hell with Cy.

The bookstore serves as a better change of pace. Even realizing I've looked at curious volumes the last few days, books always could keep me engaged. Eight years of marriage to a bibliophile like Becky have served me well.

I pull out a book promising new information on climate change and the role corporate farming plays, and while I don't ascribe to the alarmist rhetoric, the scientific nature of the conversation is more than adequate at holding my attention. I scan through the first chapter, find a stool next to a coffee bar, and keep reading for what must be hours.

A barista steps to my table, asking if she can get me something, but I ignore her. On her fourth visit, she eyes me as if agitated, but says nothing.

Before long, she's pouring a concoction, presumably for herself, then hesitates in front of me, holds it out in front of her, and places it on the counter in front of me.

"You know what?" she says. "This one's one the house. If you'll at least allow me a moment to bounce an idea off you."

I gaze at her while trying to gauge the time.

"What's that thing they're saying about fusion these days? Something about using a laser to cause a nuclear reaction in hydrogen molecules?"

Shaking my head, I continue to read.

"I'm doing a paper on it, or at least that was the plan," she rambles. "My professor at Temple considers it a great idea, but so far the research is only turning up useless tech mag articles."

"Right," I drawl.

"But if we can harness the technology, and the evidence says we can, why can't we do away with all this natural gas and solve the climate crisis forever?"

"Really, I'm not an expert," I mutter.

But a memory forces itself into my brain, and I blurt out his name without thinking it through: "Secretary Harley, he might be a good mind to pick."

Years ago, while conversing in the bakery, Harley had mentioned physics more than once. It's ancient history by now, especially in this realm, but my memory of that day is surprisingly rigid.

"Secretary of what?"

"Defense," I say.

"You *know* the Secretary of Defense?"

I stammer. Is Harley still the Secretary of Defense in this dimension? Thinking about it causes a headache to pulse through my brain. "I ... well, I guess I used to, but before he became Secretary. Good guy, better friend. Look him up, tell him I sent you, and he'll probably sit down and have a pastry with you."

"Really?" She perks up. "Wow, thanks! What's your name?"

I hesitate, glance out the window at the coming twilight, and stretch my legs. "Just call me Larry."

She's halfway through offering me effusive thanks before I'm depositing the book back where I found it and making my way through the front door. By my estimation, nine o'clock will roll around soon.

As if he hasn't moved in three hours, Cy waits at the end of the block, ready to meet the mystic. I jog up behind him, panting, and show that I'm at last ready to be healed.

The musician has long since departed, and now a lonely couple deep in conversation has taken his place. The mood has darkened, an emotion that has latched onto the fragments of Cy's persona, rendering him a shade of desperate.

Saying nothing, he turns from the sidewalk, pulls open the door, and comes face to face with Miriam, the shop owner. She has taken to sweeping the aisles in expectation, and when she sees my face, she tilts the broom against the wall and leads us past an array of crystal orbs, aromatherapy solutions and beaded keychains hung from tiny pegs on a rotating stand, which graces the top of a glass case containing what appears to be a statue of a fire-breathing dragon.

Cy tags along as the woman leads us into her den. She parts the curtain, revealing wood and glass wall cases displaying ancient books and figurines fronting a red-papered back wall. Soft carpet is compressed underfoot. She fluffs a fringed button-centered throw pillow, tosses it to the floor in front of the polished log-section coffee table, kneels, and flips through a voluminous spell book that must be six inches thick.

Resting her hindquarters on the pillow, she instructs us to follow her lead. I slip off my shoes and leave them next to the curtained door and cast my eyes in all directions. Six candles flicker on the sliced-log table before me. Seeing as I'm the one about to be healed, I settle in at arms-length from her, but she deems me too far away and leans in closer.

Flipping to what she must consider the right page, she arches her back, settles her shoulders, and inhales before resting her hands on the book and closing her eyes. As though taking a keen interest in whatever odors her nose can detect, she sniffs at the surrounding air.

"Your aura is dark," she reveals, speaking in a low, gravelly monotone. "But nonetheless complete."

"If you say so—"

"This cannot work if you don't settle your mind.

"There are passions here. Dark forces. I sense the shadow of Keres, yes, and Lethe. Poor Lethe, whose memory produces no fruit fit to eat. There is pain and death here, and a sliver of servitude." Her speech has taken the melody of a rhythmic chant, unchanging in depth or tone.

"Mother Circe, expel these demons!"

She begins yammering in some odd language that resembles Greek, but as I don't understand what she's saying, she could be cursing me to a lifetime of green extremities and verdant emotion.

*Demons?*

"It is he!" she shouts. "The One!"

I cast my eyes sideways. The carpet drifts away below me as I linger in space with only the polished wood section table, the candles, and the book swaying before me. Cy has vanished, and the flickering candles illuminate a darker shadow that lurks somewhere beyond the limits of my perception.

I'm reaching out to it, my fingers tingling in the warm air and my spirit rising. Something white shines overhead, like the pulse of a distant star beaming down on me and dousing me with ice water. Sarah's image dances before my eyes and vanishes as Miriam continues to chant.

As the memory of Sarah fades away, I linger on a breathless ether of white, as though an unseen floor of misty clouds holds me aloft. That unnamed goddess in white shimmers before me, silent but beckoning.

Before I can understand what is happening, the scene fades and stretches to black as the myriad stars blossom. I descend into a dank, stone-floored dungeon through a mesmerizing abyss—and the smell of death.

## MEMORIES:

The sadness folds in on itself, creasing my soul with an otherworldly splendor that could scatter pieces of me throughout time and space. Becky's photograph lingers behind glass, cold, tattered, and frozen in time. The darkness in the room fuses her image with reflections of shadow, as though her spirit has lifted itself from her body and is floating toward its true destination.

A hand rests on my shoulder, icy and almost subhuman. A frayed, gaunt face, shrouded by a greasy mane of black hair, skulks behind me. I study him, allowing my heart to flutter in my chest.

"She's gone, Dad," he says.

Ice water pours through my veins and freezes my spirit.

Miriam rambles on and together we hover to the floor. “We cannot mend those torn from time,” she warns.

“Her—Becky. I have to save her.”

*“She’s gone, Dad.”*

“No.”

“Do not become a servant to The One!”

That inner voice I can’t control clanks around inside my skull. *You already are.*

The wispy voice of the goddess in white echoes in my mind, pressing warmth into my heart. Tears sparkle on my cheeks. *“Use it for good.”*

*There’s no good. There is only you.*

For perhaps hours, Miriam drones on and on in that garbled Greek. Cy twitches beside me, but lowers his face when I set eyes on him to note his expression. It has gone as gaunt as the ashes of those memories that had assembled a monster when he wasn’t there.

Where did he go? That voice was there, too. And the monster grew out of the detritus that had once been my spirit and memory, to suck me into an abyssal home I could never reach.

“Cy?” Worry sparks in my voice.

“Cy matters not,” he mumbles in Miriam’s voice. “What matters is the only true reason you know within yourself.”

He closes his mouth and his face stretches into a pixelated infinity. Light swirls around me, gathers into my fingers, my arms, and my feet. Energy vibrates in my bones.

“You cannot defeat darkness with darkness. Only light can do that.”

“Martin Luther King?”

*SILENCE!*

“You can’t win,” I croak, without acknowledging that my lips are moving.

The shopkeeper stirs, pulls her hands away from the book, and opens her eyes. Oceans swim within them, the surface tossing like the last tremors of a violent tempest, and somewhere beyond the shores a simple peace settles.

She reaches down and offers me a tissue, which I dab at the corners of my eyes. The shapes and shadows in the room blur into confused, soft-edged shapes. When clarity resumes, I can see that Cy has gone stiff and pale, as if he'd just seen a horror blacker than death.

What has he seen? Judging by Cy's expression, he may remain silent for a long time, and I'd rather not find out the reason.

I can barely contain it; my fingers ache and throb as adrenaline shoots through them. The glow in the room carries a zest that wasn't there before, as if an unknown spark had ignited it into a form solid and true, and the memory is transformed into something resembling joy.

"Do you feel healed?"

It sounds like a statement rather than a question. Do I? Something new spins within me, yet the darkness that has consumed me still rages on in the background as though ready for a brutal strike.

"I ... I feel *something.*"

"What gift has Ariadne given you?"

I cannot define it. Stammering, I try to compose a reply: "Something as powerful as the dark. Something Christians call divine."

Cy looks on, as if shocked still. Yet upon mention of the word 'divine,' something in his spirit has perked up. He moves to stand, fishes out his wallet, and offers Miriam what might be more than a thousand dollars in crisp American bills.

"You must return for another session," she warns, "if you are to be fully healed. Can I schedule you in two months?"

In two months, Cy and I will be long gone, off to another dimension, yet the hope of home still burns somewhere within me. If I can still remember Becky and it's all true, I see only one solution: I've already been home and I don't know it yet.

The realization towers over me like a blackened skyscraper. Memory doesn't work in reverse. If it's real, then the laws of time and space themselves have been distorted beyond repair and home might not exist—and Becky may dance beyond the limits of my reach for eternity.

# 13

# Paradoxos

"Feel better now?" Cy echoes as we exit the store. Miriam watches as we walk away, at least until the door falls closed and the bell dings; I can feel her eyeballs boring into the back of my skull.

"Not exactly," I grumble.

"You were going to hit me again."

Allowing myself a moment to frown, I squint in the streetlamp's glare. The tourist activity has died down, rendering Market Street quieter. The throngs are now gathering a dozen blocks away in the nightlife district, known for its collection of dive bars, elite cocktail clubs, and neon-clad dance clubs. Friends and coworkers had described the scene to me back when I lived in Philadelphia. The happenings in 2059 are something I'd rather not know about.

"I bet you wouldn't like that," I say.

"You'll notice how I didn't fight back."

I only offer a polite nod. He didn't fight back because he needs me, and I'm going to find out why. Ariadne? The gift? It was vague when Miriam mentioned it, but now the memory is bleeding back into my mind.

The gift had fought back evil—the Shade. And if the power had peaked at the exact moment I punched Cy, his eyeballs might have shot out the back of his head and rolled into the sewer two blocks away.

How do I still have it? And can I use it?

"We might discuss the daemons, then," Cy notes.

"Why do you pronounce it that way?"

Cy had expected my mispronunciation. "Don't confuse them with the demons associated with your Bible. These are actual spirits with actual powers, and I've seen some of them, but never heard their names until tonight.

"What's that supposed to mean?"

He stops walking and accosts me with a scowl. "It means we've got bigger problems than Erebus, whom I've heard referred to as 'The One' only twice now. We'll circle back to that."

"Shit."

"You know *The One* can't control the daemons ... because they are associated with the underworld. There is one god of the underworld and he's arguably as powerful as Zeus himself. And he's the only one with the capacity for some of the evil we've seen on this trip.

"Don't go thinking that Hades is completely evil. He can do great works if he sees a means to an end."

"He can—bring her back?"

"I don't know about that."

I grit my teeth. "But you insinuated it. You gotta get me out of here, bring me to the underworld and I'll show him what I can do."

"You think one of the most powerful beings to ever exist is going to let a gift from a precious princess like Ariadne intimidate him?

"Well—"

"Even if you could use it. The other major problem is you can't get to the underworld unless you die, and we both know what happens if you die. It'll open up the mother of all paradoxes."

"Jesus," I say, at once breathless. "I'm not letting her go, dammit. I'll go through the fires of hell if I must, and I don't care if you come with me."

"You're missing the point."

"No, *you* are."

He paces toward the pastry shop for a few seconds as I lag behind to consider the ramifications. For my plan to work I'll need a roadmap, and I have nothing. Cy knows I need him for that and it's a partnership I'm not ready to give up yet, regardless of how deeply I want to knock his brains out.

"No one goes to the underworld and comes out. No one. It's impossible. And if you die now, you can't even go there because you ... do ... not ... exist. Don't you get that?"

My heart hammers in my chest. I can't believe I'm about to say this—"Then take me back to my present time and kill me."

"Still not thinking clearly," he dismisses it. "That won't work either, because she won't be in the underworld yet. Paradoxes don't unravel the rules of the cosmos."

"There *are* no *rules*! You're not seeing it, either. Rules are made to be broken, and if the gods are doing this, they're breaking them! You're just myopic and ignorant."

"Paradox."

"Paradoxes happen all the time. I know a big one off the top of my head: Logic would argue that twenty-four random people in a room are highly unlikely to share the same birthday. Yet mathematically, it's a ninety-nine percent probability."

"We're way beyond math here, and that's not a paradox."

"Take me somewhere." I dash across the street to the overhang of an upscale clothing shop that offers expensive tourist apparel. If I know what I'm looking for, a shadow might provide a portal.

"I'm out of destinations!" Cy shouts from behind me. He jogs across the street and meets me on the sidewalk, between two infant trees that seem to flutter in a scant breeze.

"Just this once, take me where you want to go."

"I don't know where they take me," I say. "There's another problem. One I haven't worked out yet, but Secretary Harley once referred to it as the uncertainty principle."

"Never heard of it," he scoffs. "But go on."

"Using some *portals* more than once can lead you to the same place, but every time, certain details within the destination dimension are rearranged. I can't work out why."

He strokes his beard with his right hand while he slips his left hand into his pocket, as if to make sure his tarot deck is still with him. "There could be a few reasons. Maybe a different version of you altered it? Or someone else in that dimension?"

"Impossible."

"Even in cases of destiny, the past always changes the future. Maybe that's a possibility."

"That doesn't make any sense," I grit out. "They are things that have nothing to do with the past in any way."

He considers the information and continues to stroke his chin while letting his eyes wander to the skies. "Everything we do in the past will inevitably change certain future events. Even something as inconsequential as flipping a light switch. It's hard to gauge the impact, and even when it does happen, you never think that one minor decision years ago caused something else."

I pay no attention to his rambling. His guesswork could drive me insane if I let him blather on as if he knows what the hell he's talking about.

"We need to move. I'm sick of 2059 already."

He inhales and nods. "Take note of how we got here."

"Why?"

"You'll thank me in the future."

I frown. "This *is* the future."

A blank stare crosses his face, along with a spark of uncertainty that clouds what little I can see ahead of me. Spite rises in the back of my throat, and I try to swallow it. Still, it persists.

Raising my shoulders, I sigh. "Isn't it?"

He uses this moment to speak softly, allowing a low grumble to meander through his voice. "If you insist the rules are being broken, then how can you know for sure?"

"Two people," I start. "One always lies, one always tells the truth. How do you know which one is lying? I've never been able to figure that one out."

"You don't see the problem with that? No one always lies. No one always tells the truth. So probably both of them are lying."

This discussion is getting me nowhere. I shrug and issue a final grunt, with which I intend to close the conversation. To memorize how we got to 2059, I'll have to remember where we were before and how we got here. But the events have blurred together into one soupy mess of memory where no detail can distinguish one from the other.

At least I remember the building and the elevator, which may be good enough.

Cy follows me along the storefronts of the various shops until we reach the corner.

The intersecting street usually carries more traffic in late evening, due to its connection between the tourist sections of downtown and the business district. Tonight, only a stray car blazes along its two northbound lanes with luck on its side. Lights change to green as it approaches, and then about ten blocks away, it turns right, and another set of headlights appears.

We watch as we wander the sidewalks. Scanning the buildings and their shadows, I make my way toward the garage I parked in when I first visited Harley. The years have rendered it almost unrecognizable—a decorative screen face adheres to the street-facing sides, making it impossible to make out the cars inside.

The garage had once included a ticket kiosk with an automated system that would calculate the exact cost of parking up to the minute, and take credit card payments before spitting out the ticket, which you would feed into the machine at the gate before leaving. The kiosk occupies an atrium fronting the elevator and the door to the stairwell.

After all these years the city might have updated the system, but I can confirm that the building footprint hasn't changed.

Cy lets me lead him into the kiosk atrium, which now houses a pair of voice-activated vending machines featuring candies old and new.

I stop at one of them and command it to give me a Snickers.

"Please use your digital wallet," the machine blurts out in a pleasant, mechanical female voice.

"Goddamn technology."

"I'm sorry, I do not understand. Can you please repeat that?"

Its retort leaves me dumbfounded. I say nothing and press the elevator button.

"Please insert your ticket," another AI voice says. "This action will time out in ten seconds."

"When did they give AI attitude?"

"Probably in 2058," Cy mocks me.

That rules out the garage. We make our way north for several blocks before I spy a new skyscraper in the distance: Tall enough, I wager, to affect the overall look of the skyline, the edifice sparkles with a thousand squares of light intermittently stacked behind the sheer glass walls that also reflect the radiance of the surrounding buildings. Tiny people occupy tiny residences, and when one light flicks off around the thirty-eighth floor, another turns on three floors up. I allow myself a moment to marvel at the modern architecture. Design always has a funny way of mimicking trends and invoking surroundings, and this building maximizes the lot shape, the shade of the abutting buildings, and its position relative to the river. The riverfront carves a reflective, meandering groove in the glass that terminates near a spire a thousand feet up.

Deciding it would sport numerous nooks and crannies, I walk with purpose in that direction, bypassing shorter historical buildings on the way.

Then again, for portals between dimensions to last, the environment housing them would need to endure, and that might make a shiny new building an unlikely spot. We cross eight intersecting streets before the road widens to approach the business district where the buildings sprout higher into the skyline.

Next to the futuristic condo building, a stubbier edifice looks as though age has rendered it all but useless. A boarded-up shop occupies the ground floor, and next to its entrance a rectangle in a dark inlet suggests a stairway to the upper floors.

I peer into the dark and allow my eyes to adjust to the scant light. Beyond a glass door, a set of blue-carpeted stairs rise, and to the side another glass door allows views into the abandoned shop. From the looks of it, an electronic lock keeps out intruders, and when I say "open," nothing happens.

"Attitude," Cy mutters.

He pushes on the door, and it squeaks as it opens.

Abandoning the idea of entering the new skyscraper, I study the rusting, empty shelves, the concrete floor, long since stripped of carpeting, and the yellow-tinged ceiling tiles which stretch to a back wall where a short hallway juts off.

Fiberboards covering the windows provide cracks through which only traces of light can enter, and that light bleeds into the dark to create an ethereal gray that stretches throughout the room. Where glue had once anchored the carpet to the concrete floor, swirls of yellow and white, sanded smooth, traverse between beige-painted metal shelves. Some look old and rusty, while others appear almost new. The floor sports a series of reflective metal circles arranged in a straight-line pattern along what seems to be a central aisle leading to the shelved back wall.

Leading Cy into the darkened hallway, I peer at the door labels, passing a stockroom, a pair of restrooms, and an office. The corridor ends at a heavy, unmarked door where an extinguished exit sign hangs overhead. The last door beyond the office is also unmarked.

When I push the door open, darkness greets me.

I take a deep breath while preparing to float through the nothingness where time and stars pass by in a flash.

Nothing happens.

My heart hammers in my chest.

A diamond-shaped window with a wire-mesh inlay punctures the office door. When I approach it, I allow thought to replace the need for action. I spin the cold doorknob in my hand, step into the blackness, and meet the same result.

Nothing.

Taking my cue, Cy enters every room and exits again, looking more frazzled than ever.

He looks at me, blinks, and surveys every corner of the room, searching for anything amiss. I spot a jumble of stacked furniture composed of wooden shelving, a plain laminate desk, and office chairs that rises toward the ceiling. A single missing tile paints a rectangle of dark over the stack.

I know in an instant what to do. Snaking through the abandoned aisles, I approach the stack, push at it to gauge its stability, and start climbing.

If the ceiling does support our weight, I'll be impressed, but this must mean something. The hole beckons to me.

Resting my foot on a swiveling office chair that is partially wedged between two filing cabinets, I use a bookcase shelf to pull myself up. The shelves give a little under my weight but hold as I climb higher.

Cy waits below me to observe my progress and seems to gasp when a large, hairy spider scurries out of the dark and paints a black splotch on the stained adjacent tile.

My heart beats a million miles an hour as I sense the silk of webs clinging to my face. Poking my head into the darkness, I make out what appears to be an open doorway in a duct.

Pulling myself into the hole, I watch as the tee grid buckles and shifts. The fibrous acoustic ceiling tiles could crumble under me, so I'm careful to bear all my weight onto the suspended tee grid. As I crawl, the metallic cables suspending the grid from the structure sway. That doorway must lead somewhere.

Peering into it at last, a rush of adrenaline pulses through me. Saying nothing, I breathe deeper, poke my head in, and stumble through the emptiness.

"Cy!"

My voice only exists within my head. I blink in confusion as a soft glow envelops me.

I land hard on a thin-carpeted floor between shelves of books. Feet scurry behind bookcases and hushed voices are muffled a few rows away. The room I've landed in is a used bookshop, with the same dimensions as the one I've just left. Cy might be joining me on the floor soon, so I wait, staring at a tattered paperback about Greek mythology within arm's reach.

An ironic place to land. The titles on the top shelf range from history to religion, archaeology, and astronomy, placed together in a forgotten corner of the store where few ever roam. Being forgotten and neglected, the books gather dust while they should be displayed front and center where the masses would reach out for them to grasp the knowledge they contain.

I wait for five minutes, and Cy doesn't come.

An employee rounds the corner holding a set of books and searches the shelves for the right spot. Seeing me staring at the volumes on the top shelf without looking at me, she asks, "Help you find something?"

I stammer. "What year is this?"

"Which book?"

Stumbling on my own words, I mumble something and then clarify my response: "No, I mean, what year are we in?"

She gives me a helpless, uneasy glare as she drifts away. "Um ... 2059, I think?"

# 14

# The Journey of Orpheus

The swellings of triumphant music rise and fall somewhere beyond the glass curtain wall that marks the front of the bookstore. I can hear the muffled tones each time the door opens. In this forgotten corner, dimmed can lights flicker in a brown-rimmed ceiling tile that has begun to crack from the infusion of drip-water from a leak above. If I can climb back into the ceiling, I might rejoin Cy, but the swan has grown so irritating to me that I don't care. If I ever see him again it'll be too soon.

Instead of conjuring an excuse, I exhale and study the volumes on the top shelf. Amongst well-received tomes from the superstars of physics, a few oddballs jump out. Sandwiched between a title from "the late Neil DeGrasse Tyson" and an updated version of *A Brief History of Time* rests a thick hardback with a shiny dust cover by a physicist I've never heard of.

Further down the shelf, an older book advertises itself as the complete history of the rise and fall of Pompeii. Its cover sports an ominous rendition of a cataclysmic volcanic eruption at night.

The book of Greek mythology catches my eye once again. It's no use trying to ignore it. As if something inside me controls my arms with mechanical contraptions, I find myself reaching for it. My fingers spark with an alien energy as its textured cloth exterior touches my fingers.

"*Tales from The Underworld* by Walter F. Caraggio and Stephen Lazarus," I read in a whisper that I'm not sure isn't carrying to the adjacent aisles.

*Lazarus? Please tell me that's a joke.*

An uneasy feeling creeps over me as I wedge the volume free from the shelf and peruse its copyright page. The information dates the first printing to 2043 and a second edition with a new introduction five years later. Flipping to the back of the book, I study the classic black and white photographs of the two authors, who had donned expensive-looking suits. I scan through the voluminous bio of Caraggio, before reading about Lazarus's exploits.

A fellow of Archaeology at a prestigious university, Lazarus boasts a trio of doctorate degrees and a masters. His extensive history on Greek culture includes a series of successful digs in Greece and a 'decoding' of Mount Olympus.

Another stuffy intellectual whose education could never inform him of the horrors I've endured over the last weeks, I decide.

I'm ready to pass him off as a slick know-it-all who knows little to nothing before I flip to the last page, which contains a single italicized line centered in the white sheet.

*A spectacular example of archaeology with purpose,* the blurb reads. *Caraggio and Lazarus excel in this timeless history—Harley K. Whitworth, Jr.*

My muscles vibrate. I'll be shocked if this proves nothing more than an awesome coincidence. Wracking my brain to remember Cy's description of Secretary Harley's history, I let my fingertips slacken, and the weight of the spine beneath my hands allows the book's center of mass to droop downward, causing the pages to flip and fall open to a predictable spot near the midpoint of the book. The words on the page blur as I refocus.

Below the illustrated picture printed on the top of the page, the text carries on from a previous page, which I don't care to find: "—to rescue his lover. As the story recounts, he made it back, but breaking a rule has doomed her to eternal death. Once regarded as the only mortal who ever ventured into the underworld..."

I mutter to myself. "A mortal can access Hades?"

Footsteps shuffle an aisle away as the can lights overhead flicker. Hushed voices carry over the tops of the polished wooden bookshelves like deadened wisps of memory on a breeze.

*What the hell?*

A thin veil of dust falls from above and scatters in the flickering light. It seems to pulsate like intermittent energy from a mysterious source, as the books, shelves, and carpet erode to black and the voices plunge into a silent abyss.

The book in my hands evaporates into tiny particles of dark as I witness the energy.

"Not good," I mutter, but my voice cannot resonate. The air kills it before the vibrations reach my eardrums, making every sound a lifeless drone.

Yet, where there is energy there is life. It builds within me, pushing higher and higher until it reaches imperceptible levels. Its silent shadow skulks over barren ground and broken concrete, invading the atmosphere with a dank musty scent that devours my flesh.

If I don't get back to Cy, I'll forever roam this circle of hell.

*But he needs me.*

"Why?" Again, my words die on my lips as the dark energy courses through my every vein.

A faint, gurgling voice penetrates my brain: *Because you are the link. He's never going to get back to his queen without you, your symphony.*

My eyes narrow as my fingers tremble. Alone, these worlds would be unnavigable. My ties to him are inextricable for now, a truth that burrows into the base of my spine with an impossible weight. The truth that he needs me lends credence to the idea that he doesn't care about my plight. If that's true, then we would never have met. He wouldn't just show up in my dimension without a good reason.

Before the darkness dissipates, a spark of memory blasts through my consciousness. Different dimensions of time are personal for the people involved; therefore, I have entered his dimension, and the events since that moment may not even be real for me. If I ever see him again, I'm going to hit him with a cast-iron skillet for wasting my time.

Then again, this dimension must exist for me in the same plane of reality, or I wouldn't even be here. Questions and answers form in my head in rapid-fire succession as the light gradually returns.

The books and shelves reappear as though emerging from a fog of blackness, and the carpet feels firm beneath my feet. New life infuses the voices and shuffling footsteps, but that book by Lazarus and Caraggio is gone as though it never existed.

"Sir?"

The store employee returns around the corner to gawk at me, yet she wears a quizzical expression that torpedoes me with guilt.

"Do you need help finding something?"

I stammer. "I ... that book about Greek mythology by Lazarus ... where is it?"

"Lazarus is the author?" She smiles and spins on the balls of her feet as her curtain of blonde hair twirls behind her. "Come with me—I can look it up on our system."

Hoping that Cy doesn't materialize while I'm gone, I agree to follow her. She leads me through a central aisle filled with a wide array of fantasy and science fiction books before rounding a bend into a broader area fronting a queue lined with an enticing collection of book-related memorabilia.

She slinks behind a register and taps away at the keys while I study a pack of playing cards sporting the covers of "banned" books. *Test your knowledge of the classics and have fun at the same time!*

"Lazarus?" she repeats after she stops typing and peers back at me.

I look up, expecting a pleasant smile, but she is frowning instead. "As in Stephen Lazarus?"

I nod.

"Looks like we have four books available by him through our distributors, but none are in stock. Would you like to order a copy today?"

I almost choke on surprise. "What do you mean you don't have any copies in stock? I was just looking at one, and it—*disappeared.*"

For a moment she seems bemused, but that graceful smile returns with a flicker of sarcasm. "Of course it did. You know, in that back corner, there's a portal to a different dimension."

Excitement erupts in my brain. She knows about it!

"If you go back there and pull out the three books by Vincent Price in reverse order by title, you'll find it with all the other volumes that we've lost track of."

"Uh..."

"Promise."

"*The* Vincent Price?"

"Oh my God," she says, still beaming. "You don't find another student of the theater and occult very often. What brings you in here today?"

*Is she seriously flirting with me?*

"That portal," I answer, dead serious.

She grins. "Ok, fine. I get off at six. Maybe you can explain what's on the other side? Big fan of mystery."

"Turns out," I say, gritting my teeth, "I'm kind of waiting here for someone. You ever seen him before?"

She shakes her head. "Oh, I see."

Awkward. How the hell did Becky ever fall in love with me?

"I mean—not like that."

Her smile doesn't dim. She straightens her back, pretends to peer at the computer screen, and types a few words. "At least you're cute."

"Uh, okay?"

"Yep," she says without glancing at me. "Six o'clock. Don't be late."

Stepping away from the counter, I retreat to the back aisle, determined to find that book one more time. I could be as late as Neil DeGrasse Tyson, I wager. If this is really the year 2059 for me, does the bookstore employee exist, or is she linked to me in some way I don't understand?

The memory of Cy breaks into my mind again; I struggle to push him away, but his persistence makes trying to get away from him futile. If he needs me to regain his queen, then it may be possible for us to travel to Hades together. A plan starts forming in my mind, but I'll need his help to figure out how to execute it, assuming he knows how.

Then again, I could use a few hours without him, anywhere but this bookstore. An idea pounces into my mind like a ravenous cat. Whether this is the same year 2059 as the one where we'd encountered Miriam, the building with the elevator shaft must still exist. If I can get back in that elevator shaft, I might be able to catch up with Cy right where I left him.

There would be no blonde bookstore clerk to flirt with there, and awkward or not, the prospect of seeing her again is a million times better than dealing with Cy for the rest of eternity, or at least until I can break into the underworld.

That might prove so difficult that Cy would become irascible, and if he does, I'm not in the mood to give him any slack before slapping him all the way back to the swamp he came from.

I glance back at her one more time to save her face to memory, bypass the knickknacks, keychains, laser pointers, and—*Paul Revere lanterns?*—to find the exit onto the busy street. The skyscrapers outside loom overhead like a million shimmering points of light. They sparkle in the sun as milky clouds drift across the sky. It will be a quick jaunt back to the hotel building with the restaurant if the landmarks are any clue.

Dodging scurrying pedestrians and the stray tourist who has wandered too far away from Market Street, I meander through the city in search of the building.

Then again, I could do without Cy for long enough to do some shopping if it gives my mind a break. Scanning the windows of the office towers offers nothing of interest until I make my way into a district occupied by a good range of upscale fashion and mom-and-pop décor shops tucked away from the burgeoning thoroughfares.

Three blocks away from my destination, I spy a wooden plank sign hanging from a pair of rusted chains beneath a dingy beige awning that collects dust and pollen. Up to this point imperceptible, the breeze makes the sign sway. The candlelit interior invokes a strange eighteenth century touch, and patrons sip on various drinks while seated at a long wooden-plank bar behind which a collection of bottles awaits on wooden shelves. The bottles must contain a pleasant mix of beverages both old and new, and though I've seldom indulged in a drink more potent than beer or the occasional IPA, an excellent taste of simpler times might do me good.

Stepping into the establishment, I get a stern nonverbal warning from the guests that I don't belong here, as though my attire is too twenty-first century. A man in leather chaps and tinted glasses paces behind the bar, grabbing bottles from the shelves, and pulling out shot glasses from the shelf beneath the counter.

The dust on the labels, coupled with the dark, makes it impossible to see my choices. A young woman in a cowboy hat and tight, high-waisted jeans hunches her back and sips on a glass of clear liquid. She scowls at me and then casts her attention to a man several tables away, who tips his hat and lowers his face while a cool smile parts his lips.

The bartender looks at me as though I'm lost. "Help you, partner?"

"Please tell me this is a theme," I blurt out.

The chatter around me stops as strangers interrupt their casual drinking to stare at me. I could run away screaming, if the rustic appeal of the place didn't offer comfort. If they have a batch of flannel shirts, paint-encrusted overalls, and a few cigars stashed in a back room, I might look more the part. Instead, I find an empty stool at the bar as the young woman gets up and approaches the gentleman.

"Of course it's a theme," I mutter, looking out the glass door at the cars rolling by on the street.

"You need a filler-up?"

"What?"

"What's your liquor?" He pulls out a shot glass and slaps it onto the table with enough force that it might break and ogles me.

"Maybe a ... I don't know, you got a merlot back there?"

"Only wines in here are reds and noirs," he says. "Might be a bar down the street peddling what you're looking for."

"Is the way people talk here in keeping with the theme?" I can't believe the words coming out of my mouth.

Chaps scours me with a cold-blooded glare that could shred the skin right off my bones. "What's your point?"

"I guess a noir."

The words are barely out of my mouth when the tavern door squeaks open and an imposing figure enters.

"The hell are you doing here?"

I recognize his grating voice before he's made it through his first sentence.

"What the—goddammit!"

Cy groans. "Yeah, that's what I thought."

I can only stammer one word, which makes him pause and stare at me as though hell itself were pouring out of my mouth: "Hades."

He grabs me by my forearms and forcefully ushers me out of the bar where the chill of reality (or at least what passes for reality here) lambasts me.

"You're taking me to Hades."

He shrugs dismissively and glares. "You're out of your mind."

"I know why you need me."

"Don't know what you're talking about."

Returning his glare feels only natural. He steps away from me as though considering a wealth of new information that he doesn't quite know how to process. I would consider this as a sign of relenting, but his expression doesn't change.

"Only the Gods can visit the underworld, and you're not liable to make it out alive even if you could go."

I gulp. A sudden surge of memory floods me as that dark energy floats unseen overhead, ready to douse me once again.

"What about a Titan?"

# 15

# Hands of the Hecatoncheires

Cy gives me a side-eye glance as he pores over an explanation in his mind, changes course, and then exhales as he gazes at the glittery skyline.

The sun had been scooting lower toward the horizon while I considered my drinking options, and though Cy interrupted me, I've already let the anger pass through me. Birds flutter in formation high over the lengthening shadows of the towers, themselves casting oblique shadows on the rooftops below, while puffy clouds billow in the east.

"The Titans," Cy explains while keeping his voice steady, "earned the ire of Zeus and Uranus. You don't know the tale of Cronos and Uranus, the supreme god of the universe. In short, Uranus overthrew Cronos, and the Olympians battled the Titans for control. As punishment for their perceived treachery, they were sent to Tartarus."

"Tartarus was a God, not a place."

He lets his gaze drift downward, until his line of sight settles on a window somewhere just over my head, but when he lowers his eyes to look into mine I can see the strands of regret forming. Learning how to exploit that emotion for my own ends might serve me well, but I let the moment pass so I can listen to him.

"Both, actually," he says. "You Christians believe in hell, where the wicked go. Tartarus is the Greek version of hell. Eternal suffering and lamentation, you get the drift."

"Might surprise you that I don't exactly believe in hell."

"Blasphemy."

"Common sense."

He grunts and pries his eyes away from me to study the streets, whose commotion has waned over the last hour. "Common sense is a myth."

"Ironic," I begin.

Knowing where I'm going, he shakes his head, offers a sullen expletive, and then allows himself to glance back at me as if he knows I'm about to suggest something crazier than venturing into the underworld.

"You might try explaining that to me at a later date. For now, we have—what's that American expression—bigger fish to fry?"

"Hades. You tell me how to get there."

He chuckles. "You don't just grab a passport and take a trip. Hell of a party, but you don't go without an invitation, and once you're on the guest list, you're never getting off. And then you run the risk of destroying the entire universe."

"Haha!"

"You think that's funny?"

"I was mocking your dramatics, fella."

Shaking his head and grimacing, he lowers his gaze and lets it sink into my eyes once again. "Messing with time and dimensions is one thing; there are laws that govern that, and they're strict. Now, when you involve the underworld and the dead, you can bet the gods are going to retaliate, and you don't want that. It wouldn't benefit you, your wife, or anyone else on this Earth."

"I'm not letting her go."

"You don't have a choice."

My heart lurches toward the bottom of my stomach as I growl: "You don't know what you're talking about. The hell with you. You don't want your queen back, that's fine, but I want—no, I *need* mine. Neither you nor the gods are going to stop me."

"Ker—"

"*Don't* call me that! Only one human is allowed."

He opens his mouth as if to argue, but I shut him down before he manages a single word.

"And no fowl can do it, either."

"Mighty chivalrous of you," he scoffs.

I clench my fist and notice my arm vibrating. Another word might make me snap and hurl it at him to crush his birdbrain.

"I'm going without you."

"Right," he says, nonplussed. "Soon as you figure out how, which if you're smart enough, should take about three or four centuries."

"You don't know, either."

"Maybe we can find out."

My turn to scoff. "You and your hilarious tarot cards? Very *Deus ex machina,* but I seriously doubt it."

"How many gods are there?"—he cuts me off, looking pleased with himself.

Training my eyes skyward, I offer a shrugging guess. "Fifty or so? Enough to play poker with them?"

He tilts his head. "If we're comparing them to face cards, everyone knows the kings, queens, and aces, and most would be familiar with the jacks. But the twos, threes, and fours might give you further insight into the big ones. And as it happens, the Greek deities are all interconnected. Learning about the minor gods and goddesses can flesh out your understanding of the Olympians. The ones that really matter in this case."

"Can't we just piss off Zeus?"

He chuckles, but then his face goes rigid, as if a block of ice has frozen his demeanor. "You don't want to piss off Zeus."

"What about Uranus? Or Cronos?"

"Funny thing about him," he says, allowing his expression to morph into one of pity. "He and the rest of the Titans have no power while they're holed up in Tartarus, even if some say Cronos eventually earned forgiveness and entered the Elysian Fields, where the good people go."

"But you said it yourself—you don't necessarily have to die to get the underworld."

"Same result. You're not getting out."

"Then I stay there with her, forever. Like I promised. Or we get reincarnated."

"Only the gods can be reincarnated. Look it up."

"What about the Titans?"

He grunts and lets himself drift away toward a glass storefront, behind which a collection of dusty books rests, and his screwdriver expression twists itself through my eyes. "The way you hold them up as a beacon of insight or something, you'd think they're about to climb up through the soil and save you."

"Didn't Harley ever tell you?"

"Harley told me a lot of things about you."

"Including the fact that I am a Titan?"

His jaw drops before he accesses the memory of Harley's estate, but I recognize the resistance to the idea in his eyes. For a moment, he separates his stare from my face, casts his eyes upward, and then looks sideways.

A car rips by only twenty feet away, its rumbling bass stereo providing a sonic trail that vibrates and flexes the storefronts, which catch the last gleam sunshine and the approaching headlights in a way that sends hallucinogenic reflections through the streets.

In Philadelphia, an invisible field once called the ether physically connects everything.

"You're not a Titan. I don't know who told you that."

"I—shit, neither do I. Why? I can remember that, so I should remember who said it, and why I believed them to be something of an authority."

"Can we track this person down?"

I shrug, knowing I have nothing: No physical description, no story of how I came to know this person, no identification data, physical address, phone number, post-office box, or pen with their name on it.

"Good Lord."

"Maybe we need to make another visit to *her*. Another healing session."

"I read about someone else," I interject. "The book didn't give me his name, but he was a singer or something, and he travelled to the underworld to rescue his lover."

"Where's this book?" My explanation has evoked some excitement. He stands and shuffles toward me while the sunlight stretches thin, the shadows dissipate into a deeper darkness, and the wildlife grows calm. The traffic on a neighboring street rushes through the urban canyon, creating a soup of grumbling motors, horns, and streaking tires on pavement.

"No idea."

He smirks and refocuses on me. "What a surprise."

"I was reading it in the bookstore where I landed. Which, I know, doesn't seem physically possible, when you think of the circumstances, and—of course I stood her up—"

"Slow down, my friend."

I glower at him. "Still not your friend.

"I was—well, to be honest, it's fuzzy how I got in the bookstore. But it was like reading that book put me into some weird dark dimension that broke the laws of physics, and the book I was reading eroded away and vanished. The clerk was joking about the back aisle having a portal to another dimension where all the books that disappear go. And then she sort of asked me out."

"Wait until your wife finds out."

"Don't mention her again or I'll kill you."

"Can't wait."

The falling darkness lurks to the east, where thunderstorms are rising on the New Jersey coastline. Watching the sunset unfold may have proved counterproductive if we'd had any semblance of a plan. Without that, we're just flailing bodies in the year 2059, so far into the future that I can scarcely comprehend the technology that might be available if we had any real money or a way to access it. Technology that would ultimately fail us.

A quartet of strangers emerge from a storefront, and one remarks something under his breath while glancing toward us. His compadres roar with approving laughter, double over, and stagger along the storefronts, whose lights have begun their nightly glow into the outside world.

Behind them skulks a lone invader, a man in a dark overcoat who could launch an unprovoked attack at any moment, steal the drunks' wallets, and make off evidence-free were it not for two eyewitnesses who should not even be in this version of Philadelphia.

# MEMORIES:

The eons melt into silence as Becky's voice withers in a frozen, misty universe, carrying on a merciless, icy rain and dissolving into a series of murky vibrations as the image of her melts away.

I'm reaching out for her, across the dimensions, mouthing her name as the tears warm my face. The rain falls heavier in whatever realm I'm in, creating frigid rivulets that meander through the goosebumps on my flesh.

Somewhere, Ian might also be experiencing this sorrow, but my mind and heart are so cut off from him that he hardly exists, suggesting I have been stuck here far longer than I care to admit.

This emotion is like daggers of agony slicing away at sodden flesh with dull, serrated blades. It could render me nothing more than a soupy mass of clothes, assorted proteins, and saline tears if I let it.

Yet I'm powerless to cease its destructive march. Time always powers onward, whether the souls in its path are prepared for the procession or not. Events unfold on events, some random, and some in the aftermath of more events, which had arrived from earlier ones, onward to the beginning of time itself.

My heart bleeds. All the blood in my veins pulses backward into an endless vacuum that will devour the rest of my soul. Invariably, Becky is there to gather the remains, pack them away forever in a box in the attic at the lake house, and to cherish them only on rare occasions.

Snap!

Cy slaps me across the forehead. I gather my fists in an angry mood, glower at him, and roar as my knuckles graze his ear. Dodging my attack, he readies himself for another assault that will never come, for the horizon has dissolved into a vat of reflective fluid a mile deep.

My fist prods at it as I pull it back. Here, a real ether in a real dimension isolates us in a dungeon of mist that grows smaller by the second. Like a lasso, the field pulls us closer together until we are practically hugging.

Cy lets his hand rest on my shoulder, and I yelp in pain as my knee slams into his. He groans as the circle grows tighter and tighter, and then the trembling ground falls out from under our feet. The ether lifts us higher and higher as if we're caught in a bubble floating above the destruction.

"What the hell is happening?"

"You want a way into the underworld?" Cy breathes. "You're getting your wish."

"*You're* taking me? After promising you had no idea—"

He rasps as an icy hand slaps his shoulder. Out of the ether, a thousand severed hands reach out for us, grab at our clothes, and pull us ever higher.

"You think *I'm* doing this?"

"Let us go!"

A warty hand closes around my collar. The visible cross section of its wrist reveals white in a circular field of red, while blood drips onto my clothes.

Thousands of bleeding hands, some knobby and masculine, others dainty and feminine, rain blood from festering wounds as that bitter blue ether accelerates us through an abyss of nothing. Gathering us even tighter, fingernails claw at my flesh, gouging canyons in my face, and pulling out greasy tufts of hair by the roots.

The pain pulverizes me as the ether bleeds on us, drenching us in blood that runs through my hair and my eyes, and turns me into some kind of a demonic entity that seeks to erase the entire world it inhabits.

My eyes grow wider as a spindly, bony hand covered in sagging flesh pulls me toward the circling ether, as if to guide me away from whatever has taken us in. It vibrates as it pulls at me. Ice-water flashes through my bloodstream as everything in my mind turns upside down, flips me over, and tumbles me through time and space, where innumerable stars glint in an ever-expanding darkness.

When the uncounted hands dissolve into the dark, I am locking arms with a mysterious woman with silvery hair and a gray night dress that flutters on an imperceptible breeze. Cy lands with a thump behind me and grunts in pain while I gaze at my dance partner.

Her piercing gaze radiates through me, touching me with an untold warmth that seems to split the realm of darkness into two equal halves.

Groaning in torture, Cy bellows something that makes little sense.

*Go with her.*

My legs can't help but move. Her green eyeballs carve twin craters in her wrinkled, graying face as my heart melts. With her dress flowing behind her, she turns, releases my right hand, and pushes on through a dark world that grows colder with every breath.

Her long curly hair bounces on her slender shoulders, and we walk hand-in-hand into a blackened abyss marked by the sickly sound of distant, dripping water.

We're in a cave and descending what seems to be a rocky slope, flanked by mountains of granite. I can hear her raspy breathing as I walk, and Cy limps helplessly behind us. I couldn't care less about him or his queen. This woman knows the way into the underworld, and my only choice is to follow her unquestioningly into the deepest illusion I've ever seen.

# 16

# Eurydice in Chains

Without looking back, the woman begins to descend a rough set of stone stairs carved into the bedrock. The chilly air here smells dank, like the humid, cobweb-strewn nightmare of the crawlspace. While the ceiling is not visible, it must be high enough to prevent sound reverberations from being audible on the floor. Drops of water *plip* onto stone every now and again, until one slaps me on the forehead.

"Who are you?" I ask.

Cy lags far enough behind that to him my speech may sound muffled, and perhaps that is for the better. He emits a croak and continues to limp onward. Whatever the sonofabitch is feeling, I hope it's pain.

A flat, shushing sound rips through the cave as though our escort has let it out, yet the sound is too loud to have come from a human, at least not a mortal one. If she can speak, I wager, she is still dead, and that understanding prods at the base of my spine like a branding iron dipped in ice water, which sends waves of needling chills up and down my spine.

"Do not speak," she seems to whisper.

"Uh ... okay?"

More information would be useful in this setting, even if she utters only one sentence. Instead of pushing the point, I resign to descend in silence. Another drip plops on to my brow, and as we go deeper, an icy mist encircles us. The hem of the woman's ankle-length dress is a wispy, fluttering veil of muddy gray, and the darkness makes her silvery hair appear altogether detached from her scalp.

The stairs take a hard right and hug the right-hand wall of the chamber, whose black stone is inscribed with a series of pictograms like those of an ancient language. After a few minutes, the carvings fade and disappear as we plunge deeper and deeper into the Earth's crust.

The stone steps beneath my feet have become slippery without me having noticed it, necessitating caution. If in a hurry, one could tumble into the abyss and arrive dead anyway, and that may not make any difference for us.

If all underworld travelers are dead, logic might dictate that none could exit alive. That rationale ties my stomach into a painful knot that might induce vomiting at any moment. How does one survive being dead? Finding an answer might prove difficult if it's ever happened, but then again, survival isn't my sole quest.

I'm here to rescue the woman I love. She may not make it out alive—a thought that, for a mind as broken as mine, only deepens my resolve. For better or worse we will be together forever, a promise I intend to keep, even if I must endure an eternity of darkness. To caress her beating heart, hear her voice, and wrap my arms around her once more are tantalizing prospects for which I would go to any lengths.

If this is all true, to what fate will Cy succumb? Will the great swan be reincarnated again as a reward for a life well spent? Zeus might not look favorably upon someone brazen enough to use a mortal for his goal of finding his queen. True justice would enact a stiffer sentence for that.

I grow tired of his complaints. Behind us, he has taken to cursing under his breath, groaning in pain, and shivering. Let him endure whatever displeasure he suffers, but if he could do so less audibly, we'd all be in a better mood, including our escort.

As if predestined to not utter a single word, she wraps herself in a trance of graceful silence. Again, I appeal to her.

"How far down does this go?"

The piercing, empty shushing sound returns, and she only cranes her neck as if to listen to me.

*You* will *not speak; you are cursed, my servant.*

I am no one's servant, except maybe Becky's—and I will bend to her will until my dying breath, which might be in a matter of minutes. The air becomes denser and colder as the chamber shrinks.

After we have descended over a thousand feet of stairs, the chamber constricts the staircase, which grows steeper and twists through treacherous hairpin turns that cut deeper and deeper into the bedrock.

An abyss, and it only keeps on going.

Another hundred feet, and the ceiling, which has been growing imperceptibly nearer throughout the trip, now occasionally presses against my wet hair. My clothes are soaked, and with every step the air becomes colder and heavier.

In a hundred more feet, I crouch and push myself through passages so narrow that I must turn my body sideways to shimmy through them. Because of the slope, the sideways climbing becomes harder on the knees. Before long, the claustrophobic cavern might force me to crawl through openings constricted enough to make even a snake uncomfortable.

It doesn't matter. The stairs end at an abrupt stone wall only five feet high by two feet wide. Everything around us is rock. The woman should be breathing, I presume. Remaining silent enough to hear it might prove easy, but both Cy and I have taken to wheezing in the chilly, dense air from the strain of climbing down thousands of feet into the bedrock. If the climb has pushed two fit men like us to the brink, a frail old woman stands no chance of making it this far. Not without heavy breathing and aches that make it impossible to move. Instead of reacting the way she should, she stands tall and silent. She is dead; no other rational statement can explain it.

That nightmarish reality brands it in my memory when she turns to face me. The sagging skin is peeling off her skull in clumps of flaky, grayish flesh, and where her blue eyes were, only black circles of nothingness remain. My heart slinks deeper into my chest and the knot in my stomach tightens, causing me to bend over and heave. I have not eaten in more than a day, so nothing but a stringy bile comes up, which tastes as vile as death itself.

When the woman opens her mouth, her lack of a tongue carves a deeper understanding into my stomach. My nerves turn to mush as I manage a painful, throat rending scream that dies in the abyss.

Cy mumbles something as her spindly hands slither around my fingers. She reaches out my hand in hers and presses it against the wet stone surface. Rather than retaining the expected firmness, the stone stretches like a bubble. Pushing makes it easy, and before I can understand what's happening, I am being flung forward to tumble head over heels into a wide-open pit—until I land on my side and howl in pain. The dusty earth slips into my nose as I inhale.

Rolling over and moaning in agony, a shape emerges above me. Contorting my body to get out of the way brings more pain. With a heavy thump, Cy lands in a heap next to me and does not move.

I shake him, but he has become unconscious.

Allowing myself a moment to gaze at him reveals that the fall has killed him.

This forsaken landscape stretches into the dark as far as I can see. The heavens shine down, not with stars, but with stringy bits of bioluminescent lifeforms that hang like shimmering stalactites. The ceiling must be three hundred feet high. I struggle to a standing position and prod Cy's lifeless body with my foot. Any moment now, the woman might descend to greet me, but after waiting for at least ten minutes I conclude that her journey ends at the stone wall. She's the undertaker.

If Cy is dead and I'm not, what does that mean?

I ponder on the question as I scan my new surroundings for fellow citizens of the underworld. If, in the afterlife, people move around and converse like mortals, then Cy might reanimate like a zombie at any moment.

Instead of waiting for him, I trudge onward through various-sized boulders, each covered with green, black, and purple lichen that soften the sharp edges.

*Come, my servant.*

I close my fist and batter the side of my head with it to shake out the demonic voice that has taken up residence inside my cranium. Instead of dissipating, it scorns me with merciless laughter.

The horizon is studded with signs of life: Vague shapes of rock, mountains, and trees rise like a canvas of black, and as I study that bleak line between light and dark in search of buildings or humans, I come to the sad conclusion that no one here cares to build structures. This world stretches far and wide enough, I assume, to fit millions of souls in relative comfort, and they might never encounter one another if they don't move around. It is the ultimate climate-controlled haven; the temperature may not fluctuate more than a degree or two. And that may only happen because a few different airmasses might meet at some point. In the absence of oceans or other large water bodies, the currents would be weaker, eliminating the problem of wind.

Still, shelter might come in handy if one wishes to enjoy meals or converse in private, but as far as I can tell, no buildings exist.

The path I am on winds beneath my feet, zigzagging between boulders of various sizes. In the distance, a cypress tree prods at the skyline and seems to quake. The empty landscape carves craters in my soul. I'm never getting out of here, and Cy was right. Jerk or not, he hasn't been wrong yet.

I despise it when people I hate are right. In high school I suffered a humiliating defeat in debate to one of those preppy girls who always sat rigid in class taking notes. Without half the required effort, she judged anyone who couldn't achieve the same results. She engaged me on a topic I can't remember, and while I defended my position with fervor, she blasted me with facts and figures sharply enough to cut my defenses to shrapnel. And when my position became weaker and weaker, I did what any loser might do: dug into personal attacks, and when those didn't work, sat there alone as a steaming pile of refuse. I never lived it down. Damn her, and damn Cy.

The path transverses several miles. If I have an exact destination in mind, I'm in no hurry to get there. I have thought little about Becky since I landed, which elicits a simmering sense of irony. In theory, I could search the underworld for years and never find her.

Asking directions might prove more efficient, but I see no one to ask. Being forced to travel the underworld with nothing but my own regrets as a guide helps me to succumb to my instincts of grief much faster. My body produces no tears, only darkness. Hope flutters and fades until the trail leaves behind the jumbled rocks and meanders through a barren grassland where the landscape rises and folds into a series of gentle hills. I see someone far ahead. The figure stands alone but subtly moves, as if in a tense discussion with someone.

Hurrying toward them, I watch them take shape. Twenty minutes later, I spy a woman tending to what might be a well. She wears a silver dress. Long, blond hair curls down her back and ends near her waist. Sorrow clings to her every movement, but when she sees me, something sparks in her demeanor.

I trudge nearer and try to keep my distance.

She speaks first. "Who are you?"

I stammer, "Um—you can call me Larry. Do you ... *know anyone* here?"

"I once did," she says, her voice going dreary. "But he's long gone. I don't know where I lost him or how. Every day I hope he isn't dead, but that fades every time I wake up alone."

I don't have the heart to tell her, because my words will offer no comfort. "You don't know a Becky? Or she might go by Rebecca or Susanne..."

She shakes her head. "I know none. But look for the river. Follow that, and you're bound to run into someone. I'm sorry I cannot help you."

"I—thank you. Maybe one day your man will come back to you. You never know."

"Where do you come from, Larry?"

For lack of a better explanation, I blurt out the only place that comes to mind. "Philadelphia."

"I don't—what, did they name a city after him?"

"Trusted leaders, moral or not, often get memorialized with place names. You can't pretend it's anything new."

"I once knew morality," she says in a somber tone. "But now it's just a hole in the ground. When you can do nothing to break those moral codes, you drown yourself in misery. There's no choice."

"You always have a choice," I argue. "Follow your heart. Search for your dreams and you can find them."

She hesitates. "I'm afraid you don't understand."

Ironic. If she understands anything, me arriving out of the darkness unannounced and insisting that she *does* have a choice, causes her eyes to narrow, her lips to tremble, and drives her instinct to flee.

She says nothing as she hurries away through the grass, her dress snagging on the sharper blades and prickly weeds. Her knowledge of the path makes her flight effortless.

Instead of chasing after her, I choose to reason with myself. How is it I can discern any semblance of hope? This nightmare provides none, the last of which lives in me, but even that is fleeting.

"Well thanks, I guess," I mumble as I walk away. The horizon seems to glow with predawn blue forever. Enough light resides here that I can clearly see everything nearby, but my vision is limited. Instead of a picturesque skyline of breathtaking beauty, the mountain peaks cut a zigzagging pattern of black across the blue glow.

The perception of nothingness empties my soul with every step, but I come to detect something new, as if I'm approaching what I might consider civilization.

With my heart leaping and tumbling, I stagger toward a bright flicker that can only be a blue reflection on water: the river. Meandering through the grassland and keeping to the valley so that I don't lose sight of that glimmering reflection, I increase my pace, gulp, and present myself to the underworld. And it's nothing my worst nightmares could ever have conjured.

# 17

# Shades at the Lethe

Souls without faces, names, or bodies linger over a desolate plain, hugging the banks of a forgotten river. Drifting over the water and back again, they dance in formation like shifting clouds of soot, each angling for a position to take its turn over the river. I gaze in their direction while standing motionless, and resolve to avoid them.

Still, my presence alerts them to something amiss. After a moment the shifting stops, and the clouds hover like enormous swarms of black bees.

My heart sinks as I scan the horizon across the river, where a monolithic tower separates a field of faint green from a darker landscape, beyond which an undulating orange-red glow appears.

Even with no eyes, the souls can see me. For a moment they wait along the shoreline, but when my muscles twitch toward where I perceive south to be, they seem to organize.

The river enters a sharp bend a mile from them and meanders through darker territory. Instinct guides me to alter my course so that I can cross at the crook of the bend, where the river has carved a narrower channel before the current spreads it out again.

Then again, narrower means deeper, and those deeper waters could result in stronger currents and dangerous eddies if my understanding of fluid dynamics is complete; having engineers explain it to me in layman's terms once opened my eyes to several problems regarding the design and construction of piping systems. Employing that knowledge in a place like this might make a wonderful tale for my grandchildren should I ever escape this dungeon.

Was Cy correct when he insisted that I'd never make it out alive? I gulp as I desperately try to concoct a plan. The souls, now intent on devouring me, have locked onto my position and have begun to drift closer and tighter, coalescing into a soupy black fog that erases the grassland along the river's shore.

"Run," I say to myself.

But the action is useless. My legs seem to have congealed into a gelatinous soup from the long walk, and my bones ache. Screaming would do me no good, either. Could there be a way to hide?

I scan my surroundings while opening my eyes wider to make better use of the scant light available. When my irises have adjusted, I spy an outcropping of jagged black rock that has formed a craggy line pointing into the crook of the river bend. This line, I calculate, will take me past where a subsection of the dead had gathered before the entire group became one drifting mass of black.

Pain mashes my legs and knees as I push myself in that direction. Judging my speed against the Shades', I figure that if we continue at the same disparate velocities I will make it there before they do. Instead of hesitating, I make a beeline toward what seems to be a rough triangle of black above a river of lava rock.

Hiding behind that spire will inflict pain; the jumble of sharp, loose rocks shifts and settles as I trudge through it, while the sharp spines begin to cut my shoes to rubbery ribbons. Walking this land barefoot would be torture, so I exert caution to avoid the sharpest of edges. Behind the cone, the rock dips into a crater at least six feet deep, where frosty air has gathered. My presence has disturbed the air and mixes some of the chilly layer that has settled in the cavern with the warmer air aloft.

Should I make it to the hole in one piece, it might offer a small bit of safety. The lava rock rips at my clothes and flesh as I descend. Feeling blood on my fingers makes me woozy, and the longer I hold on, the more blood oozes out. Intent on lessening the pain, I let go and allow myself to drop.

Wrong move.

What I have considered the 'floor' of the hole proves to be a mound of razor-sharp rock encrusted with ice. My feet slip when they connect with the ice, sending me back-first into the mound. I howl as it claws across my back and digs in.

The souls will have heard that. I writhe in frantic pain, hoping to burrow myself deeper into the hole.

Before I can sink my entire body into the shadow, the dead arrive. They gather in masses to search the lava field for the intruder, and a wispy howl encroaches on the land like a strong wind. My teeth chatter in the frosty hole as I hunker down, glancing upward into the open air once or twice while attempting to ignore the pain.

They huddle over the mouth of the cavern as a ravenous pack of black spirits, edging toward me. Their approach has eroded a smooth path behind them as if they had chewed up the sharp edges and erased them. Running along that path would seem like a wise investment of time, but more of them are approaching.

Numbering in the thousands, I imagine, they have homed in on me as on a feast. Fresh and mortal—nothing like the food that sustains them now, yet they still want me.

My miscalculation turns on me when I witness the wispy souls assemble themselves into a column that could twist through the inside of the hole like a scrubbing brush inserted into a bottle.

The tendrils of darkness claw at me from head to toe. My scalp erupts in agony as the black swooshes through my hair. Before my world vanishes, I see a woman standing on the rim of the cave and peering down at me. Her image flickers and wavers before solidifying as she reaches a hand toward me.

Ice flashes through my veins and my skin begins to glow. I rise through the twirling column of smoke and erupt in a flash of brilliant white light. In response the souls scatter, separating into individual smudges and swooping back toward the river.

My rising energy ceases and my feet tingle as I settle back down to the once-sharp rocks, which the dead have eroded into a smooth, rutted plain. The glow in my extremities extinguishes itself, and I search in vain for the woman who had come to my aid.

"Hello?" I rasp.

But she's gone. Erased. Did she just sacrifice herself for me?

Remorse digs into every ounce of my body as I stroll through the rocks, whose ridgeline smooths into a grassy edge where the lava rock solidified into a globular rim thousands of years ago.

In this underworld, thousands of years might flash by in mere seconds. If I understand Christian theology well enough, time is nonexistent in the afterlife. When mortality meets immortality, perception goes by unceasing, so the story goes, yet that same perception from the mortal side of the veil speeds up in comparison. One pastor Becky and I used to listen to had tried to explain evolution in the context of creation, where one day for God may equal eons to humanity.

Thousands of years in my time might mean millions could enter here; if thousands of souls linger in this one place, legions of them might stalk in places I can't see.

Another problem presents itself as I settle into a flatland shaped by a grassy hill toward the crook of the river: The intervening millennia have molded the riverbend into its current shape. Taking the path of least resistance, it would have wrapped itself around the ridge and used the stronger current to dig a deeper channel through the softer silt.

I can see no bridge, no boat, and no materials to build one. Even at its narrowest point, the river might be over a quarter of a mile wide—more than enough to drown me in various eddy currents where warmer and colder water mix into a vortex that could suck me right to the bottom, where I'd stay for eternity.

Who had the woman been? I attempt to assign reason to what has just happened to me, through whatever means I can explain, but this landscape has turned imagination on its head. Perhaps inverted or sideways it all would make some rational sense, but then again, the architects of this hell would have isolated it from reason on purpose and installed redundancy in case one part of the design were to fail.

Could she be Ariadne, whom Cy told me about? Or Becky?

I call out to her in vain as my voice wavers in my throat. Understanding claws its way through my soul as I step toward the water's edge. Becky is dead, and now so am I. If this realm has the effect its primary designer intended,

I will soon become untethered to my body, and my soul may join with the throngs gathered along the riverbank miles upstream.

"Becky," I whisper, "I'm coming for you."

Reason might have me believe that telepathy is possible in this place, but feeling takes precedence and my voice dissipates before it can create a reasonable sentence in my ears. The pain shoots deeper into my back as I search for something I can use to float across.

Even a piece of driftwood would do, but no fragments of wood lie strewn along this riverbank. The water cuts at the edges of its channel, eroding away bits and pieces of rock and soil as it goes. My heart sinks in my chest as the shame of being alone coalesces around me.

Towering above me like a serpentine monster, a dark creature emerges out of nothingness, lumbering toward the water from the other bank. Pieces of rock, grass, and other debris whip into a furious cyclone that builds it higher and bulkier. Where its head is located, a vat of snakes slithers, coils, and dances where the hair should be. It opens its eyes when it has fully formed, studies me, and splashes one massive foot into the water. The disturbance forces the stream to split, sending a murky wave of muddy water onto the far bank and raising the water surface higher. When the other foot splashes down, the flood comes, soaking my shoes and rising towards my knees.

At least fifty feet tall, it lumbers in a manner that can offer me victory. Instead of fighting, I devise a plan to climb on top of the beast as it treads closer. Confused, it could carry me across the river where I'll fight it with any tools that await there.

"Come on," I rasp, coaxing the monster to wade toward me. The water reaches its waist before it gets halfway and then begins to recede as its massive legs appear out of the reflective water, whose sloshing waves have softened the glint of what I might consider moonlight.

The bending of light rays may provide small benefits; my plan takes shape when the monster nears me. It forms a snaky fist that seems to bubble as it slashes across the darkness toward my face. If it hist me square on the shoulder, it could send me right back toward the lava field in one blinding burst of speed.

Instead of allowing it to contact me, I sidestep it, grab onto what I take as a snakehead, and let it twirl me in midair like a jump rope. The air whistles past my hair as the snake head retreats into the voluminous body and the milliseconds tick away as I fly toward the other bank.

Success is in sight, but my momentum lurches to a stop. The monster has plucked my leg from midair and dangles me over the river as though I'm nothing more than a marionette stuck to its forearm.

The shaking rattles my bones as it slaps me into the water with enough force to paralyze me. Taking in a swig of the foul-tasting liquid, I sense the frigid river overtaking and drowning me. Gasping and fighting free of the creature's meaty hands, I hedge my bets and swim away, using the current to curve me towards the shore.

The monster responds by bellowing at a thunderous pitch, scaring away any wildlife allowed to roam this underworld. Not ready to succumb to defeat, it kicks at the water. The displacement rams into my abdomen like a truck, causing the river to vomit my soaking body onto the shore.

Reeling and trying to compose myself, I limp away from it as the fear eats at my back. When I turn my head, expecting it to have turned around to defeat me at last, I gasp in horror when it all disappears: the monster, the thousands of detached souls, the lava, and the river evaporate before my eyes. And the road ahead promises nothing but turmoil.

The river has erased my memory, and as though nothing has happened, I have nothing left to fight for. There is only me, in this nightmarish world that bleeds darkness through every pore.

Oddly, the lack of memory lessens the weight on my shoulders, and here in this realm an unfamiliar landscape begins to emerge. A tower, lit by licking yellow flames, burns into the dark skyline as a plain of green spreads miles away up a tender slope. If I want to reach that verdant land, I'll have to traverse a treacherous world filled with vicious monsters.

The green represents the promised land, or what I might describe as heaven, which could mean that a shiny gate prevents trespassers from disturbing the endless peace that exists beyond.

The darkness stretches long over the ground as I gaze around me. A mountain range rises to my left, cutting a dark, jagged line across the dingy skyline. Closer, one tall mountain pokes out of the barren land like a sore, or perhaps just an extinct volcano.

I spy what appears to be someone on the hillside, huddling under a heavy stone. The figure lingers there for the longest time, as if studying me from afar. If he can even see me, I must look like a tiny brown speck in a sea of black.

Instead, he pays no attention to me. When the rock the figure huddles under shifts, my heart leaps in my chest, but he handles the enormous weight without being crushed. The stone lurches higher up the mountain, which steepens several hundred feet over his head to a near-vertical face.

The longer I gaze, the higher the stone ascends, and then my heart aches as the person surrenders to the mass and lets the stone flatten him. It can't be possible to die in the underworld, I reason, which gives me an idea.

Any monster that seeks to devour me must also know this. If it is true, would the monster hunt me for food or sport? Then again, what might feed the monsters? I plan an answer in my head as I turn to trudge on toward the fields of green.

The tower of flames stabs ever higher as I near it, yet I dare not travel too close. If its inhabitant sees me, it can't be welcome news, and a monolith like that must be home to one of the darkest figures in the underworld.

My waterlogged clothes stick heavily to my body as the chill settles in. The temperature in the air doesn't seem to change, even as I encroach on the flames. The sweat from fighting and uncertainty further wets my flesh, allowing the temperature to numb me.

Allowing my eyes to wander fills my senses with the impression of a paralyzing evil. Something prowls these lands, migrating over trampled grass, fragmented rocks, and fields of bones. I kick at a skull and leap as my heart jumps through my skin.

The tower scrapes at the sky with its flaming spires, sending twirling columns of smoke up into the emptiness, where it dissipates and joins the utter black. Heavy wings flap in the far distance, an omen of further darkness.

Malformed tiers some thirty feet high comprise the building, each tapering into a plateau that joins the next tier. Though the tiers are not uniform in height, and their tops don't appear smooth, the structure must be strong enough to offer resistance to its foes. Mountains of flaming stalagmites compose its outer flanks, reflecting the sickly orange glow of the fires as they lurch up the side of the tier as if wet with water or blood. Or both.

Screams erupt from about a dozen tiers up, sounding human. The wails are like sirens that shred the surrounding air into spaghetti. The cacophony swells and then falls silent.

Flecks of something brown and white hurtle through the sky from that tier, flinging themselves into the angle length-grass and shattered boulders at the foot of the building. Steering clear of the trauma, I decide that someone has hurled the gnashing souls off the roof for a bit of silence, if nothing more.

The resultant heartache creeps up the base of my spine until the faint thought about dying again arrests its sullen march.

The fires burn hotter and brighter the higher the structure climbs. Its pinnacle catches light like a shining beacon in the distance, as the white-hot flames tickle the skies. More wails come, and then more bodies fly through the heavens to meet their dusty fate below.

I wager the noise must be disturbing whoever resides in the tower. An impulse to scream flashes into my brain, and before I can stop myself, it rends the inside of my throat like a raspy wheeze that could reduce my larynx to a red, soupy mass of inflamed skin.

My scream ignites the ire of the one in the tower. The beacon-spire burns hotter as it roars into the night and emits a puff of white smoke.

Willing my muscles to run seems easier now. I push onward toward the acres of green as the sorrow builds deep in my heart. Though the green field offers a ray of hope, I cannot determine what else it hides. Will it be home to a vicious array of hungry beasts, or might flowers grow and harps sound the accord of peace?

No matter what the landscape promises, I am drawn to it, until the world around me goes black. Silence settles in the dark as I gaze upward into a towering vortex of bleak clouds that build thousands of feet higher than the building below.

The storm erases the land beneath it as lighting forks miles overhead and a scarring blast of wind pummels me with dust and debris. I collapse in torture as the storm lunges over me, and soon the atoms that make up my back are stripped away from the rest of my body one by one. I convulse and let it devour me.

# 18

# The Asphodel Dead

The storm builds into the stratosphere, thousands of feet up, while the vicious wind tears me apart. My limbs begin to vanish into the cloud of ash bit by bit, and the agony rends my soul from the rest of my body, which is slowly evaporating into black mist.

The current rides higher as lightning forks across the blackened clouds. Now far below, that field of green disappears into a verdant pinprick that fades into slate as I rise.

What sorcery could have made this happen?

As the last of my body turns to mist, a perception of peace washes over me. The storm clouds pull me higher and higher until the clouds thin out, providing an eerie view of space where dead stars pierce the dark like arrows of light, yet do not twinkle or move.

The absence of eyes and a body makes it challenging to perceive the scant light. My mind wants to compel movement in my muscles, to swim away from this awful expanse and to rise out of this hell. The sensation grows more dreadful as I look upon the billowing clouds of black below, which absorb my soul as the current lets me drop.

The lightning flashes once again, highlighting the nothingness that consumes me.

Dropping faster now, I feel the air seem to cool and grow dank like tides of death speeding through the soot. The clouds streak by as I accelerate downward, yet so long as I fall, the earth does not appear below me.

Do up and down even exist in this inside-out realm? Is perception merely a lingering dream?

Darkness overcomes me, yet light still spills from the stars, the moon, and even that faint glow where starlight interacts with the atmosphere. A bolt of lightning flashes nearer, and soon everything is alight. It blazes through me like a million scorching fires, the arcs of electricity flooding the remnant of my soul. The resultant glow carries on as I shoot through the clouds, down, down, down to the bottom of an ashen existence.

When the blackness has dissipated, my body emerges whole from the storm and the landscape creeps up on me. Within seconds I should slam into the ground with enough force to kill me a dozen times over. Instead, my pace slows, and I float down into a barren field blanketed with ash.

In time the sooty cloud fades away, yet my body still glows.

Ashen ground stretches toward every horizon; the field of green exists as nothing more than a memory. As I stumble through the ash, the tremors of agony return and my fall kicks up a plume of dust that settles like fine flakes of hot, gray snow. Where the ash bed wanes thinner, beds of dead flowers lie matted against the dark, sandy soil as if the lack of water has wilted their petals and the cinders have suffocated them.

Darkness extinguishes the glow within me and dims my perception of the landscape into which I have dropped.

Others roam this region—I can hear footsteps and hushed voices withering as they carry through the air. Teeth gnash nearby, producing a gut-wrenching grinding noise like two slabs of marble sliding in opposite directions. The noise chatters away as dead birds chirp, followed by a lone voice that calls out to me.

"Thou who art of light and shade, tell me your name."

I spin in the voice's direction, but she has not shown herself. She awaits my reply somewhere unseen, yet my vocal cords have been welded shut. Opening my mouth to utter anything feels like chewing gum being peeled from sandpaper in my mouth. Water would be beneficial, but it's not available.

"I.... Uh.... Kerry.... Send me to her."

But I don't remember her name, either. The evidence tumbles upon me like a thousand boulders, each heavier than the last. Without her, even the idea of existence is nonsensical, composed of neither rhyme nor reason. Yet somehow I persist in a realm where the unending tides of the present replace memory—dark and painful as it is.

"Whom do you seek?"

The desire to speak blends with the lack of memory, creating a mesmerizing heartache that exerts pressure through every joint.

"Well, if I'm dead, then she must be too. I don't know anything else, not even what she looks like. But I will know her when I'm with her."

The truth of what I'm saying to this still-invisible woman bleeds from my heart. I might not know her face or her voice, but how she feels—that intangible flare of intimacy—burns through it all, clearer than physical memory itself. How can I explain this in a way that she will understand?

"You are seventh in the line of the Cretan souls, Kerry. Follow the Six before you and you will find what you seek."

"Cretan? Six?"

"The Six," she says, her voice beginning to waver. "You will find them here. The new Titans were not imprisoned in Tartarus."

"Huh—who are you?"

Her voice muffles and her image flutters to life in a series of sparks, an alluring woman with glowing locks down to her dainty waist, and skin like glass. "I am the daughter of Demeter, carried into the underworld by Hades. Some call me Persephone."

Her image drifts away, shrinks, and fades until she is nothing more than a disappearing silhouette in the unbroken darkness.

"Wait, Perseph—tell me where to find these six Titans."

If she has heard me, she must deem it best not to respond. The despair crumples somewhere in my heart and I trudge on through the wasteland in search of six people who may or may not even exist. The sinister dark stretches further than I can see; emptiness abounds in every direction, but a mob of souls clamoring and churning amidst it all surrounds me, as yet unseen.

*None of them can know of another.* The thought pours into my head like a forced venom that surges through my veins. I cannot stop its destructive march, nor can I contain it.

*Some will await judgement. Others will join my army.*

The pain shoots through my legs, my back, and my scalp. The warm oozing of blood, seeping out of a cauterizing wound somewhere on the back of my head, stings like the blade of a heavy spear plunging through my skull.

"If none of them can know of another," I reason aloud, "I can never find the Six."

The Six.

## MEMORIES:

My heart writhes and aches as the bedspread coils around my feet. A hot sweat pours onto every square inch of my skin.

Deep within me the battle rages, and the fires burn. The centurion marches his soldiers on the village to plunder and burn it to the ground. To ward them off, a lone woman launches arrows into the advancing troops. One by one they fall, even as more in the ranks replace them, coming nearer and nearer.

An arrow splits the darkness before her face, and with a flourish of her wrist she bats it away and watches it skitter harmlessly against the stone street. But the throng hosts legions of archers, each of them spitting arrows rapid-fire through the smoke while the orange fires burn behind her.

My body blends with hers, and her pain becomes mine. An arrow plunges into her calf and I screech in agony. The flames grow brighter as the heat intensifies.

Another fighter turns to me before falling to a flaming arrow, as the smoke builds higher into the skyline. "Defeat them, Merope, Lady of the Six!"

But I cannot.

The arrows rain down as the villagers flee in terror.

As the bedspread parts, I shoot bolt upright in bed and my body trembles.

Who is this Merope? My mind aches as I attempt to assemble hidden pieces of knowledge into something resembling truth, but my memory is strained so thin that I cannot hope to place faces with names, or even cite historical events.

"Merope?"

"I know her," a female voice says.

She appears out of the mist of ashen gray like a ghost, pale and fluttering. My heart sinks when I see her blank face. She has no eyes, mouth, or nose; only a sagging gauze of flesh covers the front of her face. Her spider-silk hair floats in the still air as a speck of icy black scurries along its threads. Her ears twitch as she faces me.

*None can know of another.*

I am not one of the dead, and neither is she.

"Do you know me?"

She stands motionless and tilts her head sideways.

"She is in the stars now with her other sisters, daughters of Pleione whom Artemis asked Zeus to protect after they were pursued by Orion."

"The Six are the Pleiades? If they are in the stars, why did Persephone tell me they are here?"

She hesitates and her fragile body sways from side to side as if in a solemn dance with an invisible, ghostly partner. "I know not."

"Who are the Cretan Titans?"

Again, she falters.

"Do you know anyone else? Help me find her."

"Merope?"

I stutter. "B—Beh..."

*You cannot speak her name, my servant. She is not yours to pursue. Find yourself at my side ... only then can you find the Six.*

"The Six."

"There are seven," she corrects.

"Seven sisters." I gape. "Six Cretan Titans, and Merope is their leader."

"She was beautiful," the faceless woman drones, her voice growing darker and sadder by the word.

My heart wrenches as I listen to her description.

"Skin like alabaster and silk, emitting the softest glow, and wavy hair beyond her hips. A pale pink blush on her cheeks, and eyes an azure deeper than the sky itself. Now memorialized in the stars, they are still together.

"What is your name, weary traveler?"

I stammer: "I'm lost, I just need to find her—she's the only one who makes me whole, who makes everything make sense. Without her, there is nothing, and I am only an empty speck in a field of ash, and totally alone."

"I can help you," she says. "You must follow The One."

"I will never follow— "

*You shall.*

"Only light can drive out the darkness," I stammer, not knowing how or whence that wisdom came.

"There are devils much worse than darkness," she intones.

Her voice grows weaker the longer she speaks, and her image begins to fade.

"Foes more bitter than the blackest of scars. Follow him and you will find your precious lady. But tread lightly, traveler, for the even the mightiest cannot overcome Hades."

She disappears into a cloud of mist as I stammer a wordless reply. My heart plunges deeper into my stomach as acidic tears eat away at my face.

In an existence without aims or goals, darkness always wins. There's no way to overcome it, so there's no use fighting on. In the absence of moral choice, there can be no light.

My body hurts, my voice rasps, and every muscle aches like an augur of sorrow drilling deeper into my soul, as if to extract every photon of light until nothing remains. How can I continue when I have nothing left to fight for? How can there be hope in a limitless world of sorrow and regret?

The ash clings to my face as I ponder my options. Before me is a choice: If I choose to join the army of *The One*, I may find my origin and my reason for being, and if I choose to await judgement, I may reach a place where light rules and I may live in peace with the ones I love, forever in that field of green.

Sorrow wracks my soul, pouring a viral agony through my skin and bones. One cannot measure forever in days, months, years, or even eons. If forever is a destination, then shouldn't the path to it also be eternal?

I need her or I have nothing—no me, no her, no morality, no forever. Just emptiness. Emptiness in forever is blackness, the worst kind of hell imaginable.

Gauging the pain in my bones, I begin to settle on a solution as the darkness swells around me.

The hushed voices grow in number and the footsteps come closer, yet I cannot perceive any of those marching toward judgement. I'm not ready for that. My journey must continue, despite the dark that must dominate every step.

Speaking can only rend my heart. Instead, I gulp and face the pain as the tears of acid flow down my cheeks. At last I'm ready to surrender.

# 19

# Cerberus and the Song

Sorrow washes over me like a plague of blackness. My heart tremors in my chest, restless and intoxicated. The murk that hangs over everything here invades from every direction and leeches deep into my soul through every pore.

The mist that covers this landscape shifts, swells, and settles within pockets of varying densities, at once limiting my vision and then revealing hidden details I wish I could erase from memory.

A grim reality stands before me when the mist thins: thousands of souls are lined up among the ashes and wilted flowers in queues that must be miles long. Each of them chatters in a haunting foreign language. Though most of the souls don't have faces, scant details shine through in those nearer to me. A tall, bony woman holds a spear-like weapon, bowed toward its tip. Dressed in a tattered robe that frays along the hem, she seems to notice my gaze and looks away. I can see her wilted hair shriveling as though intense heat had singed patches of it away, and in those scars I can detect traces of humanity.

If these souls and I are not meant see one another, then how can I perceive so many of them? The question forms on the tip of my tongue, causing me to croak as if I'm about to ask Cy another stupid question.

But Cy is not here—and that suggests another query: How is it that I remember him? So many mysteries lie unresolved in this wasteland that it causes my head to spin.

To gain a greater sense of my surroundings, I survey the crowds. Human shapes emerge from the mist cloud that memorializes their spirits, cutting dense, black impacts in the fog. From here I cannot see the field of green or the tower, nor can I remember how I entered this surreal place. There is nothing I can say to anyone and no question whose answer can shed light on where I am, what I'm doing, or where I'm going.

The confusion proves disorienting the further I wander. Soon the lines of souls grow distant as I walk away from them towards the promise of solitude. If I can reason with myself, in hope of bringing logic to a puzzle so devoid of it, then perhaps I can gain a clearer understanding of what lies ahead—if an 'ahead' exists at all.

A distant howling captures my attention, and when I look in the direction whence it came, the mist obscures every square inch of land. Those dead stars linger high above; where stars should twinkle because of disturbances in the earth's atmosphere, they instead remain distant motes of light unmoving and unchanging. What could have emitted the howl? It piques my attention as I limp onward, further from the throngs. A wolf? Some untold monster that could rip me apart and spread the pieces of me across the dimensions? The questions cause my heart to sink and my muscles to spasm.

Moments of quiet in storms of torture might normally evoke a fleeting sense of serenity, where the promise of return destroys the calm in the mind; instead, these moments bring further misery.

"Persephone?" I breathe, my voice vanishing into a limitless abyss. "Are you still there?"

*Persephone is* dead.

*How can a goddess die?* I ask the darkness.

My throat goes raspy as I speak up. "Is anyone there?"

Silence, and then a shuffling of heavy feet in the soot, followed by a distant splash in calm waters. A body of water is a favorable sign. When my parched tongue sticks to the roof of my mouth, I try to yawn, letting in only dry sand. Hydration isn't the only promise within reason, I rationalize. A body of water must always lead somewhere, and if I can find the destination or the source, perhaps I can glean wisdom from the discord.

The splashing resumes and grows louder. When the vibration reaches my ears, its frequency changes. An oar is stirring in the water.

But even that faint noise fades into an interrupting sound: a gruff grumbling emanates from the fog ahead and to my right, growing nearer by the second. It intensifies suddenly, and by the time the beast has emerged from the fog, it's already too late.

It lunges at me with razor-sharp claws, emitting shattering barks that roll like thunder in the distance. Six orange eyes bleed into shadow, revealing manes of matted fur above hundreds of bloody fangs.

"Holy shit," I rasp, backing away.

The beast takes its moment to attack. It launches a dirty howl, and then pounces. Narrowly averting what is sure to be a killing blow from its claws, I roll sideways onto my back, tumble to my knees, and clamber to my feet as I yelp in pain. My outstretched hand shields those hundred fangs from digging into my neck, but leaves my flesh exposed.

Another slobbering mouth bites down on my wrist with enough force to tear off my hand, but when I scream, it relinquishes its grip, recoils, and then strikes again, but not before a third head snaps at me.

I trip on something heavy and crash to the earth as a shooting pain ravages my calf. In horror, I spin my attention towards it. Rows of bloody, drooling teeth gnaw into my jeans leg and as it shakes its head from side to side, my pants slide up and down my leg in a hot, sharp rip. When the fabric tears, the beast rears back to get a better grip, and sinks its teeth into my flesh.

Howling in agony, I bend at the waist and clutch at whatever has tripped me. My fingers caress a moist, sticky rock. Instead of focusing on how it feels, I lunge back and hurl it at the beast's head. The stone plows into one of its eye sockets with enough force to blind that eye temporarily, but before I can bask in a short-lived victory, two sets of claws shred my shirt. Blood soaks through the cotton as white-hot pain slashes across my skin.

"LET ME GO!"

The monster does not relent. The shock of being hit in the eye has angered it, and the beast retaliates by gnawing at my hair. Its maws are big enough to bite my head clean off if it wanted to, but this creature does not aim to kill me. It has resolved to rip off my limbs and let me bleed out into the dusty ash.

Punching one of its jaws does little good. It sidesteps my attacks, stands on its heels, and grabs my right arm with enough pressure to destroy my veins.

"Goddammit! NOOO!" Screaming only spreads more pain through my trachea.

The creature is not done yet.

I aim a wild kick at its outstretched front paws, and when my foot makes contact, the beast stands firm. Instead, I'm the one sent reeling. I land in a ball six feet away, which proves enough distance for me to launch myself to my feet.

Attempting to detect a weak spot in a creature so powerful is fruitless. Instead of devising a counter strategy, I resolve to escalate the violence as fast as I can. I lunge at the monster as it bears down on me with its three gargantuan heads.

I dig my nails into its shaggy hair before it can launch an attack, but that does not deter it. Again, it grips my leg and swings me airborne. Managing to land on my feet again seems like a minor miracle, but an instant later it pulverizes me with a meaty paw as its claws dig into my midsection.

"Sing," a raspy voice commands.

*Sing?* As if a magical little song can make the beast agree to not dismember me for a moment of levity. Who the hell is this clown?

The voice repeats its command for emphasis: "Sing to it."

Melody, after all, will make death less painful. But then again, am I not already dead? When I recognize that I have nothing to lose but more blood, it makes the choice easier.

The creature's fangs rip at my flesh as it wrestles one of its heads from side to side like a puppy playing tug-of-war with its favorite toy. Yet instead of my weight being enough to control the fight, the monster enjoys all the advantage.

It bites down on my shoulder, chews off my tattered shirt, and spits it into the ground as it lunges again.

Responding with a bitter, crushing heavy metal tune only eggs it on.

"Beauty," I croon, my voice wavering. "Heal me from the storm, and let me carry you to the throne. Your mercy is a joy like home."

GRROOWWLLL!

"I will be *youurrrs* for all *tiiime.*"

"Good work," that gravelly voice says. "Feel it in your soul."

"I will *never* let you *dooown*, 'cause you are mine."

Singing feels so unnatural when I am only experiencing sharp pain over every bloody wound the monster has inflicted. Soon its growls become purrs and it relents, slinking away from me and settling on its haunches.

When the raspy-voiced man speaks again, he has glided nearer, and from a corner of my blackened eye I can see the water's glassy surface emitting a tangling mist, like tongues of flame lapping at the air. He wields a single long rowing oar and stands alone in a wooden craft made to ferry a dozen souls across the calm waters.

"See," the man explains, "he's not so untouchable when he's charmed. You're lucky you had the chance. What's your name, partner? And who taught you how to sing?"

The man's voice seems to drawl as with a thick Louisiana accent, and while it emanates a rustic charm, its simplicity bores heavy blocks of granite into my mind. I don't want to listen, but his tone intrigues me. He at least looks alive and has a face. The fact that he neither speaks in riddles nor seeks to destroy my mind is a rare treat here.

"Um, my name.... Some people call me Larry."

"Where are you from, Larry?"

My mind draws a blank. "Uh ... I don't remember."

"You crossed the river Lethe. There's not much you will remember from before that."

I pant and groan with agony as he reaches out his free hand and welcomes me aboard via a narrow wooden plank that extends a few feet into the water. His hand seems to shake and undulate in rhythm with the surface of the water.

"You seem not quite here," the man explains, "which makes you mortal. I hope you know there's no getting out of Hades, son. Dead *or* alive. So tell me, what's your quest?"

"Tell me about the Lady of the Six."

Hedging my bets might give me thin odds, but cutting the bullshit and getting right down to it promises to save time. When confronted with such a disorienting question, he lets his shoulder settle as he pushes the craft away from the shore.

"Legend has it, one of Phaethon's sisters was reincarnated for a noble purpose, but she's never been seen, even a thousand years later."

"Her name was Merope," I grit, my teeth gnashing together as the waves of torment devour me.

"You have a good ear," he complements me. "Where did you hear that name?"

I shake and attempt to steady myself as the boat shifts under my weight. Expecting this, the man lurches sideways to counteract the motion, pushes the long oar through the water, and regards me with a careful frown.

"It might have been a dream, but I remember speaking with Persephone," I say, unsure of whether my memory is correct.

He rasps and rows again. "Impressive."

What? What's so impressive about dreaming? Perhaps here in the underworld, few even are able to dream, but wouldn't that overrule the nature of a chaotic world, which dreams should serve to enhance?

"I need to find the Cretan Titans," I manage, biting my tongue to seal in the searing pain.

"The only Titans are yonder." He points to the orange-tinged horizon. "Beyond the river of fire, from whence no soul ever comes out. If you're prepared to endure the pit of Tartarus for such a trivial query, you're more foolish than a human trying to take on Cerberus. That's an eternity no soul would ever want."

"I'm finding them. Even if I have to go through hell."

"Grit and determination still won't get you out."

"I bet I know one way," I rasp.

"You think so? Funny, Larry."

This man talks like Cy, and I hate it. Remembering his name again smashes into my consciousness like a heavy, saline wave. Who is Cy? I narrow my eyes, trying to make sense of it, but the memory of him burns brighter than everything else in this realm. If he's important enough for the memory to survive crossing the Lethe, as this old man says, then it must mean I have encountered him...

...in the future. Realization crushes my skull and spreads pain through my scalp.

"The future," I whisper to myself. "The dimensions of time are intact in the underworld."

Still, a future I have never encountered should not allow memory, should it? Unless the past shaped that future. Stretching it all the way back causes events to stack on top of other events. At some point, the lines between dimensions must have been disrupted, allowing for the possibility of memory.

Before I can rationalize it, I speak his name louder. "Cy."

"What's that?"

I turn toward him. "You don't know a Cy, do you?"

The old man seems to glower. "I seem to remember a Cy Young I ferried across here some time ago."

"No, not that Cy."

A black bird caws high overhead, its shadow opaque enough to dim the light reflection on the water.

"He claims to have been a swan in a past life."

"Only gods can be reincarnated," the ferryman says. "And only by the hand of Zeus."

"Then he was a god?"

"A god who became a swan among the stars," the man intones, "might be King Cygnus according to legend. But no one's seen him, either."

Speaking quicker soothes some of the pain. Adrenaline might do that, I reason, so I plunge onward with the beginnings of a plan.

"What's your name?"

"Me? I am Charon, the ferryman of the underworld. Escorting the dead across the river Styx has been my job for thousands of years."

"If you can help me find Cy—" I launch into my plan point blank without slowing to think about the logistics of it all. "Help me find him. Then he can explain to me how time dimensions work down here. Once that's done, we team up with The One to track down the rest of the Cretan Titans, find a hole to crawl through, and emerge on the other side fully alive."

"Tartarus is eternal, Larry. Time dimensions or not."

"You don't know what I'm after," I shout above the silence. "Darkness isn't the worst foe one can meet—sometimes you must ally with it. I'm going to win this time, against all the odds."

Charon offers a merciless chuckle. "Confidence is the quickest way toward defeat. It makes the odds untouchable. Let me repeat for you: no one can get you out of Tartarus, not even Zeus himself."

I grind my teeth. "I'll take that bet."

"I won't stop you," he growls. "Not my job. Where do you think this Cy is now?"

"He's dead,"—I rattle it out without understanding how I know that—"and recently, I think."

"Do you know the consequences of meddling with time?"

"Not exactly," I say, relenting. "But it's a risk I'm willing to take."

He shrugs. "Could unravel the idea of existence itself, but you have fun with that."

Watching him use the oar to paddle us farther away from the shore allows the sting to wear off. The wounds from the beast will weigh me down, but for a fleeting moment or two the agony abates.

"So you admit there *is* a way."

Charon allows his countenance to darken. He twiddles the tip of his stringy gray beard as if contemplating something amusing, and then sharpens his expression to gaze right through my eyes to the center of my soul.

"You're not listening."

"Really good at that," I interrupt him.

"Have it your way, this time. If you're so sure Cy's dead, he might be waiting on the other side of the river to be ferried over to await judgement."

"Works for me."

"Then you can scheme with him and let me go about my job. Is it a deal?"

"Whatever gets me out of your hair," I say, trying to be funny.

The ferryman has no sense of humor. Then again, can humor be at all valuable in this realm? Doubt crosses my mind on that front, but I let the mood linger for several minutes while I concoct a haphazard plan.

Allowing me to ponder it seems to suit Charon well enough. Instead of protesting, he rows faster as the minutes fade away.

This river must be wider than the Potomac where it dumps into the Chesapeake; over time, the shore we started at has faded into the heavy mist and only a faint outline of what might resemble land makes a scattered silhouette in the fog ahead.

After another fifteen minutes of silence, he angles the watercraft toward a long wooden pier, where a line of the dead await their turn to cross. Trying to count them numbs my brain, but here at least I can see them. Some have faces and others comprise only bones and tattered clothes.

The idea of infinity has always been unnerving, and even here it lends itself a mystique that I cannot wrap my mind around. Human thought must be frail according to the gods, and though our imagination and ingenuity are our most notable traits, rationality cannot explain some phenomena.

When the boat bumps against the dock, I leap out, allow a moment to regain my balance, and search for someone that looks familiar. After scanning those souls for over ten minutes, I cast my eyes on someone tall and mysterious. It can't be Cy, but I'd remember this face from anywhere. My heart pounds in my chest as I approach.

# 20

# Dreams Beneath the Elm

Only one word can describe how I feel—agony. An utterly dark, hopeless pain that rides on a mare of purest torture. I have felt suffering before, but none like this. Everything hurts. The bite and claw marks from the monster, the headache, and the untouchable grief concoct a cruel poison of torment for my soul.

Among the hundreds of the dead, I look upon myself for a moment, yet something in my eyes is detached and strange. The last piece of the puzzle falls with a heavy thud against my heart. The face in the crowd does not belong to me; it belongs to Ian. Beaten and bruised around the left eye, he peers at me as if disbelief swims in his thirty-odd-year-old eyes. A patch of blood dominates his scalp, and his hair seems corroded and shriveled. His chin is wet and tangled with a streak of blood where a wound bleeds into his facial hair.

I gasp as I approach him and a spark of knowing crosses his eyes. From closer, I can see that the knuckles on his right hand carry the same blue and purple bruises that mar his eye. "Hell of a fight."

His voice sounds gruff and untamed. "Hi, Dad."

Hearing him call me Dad bleeds into my soul and uncorks a potion of tears that might have erupted from my eyes if I'd had anything to drink in days. Now they can only emit perplexing guilt. First Becky and now Ian.

Her name fights into my skull. Becky. I suddenly know what I'm searching for—how did it happen? A million questions brandish in my mind, but I stutter and can only ask one.

"How have you been?"

"Well, he was bigger," Ian begins. "And drunk. But I think I held my own. Where am I?"

I don't have the heart to tell him. My heart hammers in my chest as I scan the hundreds of faces for the one who might help me to find the six Cretan Titans.

A man and a woman, elderly beyond the grave, seem to shrivel and decay before my eyes. Their faces hang low from gravity and age. Conflicting emotions of sorrow and relief dance in their expressions as they wait for Charon to ferry them across.

In the distance, a range of black mountains saws across the night like an animated black silhouette. A single tree occupies the foreground perhaps a hundred yards away from the pier. It looms tall and is bathed in perpetual dark. A few of the dead linger beneath its branches and then fade away to oblivion as I resume my search for Cy.

"I don't understand it," he breathes, his face drenched in misery.

I likely possess more knowledge than he does, but my grasp of the situation remains limited. I might say age has shown its effects in me, but I'm not much older than he is. He gazes into my eyes as if he too sees this truth but wishes to swallow it in favor of something more wholesome.

"Maybe we should chat, son," I stammer, glancing away toward the tree.

In front of it, the crowd thins out. One or two people pass in and out of existence somewhere beyond it; gravity tugs at its branches more than it should, as if carrying the weight of an invisible snow.

Leading him away from the group, I step onto a patch of dry, sandy soil, and meander through a loose group of five women with only eight limbs between them. The nearest woman gasps when she sees my face and then glances in horror at the other deceased. She wears cool pastel colors, as though to carry on the mood of spring. A flower in her hair has wilted and casts seeds into the air as she limps along on one foot. Somewhere below her hip, her excised thigh sports a thick stripe of blood that stains the empty, tattered leg of her shorts. Her partners, some missing hands and others missing feet, stagger toward the ferryman as if uncertain of their own mortality. They don't have to speak in order for me to acknowledge the hell they've been through.

Were it not for the ferryman's advice to sing to the beast, it might be feasting on my carcass right now. I'm surprised I haven't succumbed to purest black.

"What is this place?" Ian asks again once we have passed the women. "It's like one of my worst nightmares, but it feels too real. Please wake me up so I can kiss and hold Brianne one more time."

I say nothing for several moments as we grow nearer to the tree. Before I can piece together a reply, he changes the subject: "So this is where you went all those years ago? Why here?"

"Why indeed." I don't intend the grave tone of voice, but emotion is driving my inflection.

"Why did you leave? I thought you loved Mom."

The makings of a dusty tear assemble at the corner of my eye, as though concrete has formed a barrier that will not allow moisture to pass. In the absence of any displayed emotion, my face must look like a decrepit pit of stubbly black.

"Nothing I love more," I say. "I didn't leave. I just.... Actually, I have no idea how I got here, probably by design."

He narrows his scarred eyebrow downward, and his bruised knuckles vibrate as they sway at his sides. As though the drunken brute has damaged his leg, he strides gingerly. "What are you ... I mean, this can't be real, can it?"

"What even *is* real? One minute you think you can define it, and then there's this."

"I *used* to know." His voice sounds pensive, as though a rage of torment passes through him. His bloody lip quivers a moment before he ices it away. "Everything used to happen for a reason. But after Mom died, something changed."

Agony floods me. "She *died*?"

He hides a sheepish sadness that seems to weigh down his words. "I mean, they assume so," he says. "Missing for a year, and they just gave up after Philadelphia was sacked."

His explanation sends another rush of pain through my heart like a poisoned spear. "Philadelphia, too? My God."

"Yeah. Papers have been talking about it ever since. Criminals run what's left of it when they're not hiding out from the suburban militia groups that impose their version of the laws, which they've distorted over time. Society has fallen victim to itself. I just thank my lucky stars I don't live there."

"How does the state handle all the lawlessness? The Fed?"

He shrugs and shows a decisive frown. "They don't care. Turn the other cheek because it looks like things are going smoothly. The militias aren't shy about executing anyone they accuse of being a criminal. That mask of vigilantism is enough to placate Washington and Harrisburg, while most of the country thinks Philly did it to itself."

"Sounds like hell," I offer. "A least I might say that had I never set foot here."

"Might agree with you," he says, casting his eyes at the black mountains and the tree. "Wait ... are we in hell now?"

I shake my head vigorously enough to cause a knot of pain to erupt behind my ear and my heart to flutter. The voices of the dead hush as Charon calls out a bunch of foreign-sounding names from his boat. "Hyrum Svarbard, McEnroe Wilson."

"There's a weird name," Ian chimes in.

"No, not quite," I answer, trying to build a solid explanation. "Although I'll be headed there soon. To Tartarus."

"Tartarus?"

"It's what I used to know as hell," I say, my throat going raspy. "How did you meet Brianne?"

"College," he says.

"Say you went to Temple."

"Penn, actually."

I widen my eyes and force a peculiar frown to communicate surprise. "Wow."

He lets the moment pass. "We took a psych class together—academic, nothing like real life, where the id and the ego only register in the aftermath of a bar fight."

"What happened there, son?"

He looks at his feet while attempting to square his shoulders. "I went there to confront her over something someone said on social media. You know how rumors are, but I had evidence for it, or at least I thought so. She wasn't there, but one guy didn't like the way I looked at him, I guess. Messed each other up."

"Shouldn't have done that," I say, gulping. Somehow, I can anticipate where his story is going, but trying to turn the page onto something else fails me.

He continues: "When I get home, she's there, she sees my face, tells me I'm not the guy she fell in love with. Leaves, says she needs to think it over, but that I should not try to call her again.

"God, it made me go crazy. That moment. That temporary weakness. And suddenly, I'm here with you."

"You..." I cannot finish the sentence. The pain blinds me.

Purple spots appear in my peripheral vision, like the blurred kaleidoscope of semi-consciousness before a purposeful sleep. The tree and the mountains undulate as though I'm rocking up and down on subtle waves in a narrow wooden watercraft, and the darkness dilutes the crispness of reality, numbing everything but the pain.

"I don't know."

"You're too young."

"How ... how did it happen for you?" A morbid question like that has to be the product of curiosity rather than a request for confirmation, but trying to answer him is useless.

I stammer something nonsensical and take a deep breath.

"Dad?"

A corrosive *humph* isn't something he deserves even if half his story is true, and while I have no reason to doubt his recollection, betraying myself with a colder remark could reduce me to rubble.

"Are we going to meet Mom here?"

"Of course we are."

Hope. In a landscape so devoid of promise, where emotion rules until the end of time, hope is a rare delicacy.

*Do not partake, my servant.*

Servant. I've been called many things and have appealed to the title with zest at times, but the word has always carried an air of humiliation. Becky used a million words to describe me, not all of them complementary, but none had ever struck me so hard right where it hurt.

Now that I can recall some past events, I can start rebuilding my life into something better. A sudden surge of energy highlights the tendrils of my heart, raising the tempo of my breathing and cooling the throbbing, scorching wounds where the monster bit and clawed me.

In a way, I defeated the hellhound; even with advice from the underworld ferryman, the previous me would have considered the battle a success for the simple fact that I remain in one piece.

Servant—that word doesn't sound so destructive to my personality now. Instead, it seems to invigorate me and give me purpose. If darkness is not the worst enemy, then I have yet to meet it. The One will guide me, not because I need him, but because he needs me. An untold quest for victory pushes him to gather an army for a coming war, one that cannot produce either victor or vanquished.

## MEMORIES:

The wind outside howls like a thousand agonized banshees as the choppy yet vibrant waters reflect a million shimmering stars. After sunset, the beach has died down; fathers and sons with kites and footballs have all retired for the night, retreating to the inns and vacation rentals that dominate the shore. Later, the few canoes and fishing boats have retreated, and lights have turned out. This is when the lake comes alive.

Her heartbeat simmers as we snuggle next to a fire I had built with my own two hands. The yellow and orange flames lap at the sky and send showers of sparks and a twisting plume of smoke up toward the heavens, where the gods and angels of legend watch over us.

Nocturnal life thrives along these shores after humanity disappears, but if someone is peaceful enough, he can become one with that nature that heals the soul.

I can barely remember shouting at her now as I wrap my arm around her, and she rests her head against my shoulder. Her shoulder-length dark hair tickles my neck as cooler air drifts ashore. Between the distant sounds of birds and the shuffling of shoes on coarse sand, I can hear her heartbeat as the rise and fall of her breathing is tuned into mine.

"I'm sorry," I whisper as an afterthought.

Her eyes close as she glances up at me, and before my heart can prepare for the fleeting bliss that is to come, she kisses me and presses her hands against my back.

I kiss her lips as passionately as I know how, lay her back on the sand, and squeeze her shoulders. But it doesn't last.

A sudden wave of frigid water washes toward our feet and the moonlight fades to a hazy red. With the waters thrashing, my heart rattles in my ribcage. I help Becky to her feet as the heat of action plunges into my veins.

As I whisk her away, I glance back at the turbid waters; an eruption of slimy green precedes a tempest of flailing tentacles as the monster lunges toward the shore. After a moment, the appendages retreat into the water as a thousand bodies surface. Bloodlust has transformed their faces into a soul-sucking rage and sharpened their fingernails.

Before I can blink, a thousand nude women gather into a monstrous wave that aims to swallow us whole and which then dissipates into a chilly mist.

I awaken to Ian standing over me in the shade of the large elm tree. Beyond his head, the myriad stars signal the beginning of a lifeless eternity untouched by the decay of humanity. My heartbeat rages out of control as I gaze up at my son with only pain in my mind.

The possibility of spending eternity in the underworld is worth the success I might achieve.

First things first, I must find Cy.

Ian leads the way, and when he turns his head, I spy the one wound no father ever wishes to see: the blood has soaked his shirt in a dirty red as a soup of hair and mangled flesh behind his ear mar his appearance. Only one weapon could have made that hole.

To prevent my mind from wandering and attempting to confirm my worst suspicion, I press onward. Trying to count my steps while watching my feet thrash through the sandy soil only offers a mild distraction. When we reach the back of the crowd, I peer into hundreds of desperate faces one by one.

Cy should be recognizable if I see him, but the river Lethe's effects block out any memory I had of his face.

He's the only one I can count on to lead me to the Cretan Titans. No one else will show me the way if they know, because no soul would agree to traverse the worst of the underworld.

The darkness grows soupy as I look on. Before long, the faces begin to appear alien and discarded. One man, whose gaunt jawline highlights an air of humility, appears to grow miniature winglets high on his cheek, but when I study his eyes, they disappear along with the rest of his skin until only a pair of shimmering gemstones remain.

Reaching out for them is almost automatic, but when something slaps my hand away, I refocus my gaze and allow a vein of shame to seep through me. The woman who hangs on his left arm is scowling at me with a rigid sternness. She bares irregularly spaced teeth when she passes, and her fluttering locks freeze in midair as I shuffle onward.

For a moment I study a man's vacant expression hiding behind splotches of brown and black on pale skin. A narrow plastic tube runs through holes in his nose to help him breathe, and his bowler hat conceals a mop of ratty gray hair. The skin on his neck droops low enough to cover his Adam's apple and detaches itself from his body.

A hundred faces, and not one of them is recognizable. Hoping I have not seen him and failed to recognize him, I trudge onto the pier and stare out at Charon, who, having led a dozen people aboard his ferry, drifts across the churning, reflective waters.

Calling out to him could disturb the throngs of dead awaiting their turn to cross, provoking retaliation. Ian and I would be no match for hundreds of angry spirits, I decide, so I let the ferryman disappear into the mist before opening my mouth and blurting out his name.

"Where are you, Cy?"

"Dad? Who's Cy?"

"He's a fowl creature," I garble, "but I need his help. I should tell you all about this, but I doubt you'd believe it."

He gazes out over the water for a long time, perhaps considering how best to respond to my insinuation, yet ready to accept it. When he does speak, his voice registers no higher than a whisper. "At this point, I'd believe anything."

"You know Orion used to pursue seven sisters for their beauty," I explain, my voice alternating between grim and hopeful. Though my understanding of the story might be flawed, I find it easy to recount. "When their mother made a deal to protect them from him, they were sent to the stars. I know one of them is also the Lady of the Six, a warrior who protected innocent villagers from the Roman army. And I believe part of her soul lives within me and that now I am the last mortal Titan of Crete."

He gazes on, unflinching. "Did you hit your head on the way out the door?"

"So, Penn," I say, changing the subject. Knowing the tactic won't work, I waver and let him answer.

"Yeah. Great education and now it's useless."

"Brianne isn't the only woman who will ever love you," I reason.

"Maybe not," he argues, "but she's the one."

I gasp at him calling her 'the one.' The words echo around inside my skull for nearly a full minute before I can extract and investigate their context.

"She's not The One," I say without turning my head.

"Mom?"

I recoil. Even anticipating his guess, I let the heartache it brings slam me square in the chest as black envelops every corner of my soul. I don't dare let him follow on this expedition. He has better things to do, and a lifetime of healing to undergo. If he weren't in the same peril I'm in, I might consider leaving him here and coming back for him later.

But if he stands before judgement I'll lose him forever, and so will Becky—and that's a risk I cannot take. Saying the words I'm about to utter will shatter my soul into a billion pieces that will scatter in the wind like specks of coal dust, but I can no longer hide it.

"No," I repeat. "She's not The One."

# 21

# Finding the Minotaur

Because Charon has already begun his ferry run, Ian and I stay with the hundreds of dead waiting to cross. In any other realm, this situation might prove unnerving, yet a shared camaraderie exists between us, even if the others look at me with mistrust. After all, each of them shares a single trait: a deep ache that meanders just below the surface, to muddy every expression with pangs of regret.

This phenomenon manifests itself most clearly in an isolated young woman with her whole life in front of her. Although her face bears no signs of trauma, and all her limbs are intact, a pale sickness mixes with her dreary frown. In order to comfort her, I say something I can barely hear myself, but which in my mind evokes powerful imagery: "You are stronger than your frailties."

Still, all these people have let their weaknesses defeat them, succumbing at last. In my mind, they will experience healing on the path to their final destinations. In the absence of illness, the young woman might be whole again and able to enjoy a full postmortal life.

Ian clears his throat as he stands on the pier, gazing off into apparent nothingness. "I don't suppose you know where to find this Cy."

Allowing myself to frown in this scenario feels too natural, yet when I attempt to express something else, everything about me comes off as both mechanical and artificial. Pathetic as he is, the real me is the only personality that can draw others in, a tacit truth that Becky taught me a year or so after we met. "No idea."

"You can manage," he says, witnessing my weary look.

Can I be such a hero to him when I disappeared in his youth, never to be seen again? That he recognizes me at all is something I might ask him about later if the opportunity presents itself. Instead, I can only grimace in pain.

"If you need to leave me here, I understand."

Trying to calm the tempest on my face, I offer him a sincere expression. "You wouldn't encumber me. I know what will happen when I try to disrupt the system. Registering your car at the DMV doesn't work if you don't take a number and wait in line."

A brief chuckle escapes his lips. "So *that's* where we are." Looking around, he adds to his statement: "It tracks."

"Your professors at Penn have done a remarkable job in making you look like an intelligent human being."

"Would have thought it was more than looks," Ian notes. "But then again, smart people don't experience what just happened."

Regret hits me—"Not exactly what I meant. I guess I still have problems verbally expressing the thoughts inside this head. Your mom hasn't yet trained the *me* out of me."

"Give it time."

Time has proven to be a more elastic entity than even Einstein predicted. While he reasoned that time and space bend and contort near massive celestial objects, that legendary mind never decoded the true mystery: If time is subject to the whims of the gods, then they exert more power than the laws of physics themselves.

Given time, Becky could shape me into a better version of myself, and we'd both be better off. But for now she's lost. Ian proposing that her wisdom can transcend time might prove brighter than any advice I've ever heard.

Finding hope in the mundane has never been my strong suit, but if some version of me is to survive the underworld, I must embrace such a skill. In that regard, Ian's accompaniment might benefit me in more ways than one, regardless of the odds.

"I know one way." My voice rises in pitch midsentence, allowing me to elevate my mind to see the landscape ahead from a different perspective. "We'll have to face judgement."

"Judg—already? Usually, God lets you cool off a bit so that a level head can prevail."

"We're after one god in particular. Maybe not one so hellbent on destruction and salvation, if you'll forgive the insinuation."

For a moment, he struggles to square what I've just said with the truth his pastors have taught him since he was young. I don't intend to set him straight, but my opinion might appease him enough to open his mind that not all gods demand the same things as God does.

"What are you saying?"

"The Greek world knows many gods. Some are more powerful than others, and they each have their own domain. You know God as one supreme being that controls everything."

"He doesn't control everything," he interrupts. "He gave us free will. You can't blame God for getting hurt in an accident involving a drunk driver when the other person exercised his will to get drunk, and you for not putting on your seatbelt."

"What if not all gods merely offer a choice between grace and damnation? What if everything we believe about the afterlife is inaccurate?"

"Sounds like blasphemy to me," he counters. "I'm surprised you haven't been smitten yet."

I struggle to offer a cogent response. His reasoning is sturdy enough to weaken everything I think I know, but seeing is different from believing. His faith guides him, while my experience guides me. "Maybe I have."

He thinks about this far longer than I had expected, yet when he's ready to open his mouth to defend his position, his expression changes to mirror mine.

"Then where is the judgement party?"

I nod into the mist, which still hangs heavy toward the water and draws in streams of moisture from its surface. "Let's cross the river, mess with the hound again, and stand in line with the spirits."

"Good way to get lost."

"Any better ideas?"

He lowers his battered eyebrows, curls his lip into a frown, and waits for me to explain my plan, which I don't have.

"Charon might not be keen to offer us a ride, especially you. You would have to wait your turn. You up for a swim?"

He nods slowly. "How far is it?"

"Far enough to drown—maybe. But if we go far enough upstream, there might be a narrower part. Unless Penn taught you how to fly."

"'Fraid not. With enough wood and some tools, we might fashion a boat, but I doubt they designed this realm to make survival easy."

"Good point," I say. "There's one other way, but it's probably worse than waiting for the ferryman and begging for a ride."

"What's that?"

I point across the river, trying to guess the tower's location. "There was a storm over there, I don't know how far away. It sort of swept me up into the clouds and dropped me on the other side before I caught a ride and found you."

"Summon it."

My heart sinks to the bottom of my chest. "It spit me out for a reason, I think. Not sure it would do the same for you."

"Only one way to find out. Besides, what's the worst that could happen?"

I tilt my head to the side and consider it. While I have always considered my sense of reason logically sound, he's running circles around me, proving that he's in a different class. I might reconsider my skepticism of higher education if it made sense in the here and now.

"Well, besides the likelihood that it will erase you."

"I've been erased already."

"Not what I meant."

"So explain it to me."

I bite my lip and reconsider my options. This is an argument he's never going to win, whether or not his assertions are based on impenetrable logic. "Now's not the time."

"Always with the lessons in their own time. Sometimes lessons don't need a specific time and place to be effective. You used to tell me that before you left."

Sadness replaces the thoughtful logic on my face. If he thinks he's hit the mark by using my own wisdom against me, he's mistaken.

"I didn't leave," I whisper. "I guess I don't recall how it happened. That river does a number on your memory. But I never left. Just wish I could tell your mom that."

"You can." His voice is firm but understanding. Instead of pushing his advantage, however, he relents. "If we can find Mom. She's still your one and only—I can sense it in you. A certain resolve, and it's not just about these Titans or Cy."

"You don't know the half of it."

"Maybe just enough to get you going."

Adrenaline vibrates in my fingers as I try to muster the strength to do the only thing that makes sense to me. Abandoning the promise of forever will devour my soul and leave me isolated in a barren landscape with no end, but if it helps me find Becky, it will be worth it.

Calming my emotions, I close my eyes and reach out into the dark. Speaking the words might retard the message, especially in the presence of my son. *Help me get to the other side, and I will serve you, master.*

The ground trembles beneath my feet. Feeling the same thing, Ian tries to stabilize himself by grabbing the crook of my arm, but his weight pulls my shoulders down with enough force to send a shockwave of pain up my back. I groan in disapproval as the tremor ceases.

*My will be done.*

Silence resumes, and then faintly at first, the anguished cries of a thousand souls fill my ears. The mist does not part, but as I gaze into it, something appears. Fuzzy at first, crossing over the water—and flying perhaps low enough for me to grab onto it.

Before I can prepare for what is coming, scaly snake tentacles shoot out of the mist, wrap themselves around us, and carry us twenty feet above the surface of the water. From above, the mist conceals the water, making the promise of falling that much more treacherous. The snake heads retreat into a massive body standing knee deep in the river as a pair of gigantic hands grasp us and carry us farther from the shore.

"What the...?"

The creature that is carrying us groans. At least seventy feet tall, it lurches its monstrous bare chest as it breathes in a gale of air and mist. A pair of thick brown corduroy pants made for a giant cover its legs. Its belt comprises a chain of snakes biting each other's tails as they constrict and squirm in belt loops big enough to fit my legs through.

A screeching howl of wind erupts into the dark every time it breathes, and as it carries us out over the mist, I can sense the disease that supports it. A thousand bodies have assembled on the far shore, staring up at the monster, whose red-eyed snake hair twists and writhes atop its head.

Below, a pile of debris twists into a cyclone, like a whirlwind of garbage. From aloft, I cannot make out any detail, but one thing catches my attention: shredded newspaper scatters into clouds of gray and white around its knees. The souls that await on the other side guide the creature with ropes of fire, which illuminate a host of scarred, eyeless faces.

I writhe in horror as the monster grips us and carries us toward the awaiting spirits. It bellows discordantly as I shout for Ian to hold on. The decaying bodies on the shore resemble an army, their slackened ropes and howls foreboding doom.

They gather below us as the creature drops us from a height of at least thirty feet. Before we hit the ground, our pace slows as a million hands reach out from the darkness and seize the hems of our clothes.

*"You who have not committed,"* a raging voice bellows. *"Follow The One or wallow in misery forever!"*

*You're not getting him that easy,* I warn.

*SLAVE!*

"I will do what I must," Ian says as the hands lower us to the dusty ground and dissipate into thin air.

Though the legions of the dead resist, I feel safe from any harm. Ian, on the other hand....

Dozens of animated corpses rip at his skin, dividing into two groups and grasping his arms. Together they pull in opposite directions as Ian pelts the air with a desperate, agonizing scream.

"Leave him be!" I shout.

The two groups only bare their stained, bloodthirsty fangs at me in disapproval. I spark with energy from some reserve within, and when I gather the power to command them away, every ounce of it flows from my heart into my bones. Lightning shoots from my fingers and the legions of the dead scatter into the darkness.

A powerful burst of light plows them all away, and I black out.

"Offer you a hand?"

I can hear a warm voice emanating from somewhere above me, but without shape or emotion, it merely drones.

"Careful, young one," it says, sounding all at once bestial and gruff.

"Dad?" My son's voice invigorates me more than the stranger's.

I wedge my eyes open and find myself gazing up at a sea of stars that goes on forever. Reaching out toward the heavens, I let my peripheral vision fill in the scene with what must constitute dingy colors. The flatland stretches farther than my eyes can see, yet seems unchanging even in the distance.

The mist has evaporated, leaving behind thin wisps of fog that rise into the air like puffs of cigarette smoke on a wintry day.

My voice catches in my throat where a lump has formed. It prevents me from speaking, but the souls who hover over me seem to understand what I need. I see Ian kneeling as a hand reaches out. His bruised face looks more forlorn than it did when we first met.

"Take a drink," he says, offering me a thin metal flask.

I struggle to control the shaking in my hands, and when I regard him with a questioning gaze, he offers to reassure me: "Yeah, it's safe. And delicious."

Guzzling may be terrible manners, but I cannot resist. The flask shakes and its contents slosh as I hold it to my lips, open my mouth, and take a swig long enough to drain it. When I'm finished, Ian takes the flask back, screws on its cap, and holds out a hand to help me up.

His stance is firm, suggesting that the army of souls had not injured him enough to cause a limp. Instead, he looks beaten in other ways. A sudden dreariness plants itself on his lips as he flits his eyes to his partner.

Upon seeing his face, I recoil in fear as the man reaches for my other hand.

On his stretched-out snout sprouts a musky-smelling beard an inch long, but where the nose should retreat toward the eyes, it stretches backward. The matted and grizzled hair atop his head carries an array of tiny insects, yet horns coil out of the mop and rise to a pair of bovine points above its head.

"Good to see you again, friend," his gruff voice says.

He's a man, but what has happened to his head? A metal loop ring pokes through his nose as his pair of dark eyes study me curiously. A man, yes, but he has a bull's head.

"Again?"

"Been a long time, but you may not remember."

"Who are you?" I stammer. A twinge of pain prods at my joints like needles, causing me to waver; still, I can stand without my son's aid. And when I gaze at the Minotaur's face, a vein of understanding breaks over me.

"I'm a friend of Ariadne's. You seek my father. Let me take you to him."

"Your father is a judge?"

His beard dips and his horns tilt forward—the gigantic eyes don't change expression so freely. When I regain my balance, I look upward at least a foot to study his nose ring. "And a king. He can help you."

Saying nothing, I allow myself to follow his gaze as he turns his head. Beyond his field of view, a vast plain stretches out. That same ash that is layered over fields of wilted flowers now garners loose stones of various sizes, each coated in a thin dust. The air hangs low with humidity as Ian stands next to him.

The Minotaur leads us headlong into the ash without saying much. Ian tries to regale him with his story, but the lack of a reply shows either that he is not listening or is lost in enough related thought to keep him silent.

Before long, a series of voids appear like black silhouettes. As if living, these voids part as we press into their company. "Excuse me," a man says, yet I can see no human presence. "Go ahead," another says.

"No cuts!" shrieks an invisible, indignant woman.

We curl our way through the throngs until a giant archway of dark stone holds back a veil of darkness beyond. Three people man the archway where the souls await their judgement.

Dressed in a robe of gray and white and sporting a long, graying beard, a man with a staff locks eyes with the Minotaur and nods. Together, we step toward him. His voice is powerful and opaque, yet within it reigns a sense of empathy.

"Who have you brought me, my son?"

"Ian," my son speaks. "And my dad Kerry."

"I am Minos, king of Crete. Ian and Kerry," his voice rises in authority, "you seek judgement on this day. What do you say for yourselves?"

"Not judgement," I stammer. "We have already made our decision. We're looking for a man called Cy. Do you know him?"

Before me, a face appears out of thin air. I stare at it in disbelief. Now detached from his own body and somehow looking more mortal, Cy has taken on an air of solemnity. Trying to see him speaking with any other emotion does little for my imagination. I nod and wait for the king to answer.

"This is Cygnus, reincarnated in human form. I have not seen him in centuries. Tell me why you seek him."

"He's going to help me," I blurt out. "He must be here somewhere, in search of his queen. I need him to lead me to the Titans."

Minos shows a look of deep concern and watches me without blinking. "What must drive you to the abyss of Tartarus?"

"I'm going to find out who I am—who I really am. And then I'm rescuing Becky."

"You can never leave that place," he warns. "No soul has ever escaped the pit, and none ever shall. There is evil there, and dark. It will devour you, convert you to its realm, and seal you in for all eternity. It is forbidden."

"I don't care about your warnings. I'm going to find her, and I don't need you to try to stop me."

The king of Crete bows to me, a stolid expression of alarm crossing his face. Given that we share the same ancestral home, he must know of the Titans I seek and my relationship to them.

"I have no authority to command your choice, but I will not condemn you to that awful place. If you must go, only one shall guide you. You understand what this entails, don't you?"

"I do," I say, swallowing. "And I accept it. My son will be taking the journey with me because Becky is his mother."

"Depart, Ian and Kerry. I bid you farewell and beg you to travel carefully."

I gulp again and let the pain rise to my face. "Just one more thing, your Highness. Tell me how I'm related to Merope and the Six, and the Titans."

The king frowns, squares his shoulders, and mirrors the pain in my expression. If he can tell me the entire story, it might make the journey easier, but he has chosen silence. Instead of answering directly, he poses two questions: "When did you learn of this? Who told you that you are a Titan of Crete?"

# 22

# Tears of the Heliades

King Minos of Crete flashes a dark frown when I turn to face him. Uncertain of my answer, yet finding resolve somewhere deep within, I utter the only name I can think of.

"Persephone."

My answer does not impress the king. Straightening his back and stroking his beard with a fist full of iron rings, he allows the frown to linger.

Does he expect me to say something, or should I just walk away? The tension tightens as I gaze at him, and soon I allow my frown to mirror his. Each of his fingers bears a simple ring, which has oxidized and turned red enough over time to stain his fingers orange. The pain must be unbearable, but having worn them for so long I figure he has gotten used to it by now.

"Yeah, I guess you're not going to help after all."

Still stroking his graying beard, he lets his eyes flit sideways and then impales my soul with his gaze. "Find the poplars. It is said that they grow here along the river Cocytus, near the confluence with the Styx. But be wary—the daemons prowl those lands."

I shrug. He might as well have told me to find a minor intersection in Tokyo without a map. People here could be infuriatingly vague, and for me clarity is one of the true pillars of a project. Without it the plans and specifications are useless, and construction will result in poor workmanship or outright disaster. I've spent long enough answering questions and interpreting prints for it to become second nature.

*How do I remember the details of who I am?* The question lingers in my mind for so long that the king begins to lose interest in me. He motions for another soul to join him, and a dark-haired woman materializes out of the mist. She offers him a bow, and with her knee still bent, glances toward me.

"I'm not really worried about daemons right now," I say as my frown intensifies.

"Have you met the ferryman?" Minos asks.

I nod, awaiting more.

"Follow the river from the landing. You'll know when you get there."

His voice sounds all at once dismissive, and he doesn't look my way during his brief explanation. The best I can do is follow his instructions and maybe I'll get lucky. But how long will it take?

When the woman speaks to him, the king listens as she attempts to describe a choice she made when she was alive, one that seems to have resulted in an injury to a child. Her pleas for mercy puncture my ears and my heart as I back away and bump into a woman somberly stepping towards the stone archway.

Beyond it, a veil of blackness awaits. Mourning. Sorrow leaks through from the other side to invade my soul with the subtle tendrils of dark. When the woman crosses my path, she attempts to tiptoe around me, and in so doing, trips over one of my feet.

As she tumbles toward the ashen earth, I hear her whisper something that sounds like my name. Could it be?

Her eyes sparkle with a deep blue as I reach out to grasp her spindly hand, where a single golden ring adorns her left hand. I react too late to stop her from kicking up a plume of ash, and her knees collide with the ground.

A cough escapes her lips when she lands, and searching the darkness for her fate, she lets out a single, heartbreaking breath.

"You came."

"I—this can't be."

"I'm afraid it is," Minos explains, having turned away from the woman he's questioning long enough to see the source of the commotion. "She was mortal. And memory always transfers between partners."

"Memory..."

"It's you," she whispers.

I clasp her hand and bring it to my chest before bowing to kiss her fingers. "It's been so long, and ... so many questions. Please stay and tell me how this all happened."

"I cannot, Kerry," she says. "I must say goodbye to you forever, my friend."

Finality has never felt so bittersweet, so relieving, and yet so agonizing. Memory always transfers between partners. That is how I recognize my son, who now stares at the woman whose judgement I interrupted, and how I know about Cy.

The missing link—and Cy must know about it. If I ever find him, I'll beat him to a pulp. Still, I'm no closer to finding him than I was hours ago.

I mouth something nonsensical, searching those lost memories for a name to which I can assign the face, yet her gratitude spells it out for me with every mournful stroke of my heart. "I ... I don't even know how I got here, but I have to find her."

A tear sprinkles onto her olive-toned face. "I know. You love her."

All at once, her name trembles at the tip of my tongue. As she releases my grasp, I mouth it and then whisper it again from my dry, raspy throat.

"Vanessa."

Her voice wavers. "I'm going home ... look to the stars and you will find me."

And suddenly, I know to look for the Big Dipper, where Callisto the Great Bear watches over her son in the sky. My heart flutters as her image fades. The veil of mourning ravages her body piece by piece, absorbing it into the dark as though she's stepping into a whirlwind of black sand. The tears in my eyes transform into energy.

Persephone referred to me as a person who carries both light and dark. My tears sparkle on my cheek as the last vestiges of Vanessa's face, and those long, well-manicured braids, lose focus and shape.

My heart plunges into my abdomen with a thud, causing me to stumble. Ian tries to catch me, but not before my face crashes into the bitter earth.

"Vanessa," I weep.

"Dad?" Ian whispers. "Is that who you left Mom for?"

I cannot voice my sadness without my heart heaving in the destructive force of my pain. "I didn't.... I never left her.... She left me."

"She didn't," he says, bending at his knees and wrapping an icy hand around my wrist. As the moments bury themselves in oblivion, his words sound like brine to soak my hurt. "And we can still find her. You just have to find this Cygnus guy. And now we know where to look."

"They took everything from me," I bellow, the anger and pain scouring my vocal cords with acid.

"Who is 'they?'"

I bite my lip and pour rage through my veins as the tears crystalize on my cheeks to glitter like pure diamonds. "I don't know. But I'm going to find out. And they're going to pay."

"Dad.... This isn't you."

It's all me. When you're a father, you try to hide your darkest secrets from your children for fear of them adopting your bad habits and destructive tendencies. Success always comes in fits and starts, and now understanding how Ian came here, the sting of failure morphs together with the pain. Now that we're both adults, I find no shame in revealing everything to him. He'll know I'm mortal and will empathize in a natural way, but that can't compare to the love and anguish that rends my soul. In what way have I contributed to his downfall? If something sinister didn't pull me away from his mother, I might be talking to him on the phone right now, meeting my first grandchild, and embracing the sweetest pleasures life has to offer.

"If you can't walk," he says, "I'm going to carry you."

His strength surprises me. Without breaking a sweat, he pulls me to my knees, wrestles me up to my feet, and then lets my weight rest on his shoulder as I limp away from the archway that had consumed Vanessa.

"See? Not so hard when you get moving. You taught me that."

Time has destroyed my memories so that I can't remember ever teaching him, so I concede that his recollection is sharper than mine. He half-drags me away from the lines of souls awaiting judgement and trudges on for what seems like miles as I gradually regain enough strength to support my own weight.

# MEMORIES:

Religion has always described patience as a virtue standing next to godliness. According to Jeff L. Martin, the pastor Becky and I listened to in our first year together, patience has a special way of reminding us mortals that we are subject to life's perils, but can find great reward in seeking a path based not on vengeance, but upon hope. Patience makes us resilient and fortifies us for the journey back to our Savior.

Years later, I learned the hard way while driving home from a long day at work. Frustration was running rampant through my thoughts, and I was on edge all day. Orders were late, vendors were making excuses, and the project manager had put the responsibility on me. Another impatient driver crept into my lane, all the while glaring at me, so I gave him the finger, accelerated beside him, and raced him down the freeway until we were both doing ninety. The interaction crushed me, and it took weeks for me to get over it. If instead I had taken a deep breath and realized the other driver was just as human as me, anguish might never have scarred my heart.

"Here's how you do it," I say, kneeling in the grass beside him and taking his hands into mine. "You gotta look down the bat the whole way. Don't lose sight of the ball. And step into it by leading with your right foot. It's all one motion."

He swings the bat and misses. Slipping off the helmet and throwing it across the diamond, he loses his temper.

"Just keep practicing."

"I'm never going to get it. I quit!"

I emit a muffled sentence, trying to soothe the wound to his ego with my voice. "Try it one more time, and we can get some ice cream."

"No."

"Just try. Practice swinging the bat. Practice stepping into it. You'll find that just the act of the work can give you new ideas and fire."

He shrugs, picks up the bat, and slices it through the air a few times. His footwork could use some fine tuning, but he's seeing the swing at least.

"Now get ready, and don't try to slug the skin off of it."

A smile flashes on his lips. Maybe I've reminded him of one of my favorite childhood movies, which I'd made him watch at least a dozen times.

He grips the bat. And swings. Another strike.

He gulps and frowns at me. "Now, about that ice cream. Can I get fudge?"

Wrapping my arm around his shoulder, I take the bat with my left hand and toss it aside, where it clinks into a loose pile of bats at the edge of the dirt. "Only if your mom says so."

The trip takes a lot longer than I deem necessary, but without me having noticed, we are now parallel to the rocky shore of a wide river that reflects the starlight back into space. I might judge the setting to be surreal if we hadn't been trudging through this paranormal realm all this time.

"That's the Styx," Ian says. "We're almost there."

"Not quite; we'll need to find weapons. I'm not going to Tartarus unarmed."

He escorts me through a grassy area littered with large rocks the closer we tread to the shoreline. We will cut the expenses of weariness and distance by going through the rocks instead of around them. Still, traversing a rocky landscape will require energy I don't have, making the journey more dangerous.

"About that," he says, suppressing a dark groan. "What happened to all those people with no eyes? I thought it was them, but now I've been thinking about it, it was you. You did that."

"What did I do?" My question is sincere. I can't remember any of it, as though losing consciousness has erased it from my memory.

"I don't know how to describe it. There was a bright flash. They went away running, and you fell. I thought they'd set some kind of light bomb off on you. But I saw echoes of it a while ago when you were talking to your ... Vanessa."

*Thou who art of light and shade.*

"How? Doesn't make any sense."

He shakes his head. "No. But if you can do it again—maybe train yourself how—it could be useful even if we don't know what awaits us in hell."

"Are you kidding me? You can't train yourself how to do something you only did by accident."

"Sure you can," he argues. "That's what happened to me in calculus at Penn. The equation looked like something you'd find in one of those graduate-level physics books, where the author is trying to impress his readers how special he is with this simple equation, which takes two pages to break into smaller, but somehow more complex statements to derive a—"

"What?"

He chuckles. "Lost me, too. But after class, I was scratching some things down in one of my notebooks. Late night, lots of pizza. And I started to riff on some of the variables, what they might mean, and experimented with different ways to apply them. Taught myself a different equation that the stuffy physicist hadn't thought to explain, but I didn't know if it'd work in practice. But you know what? It did."

"That's what study gets you. Not dumb luck."

"But is it really just dumb luck with you? Because you've got something we can hone into a weapon."

"What are you doing here? Why aren't you taking graduate classes somewhere even bigger than Penn?"

"Maybe a story for another time," he says, nodding to the horizon.

A series of tall trees occupy an expansive plain, beyond which rolling hills surge to where green underbrush colors the landscape. The trees rise fifty to sixty feet if I apply my best guess and factor in the distance. Their slender trunks support branches that curve upward and grow what looks like a dark, verdant moss.

As we get closer, I watch them sway. Stepping through the grass, I trip on a protruding rock and catch myself before falling at the root of the nearest tree.

"This must be it," Ian says. "Two rivers. Poplar trees."

"And no Cy."

"You know him," a distant voice says.

I watch as a thin, lanky man grows visible between a pair of the trees. Instead of speaking, I gaze upward at the spot where the trees point into the heavens like daggers, and then peer by my feet when a golden glint catches my eye. Bending down, I pick up a yellow resin stone that takes in all available light and glows.

"You've met my sisters," the man says, limping forward. "Never thought I'd see them here, but sometimes you get miracles, even in the underworld."

I glance around to question him in a nonverbal way. There's no one here. If the miracle is that Hades has made him delusional, I might agree. But he means something. I can tell by his gentle, piercing gaze.

"You stand at the feet of Merope. She's a beauty, isn't she?"

"Merope? You're related to the Seven Sisters?"

He tilts his head to his right side and Ian looks on as if unsure whether we can trust him. The way the man leans into his step brings out an uneasy feeling, but he means us no harm.

"I had seven sisters, yes," he says. "But not the same sisters you're probably thinking of."

"Orion, the hunter—"

"Nothing to do with it," he says, squinting. "You found yourself one of her tears. See, my sisters loved me so much they came here and transformed into the Poplars after I fell into the river. They weep amber. It has several special properties, you see."

"There's another Merope?" I ask, narrowing my eyes and frowning.

"Several others, but my sister—"

"And you fell into the river?"

He shifts to his side and grimaces before running a wrinkly hand through his graying stubble. "A story in itself, which I'm sure you're not looking for. Your Cy is better known as—"

"The swan."

He raises his eyebrows. "So you've heard. Have you also heard I knew him? Best friends, he and I. Zeus transformed him into a swan and sent him to the heavens that day so he could have peace."

"Didn't really work," I suggest.

"You're wondering why?"

"Not really."

"Because he was in love with me. I knew it, my sisters knew it."

Nonsense. He's looking for his queen, and my aid meant everything to him, despite me assaulting him more than once. "No, that's not true. He's straight."

"Straight? What do you mean?"

I gulp and try to steer clear of an argument. "I mean, as in not ... you know ... gay."

"He was happy when he was around me. Is being gay not a good thing?"

"Uhhh."

"He liked men," Ian interrupts.

"One."

"I see," I lie. The shock builds through me until it makes breathing difficult. He'd never mentioned this man before. Why? Is this why he kept his true intentions a secret? If I meet him again, I might slug him for the deception. But then again, I recognized his deceit from the start, whenever that was.

Looking back, I try to access a memory that has been sealed away. Cy in love with a man who has seven sisters, one of whom is named Merope?

This can't all be a coincidence. Advice I received from a friend long before I ever met Becky insisted that coincidence is a myth. I was skeptical, and maybe for a good reason, but this is too much.

Instead of confronting the man over it, I run it through my head in search of an intangible answer destined to remain out of reach forever. Turning the amber over in my fingers reveals starker emotions that linger somewhere beneath the surface; that memory has been hidden for ages, but now that it crops up I allow it to fester within me until I can only shed another tear of regret.

We all have artifacts of our own—things precious to us for reasons only we can comprehend. The welded washers became a part of me, and because of that I gave them to Becky, who in turn made them a part of her. Two souls forever welded together through an unbreakable electrical bond.

"You look like you have a million questions," the man says. "So start with just one."

"You and your sisters," I stammer. "Why does the amber have properties? Why does any of this make sense? I want you to tell me everything. Especially about Merope."

"The daughters of Neaera or Daughters of the Sun, children of the Titan Oceanus. Merope was born on the island of Crete."

"A Cretan Titan," I say. "Not a prisoner of Tartarus. She's one of six."

"You're putting a lot of thought into your imagination," he warns, seeing my vacant expression and glancing past me where the river meanders along the rocks.

"I know they're real. And I'm..." I cannot say the words. Instead, I breathe them in a voice so muffled that he cannot hear me. *And I am her descendant.*

*And now you are mine.*

"Tell me," I choke on my own words. "Where is Cy now?"

"You tell me."

"He, uh..."—my voice catches in my throat—"he died when he fell."

"The swan does not fall," the man whispers. "He flies."

When I see it, my fingers spark with an unseen energy I have not felt for a long time. As that warm glow surrounds me, I notice that Ian can see it, too. How can we harness this energy when I'm unfamiliar with how it works and can't contain it?

My fingers tremble as I step away from Cy's lover and try to wrap my head around it. I may never understand what any of it means, but it's becoming increasingly clear that the way forward will be through this man's sister, my long-lost ancestor Merope.

"Dad?"

He sees the swan, too. It drifts overhead with a graceful swoop of its wings, its graying feathers painting a streak across the star-encrusted sky. Expecting it to land, I watch it instead fly away, off towards a thick cloud of utter black stained crimson with a raging inferno of death. And then it circles back as if to point us in that direction.

I'm going to experience hell, and I'm unprepared for the agony and torment that await me. There is no other path. Foreboding flushes through me as Ian points his feet in that direction and limps away to a blackened fate from which there can be no escape.

# 23

# Algea Metempsychosis

The amber warms my palm as my fingers curl around it, almost as though it conceals a small heating element, and when I raise it closer to my face, the radiance transmits some of its latent energy into my spirit. I watch it glow as we trek away from the tranquil waters of the Styx.

They took Becky from me, but who are they? My mind can't fill in the blanks, and that causes a stir of anger to bubble in my brain. I glimpse the artifact at that very moment and, certain that it has lost its luster, I conjure a quaint feeling of peace that causes it to pulsate with warm, radiant light.

It responds to my emotions. Trying to work out how may not seem important, but my brain copes with confusion by assigning cause-and-effect scenarios, which may or may not be true. Achieving healing through this means might be unconventional—but then again, 'unconventional' is a synonym for weird, a label I've long thrived on.

Positive emotions make the amber glow brighter, and negative emotions darken it. How can it read my brainwaves through my skin? And if I were to combine this with the phenomenon that Ian saw, could it be a defense against the evil that awaits us?

"You know," Ian says, lowering his voice. "I'd say you don't really know Cy as well as you think. At least if whatever-his-name-was is telling the truth."

"In a contest of honesty," I wager, "I'll take him over Cy every time."

"Why don't you like him?"

A sigh escapes my lips, and the shine in the amber flutters in response. "Long history of hard lessons and half-stories. The fact that he'd use me to find that man pisses me off."

"Why should it? Think of it as a symbiotic relationship."

"They teach psycho at Penn?" I ask, raising my eyebrow to indicate humor.

He shuffles as a patch of sandy earth gives way beneath his feet, sending him sliding back at least six inches for every step he takes. When his shoes land on a grassy section, where the roots dig deep into the soil, his footing grows surer, and he can walk faster. In some ways, confusion might cause every step of our progress to lose its effectiveness and waste our energy.

"I mean, hear me out. You want something and he can help you. He needs something in return and helping you can help him, and vice versa."

"Not like I haven't thought of that before," I argue. "But he's still a bastard."

"Negative emotions make us want to judge others more often," he laments. "A fact I learned before I met Brianne."

"Listen to this," I exclaim. "My son, trying to teach his old man lessons in wisdom. Ironic."

"Maybe. But it's still true, and don't you agree that wisdom doesn't always boil down to age and experience?"

I shrug and follow him up a shallow slope, to a flat-topped hill overlooking a narrow ravine and the babbling, reflective waters of a stream. "Not at all."

"Then maybe you're wrong."

At the V-shaped bottom of the creek channel that must feed the mighty Styx, a grove of trees grows high and waves in a breeze I cannot perceive from where we stand.

"I've been wrong before. Your mom probably told you all about it, and she'd have been right. I'm wrong often—but not this time."

"I'm just saying, maybe you owe it to yourself, and Mom, to open your mind to explore distinct possibilities of thought."

"I don't think you're hearing me," I say. My position is not negotiable, and he must know it. Arguing for argument's sake is only a recipe for discord, which comes with too many drawbacks in this realm.

"Fine," he says, somehow a signal that he's not yet ready to concede.

And that means he's sure to dispute the idea again at a bad time. Of course, the way he came to the underworld, if his story is accurate, doesn't evoke confidence on the topic of wisdom. A fatal flaw of logic everywhere revolves around the fact that using rationality to describe the error of others fundamentally ignores the error we ourselves commit. If Ian hasn't yet figured that out, any debate will only frustrate us, and when two opposing viewpoints entrench themselves, they can achieve no consensus. When that happens, the perils that stirred the debate continue to rage unabated.

The ridgeline extends a few hundred yards, before tapering off to an acute angle and falling at perhaps a ten percent grade. Then it reaches a crook in the valley where the creek doglegs hard toward the river, and down there, a more destructive darkness hides.

I decide that Ian can sense that darkness but is leading us there anyway. He glances skyward to search for the bird, but when it fails to show itself, suspicion churns within me. Cy likely knows what dangers lurk down here, and leaving us to battle them alone is the coward's way out.

I grit my teeth and notice the shine pulsing between my fingers.

No, it's not responding to my brainwaves—it's responding to my heart. Even the calmest heart reflects emotion in its constant beating, and it must be picking up these subtle signs by interacting with my blood vessels. A prehistoric mood ring fossilized to commemorate sadness. Ingenious.

Far beyond the valley lurks the paralyzing darkness that towers over the landscape and hides the moon and stars in the perpetual gloom. Yet even that darkness can't defeat the light from those fires that burn deep within me. Before long, I may sense hope when I gaze into the black.

We take ten minutes to descend the grade, and Ian, having composed a silent plan to quench our thirst in the tributary, hurries toward it.

A brush root grows in a gigantic boulder's shadow, but Ian doesn't see it obstructing his path. He twists his ankle, falls like a stone, and groans when he tumbles to rest at least five feet down the slope. When I hurry to help him, the darkness begins to chatter like the grinding of icy, rigid teeth against bone.

The murk snarls, and before I can determine from whence it came, the amber in my hand goes black as squeals, shrieks and grunts fill the air on all sides.

I hunker down to defend against them, but all light has left me. Seconds tick by as a hundred souls materialize out of the dark, animating the trees and conspiring against us. Their bodies are fraught with scars, boils, and rotting flesh and their eyes reflect only flame.

Recoiling does nothing to slow their march. Ian bats away a decaying hand and shrieks when it multiplies. The hundreds become hundreds more, and each time another one appears the agony stirs deeper within me.

Collapsing in sheer torture, Ian groans and yelps as though something has enraged the bruises on his face and the gunshot wound behind his ear. His eyes show desperation, as though he's bleeding out.

In my quest to help him, I can do nothing but surrender to the torture. Anger blossoms somewhere in my heart, sending pulses of white-hot fury into my fingers. I swat at one of the corpses, and when my fingers brush its thin, white hair, my skin burns. The daemon grins at me through sharpened, bloodstained teeth that look as though years of gnawing at loose flesh on discarded bones has transformed them into predatory fangs.

It shrieks as I close my fist, grip it around the neck, and squeeze. In response, it kicks at me, bites at my hand, and attempts to climb up my body. Its weight sends a tide of pain through every part of my soul.

I want to retaliate and destroy the creature, yet every action I take to defeat it seems to further strengthen it. The torment is a guile that I cannot defeat, no matter what logic says about positive emotion. There is none left.

Pain has stripped me to the bone and left my carcass to be consumed by hundreds of carnivores bent on causing grief.

"AUUGHHH! Make it STOP!!!" Ian screams.

I grab hold of the next daemon to bounce my way, dropkick it in the crotch and watch it roll away howling. The minor thrill of victory doesn't swell within me. Instead, the creature rears back to attack once again with its support troops backing it up.

"Son of a bitch, NOOOO!"

"Ian!" I scream. The daemon spirit falls at my feet and gnaws my ankle, sending jolts of agony up my legs to meet with my spine, which another spirit is ravaging with razor-sharp claws that protrude from bony hands.

The monsters have descended upon Ian, and I growl while fighting my way toward him. Punching one of them in the face shoots shards of ice through my hands and the resultant smack sounds like a fist punching into foul-smelling raw meat.

The shrieking continues, and then the pain grows deeper. Physical agony dominates every inch of my body, but the emotional stress begins to rise with every swipe I take. Still, the daemons do not let any action I take deter them. They feed off my pain, and feast on the will to create more.

Hot tears erupt from my eyes and wash down my bloody face like rivulets of hydrochloric acid. The sting feels corrosive and vile, as the sadness melds with venomous rage to induce an emotional hell like nothing I've ever experienced.

"I'm going to kill you!" I rasp. "And your masters!"

Laughter. It has provoked them—instead of feasting on the festering pile of defeat that is my son, the legions of them encroach from all sides, battering at me with ear-splitting howls, gnashing teeth, razor-like claws, and stinging flesh, even as the torment crushes my soul.

Becky. The washers. The vanishing, the monsters, the guilt, and all the energy of self-deprecation I have ever heaped upon myself swirls like a vortex deep in my heart, where the remains of my tattered soul are being devoured piece by piece until there is nothing left to suck up from the storm of confetti that surrounds it.

*You're nothing, Kerry.*

*You fat, insensitive slob.*

*Idiot. Fool. Naïve little punk.*

*Are you going to cry?*

A sob works its way through my nostrils and burrows deep, as though to destroy the only sound I can emit. My airways seal themselves off as the daemons pile on top of me like a haystack of sweaty, grimy bodies.

And then, something I can't explain happens; one by one, they lift off of me. A voice penetrates my ears, and her sweet, humorous charm sparks my spirit. Sarah wields a weapon that can defeat them all, and now that I can sense her power, it repels the dark spirits that entangle with one another as they rise high into the air, as though gravity has lost its hold on them.

By the hundreds, they suspend themselves in midair, screeching and howling as they reach out toward Ian and me, their two helpless victims. But they are not done with us yet.

Sarah's voice evaporates, and with it, gravity reclaims the spirits. They land on their hands and feet in every direction, baring dripping, bloody fangs and glowering with the infernos consuming their eyes.

Now, instead of reflecting fire, those hellacious eyes emit flames tall enough to scorch the thin hairs on their bleeding scalps. If they can sense pain, they can also inflict it.

With each excruciating blow, they crowd around us to consume everything that composes us.

*You asshole.*

*They lost. Because of you. She's gone. Because of YOU!*

"NOOOO!!!"

"D...d—daaa," Ian croaks beside me. "Use it."

But I wield no weapons; I am already defeated. Hundreds of bloodthirsty monsters pounce on my body, shredding me with a pain deeper than anything imaginable.

*It was popular before you adopted it.*

*You look like hell.*

If nothing can defeat these hungry zealots, I must purge every ounce of pain from my body and expunge the demons that rage through my spirit.

Before I know what I'm feeling, a foreign memory sparks in my heart.

## MEMORIES:

She floats above the dusty floorboards, suspended in a blue ether of sadness that collects her tears and transforms them into a wispy mist that escorts her toward me. Floating as though gravity has no effect on her, she breathes my name, solidifies, and then vanishes before the stars swirl around me and a howling wind replaces all thought. When we reappear, she is holding my hands in her palms and guiding me towards a distant red giant star.

Her tears give way to a simple, solemn smile, and energy builds within me, stoked by a light I've never known, and my heart flutters into overdrive.

The amber senses it—in one bright flash, lighting forks out from my chest in every direction, zapping each one of the demonic creatures that aim to devour us.

*Light and dark.*

The electricity emanating from my chest blazes to life as Ian struggles for breath next to me, and before I have understood what is happening, I'm standing, raising my arms like Moses before the Red Sea, and driving away the evil.

*That is how you do it, my servant.*

Their howls grow distant and fade away into nothingness as their disfigured bodies vanish, revealing a new kind of terror.

Before us, a hundred mangled bodies lie dead on the rocks in the creek. Their amputated limbs, a buffet for a million bugs, lie in heaps along the water. Gaping wounds slash up their midsections, revealing bloody stinking entrails that draw in the insects by the billions to lap up the riches of their sustenance.

A pang of sickness punches me in the gut, and I let out a dry heave that would contain a soup of my earlier meals if I'd had any.

Ian has still not gathered the strength to rise, but when I help him to his feet he sees the carnage and reacts the same way.

Tears roll down his cheeks, and he doubles over.

Heads removed from their necks, a pair of bodies caress one another with bony, decaying hands as millions of insects feast on their innards.

"God!" Ian says, heaving again.

"Don't look at them," I say, my voice wavering.

Being advised to look away from something awful somehow intensifies your desire to stare. The psychology textbooks have never figured out why, but I already know that human nature attempts to make sense of the senseless, and there's nothing more senseless than the carnage that litters the path ahead.

Tiptoeing between the bodies, careful not to step on rotting flesh, I half-drag Ian onward, skip-hopping across the rocky creek and hurrying toward a hillside that must overlook the devastation. Together we climb in silence, murmuring with the remnants of pain and disgust.

Where had that power come from? Did remembering Sarah somehow ignite me? I resolve to test this theory at my next opportunity, but for now, my only quest is to get away from the daemons and the slaughter along the creek-side.

Twenty minutes later we stand atop a hill coated with yellow and gold grass and a thin layer of lichen or moss devouring the nutrients in the rich soil.

When I look back, it appears as though nothing has happened. The dead have vanished, but the pulsing sorrow and sickness remain deep inside me. Understanding that the horrors are only just beginning to unfold wracks my midsection with a powerful ache. A worse fate must await us once we reach the abyss of Tartarus.

# 24

# Phlegethon Desire

Our pain is beyond words; to say we're hurting understates the agony that ravages us, yet the glowing amber offers only limited visibility. Shivering, straining, and grimacing with every move he makes, Ian emits low grumbles and moans between steps while I trudge on through the wild brushland for what seems like hours. My gait has become a somber limp, and when I see Ian has bent over to gasp in the warm, sterile air, or to vomit, I offer him my arm to keep him from falling face-first into the thorny grass, which may share the soil with invasive nett les.

"You doing okay, son?"

He wipes his brow and coughs, emitting a bit of bloody spittle onto his lip, which quivers in obvious torment. I'd say that he's got it worse than me, but I have decided to use the pain to propel me onward.

"No," he says, "not even a little bit."

"Then let's stop and rest a few minutes."

With a slow shake of his head and widened eyes, he glances in both directions before speaking: "I'm worried more daemons will attack."

"Might as well," I reply. Rather than admit defeat, I speak in a falsely optimistic tone to intensify energy. "What's going to happen?"

He takes a deep breath and rubs his knee, which is oozing a circle of crimson and black blood through his trousers. "Dad, are you dead?"

I recoil at him using the word.

My reaction only provokes him. "We both know the topic had to arise sometime. There's no sense in letting it drag out."

Swallowing, I attempt to gather my thoughts, and failing, I let out a slow, raspy breath. "I thought so when I arrived, but I'm just not sure anymore. Everything's so jumbled and confused here; differentiating up from down is useless."

"How did you get here?"

"I still don't know." Memories of Cy, while vague, still resonate. Seeing Vanessa earlier, and with Ian accompanying me, I can at least make out a few ill-founded guesses, but the crossing of the Lethe has eroded my memory. How I can remember anything at all, especially now-distant experiences, is a mystery.

"No,"—he curses as a sharp sting jabs at him—"no idea?"

His leg twitches and his grimace sharpens when a new shard of pain shoots through his limbs. Seeing his reaction only deepens my agony.

I huff in the warm air, cross my arms, and lean over to continue the conversation.

If a discussion can achieve anything now, it can at least reveal hidden truths. Perhaps sharing observations and swapping notes can prove advantageous if we can predict what lies ahead.

A place like this shouldn't feature predictability. Architects design every detail of a project for a purpose, and if weary travelers, the dead, the spirits and everything else that lurks in the underworld can expect anything, they will defeat the design. Then again, even nature observes certain patterns, and understanding and exploiting those details can be the difference between life and death in the wild. The underworld may not qualify as 'the wild,' but it adheres to some of the same general rules.

"None whatsoever," I answer. "But I do have an idea as to how you got here."

"Don't judge me," he interrupts. "Please. Now's not the time."

"I'd never do that. Just maybe we should discuss it."

"Everyone does things they regret," he explains. "And I know that penance doesn't erase the deed. I just need time to process that on my own and come to terms with it. You'd ask the same of me."

"I guess I just don't understand." My lip quivers and my hands begin to tremble as though my nerves cannot withstand another moment of hurt. Every part of my mind and body is bleeding, and every pang amplifies the next like thousands of cheers at a football game.

"I know that, and neither do I."

Another question springs to the front of my mind, but judging whether I should risk it might overload my thoughts. A vicious headache is boring into my head like monstrous drill bits from both sides to pulverize my brain. "Don't you wonder what your loved ones might think?"

He groans and spills a batch of tears onto his face. The anguish is melting his soul. His abdomen lurches as he buries his scarred face into his bloody hands. "Not exactly ... something you think about at the time. When it's all internal ... but you're right, if there's anyone I really love left."

"What about Brianne?"

He continues to shake. "I ... I don't know. I guess I thought I was in love with her, but was it really that or just the excitement of finally having a steady girlfriend with whom I could share everything?"

"Is there a difference?"

"It never felt like I remember you and Mom being."

"Relationships often feel different to the people in them than to outside observers," I wager. My own romantic life was a series of spectacular failures and pathetic fear before I met Becky. But somehow it all worked out.

"Dammit," he whispers. "I guess being smart doesn't make you wise."

"You're wiser than I was at your age." Then again, I've lost track of time to such an extent that my age might not even be a ballpark guess. Judging from his looks, I'd estimate he's about the age I was when I met Becky. My statement is genuine; too often, I look back at choices from months or years ago and see how foolish I was. Learning is a lifelong endeavor, and if I am dead, then it must continue into the afterlife, if one exists.

"God. It hurts like a sonofabitch."

I wish I could give him some reassurance, but hope is running low. What makes the amber shimmer must result from the energy spent in exerting love. Another of its properties? I glance at it to make sure my eyes aren't deceiving me. Ian pulls something out of his pocket and examines it.

He'd also taken a piece of the amber. As he rolls it over in his hands, it shines with a dull orange ambiance that might communicate uncertainty and clouded judgement. And that gives me another idea of its properties.

If hope can offer clarity, it can provide comfort, and positive emotions tend to make the amber shine brighter. Clarity might be a wildcard in this wilderness. This might be something I can fashion into a weapon if I can figure out how the tears work.

"What do you say we keep walking?" I say, helping him to stand upright.

He wipes a spot of blood from his lip, breathes into his palms, and then gazes into my eyes for a split second. A vein of distrust weaves through his eyes, yet his expression doesn't direct the emotions at me.

"Where did that swan go?" he asks.

"Probably having the last laugh right about now," I say, remembering some of my violent thoughts toward Cy. Had I really fought him?

"He doesn't like you?"

"Best I can figure, he's neutral. He needed me, and now I know why. Now that he's got what he wants, he's under no obligation to lead us anywhere."

"Debatable."

"Why?"

"Camaraderie," he says, grimacing and limping under his own weight. "Have you ever felt that with strangers on a train? After a while, you start to form a basic understanding of their personality, and their expressions tell the same story. Even if your exchanges aren't friendly, you're in a familiar situation, and that forms a bond."

"Never thought of it like that."

"Neither did I until a year or two ago. A friend of mine met a guy at the bus stop and since they were both running late, their conversation led to a friendship."

My mind works in overdrive as I scan the surrounding terrain for something that might resemble a trail, anything that might give a clue that we're going the right way, apart from the incessant orange glow on the horizon.

We're following a narrow ridgeline that juts back and forth between narrow washes cut into the hillsides. A gentle slope provides us ample elevation to view the horizon, though the dark distorts and limits our view. Without that glow, our perception would only extend twenty to thirty feet. With it, I estimate the distance to the source of the light to be ten miles. Four hours, at least, and maybe five, considering the pain we're in. And that doesn't factor in the possibility that we might run into more terrifying ordeals before we get there.

We press on in relative silence for more than an hour, interspersed with whimpers of pain and passing observations of the landscape.

After another hour or so, the bird appears overhead and swoops low enough for me to talk to it in a normal voice. If it can understand what I'm saying I might consider it lucky, but I can't resist.

"Worked out real good for you, didn't it? Except now you're dead."

As if it understands me, its wings flutter in fury and it flies higher into the foreboding dark. Before it soars away, it cranes its head to take in one last glance at us. The fire grows nearer as we traverse a woody and grassy terrain filled with various dominant shrub species that live in harmony with the grasses and thistle weeds that jab constantly at our ankles.

Pain has numbed my extremities enough to obscure the poky thistles. Over the last several hours, the agony has sunk deeper, and every sensation has coalesced into a simple, crushing ache over my entire body. The mental anguish is even more profound. Every thought reminds me of Becky, my son, and loss, while the discordant fires of confusion burn into all corners of my mind.

When we ascend a hill, I can see a line of flames that stretches for miles ahead of us. After trekking down a hundred yards of uneven slope, we take a more direct route over a range of grass where the brush and trees grow thinner. With every step, the flames arch higher as they dance to a terrifying disharmony.

The heat intensifies as we near it. Before long it will singe our hair and leave us sweating. I haven't had a sip of water for hours, but now I see something promising before the flames. If it's water, it would be warm and disgusting, but in our state any form of hydration will do.

We head in that direction, and relief spreads over me when I see that we have entered a circular marsh fifty feet in diameter. Despite the algae and whatever organisms that call the water home, it will be a treat. We drink and savor it for over ten minutes. In truth the water tastes awful, but it's good enough to keep us going.

The ground between us and the fire shrinks as we lumber in its direction. The flames lick at the sky at least fifty feet high, and the inferno radiates an intense heat that would evaporate the marsh if it were closer.

Ian gawks at the spectacle when we arrive at a rocky precipice overlooking a jagged canyon cutting through the rocks. The heat is powerful enough to boil any water that trickles along its bottom. A jumble of independent boulders makes up the cliff, as though a builder had stacked them, and the stones create a zigzagging pattern paralleling the other side of the gorge lying in near blackness a hundred yards away. Erosion has reduced the rocks to a settling heap of shattered stone a few feet below the corners of the vertical walls.

Few plants grow in the ravine or along its walls, though some hardy vegetation pokes through cracks where the heavier stones provide ample shelter from the raging heat.

Panic strikes within me as I see the only way across. If The One has a plan to help us reach the other side, now would be a good time, but I'll be better off the less we communicate.

"They didn't say there would a be a canyon of fire," Ian laments.

"There's a way across," I say, peering toward a narrow opening between the towering flames, where a rope and plank bridge stretches toward the far rim.

"Right," he says. "I'd just as soon burn to death."

It might be a painful way to die, but could the agony get much worse?

The bridge's first plank lands at a level outcropping of rock twenty feet below us. Descending to the bridge promises danger; the treacherous slope could send us plummeting to our doom if we step onto the wrong rock or shift our weight around too much.

Determining that the stronger between us should go first, I step down from the rim onto a rounded boulder that jostles atop the smaller rocks beneath it. A large crack runs along its domed surface and ends in a sheared-off vertical section where tiny ledges accumulate dust and ash.

Judging the rock to be stable enough for Ian to join me, I reach out for him and ready myself to break his fall. He turns backward so that he can see his hand and footholds as he goes. The rock shifts again when he lands on it, but it starts to give way as I bounce to another rung and help him down behind me.

Being careful makes the climb take far longer than it should, but once we have made it, I peer out over the canyon floor, a hundred feet below us. From this vantage point the flames lap so high that I can't perceive where they end.

The sides of the footbridge comprise rather slack, one-inch-thick braided ropes tied together with vertical strands at twenty-foot intervals. Footer ropes that sway with our movement are lashed to the vertical strands. Centuries-old sawn wood might carry the scars of termite damage, making the bridge even more treacherous.

The structure teeters and sways as we step away from the outcrop and cling to the handrail ropes to keep us steady.

A gust of torpid wind blasts us before we've even made it halfway, and propelled by the gale the flames only dance higher, until they seem to caper in lockstep with a discordant drumbeat miles away.

Ian groans and swears as he hovers behind me. When I step forward onto the next plank, it snaps under my weight and its halves catch fire as they descend to the riverbed below. When he groans again, I make the mistake of looking back.

Hands of flame have wrapped their fiery fingers around his ankle and are trying to pull him into the abyss. Abandoning all sense of precaution, I hurtle backward to help him, but another pair of hands reach out of the inferno to strangle me.

I scowl as my collar ignites. A scorching pain rings my neck where the flame hands grip me, and as I struggle to break loose, another set of hands reaches out. Before long, the walls of fire sport angry faces in the conflagration. They scowl at us, emit towering, guttural grunts, and torment us with cascades of virulent laughter.

"DAMMIT!" I scream as the hands grasp me tighter.

Having put the piece of amber in my pocket for the descent, I cannot see what emotions it senses in me, so I try to gauge how I feel by slowing down. When moving, sometimes emotion gets lost behind the range of decisions.

Desperation claws at me, and before I know it, the ropes holding the bridge together have combusted into linear strands of fire a hundred feet long. The flames burn at the rope from the center outward. I vault back over the missing plank, make a steady landing, and coax Ian to join me.

He yelps in pain as the fire hands drag at his ankles, but they allow just enough movement to catch the other end of the flaming rope.

I hang on and sprint towards the other side, but way too late. The fraying ropes give way from the fire devouring them, sending the footbridge cascading to the depths.

Wedging my foot into a gap in the planks, I hang on as the flaming ends of the ropes scurry up to eat at us. The swaying slows as the inferno demolishes what remains of the bridge. We will have to climb the last hundred feet up a vertical rope-and-plank ladder with dry rot- and termite-damaged wood.

With white knuckles, Ian clings to the ropes as I pull myself up step by step. The fingers of fire have released him, allowing him to climb faster. I try to match his pace while batting flames away from my face. The blaze responds by scorching my arms. Above me, standing atop the rock, is a single standing flame-being glowing with rage. It wields a white sword of fire and taps its coal feet as I ascend to meet it.

"Stand aside," I rasp, cowering at the figure's feet.

"You shall not pass," it roars, "unless you claim fealty to The One, and tell me to whom I was born."

"Fine," I growl. "I am a humble servant of The One, and you're a son of the Titan Prometheus."

Merciless laughter bounces off the canyon walls and the dozens of faces in the towering walls of flame sneer with delight. The fire monster steps aside and brands my arm with a black mark that can only be the signet of Erebus.

Howling in pain, I tremble as I walk away to climb the last few steps to safety with Ian on my tail.

Instead of refuge, the landscape presents me with a peril not even my darkest nightmares can conjure.

# 25

# Water for the Danaïdes

Darkness rips the world asunder. An extensive network of cracks, some hair-thin and others as wide as streams, coil around a deep pit that spirals down into utter black. Ian and I gape at the spectacle as I try to plan our route.

A huge section of the opposite rim, over a mile away, splinters and falls into the abyss as I watch. Its rocks collapse into clouds of dirt and pebbles as they fall, down, down, down into the seemingly bottomless p it.

Sore from the burns and the daemons' torture, we limp to the shoulder of a cracked trail that snakes along the cliff walls at steep gradients, through switchbacks and banks so tight that we must turn sideways to avoid falling for an eternity.

Chattering teeth signal unrest, and I tiptoe along the rocky, clay-bedded trail. Interspersed between sheer rock faces, a honeycomb of caverns resembling black blobs on a canvas of dark brown pockmark the cliff wall. These caverns might serve as a refuge from what lurks below, or they could house myriad creatures of the abyss.

Ian hugs the wall of the precipice, guiding himself through the darkness with sharp jutting pieces of rock, while I occupy the center of the trail. A voluminous crack splits the trail in two parallel halves as I try to regulate my speed by lengthening my strides and fixing my eyes on the path. The resultant ache hammers into my thigh muscles with every step. I follow the crack on the safer side, should the cliff wall shear off and slide into the nothingness below.

Ahead, screams and wails disturb the ambiance. Trekking downward produces stratified temperature zones as the colder air settles toward the bottom of the gargantuan cavern, which must be miles deep if it even has a bottom.

To protect our ears from the discordant sounds of suffering, I offer Ian the chance to talk about his past by asking a series of questions about his teenage years before he met Brianne. His simple, one-sentence answers might seem textbook, but he has chosen to listen to the pain and sorrow lurching amongst the thousands of dark souls clinging to the walls, skulking in caves, or jumping feet first to their doom.

Monstrous agony. Every few steps, I hear sniffles, guttural moans, gnashing teeth, and the *zhug-zhug* of metal grinding against wood.

"No, I didn't know. I—they told me—nooo. AHHHHH!!" a woman screeches, somewhere unseen.

"Torture, my friend," a man maybe forty feet away says, possibly to himself. "No way out."

I cannot see who has spoken any of these despairing words, but each of them claws deeper into my heart the longer I wait. What must they have done to deserve such endless suffering? How many souls have they tormented, to deserve the eons of blackness forced upon them? Tears squirt to my eyes before I can wipe them away, and before long I hear my own teeth chattering as I step downward into the frigid dark that seems to have no end.

"Light ... light? What's ... I do see it," a man growls.

When he thrusts his face out of a dark tunnel, I can see that his eyes are missing: black voids, ringed with sagging, wrinkling skin, crater his complexion. Crusty splotches of blood stick to stubble on his chin in flaking, crimson rivulets like tears of blood from his eye sockets. He moves as though he can sense our presence.

From his own admission, he can detect the light, but its radiance may be so foreign that he doesn't know how to react.

"Who—who are you?" his wavering voice scrapes at my ears.

"We mean you no trouble," I say.

"T—trouble. You won't find much else here. Don't you agree, m'lady?"

Her looks mirror her companion's. Peeking around the corner from their lair of black, she aims her empty eye sockets at us, a lustful longing at the flickering shard of amber I hold in my palm. Its light fades and dies the longer she stares, and her man can't help but reach out for it.

Trying to be gentle, I bat his hand away and teeter for a moment on the precipice of the trail. Overhead and to our right, part of the rim collapses and erases a section of the trail we've already traversed. Instead of reacting to the destruction, the expressionless couple sense the rumbling of the ground and listen to the thunderous cascade of dirt and rocks.

"How ... uh, how far down is it?" Ian asks, still clutching heavy stones embedded in the cliff face.

The woman utters a cackling, merciless laugh. "Is what? This 'it' that you seek."

"The bottom," Ian corrects himself.

"There's no bottom," the man growls. "You fall from here, you fall forever. No one to save you."

"We're always on the edge of nothing. A reminder of our..."

"We'll let you get back to ... whatever it was you were doing," I say, still balancing on the ledge of the crater.

"Carry on. Find your 'it.'"

A pang of remorse skewers my emotions as I return to the center of the trail and continue climbing down. A switchback digs into a crook in the rock face just ahead, and the next leg bolts twenty feet below my feet. The switchbacks continue until the blackness obscures them a hundred feet down.

*You'll never know what they feel.*

My heart folds in on itself. "But I can still express empathy," I whisper so that Ian can't hear me.

He has taken to listing to muffled moans ahead, clinking sounds of metal on metal, and heavy glass dragging across a broken slab of slate and granite. "Mmmm ... ugghh...."

"Son. You don't need to listen to them."

"This is," he says, shivering, "the hell they always described in Sunday School. But suddenly now, it's worse, because it's not hypothetical suffering anymore. It's real. And they—they can't even undo what brought them here."

I can only nod in agreement, doubting whether he can see my body language.

"No, not again," a woman whines from below.

"We can try another time."

"What's the use?"

*They will never be clean.*

My heart skips a beat as something swoops above the pit's rim. It screams and howls into the dark, a furious cacophony of noises from jack-hammers to a chorus of crying babies. Fire shoots out from its mouth, fogging a hundred red eyes with thick, black smoke, while its heavy wings beat against the darkness with repeated *whoops* before it settles into an effortless, downward glide.

Avoiding gazing up at the beast for too long, I scan a dented part of the trail near the switchbacks. A hundred hairline cracks scatter into the crusted surface, and some flake off pieces of the stone wall and allow a pile of dust to gather.

We take the switchback in silence as the ache digs deeper into my thighs. I don't want to know what the voices are discussing, but as we grow nearer, I can hear more of their predicament. Maybe a dozen women are chattering in dismay from a black alcove dug into the rock face beneath the section of trail we've just descended.

"No," one woman says.

"No," another repeats.

Splashes and sloshing water echo in the den. Ian and I could use a drink, but if these women have a monopoly on the water in this place, I dare not ask for any. What kind of payment might they demand? And will any price get them what they seek?

In silence, we slink down the trail until we reach the mouth of their cave, which comprises a circular hole thirty feet in diameter dug out of the rock walls. A pebble falls from above, followed by a sifting veil of dust. One woman shrieks as she notices us.

Ian gapes into their lair first. Dozens of pallid faces shrouded in darkness lurk in the black, and when the first woman panics and backs away, the dozens of others seek to offer her shelter from the strangers.

A trickle of water escapes the cave in a narrow, rope-surfaced rivulet that seeps from beneath a large, circular pot. The continuous flow of trickling water suggests that the tub is emptying, yet more than one woman carries a jug of water and pours it into the basin while glancing up at us.

"I beg your pardon," I stammer. "But what is it you're doing?"

"The filth," she mourns, scowling. "We must wash off our sins. Can you help us fill the basin?"

"It's got a leak," I say, noting the trickle of water, which seems to have grown with the water she's dumped into the tub.

"No ... no...." she says. "It's filling up. We'll get there."

"Why do you do this?"

"We do not discuss it," another woman says. Her stapled-shut eyes churn when she moves her head, and a tear in her gown has created a tattered V below her left breast. Her hair drapes in a brown, ratty sheath down her back, and when she turns her shoulder, the frayed ends scatter in a breeze that tries to escape the chamber.

"Pain," a woman's voice screeches from a cave further ahead. "They *murdered* their husbands. All forty-nine of them! On their wedding night!"

"No...." the woman with the stapled eyelids mourns.

"They were brothers!"

"Shhhh ... do not pity us," the woman says.

Pity is all I can relate. Their den with its enticing moisture stretches deep enough into the darkness to reach a spring or another source of water. If they're seeking to bathe, then perhaps they could shower in the source. Trying to problem-solve for them introduces yet another wave of pity.

Instead of listening to the scorn of their neighbor, the forty-nine sisters form a chain that stretches into the dark. When one empties her bucket, she loops back to the source to allow her sister to drain her container. On and on it continues. Without tiring, they labor to fill the leaky tub.

They must realize the tub is leaking, so why haven't they attempted to patch it?

I don't pretend to know an answer, so I watch as they labor away. The water sloshes in their pails as they carry them, sometimes splashing over the edge to douse their colorful dresses, yet every dribble spreads red like blood.

"Everyone down here has a fatal sin," Ian laments, quietly enough to prevent the clarity of his voice from reaching the women's ears.

I can see that. How many souls with similar stories occupy holes in the cliffs? My eyes ache as I scan the abyss.

Faces appear on the edge of the darkness, observing disturbances all around us. Tears flow, and dull moans fall dead into the pit, draining into a throbbing chorus of dismay that joins splintering branches of sound like a vibrating tree of black sinking deep into the earth.

"I can see it now," Ian says. "We're just going to have to endure."

"No. Far worse lurks down here. We have to be prepared."

"Prepared for what?"

"I don't know." The finality of my admission carves a crater in my soul as the dread of agony slides deeper into every extremity of thought I ever knew.

Without answers as to what might lie ahead, we cannot make plans to ward off that evil, to fashion weapons or to devise any defenses. Instead we must adapt on the fly, a promise that may prove deadlier than walking in unprepared.

Something hides beyond the edge of the shadow. I can sense motion, and for a moment the shadows swell before settling into a wispy soup of black. Somewhere a hundred feet lower, I see an arm shoot out of the dark, but instead of pulling back in, it continues outward and then falls into the hole without its body.

With every step, the aching figures gather into groups and their cries for mercy grow more fervent. Each sound wave smashes into my spirit like a spear, and with that weight of endless torment, the amber flickers and dies.

*Now you must use the dark.*

I don't know *how* to use the dark; darkness has always intruded as an obstacle or a weapon of chaos. Where murkier souls might take advantage in the relative shelter of shadow, to prowl behind strangers as if on the hunt, I allow the disquieting strain to bludgeon me from all sides. Rather than a repayment, sin has always affected the dark. And now that it batters me, I can only wander haplessly in its eternal wilderness. I cannot use it.

What am I supposed to do with it?

No answer comes, but the soul ache grows heavier with each step.

Together, Ian and I meander down the trail as it narrows toward yet another switchback. Beyond it, carved-out steps are formed in the rock, allowing a steeper descent into the maddening crater. We stagger toward the end, lean against the rock face, and gaze into the expanding nothingness below.

"I don't think I want to know what's coming," Ian admits. "It's like an omen: something you've worried about forever, and yet now that it's here, you can't stop it."

"I know how you feel."

"We should be glad we have each other here," Ian says, watching a skinny, emaciated man saunter to the edge of the trail, peer into the black, and jump in to be devoured.

"And not even that will help him."

"Forever," I sputter. Even now, I can remember the washers, the way they cling to each other and cycle to infinity. The bond that can never break, yet now it's finally severed, always.

"It's hard to get a concept of infinity," he says. "Everything you ever knew and saw exists within a few-light-year-sized bubble. When you think of what lies beyond that ... what happens beyond the limits of our universe? Does it run up against a white wall, or does it just stop? We'll never know. It's perplexed scientists for a thousand years and humanity might never know why God created infinity."

"Did he?" I reason. "Or does He simply exist in it?"

"Cosmic chicken and egg," he whispers.

The darkness swells as though some dark mass stirs within it. A thousand souls peer into that circulating hole of black, looking across at those mad strangers who dare plumb the aphotic depths."Has your amber gone out?" I ask.

He unfolds his palm and gazes at the lifeless stone. "Useless down here."

"Keep it," I say. "You never know when you might need it."

He shakes his head. "I'm not like you; I don't have that gift of lightning and light. Frankly, I don't care how you got it, or if it even will come in handy from now on."

*Use the dark.*

The dark is both nothing and everything. I must cling to it to survive, and that is perhaps the most paralyzing, traumatic truth I have ever endured. To rely on it means to give into its destructive power. After all, how much is left of me to destroy?

Ian stirs beside me, and pushing away from the wall with his feet, continues through the switchback to plunge deeper into the dark.

Keeping my eyes glued to the trail, I follow as we descend an endless, broken-stone staircase littered with dust, loose rocks, and scattered human bones.

A femur teeters on the trail's edge and settles, while a pair of intact ribcages lean against the wall in a two-square-foot landing a dozen feet down. Beside them, empty skulls missing their mandibles peer up into the black, yet their eye sockets carry something I might consider to be life. A serpent pokes its head out of one, coils around the ribcages, and slithers through a crack and into the sheer cliff wall.

I nearly faint when I see it. Ian steadies me by grabbing my hand and pulling me closer to the wall. Avoiding tripping on a loose, chipped stone, he levels his eyes at me as if to ponder something deep. Reflected in his eyes, I see a shapeless mass lingering beyond him. It shifts to his left and disappears, and when I crane my neck to look at it, it slinks away and disappears.

"What was that?" I ask.

"Don't want to know."

"I have a feeling we will, sooner or later. Keep an eye out for it and get ready to fight."

"How are we supposed to fight the monsters of the underworld?"

I gulp and allow the ache to spread through my thighs as I follow him down the stairs, careful not to let momentum trip me up.

"It's the underworld to the underworld," I say. "Tartarus, a pit no soul has ever escaped from. And we're going to be the first."

His eyes dart back and forth before settling on my expression. His piece of amber emits a low, resonant glow that vanishes as quickly as it arises.

The foreboding darkness has not yet extinguished its luminance, so some semblance of hope must extend into this hell. I let myself gaze at it far longer than I should, and when it fails to illuminate again, I resolve to keep an eye out for any sign of it changing.

Another hundred feet and another switchback awaits, the stairs appearing to narrow in the approach. I gaze up at a disc of stars beyond the hole's black rim. We've descended over three hundred feet so far, yet the darkness plunges far lower.

I gulp and peer over the edge as I saunter back and forth in pain. A cry erupts from a cave somewhere beyond the switchback; it wails and sobs louder the nearer we come to it. Without knowing the torment that person must be dealing with, I can only carry on as that faint wisp of hope fades. My heart sinks lower in my chest as I go, and before long I can hear Ian whimpering in pain.

"Help me, Dad," he says. "I can see her."

"Who?"

"M—Mom."

Becky. Rage pelts me. I gaze up and down into the dark, see no one, and then rest my attention on my son, whose face has gone ashen. Somehow, the wounds and scars have blackened further around his eye and his lip, and his eyes have gone glassy as if he's just seen the most painful apparition he's ever set eyes upon.

I gulp down the misery as I lift him away from the bedrock. Securing his arm around my neck, I trek toward the switchback, and by the time I get there I'm overcome with a nightmarish hallucination that tears my heart from my body and tosses it over the precipice into the swirling maw of eternity.

A bloodstained burlap sack shrouds her face, yet I can hear her pulverizing cries emanating from beyond. The harrowing emotion that batters and bruises her heart leeches into mine. Reaching for her hand feels like death having reached up from the darkness to claw out my innards. Her icy palm slaps into mine and collapses as a long, dreary sigh filters through the mesh of the burlap. Water trickles onto her head from somewhere up high, and soon a cascade pours over her, wetting my hair until it becomes as brittle as new frost.

I hold her hand until her last breath leaves her body, and soon I'm transported to a realm that burns into my corneas before ceasing to exist. I can only surrender to the pain in this place.

It somehow holds me together, yet some unseen promise rises like an oil stain on white paper.

Dark. It leaks into me through every pore, covers my flesh, and erases my eyes. I've become nothing but a Shade, and I search the abyss for any sign of The One. Not knowing how, I can perceive Ian sifting into the dark to join me in a new reality.

# 26

# Arachne's Tapestry

Everything is smoke, and fire. That burning, lustrous flame shimmers somewhere beneath the smoke, blending fine black soot with a red-orange glow as we spin through a torrential abyss. I reach out to Ian as if to save him from the same fate we will both meet, but I cannot touch him. His image freezes in time as he spins.

"Ian."

He doesn't move.

I blink with remorse as everything goes white, as if I'm in the middle of nothing. No walls, floor, ceiling, entry or exit constricts my movement, yet I stay tethered in place.

"Ian!"

No one is here. I am utterly alone.

"Dad. Dad!"

I can hear his voice clanging around in my head, and rough hands are shaking my body. When I fling my eyes open, a terrified expression spans his face. His eyes dart back and forth as if he's gone mad, and his hair droops like a cobweb-strewn mop left abandoned in a corner.

"Wha—"

"We gotta move," he says with an edge in his voice. "It's coming back."

I squirm as he helps me sit up. Viewing the never-ending pit from a different angle only increases its scale. The hole stretches so wide that its opposite wall is visible only as a shapeless mass of brown and black. The stars still shine high overhead, yet they gleam down on this world's inhabitants with a baleful shame.

"Wh—what's coming back?"

He pulls me to my feet. The trail has led us into a cave dug into the side of the rocks. Its stone ceiling arches higher at the mouth, while the clay and stone floor slopes downward towards the path outside. Enormous rough-edged boulders, having fallen from the ceiling, litter the floor with many obstacles, while a narrow path meanders through piles of debris and dust into pitch black.

"Let's get back outside," I say, coughing in the dank air.

"Can't," he answers. "Trail's gone, collapsed. I'm just hoping there's an exit."

"How did it happen?"

"Well, you ... I don't know exactly. You sort of fell into a trance, and no matter what I did, you wouldn't wake. So I half-carried you down and escaped just before the cliff gave way."

"It was like a nightmare."

He coughs. "All of this is. Probably better to be quiet in case it hears us."

A wet, phlegmy cough spatters my lips with a soupy concoction of mucus and stomach bile, which tastes revolting. Swallowing it could cause me to outright vomit, so instead I spit it out onto the scarred floor of the chamber.

Still grasping my hand, Ian leads me around a monstrous rock that has fallen from the ceiling. A sticky wetness, reflecting the scant light coming through the entrance, covers every razor-sharp edge.

It's an extreme understatement to say that this doesn't feel right. Everything about it screams that I should flee, but now we can only travel one way. If we stop, we will be stuck in this catacomb forever. I don't want to know the horror that awaits us in this cavern.

"We've got a real problem," he whispers, gazing at his palm. "We're going to need light, but both yours and mine have gone out."

"I have a feeling that's only going to do us good in fits and starts," I hazard a guess.

"We need to force our emotions into something positive."

I shake my head, cough again, and try to explain something I have already observed: It responds only to genuine emotions from the heart, and pushing those emotions through from the brain does nothing. "Not going to work. Whatever it is, it needs to be real."

"Then you can use your lightning trick."

"That's mostly involuntary. Can't predict when it's going to come."

"Any other ideas?"

Something moves in the darkness, prowling along through the confines between the rocks, tiptoeing deeper into the lair.

"Ideas aren't going to get us anywhere," I say.

The creature's shadow scampers across the walls and ceiling. As the light from the mouth of the cave grows ever dimmer, a similar darkness covers my soul.

I will have to use the dark.

Instead of offering a few well-timed thoughts, I press myself against the wall, where a sticky substance pokes at the skin on my arms and tangles with the hairs.

This is all wrong. My heart wrenches in my chest, causing a pain that might make me keel over. Only one substance I've ever seen could feel this way. I slink lower and peer towards my feet, where a gray, stringy goop cocoons my shoes. It restricts my movement, but with enough muscle power, I free myself.

The lurking pauses as the creature stalks us in silence. Trying to discern where it must be hiding, I reach out with my mind into the dark. Somewhere black and foreboding, a cave within a cave.

It hasn't seen us yet, but it will.

A long, sagging cloth of purple, embroidered with golden highlights and symbols, droops from silky appendages that dangle from the damp ceiling. Its grandeur might be worthy of display in a world-famous art museum, yet its unique qualities only make it personal to its creator.

Swallowing a pocket of bile, I let my stomach churn. Keeping it down will require resilience in an environment like this, but whatever monster hunts us in the shadows, Ian has already seen it.

I hunker down and wait in the shadow of a large boulder, behind which something lanky protrudes into the faint light. The spindly hairs on one leg stand on end like strings of black in the dark. Its prey skulks past it, and before I can prepare, the creature bolts out of its hiding place and pounces on us.

Eight legs the length of my arms, each covered with a spiky mane of black hair, dance before us. Ian screams and loses his balance. Falling right into my hands, he thrashes against the creature's vice-like grip. Its pincer-mouth chews through his pants leg and tries to pull him away as he shrieks. Using the rocks to leverage myself, I engage in a game of tug-of-war with a four-foot-tall spider with a hundred black eyes.

No matter how dark its habitat, it can see us.

Screaming as he kicks one of its eyes, Ian slams his head back into mine, smashing his cranium into my nose. I croak as I tug at him. When his leg is free from the creature's mouth, Ian attempts to propel himself back towards the mouth of the cave. The creature will have likely created a trap to keep its prey from fleeing, so that doesn't present itself as the best idea.

Instead, we must fight it. Stopping Ian from running away takes all the strength I can muster. In the moments between strikes from the spider, I press two fingers to my lips to shush him.

If we're to escape, we must occupy darkness deeper than the arachnid's hideout. Thinking about death, destruction, and hopelessness, I press forward. This seems to confuse the beast, but it can still sense my movement. It scurries in a weaving circle and squeals as it sprays a fine white string of silk at the boulders.

Using this distraction to my advantage, I thrust at it, kick out one of its legs with enough force to hear it crack, and then attack the next.

The predator reacts to the pain by springing at us out of pure instinct. Shooting its sticky silk at my face, it scampers away to hide in another void, as if to make us think it has given up the fight. Instead, it's planning a counter strategy.

I plunge my thoughts deeper into the dark territories of my brain while inching on through the marred sea of granite boulders, pebbles, and dust. I can't see any of it, which makes my footing treacherous. My ankle twists in a crevice of rock and I fall face-first into the silk while groaning in pain. Attempting to catch myself dislodges the piece of amber from my hand, and it tumbles across the stony floor until a watery *plunk* sounds.

I crawl toward it, but before I reach it, the amber has transformed. It grows the dark legs of a woman, tall and curvaceous, yet it stays submerged. The tiny figurine completes itself before my gaze, tilts her head sideways, and stares into my eyes.

Before me in the puddle, she dances and shimmers. To see the source of the commotion, the spider bolts out of the dark as its eight legs batter the floor with a thunderous drumbeat. Seeing the woman spin on one toe, the creature pounces on it.

Once again, the tiny woman transforms, rolls away from the attacking monster, and takes the shape of a nymph. I gulp as it prowls the edges of the water, never letting its head break the surface tension. The spider, having missed the confusion, removes its eyes from me and focuses on the nymph.

Getting the piece of amber back might prove problematic if it keeps luring the spider. The light attracts the beast, and focusing all its attention on that small prize denies it its meal. I rise to my feet while attempting to devise a plan to deal with it.

The distraction morphs between forms beneath the water, and each time the hunter homes in on it, the nymph moves to another spot a few feet away. The arachnid's hiding place might be a dead end, but I saunter in that direction while Ian scampers along behind me.

When the nymph loses sight of me, it disappears, extinguishing its pale white glow. The monster, realizing I have fooled it, shrieks, spins on its eight hairy feet, and slams itself into a boulder with enough force to vibrate its home. Ian struggles in its webbing, breaks free, and stands up beside me.

Rather than focusing on him, the spider launches itself at me. Using its silky spray as a diversion, it darts at me, kicks at my leg, and then clamps down on my ankle with its fangs.

I will not give it pleasure by screaming; Ian does that for me.

"Nooo! Leave him alone! It's me you want."

"Ian!"

He kicks the spider's nearest legs as it peers at him with several of its eyes. Still, it aims to devour me. It bites down on my ankle with enough force to crush the bone, and then, as though it has lost its appetite, lets me go.

I scurry away by dragging myself across the rocky floor while it engages Ian in a battle of wills. He loops around it, climbs up a rock, and pile-drives it from above. Disoriented from the assault, the spider realizes that another trick has confused it.

It redirects its attacks upward while using its hairy legs to thrash at him while he's low. In the confusion, I reach back for the piece of amber, still submerged in the puddle. As though it hadn't transformed, it retains its original shape. Waiting for the glowing nymph to reform, I listen to the screeching noises as Ian slams his fists into the monster's eyes.

"How do *you* like it?"

SCRREEECH!!!

"Come on," I whisper. "Transform."

It remains still. Frustration overwhelms me as I splash my hand into the puddle to retrieve it. When it breaks the surface, its glow returns, but it gleams white. Again, the spider darts its many eyes toward its prize, but aims its venom at Ian's shoulder.

He slams into its fangs with his elbow, rebounds off the rock, and twirls free from the spider's grip.

"Toss your amber into the pond," I yell.

He flings his hand through the air, and the stone splashes into the water. Instead of mimicking mine, it rests at the bottom of the puddle as if nothing has happened.

He needs to be watching for it to happen.

I need to take his place for him to do that. The monster sees the white-glowing amber in my palm, squeals at me, and attacks.

I hammer it with my right hand while holding the object of its attention aloft in my left.

"You looking for this?"

WHAM!

SQUEAL!

"Yeah, that's right. Come and take it." I kick one of its legs as it bites at my raised hand. The creature is not tall enough to reach that height without climbing onto just two or three of its feet and hoisting itself by the nearest boulder. As it does so, I kick another of its legs. It claws at the rock with five of its hairy appendages while a satisfying snap dislocates the one I've kicked.

Struggling to catch its prize, the predator works up a new strategy: spraying me with its silk. It hits me with enough of the sticky stuff to restrict my movement. Once satisfied with its work, it opens wide to plunge those venomous fangs into my forearms.

With a single swoosh of my left hand, I yank it away like Lucy pulling the ball from Charlie Brown.

It tumbles toward the floor and nips at my sides. Before I can move, it grasps me with its meaty legs, holding me still for just long enough to bite down on my hip. As it lunges to do so, Ian arrives at my side with his shining bit of amber held high.

With two lustrous prizes at stake, the monster divides its attention between them. Ian, having expected this, sidesteps a swipe from its legs, forcing it to release me.

Once I'm free from its grasp, I can pummel it from above. Keeping the shining amber held aloft, I climb the rock it attempted to scale and let the dark thoughts of desperation plunge deeper into my spirit. The beast loses track of me but keeps half its eyes on my amber.

Ian lands a couple of smart jabs on the monster's face while I climb towards the chamber's ceiling. Gathering enough momentum to make my fall painful, I tuck my head and aim at it like a missile. Ian disorients the creature by reaching out and leading with his amber-holding hand.

THWACK!

The collision forcefully dislodges the amber from my hand, causing a dislocated shoulder, but the nymph transforms into a silvery spear at the perfect moment.

The monster squeals and thrashes as it oozes with what must constitute blood. Pulling my arm from the hole the spear has impaled it with, the gooey substance clings to the hairs on my arm as the spider flails in every direction. To immobilize it, Ian slams the amber down into its eyes, blinding it.

And somehow, the two pieces of amber unite themselves for one last strike. Cleaving all eight of its legs clean off, the device swoops through the darkness and returns to our hands.

Ian howls with delight as the spider lies dead in its own lair.

Fearing the worst, I pull him away from the creature's corpse. We make it about twenty feet before the beast rises to reattach its legs like a spider-zombie. It runs at us in fury as our weapons return to their amber state.

*Use the dark.*

My mind goes numb as the thought of Becky's bones and the image of the welded washer-pair at her fingertips works its way into my brain. Years of agony roll into one common emotion as the darkness digs deeper. In the dark, we can escape the monster's lair.

The light returns around a bend, and we accelerate toward it as the spider fumbles around for something it can never taste. The amber has saved us, and I begin to realize why—water. In order to use them as weapons, we need water.

But what works for one creature of darkness may not work for others. We're not out of danger yet.

Agony hammers at my bones as we emerge from the opposite mouth of the cave onto the start of a trail that switchbacks into blackness beneath us. Four hundred feet above, the stars shimmer and those beating wings swoop high overhead.

The sounds of squealing tires, honking horns, and guttural roars combine as the flying creature bellows smoke and fire above the rim.

To stay hidden from its view, we plaster ourselves against the wall and descend one cautious step at a time.

The spider-zombie has other ideas. It screeches as it emerges from its cave, thunders toward us along the narrow trail, and strikes. Its fangs graze my arm as I shift against the wall. The changed angle of attack forces the beast to alter its trajectory right at my abdomen. It slams into me, pinning me against the wall, and rebounds towards the edge. Four of its legs dangle over the abyss as it attempts to right itself. Seeing the precariousness of its balance, Ian shoves it away from the wall. One of its legs wraps around his ankle as it struggles against the cliff.

To stop the enemy from dragging him into the abyss, I stomp on its leg with enough power to stun it. That leg slips backward, and soon, the spider cannot stop its momentum from dragging it into the vast emptiness below. It screeches and cries as it falls, the sound reverberating upward until long after it has passed into the utter black.

The spider's neighbors emerge from their caves to see the source of the commotion, yet their expressions do not communicate surprise or victory, but only anguish. Their baleful looks bore into us as we limp down the trail covered in sweat and spider silk from head to toe. A week's worth of showers might not be enough to cleanse myself from this torment, but for now we are free.

# 27

# Prison of the Titans

We descend into a realm of utter blackness, the kind of dark where you can't see your hand in front of your nose. If you're exposed to it for long periods, it can drive you mad.

Neither of us speaks for hours, even as we listen to the tortured cries and wails growing clearer and more desperate. For me, the quiet promises a coming doom, as if we are marching to our own executions. Perhaps thinking about how he wasted a successful life in one moment of rage, Ian seems to shake increasingly the further down we go. I cannot see him, but I can hear his footsteps gain a tinge of rigid over-caution and in one step, he taps the same toe on the trail twice.

I once decided that rather than expressing it, leaving my inner turmoil to wither inside would serve me better. But now that I can sense it eating him alive, I can only wish for him to say something, even if it describes the utter anguish taking hold. Concealing that grief can only bleed into further misery, and in darkness this deep, I'm helpless.

The trail switches back a half-dozen times in the murk and seems to steepen somewhat as we go, often breaking into cracked and uneven staircases, which, if we treat them like a normal flight of stairs, could send us tumbling into the rotten abyss.

When our chattering teeth subside, a warm ambient glow pulses in another world. The terrain of the path evens out, rendering the grade less treacherous, and soon the bottomless pit we encountered before indeed has a bottom—a hidden one beyond the reach of the souls higher above.

For a moment I wonder why the cries have gone silent, but when the truth confronts my mind, it rattles my very teeth. The pit is a ranking system, where the less evil souls reside at the top, and the vilest, foulest cretins that have ever lived reserve the lowest levels. People like Stalin, Hitler, and Bin L aden.

Should I run into those villains, I might ask them to explain their rationale for such horrible deeds before punching them in the mouth. Then again, my journey has a deeper purpose, one I don't yet fully understand.

When the terrain levels off, my feet collide with heavy stones as I stroll across a desecrated monument whose once-majestic pillars and sculptures now lie in ruins. A billion fragments, from ones smaller than pebbles to those weighing several tons, make up the debris. I can see it because of the dim light, which might emanate from a distant fire.

So far, Tartarus hardly resembles the fire-and-brimstone version of hell that Chistian theology preaches. Instead, it showcases something crueler and more desperate—utter isolation from those whom the lost souls love, and an eternity remembering the abominations that led them here.

Agonizing as it seems, this little light presents an opportunity for peace. Checking the fragment of amber for signs of hope, I allow my heart to sink when it emits no light. If it even works as intended this deep, it might be a miracle.

The ruins, I decide, had once consisted of a temple or public meeting space sporting classical Greek architecture. Stone columns, which sport ogee shapes and squared-off reveals like crown mouldings at their bases, lie shattered into a million pieces. A triangular gable, also broken into jagged pebbles, displays carvings of rulers, nobles, and gods. A set of intricate inlaid steps lead up to what appears to be a doorway, a pair of keystone columns perhaps more recently carved out of the densest granite. Above them spans a rectangular lintel designed to carry the weight of a larger stone face, but with that structure collapsed, the doorway only leads to another part of the ruins.

Ancient builders must have carved much of the interior out of the cliff faces, I surmise. But before I can explore the idea, Ian leads me up the wide staircase, sidestepping sheared-off pieces of column that must weigh several tons each. His feet kick at some of the limestone sand and pebbles that have accumulated over thousands of years while he glances back toward me.

His expression has been carved from a monolith of worry if I've ever seen one. Although I cannot hope to deconstruct everything going through his brain, I can on some level understand the associated pain. With that kind of hurt, the pain isn't the worst of it. Instead, the very understanding that you've hit rock bottom and can alas go no lower, plunges the heart into deeper woes. Only a rigorous counseling regimen in a series of predetermined steps can wash away the self-loathing that accompanies it.

And this place clearly lacks qualified psychiatric care physicians.

Beyond the reinforced columns and the stone lintel, a gray darkness awaits. Filtering that ambient orange glow, it has transformed the color and intensity into one of pale remorse. Ian enters through the doorway without seeming to have given it a second thought.

The murk stretches onward to a black wall a hundred feet away. The corridor widens to an impressive thirty feet, and when I notice the dust-caked marble floor, I allow a sense of grandiosity to invade my mind. The ancients could only have constructed a building this ornate for one purpose, but now it serves a different need.

I recognize it a moment too late. Metal on metal clinks to my right, following the clank of a heavy chain being dragged across concrete. The sound is emanating from a chamber off the main hall, and when I try to readjust my eyes to the dusty shade, the purpose of this edifice comes into focus. This is no longer a seat of political power; it now represents a crumbled authority, leaving behind an apt prison.

Thick bars over wire mesh glass windows, cut into reinforced iron doors, represent the danger inside the cells. I can't have stumbled onto it by sheer chance. Rather than dwelling on the odds, I let the studded iron doors draw me closer. The chains drag across the floor again, and when I reach the door, I gaze through the glass at the cell hidden within.

The emaciated body of the prisoner carries a forlorn aura, one that tells not of wisdom, but true evil. I can only guess how long he's wallowed in this hole, but I don't care to know.

The inmate avoids eye contact as if he can sense my presence, and when he turns his head, I can see the signs of what might be an extrasensory perception. His skin sags around his bare pectorals and shoulders from the receding of his malnourished muscles. In his chained hands, he wields a dim orb of light that seems to flutter as though made of the same amber I hold in my hands.

"You ... mortal ... what do you want?"

I stammer, letting myself back away from his cell door. "I ... well—I think I should ask your name."

Although his voice exudes patience, he seems to rage at me for asking such a stupid question. "Why do you think names matter?"

"I don't—now that you mention it, I do have a better question. Where are the Six Cretan Titans?"

"There are twelve of us, and we hail not from Crete. We are the sons and daughters of Gaia. Imprisoned for challenging the gods for their hubris."

"What hubris?"

He growls at me, a deep low rumble that I could mistake for a distant earthquake. "Of claiming true power while extolling a system where the people have a voice, yet leaving out large segments of the population. Those born of privilege, esteem, or wealth deciding for the rest of humanity how things are and should be. They claim a moral superiority while failing to grasp what 'superiority' really means."

"You must realize that you were doing something wrong. Why else would you lie at the bottom of Tartarus looking like a bunch of washed-up bodybuilders?"

"Speak not," he warns. "We may have been thrust down to eternal damnation, but we still hold powers you will never comprehend."

"Such as?"

He grunts. Refusing to explain might be par for the course, I reason, yet a nearby weakened feminine voice reaches my ears from the next cell.

"Such as the power over memory."

"Mnemosyne thinks that's a unique gift," another female voice sounds from across the hall, where Ian appears to have caught sight of a commemorative plaque. "Memory is nothing compared to fairness and justice."

"Justice cannot exist without fairness," Mnemosyne responds, sounding cheerful.

"What have you come for?" the first voice demands.

"I am a descendant of Merope, Lady of the Six," I announce, trying my hand at assertiveness.

"You'll never find her, mortal."

"You know!" I shout, breaking Ian's gaze from the wall nearest a cell door, behind which clatters a heavy chain and a throat-splitting groan.

*Free them.*

How am I supposed to do that? And for what purpose? If they've violated more than the decrees of the gods, they deserve their current plight, and I'm in no mood to help them.

*Set them free, or you shall never see your beloved again.*

"Miss Justice," I say, hesitating. "Don't exactly remember your name. Don't you agree that honoring the requests of a mortal who has no business being here merits at least some form of consideration? After all, he's endured far more than any mortal since."

"And for what ends?"

"The chance to discover who I really am," I plead. "To regain the hand of the woman I love."

"That woman is not down here, and neither are those six so-called Titans."

*Down.* Another indicator that these Titans understand their sins. It is a single word that denotes an air of negativity for a person of high aspirations, an honest interpretation of severe struggle. And they deserve it—all twelve of them.

*No,* I think to myself, *I won't do it.*

"Say we do help you find your lover," the woman says. "We can bargain."

"We shall do no such thing!" The tortured voice erupts from across the hall behind the door where Ian stands.

"We were born to serve the people," Justice says. "Not bend to the yearning desires of one who has lost his way."

"How honorable of you."

My sarcasm misses the mark. All twelve voices remain silent, but a red-orange glow in the door's window behind Ian flourishes in that instant, as if dim hope has ignited his spirit.

"Mnemosyne," I say, pausing for effect. If I'm right about her name coming from the same root as the famed mnemonic device, my request could have far-reaching consequences. Instead of fumbling over the words, I say it directly and repeat it for emphasis.

"I need a refresher, because I really don't understand how I got here. Help me with that, and help me find the Six, and consider yourself freed."

"Freedom," Justice considers in a thoughtful voice. As if becoming pensive, she prowls toward her door to peer through the glass.

"A promise no one has given, and which Tartarus has decreed shall never happen," the patient voice says. "You have no power to do it. I betrayed my father for the truth, but you cannot betray your true intentions."

"My true intentions are what I have told you," I argue.

"HE LIES!!" A mushroom of fire erupts in the room containing the angry voice, and I now remember who he is.

"Tell us the truth, oh mortal," Justice pleads.

*Tell them, my servant.*

I have no choice but to relent in the face of the power of The One. My voice flutters in my throat, a sign of meekness I've never seen in myself.

"I was commanded by The One."

"The One, as in the One True God of Darkness, Erebus?"

"The same."

They stay silent for several minutes, as if engaging in non-vocal communication. If they have mastered telepathy, it makes no sense that they've remained in prison for over two thousand years.

"The truth," Prometheus says, "shall set you free."

"You cannot do it," Mnemosyne says. "A mere mortal cannot beat the guardians."

"I'm a Titan. Do what I ask, and I'll do it."

More silence. If they intend to disarm me, the tactic is proving efficient. Instead of demanding they answer and raising my voice, I can only wait, as if their decision burdens everyone and drives my reactions.

For his part, Ian seems to have taken up the role of silent advocate. He peers in through a window that has become clouded with a brown stain from years of heat and has yet resisted shattering, as if trying to plead my case using only his facial expressions.

After over two thousand years in the most impenetrable fortress in the universe, would they even be able to read facial expressions anymore? Doubts swirl within me, but for a moment, I let them settle.

The fire spirits guarding the entrance to Tartarus had asked for my fealty to The One, and I'd given it, which must mean that they too are working for him. If that's true, they can earn no one's trust, even if Erebus demands it.

## MEMORIES:

I linger in a shadow in the bedroom, caressing the spine of a book Becky has poured her heart and soul into reading the last few weeks. Wondering if it has done anything for our relationship, I consider the power of just one kiss. One kiss can lead to many futures: It can lead to an everlasting partnership powerful enough to weld two souls together forever, or it can lead to isolation and destruction if not carefully nurtured. That power has drawn us through nine years of trial and joy, helping to deliver happiness.

Falling asleep watching cheesy chick flicks, just because she values quality time and touch, melts her heart in such a way that I cannot grasp it. Tonight is going to be wonderful, I can feel it. I will whisper in her ear that I love her, and when the hormones make it just right, I will—

It all turns upside down in an instant. The bedroom stretches and morphs into a sodden, misty farmland, which I wander through in only my pajamas to meet a man who calls himself Cy. He speaks to me in a series of riddles and logic tests before leading me upstream to a stately mansion owned by our old friend Harley.

One quick discussion, and I'm being whisked away into a confused dreamscape where reality may be nothing more than the judgement of a moment.

I love her. I'm coming home. Someday.

And then I see the welded washers I fused all those years ago. I remember the puff of smoke and the cool sensation in my fingers. I remember the rationale that went into the ultimate metaphor that has forged our relationship; it lies isolated next to the metatarsals of a female skeleton missing its skull. It rends my heart into a billion pieces, and I blame Cy. After all, he's the one who took me from her in the first place.

Or is he? He'd never admitted that. While he doesn't argue when I accuse him, his expression remains grim.

In another place and time, I'm descending a tight staircase through a deep cave, only to fall out into a landscape devoid of life and light. A lonely woman resides there, and then I find the Shades who chase me to the river Lethe, where I lose sight of everything that has brought me here.

I now know why I'm here—I'm here to save her life. Since our dimensions are forever intertwined, I cannot fail at this, or I will lose her forever. I must bend to the wishes of The One.

"What do you call yourself, mortal?" the one who betrayed his father asks.

"Some people call me Larry. Becky calls me Ker because it makes me sound cute and cuddly. And this is my son Ian. We're going to save her."

"Free us, and we will lead you to the Six," Prometheus says, the tension in his voice cooling. "But only if you can get past them."

"Who is 'them?'"

# 28

# Cryptid Palace

*Them.*

Adrenaline rakes through my veins as I spin to face the door where the light is filtering through. A monstrous, drooling shadow now darkens the passageway, and as it steps forward, it bares a hundred razor-sharp teeth and blinks its four glowing ruby eyes.

Its growl vibrates the floor beneath my feet. Creeping forward it sizes me up, and I gasp at the sight of its hulking, double-headed form. I put its brother to sleep by singing what feels like a century ago. Although it boasts one fewer head, it looks no less ferocious than the mighty Cerberus.

GRROOOWWLLL!

"Dad?"

"Run, Ian."

Ian has nowhere to run. We can only exit this hall the same way we entered. Instead of running, he backs away from the eight-foot-tall two-headed dog with its pair of metal-spiked collars.

It taunts us with a thundering boom of ear-splitting barking, lowers its meaty haunches, and lunges at us.

The first strike is easy to sidestep. It misses, and one of its heads collides with the stone wall next to a metal cell door. With a heavy crack, it twists its neck, steps back, and launches itself at us again. Would singing to this one work?

I try to whistle, but the only thing my lips can emit is a harsh, dysrhythmic screech that irritates the beast. I wave my piece of amber before its eyes, hoping it will get a hint of what I possess, but instead of showing fear, it mocks me with double snarls that join in unison like an angry choir.

"Ian?"

He trips over a broken piece of stone from the ceiling and falls backward on his butt as the monster eyes him with rage.

"Nice doggy."

BARK! HOWL!

It darts at me before I see it coming. To save myself from a fresh round of pain, I dive between its massive-clawed front feet, each bigger than my head. It swipes at me as I slide under its belly. Momentarily confused, it spins around so fast that its tail lashes at the air like a whip. In a split-second decision, I grab onto the tail with both hands as it slaps past inches from my face.

In just a second, the most terrifying ride of my life is finished. With a whip-crack motion the tail flings to a stop and sends me airborne head-first into the same wall it has just collided with. The force could be enough to break my neck if I don't break my acceleration with my hands.

Both of my wrists smash into the stone wall and send shockwaves of agony through my arms. I growl at the creature as it pounces on me, tries to sink its bloody fangs into my neck, and thrashes at my legs with its other mouth.

I manage one kick to its face as its fangs shred my other pants leg. The muscular jaws lock around my ankle and it thrashes its head, tossing me three feet in the air before I land with a painful crack on my pelvis.

Lurching to my feet, I can feel my body slowing down, providing the beast with another advantage. Instead of using that edge to maul me, it torments me with a volley of ear-splitting roars and howls as it glowers at me through those four red eyes.

"You enjoy music like your brother?"

It answers by sinking its claw into my leg. Twisting on the ground, I launch a furious kick at its face, successfully nicking its tooth, and scamper backward into the wall. Ian bolts from the far end of the corridor to shield me from the monster's lunge.

A sound idea, but the monster has marked us as a two-stage entrée. It bites at Ian's face as its other mouth snarls. Having lost track of me, it changes focus to him instead. Once I'm on my feet, I aim to make my attack count. I dart around Ian as the pain flares in my leg. One hit to the dog's face sends it reeling.

With a newfound edge, I jump on it, curl my hands around its bushy mane, and ride it like a ferocious bull. It bucks me high enough into the air for my head to brush against the stone ceiling.

Gathering a fistful of its fur, I pull tighter to command it. Instead of complying, it twists its neck, inflicting further whiplash. I'm too far back for its fangs to reach me, so it lies on its stomach and scratches at me with its even bigger back claws.

With it lying prone on the floor, Ian lunges toward it, kicks it in the face, and then hammers one of its eye sockets with his boot. The monster recoils with shock, flips its back, and sends me sliding across the dusty floor.

The next surprise slinks through the door before I can gather my bearings.

A powerful lion body with the face of a woman greets me and whispers my name.

"Kerry, you will not succeed."

The dog hasn't finished with Ian yet. It flips itself back to its feet and regales him with a series of bloodthirsty growls as it attacks. Ian parries by dancing around it in circles as I stare down the sphinx with an air of misplaced confidence.

One heavy paw is enough to launch me off my feet, but it slows its attack, angles its claw, and picks me up. If its mouth were big enough, it could have eaten me whole. Instead, a slimy tongue slithers out of its mangy mouth, licks its chops and then it drops me with a heavy thud to the floor.

With every ounce of adrenaline I can muster, I scoop myself off the floor, run at it headfirst, and collide with its ribcage. It emits a hiss of surprise as its claws pinch at my shirt.

Ian has made no headway with the hound. Instead of striking, he dances around while the monster lunges at him. It could take him down with a single bite, but Ian proves limber enough to outmaneuver it.

But not for long—a third beast lumbers through the open door. It sports one head of a bulky lion and one head of a twisted-horned goat, with blood congealing at the corners of its lips.

The goat's head brays at me while the lion head seeks to gnaw on my chest. It charges with enough force to prevent me from stopping it. Instead, I dive to my left to give it a clear path at the sphinx. Its goat's horns gore the sphinx in the posterior, to which the sphinx responds by hissing and flipping its claws at it.

Their split-second spat proves enough time for me to stumble to my feet. The dog proceeds to maul Ian. Instinctively, I sprint toward him, bypassing the sphinx and the goat-lion hybrid.

Its tail sees me as I spring past it. A forked tongue shoots out of a fanged mouth as I dodge its swipe. The monster lunges at its sphinx opponent before wrapping its leathery snake-head tail around my wrist. My momentum grinds to a halt as the hound attempts to devour Ian.

Ian's scrappy fighting style surprises it at a few intervals, but he is no match for its power. To defeat these three beasts, we must strategize on the fly.

Before I know what I'm doing, I open my mouth, insert the amber, and suck on it like a piece of candy. I can feel it stirring in my mouth, and when I pull it out, it shimmers like a molten, misshapen piece of silver.

Its shape morphs as I pinch it between my fingers. The sphinx growls as if unsure how to react, but the chimera locks onto me with all three heads. Allowing its snake tail to uncoil itself from my arm, the beast lowers its body to the floor and launches itself at me horns-first.

Thinking fast, I fling the misshapen piece of silver at its lion's head. I miss the mark by a mile, but as its snake-head tail whips back around, the amber weapon molds into a short blade just in time.

The monster reacts in shock as the blade slices through its necks, hissing as the snake tail watches its other two heads tumble to the floor. Instead of backing off, the creatures intensify their strikes. If the dog and the sphinx attack in tandem, they will overwhelm me.

A split-second delay allows me to wonder why the Titans aren't attacking. Perhaps their bonds prevent them from using their powers. Instead of cowering in the corners of their cells, they all watch through their door hatches. I hear a whoop from one end of the hallway, but before another voice can join in to encourage the two underdogs, another foe smashes through the wall at the end of the cellblock.

The roof cracks and crumbles as Ian darts out of the way. As part of the ceiling collapses, the hound issues a whimpering roar as a heavy stone slab slams down onto its twin craniums. Its muscles flex as it attempts to free itself from the debris.

The sphinx and dog back away from a twenty-foot-tall, muscular woman as if terrified. Her bulky arms swing like meaty pendulums as she stomps at the debris. Unable to fight back, the two-headed dog emits a nasal yelp and lies there, helpless.

The twenty-foot woman lets her dreadlocks tangle and flutter as she lowers herself to pick Ian up by the waist. Ian flits his eyes sideways at the last second. Hundreds of red eyes gaze out from her dreadlocks, and they begin to twist and thrash like a pit of angry vipers. The snake-hair knots itself around Ian's torso as he looks away only a split second before being turned into a statue.

"You!" I scream as the memory of our last encounter rages through my head.

The monster again spins a whirlwind of debris around herself, and even as the rocks are heavier, the whirlwind manages to pick several of them off the floor. The blade in my hand shrinks away as I lash at its snake heads in no particular order.

Rejoining the fray, the sphinx and the dog flank us by pressing their tails against the cell walls.

Ian recognizes the tactic and frees himself from the tangle of snake heads before twisting away and colliding with Prometheus's cell door. A blossom of flame erupts from behind it as the Titan watches the chaos unfold.

Having baited the snake-haired woman, Ian takes to taunting the other two attackers. They march on him two abreast while licking their chops and emitting low, rumbling growls.

This presents itself as the perfect opportunity for me to strike from the side. I lick the amber again, which had begun to transform from its silver state. Hoping that it takes the form of something useful, I wait for the metal to shift and swirl before feasting my eyes on a dull scythe.

The dog lurches back, growls, and sprints along the hall as I twist the scythe blade in my hands. It emits an excruciating howl as the steel slices through its neck, sending the beast sliding to a halt at the giant woman's feet.

Now taking me more seriously, the sphinx charges me, and I have no time to react. Instead of inflicting much damage, the metallic scythe tip draws only a scratch of blood through its golden coat. Its enormous front claws slash through my forearm, inducing scorching pain. The sphinx skids to a halt, turns around, and charges again. A half-second before its claws rip through my stomach, I leap high enough to avoid the swipe. I curl my hands around its torso as it thrashes.

The medusa-headed witch hisses at Ian through a hundred mouths as she takes him up in her cyclonic gale. He spins around the vortex in a blur while the sphinx attempts to throw me off. It manages to dislodge me by clawing at my midsection, which I dodge with my wrist out-thrust. I shave off some of its mane with the scythe, dive off, and finish it with a single, ferocious swing. The blade slashes across the lion-woman's face. Surprised, the beast covers its head with its paws but readies to pounce. Still bleeding from its facial wound, it roars and thrashes. The extra movement gives me ample time to lop its head clean off.

The sphinx's head skitters across the floor to join the dog's carcass while its body collapses into a pile of fluff. Instead of reveling in victory, I take on the gorgon the only way I know how. One of its snakes coils itself around my forearms, and as the woman flings her waist back, she sends me flying right up into the crumbled ceiling.

WHAM!

Ouch.

Pain scatters through my body in a spreading ache. The blade in my hand goes limp before it can dislodge a single head. I avoid eye contact with her as the snake's heads toss me through the air like a ragdoll.

Ian, spinning helplessly around her waist, reaches out to grab something.

He has mimicked my idea by inserting the amber into his mouth. When he withdraws it past his lips, it transforms into a blood-red blade.

When it takes the shape of a sword, he slashes at the woman's side. She shrieks as the blade gouges a two-inch deep incision in her waist, causing her to double over in pain. Rather than giving up, though, she intensifies her attacks.

The mop of snakes' heads slither in every direction, carrying me in circles over her head. When she reaches out her hand to squeeze the life out of my son, she makes a fatal error: Miscalculating the odds of the sword doing further damage, she slaps at him. The sword shears three fingers from her hand.

The shock gives me a second to wet my piece of amber again as the snakes' swaying heads cease for just a moment.

She howls in pain as the whirlwind around her settles. I waste not a second before my scythe materializes once again. She overreacts by punching at me with her one good arm, allowing precious seconds for me to shave half the snakes from her head. They fall to the ground, hiss at me, then slink away into the darkness.

Ian eyes his next chance at getting in a hit, but misses the mark when she parries with her two-fingered hand. Despite her injury and weakened grip, she knows how to deal with me.

Her fist closes around my waist as I lunge away in horror. The scythe falls from my hands, reforms into amber as it drops to the floor, and rolls away.

She bores into me with her angry red eyes as I look away.

"Look at me!" she hisses.

*Use the dark.*

I'm going to kill her. The dark coils within me as every heartbreak I've ever endured boils somewhere deep in my soul to emit a broth of steam and rage I've never let myself express.

I hurl obscenities at her like they're nothing, and she has the gall to grin at my pain. The rage grows into a darker storm and as I lose consciousness, half my body dissolving into a soupy mist that envelops her entirely.

*"Larry."*

My eyes wedge themselves open. A red star hurtles through space far off in the distance, while Sarah's amber hair forms a curtain before it. When the tears leak through my eyelids, I feel as though peace has scattered the agony and replaced it with hope.

"Sarah."

*"Having a good day?"*

"Um."

Yeah.

"Just got done destroying three enormous monsters, and I don't even know what's going on with the big one. Just peachy." The sarcasm bites through my voice, which causes her a moment of alarm.

*"Do you remember when you found me?"*

I do not.

Watching my hesitation, she searches my eyes for something that might resemble hope. When she finds none, she closes her eyes and looks away to the red star behind her ear.

*"You were in love—I knew it then. But you saved me anyway because there's still something good in that heart. You know how to find it."*

"I have nothing but the dark," I say, defeated.

*"You have so much more than that. You once defeated fear; now you must defeat the pain. It's a lot harder, but I know you can do it."*

I exhale as the icy vacuum sucks the life out of me.

*"You still love her, and you always will. There isn't much that conquers love, Kerry. Not even the darkness of the devil himself can do that."*

"How—I don't even know how I ended up here."

It hits me before I can finish my sentence: I'm having a classic out-of-body experience, only this time, my body has eroded into a cloud of coal ash that billows as thick as the darkness in my soul.

Her words sting me, and pour energy throughout my body. Somehow it absorbs all the pain, gathers it into a single point, and preserves it as a weapon.

✦

Ian struggles in the medusa-woman's two-fingered grasp as she realizes a cloud of coal dust has devoured her entire left arm.

I see myself materialize out of the cloud, with a newfound energy broiling in my soul, yet gravity is inexplicably allowing me to float at her eye level.

She hesitates and flails, as if trying to swing her missing arm around my neck. I'm only getting started. This time, I don't even need the scythe.

All that anguish and pain has become a glowing orb within my body. As I roll my hands together, the ball of energy grows in my palms.

I clap my hands together on either side of her head while the remaining snake heads lunge at me. As if constructed of heavy golden cymbals, my hands smack into the sides of her head, the resultant concussion wave drawing blood through her ears.

Outraged, she screams at me with a tidal wave of foreign-language obscenities. The snakes are helpless; having become immobilized, they flop around her hulking shoulders. When she draws Ian up to her mouth, I can tell she aims to bite his head off.

"Don't try it," I warn.

"You don't know what you're doing," she hisses. "They will not honor you—the Titans will kill you without a second thought. They'll organize for universal domination and not even the gods will stop them."

"I already have a plan for that," I argue.

All that pain brims within me as though it needs an outlet. I settle to the floor as I gaze up at Ian.

"Put him down and I'll spare you."

"Spare me?" She laughs. "We're already dead."

"Yup, that about sums it up," Ian rasps as he watches the debris shift and the bodies of the creatures reanimating themselves. As if the creatures weren't ferocious enough, zombified versions of them might be even worse.

They regain their feet as they reattach severed limbs and heads.

Instead of attacking or retreating against the cell doors, I inhale, close my eyes, and imagine Becky's warm embrace.

With that thought, the pain ebbs. And as if the agony has strengthened the memory, I allow it to swell within me. I can do this only once. And as my skin opens pore by pore, the power of a star streams through me.

Lightning arcs around me as my glow burns brighter.

The creatures, filled with horror, watch in disbelief as they experience something they've never seen before. I allow myself a gaze into the medusa-woman's eyes and explode in a brilliant flash of energy as bright as the sun itself.

The creatures evaporate in a flash, and I catch my breath as the lightning disappears into the darkness.

Ian has caught the full brunt of my outburst and lies motionless beside the disfigured bodies of our enemies. Alarmed, I sprint to his side, press my hands into his chest, and attempt CPR.

All hope has faded, yet I haven't seen the worst of it. Another dark creature skulks deeper in the chamber beyond the crumbled walls the woman had smashed through. Something big and scaly drags across the stone floor within the antechamber.

I've used up everything I have. There is nothing I can use to fight. An impossible task awaits, and I must face it alone, because Ian isn't moving.

# 29

# The Wrath of Echidna

Ian's pulse is flatlining, as if echoing the destruction within the chamber. As if a nightmare paralyzes him, his eyes flit from side to side, never focusing on me. I pump at his chest with all my might as desperate tears cling to my cheeks.

"Come on, son," I plead. "Ian. Please don't...."

Something in the darkened antechamber hisses as it observes, but instead of giving it attention, I focus all my energy on reviving my son. That his condition is a direct result of my action crosses my heart with guilt. But had I succumbed to the monsters instead of fighting, I doubt his condition would be any better. Even if I had no control over it, something deep within has made it possible. There's no denying that.

HISSS!

"Be with you in a moment," I mutter.

That venomous hiss shatters the heavy air in the hall as the scaly dragging continues.

"You will *die* in a moment, Mortal!"

Nothing I haven't heard before, even in my own voice.

I let the threat bypass me as I force huge breaths of air into Ian's lungs and listen for signs of a heartbeat. Surely this thing, whose voice sounds female, has better threats.

Such as a powerful scaly body that could squeeze me to death in a matter of seconds, or razor-sharp nails at the tips of twenty gangly fingers.

I glance up as it awaits my attention, as if it knows I'm going to give it the time of day.

She looks at me through fiery eyes that cut narrow slits into her slender feminine face. Though weathered with age, she still manages to look genuine and stately. A tight-fitting tunic of some sort wraps her torso just above where the snake scales gradually transition to skin. She looms high above me, filling the chamber with her enormous, muscular tail that, if stretched out, might span a couple of city blocks.

"You—" she hisses, eyeing me with rage. "You slayed my beloved Typhon."

"Never met him."

Predicting her reaction proves easy, though instead of spitting an enraged reply, she slithers higher and arches her back while allowing her hiss to become a solemn whisper.

"You cannot escape ... he is doomed to torment forever as a spirit without a body."

"Come a little closer," I taunt her, "so I can see how big you really are."

Instead of moving to strike, she stands aloft like a cobra, unfurls her four arms, and brandishes four bladed weapons. In one of her right hands, she wields a long cleaver twice as large as a butcher's knife, while the other right hand sports a curved katana. Her left hands hold what I could describe as a longsword with a dainty hilt and a reaper's scythe. As if she even needs weapons to kill her enemies.

I am unarmed. Unless I think fast, she's going to slice and dice me into fine chunks to use as protein on a salad.

Rather than fear, anger lashes through me. If I must go through her to bring my wife out of Hades, I'll do it without a second thought.

Her tail slithers across the stone floor as she waits for me to come to her, calculating my every move. There's only one thing I can try—the idea came to me during our battle with the spider. Now that I can wield both pieces of amber, they might make more formidable weapons, if only I can find the water to *activate* them.

Searching the darkness and debris presents a challenge, and trying to do so in silence proves even more difficult. After I have them corralled, I gather both fragments in my right hand and roll them in my fingers, as if expecting them to transform at my will. Instead of plunging into a pulverizing black, they sparkle to life in a way I have not yet seen. Not only do they glow with positive emotions, but they also crackle like fireworks when my emotions exert enough power.

I suddenly know how to use them; the energy might manifest in the power I used to defeat the medusa woman.

*Use the dark* indeed.

Limping into the antechamber with only thoughts of finding the Six and bringing Becky home feels cathartic, as though I'm releasing a piece of my soul that has remained dormant for eons.

If she plans to keep the Titans in prison, she'll have to get through me, and although I weigh a fraction of what she does, I'm not as feeble as I may seem. I will have to use my size as an asset. If she wants to kill me, she'll have to be precise.

"That's it," she says. "Step forward."

In a flurry of simultaneous action, I leap over a pile of crumbled stone along the wall as she moves to strike with her longsword. As if mirrored in the sound of her wheezing hiss, I hear a *plip* that can only be a small droplet falling into a puddle.

Humanity thrives on water; it is the basis of our entire civilization. It breeds cities and agriculture and even sparks wars. No human being has ever used water for what I'm about to do.

Locating the puddle with accuracy is not so easy in the dark. Instead, I must use the echoes and basic triangulation to find it. The splash must have come from above. Either a stalactite or fissure might have allowed the puddle to form, if I'm correct that the contractor had originally carved the room out of bedrock. Any such feature should be more likely to form at a high point, where gravity would overcome surface tension.

Since the echoes deaden near the center of the room, that's where the water must be. To get to it, I'll have to contend with her tail, which even uncoiled stands nearly as tall as me. If she feels me climbing over her, she'll squeeze me into oblivion. If I want to reach it, I'll have to move faster.

With adrenaline blasting through me, I bounce off the concrete floor, claw at her scaly sides, and leap onto the ground again. The snake tail in the distance sidewinds through the chamber into a tightening coil beneath her torso. She shrinks my landing spot just in time for me to douse my prize belongings in the chilled water.

True to expectation, they blaze to life, and before I know what has happened, I'm dragging the tips of twin glowing swords on the floor.They sparkle with my potent aggression, which, born from the promise of finding Becky, blazes with pulsating beams that mimic my heartbeat.

"Die!"

She moves faster than I could have planned for. Her tail squeezes me like a noose. The only potential reaction is to slice at her body with both blades. They pulse as they draw a sticky red resin on her serpentine skin.

Demonstrating her pain, she shrieks, regathers her tail, and flexes the muscles with enough power to suffocate me. Anticipating this, I leap up to the top of her tail, bring the swords together high over my head, and plunge them down into the appendage.

She reacts by flexing again, only in the opposite direction. My first take is that her body is slithering away, even as her torso remains stationary. Though agile, her size and length come with a notable drawback: no matter how fast it moves, her center of mass will stay put long enough for me to place well-timed hits in the right places.

Instead of flitting away, her tail forms a whip. It slaps at me so fast that my eyes can't react to the blur of motion. She bats at me like a kitten with a ball of yarn, and then slams me harder. With a whoosh of chilly subterranean air, the scales plow into my chest, lifting me off the floor and tossing me at least fifteen feet toward a crumbling yet ornate sidewall with built-in alcoves for art objects.

"Fool!"

I grumble and wince in pain as I struggle to my feet. I'm not going down like a chump—if she's going to defeat me, she'll need to earn it.

"Nothing more dangerous than a fool with nothing to lose," I snarl, launching myself toward her.

She squares her hips and readies all four of her blades as I charge her with the tips of my glowing swords pointing right at where her heart might be, if she had one.

One clink is all it takes. She hits scythe and the longsword together and steadies her hulking body. Though her tail remains in motion, she brandishes the weapons and strikes at me with all four in one fluid move. A quartet of metallic clinks echo in the cavern as I parry the most forceful of hits.

Before I allow satisfaction to form in my brain, her arms move faster. Flailing about as if in a rage-filled tantrum, she spins the four blades into a sharpened tornado. If I get too near her, one of them could remove my head from the rest of my body before I have a chance to cower in shock.

Lucky for me, her steady stance allows me more room to maneuver. Altering my trajectory to my left on the next charge takes me to something I perceive as a weak spot; she will have trouble spinning her body fast enough to meet me there before my swords impale her back.

Except that her tail has gained enough momentum to knock me off my feet again. I cling tightly to my weapons as I am once again airborne. Pain rockets through my shoulder as I land hard on a protruding altar I hadn't yet noticed. Wincing only increases the flow of adrenaline. Before I know it, I'm springing to my feet and assaulting her yet again.

She anticipates my move to perfection. The katana whips through the air right in front of my nose as the scythe follows below it. In the nick of time, I contort my body to avoid both, but her tail slaps at me again.

Its angular momentum lifts me higher this time, and lobs in a steeper arc just high enough for the scythe blade to slash harmlessly beneath my feet.

She growls and hisses at the same time while baring a set of snake fangs dripping with venom. Hoping she can't dislocate her jaw to swallow me whole, I meet her eyes with my gaze as the heat of my passion burns a hole in my heart.

The swords flash with every note of aggression, in tune with my heartbeat. Paying attention to the rhythm the whole time has given her an advantage. She fine-tunes her strikes and reduces their ferocity to allow for greater precision, so that her hits can come between flurries of my heart.

Then again, adrenaline can have peculiar effects on even the most resilient pulses. In me, the flow modifies my heartbeat, rendering it erratic enough to foul her timing.

One pulse, *clash*; two pulses, *clash*, *clash*. The second parry misses the flourish of the blade's glow by a fraction of a second.

Power surges through me as I reimagine Sarah's face into something more luminous. My frown deepens as I smash one of my swords against her scythe. The curve of the blade catches the arc of my swing at an inopportune moment, and on the follow-through, friction tears it out of her hand and sends it flipping through the air at least a dozen feet behind her.

Instead of allowing herself to fret over the loss of a weapon, she intensifies her swings as her tail seeks to entrap me. I dodge the tail while parrying her longsword, but her katana hits with more precision. The sting of contact rips across my forearm as a flow of blood escapes from a narrow wound.

Not deep enough to bleed out from, the scar seems to heal itself as I swing my second sword toward her face.

She parries it while launching a double-strike toward my chest, but I'm too nimble for her. My feet dance on the cracked stone floor as I swing at her again. One blade glows hotter as it grazes her serpentine tail, and the blood oozes black onto the surface of her scaly skin as it peels away from her hip and loosens along her extremity. She's molting right before my eyes, but this doesn't distract her in the slightest.

My next hit is far too casual to do any harm. The blade misses behind her back as she bends forward to impale me with the longsword. My swipe to counter it misdirects her aim just enough to make her thrust miss; she counters with an angular swing of her longsword aimed at my neck, but I duck so that it only gives me a haircut.

Both blades glow as I ready them for a double-tap slash at her midsection. She swipes away one of them while absorbing the other with the katana.

With every swing, adrenaline supplies me with enough energy to counteract the creeping loss of power from my emotions. A battle like this can't survive on emotion alone, since the slicing and dodging saps me of the energy needed to direct my feelings.

She levels her longsword and comes at me with the other. The momentum her shoulder puts into the swing pulls her free hand with it right into the path of one of my swords.

The hand pops off her wrist and tumbles toward the floor, and a thick ooze of black blood spouts from the wound. She shrieks with pain as she scours the surrounding space with furious strikes that grow clumsy from her rage. She'll have to step up her game.

I don't have time to finish the thought before I glimpse her tail whipping toward me so fast that any reaction of mine would be too slow. This time, instead of sending me hurtling across the room, it launches me into another fold of her tail. She has managed to sidewind into an excellent position to trap me. I scurry to my left as I land with a thud against her tail.

Pressing her edge, she squeezes until my swords gore her tail.

Fury paints her face with something otherworldly as she snarls. Having rendered my arms momentarily inoperable, she now has me right where she wants me. Against the embrace of her tail, I can't do much to stop her. She sends the katana hurtling through the dark at my neck, but I have just enough wiggle room to dodge it. Instead of dismembering me, it gashes a linear incision in her tail. She screams in horror as the pain flashes a horrific scowl across her face.

The tail squeezes tighter, and I draw in failed gasps of air to loosen it. Her strength is too much for me to overcome. My face grows dark as the glow of my swords flounders. Still stuck in another segment of her tail, they seem to lose their luster with each passing second.

As the breath leaves my body, I see visions of spinning circles, stars, and a different place and time.

## MEMORIES:

Becky caresses my back as we sit on the beach and gaze in wonder at the wooded island. Somehow, I can remember what once transpired there. *The Soul of the Baron* rests forgotten on a dusty table, and as I visualize its spine, an incandescent glow surrounds my fist. Transferring the energy into the rock, I hurl it at a flying, fire-breathing beast. It shoots through the air like a bullet and punctures the monster's brain.

The stars swell overhead as she grips my hand, pulls it towards her face, and kisses me.

In the blink of an eye, she vanishes, and everything fades away until I lay eyes on the ghostly, undulating image of Sarah, her sadness having rendered her translucent.

I can hear her speaking as the scene floods away.

*You know how to find me.*

*Use the dark.*

One of the best things about darkness is that it masks intent and reactions better than any human expression can. Without visible cues such as body language, any attacker must rely only on instinct through experience and expectation.

I've never understood how to harness that dark energy. According to physicists, dark energy drives the forever expansion of our universe, propelling galaxies away from each other as the visible energy stretches farther and wider, leaving a frigid emptiness in its wake.

It drives objects apart. And Persephone admitted that I'm able to harness the power of both light and dark—how can I pull off that feat without knowing I can?

Since we cannot detect or measure dark energy by any scientific means, it remains a theoretical force, at least in terms of what it is and how it works.

Rather than attempting to understand it, I allow it to burrow deep within me. The glow of the blades disappears as the snake body constricts me tighter.

I gaze into her fiery eyes like a man on the brink of death. In a sudden flourish, it all makes sense: surviving this hell was never in the cards. I can only succumb to it. Defeat can manifest in various forms, much like the power of darkness.

In the prison hallway, I can see its disastrous effects. Ian lies limp and bruised beside the scarred and blackened corpse of a twenty-foot-tall medusa-woman. I have battled the snake woman for so long that reviving him might be impossible.

Ian isn't meant to survive this, either—in fact, he has been dead from the moment I first met him. A soul without a body. Dark.

It draws itself deeper within me as the snake-woman squeezes the life out of me. Agony pours through every crook of my being as the towering vat of darkness consumes me. If I'm not meant to survive, I will become a Shade, forever in the service of The One.

And Shades don't kill people; they devour them whole and absorb them atom by atom.

My body begins to lose focus as consciousness fades from me.

The dark energy pushes away every bit of positive energy until only a bitter vacuum remains to draw in the inherent darkness within the other soul. And that dark power imbues this creature; a monster guarding the cells of the Titans in Tartarus must depend on it.

I grow weaker as she grows stronger.

And then, before I can sense myself giving in, the terrible consequences of my decision play out like the inevitable rip of the cosmos speeding up the expansion of the universe. The One has now amassed such power that no one can stop him, unless the Titans intervene.

I must depend on them if I can. Then again, they have not shown their true motives.

Now it all makes sense. The only way I can free the Titans is by harnessing this dark power and absorbing the monster as a Shade.

She squirms and squeals as I evaporate her, particle by particle. Every pain I've ever felt magnified by a factor of a thousand surges through her, bringing an immobilizing agony as I reduce her to little more than coal dust.

With one last pulse, her movement ceases as I erase what remains of her. The weapons clank to the floor and all the atoms float off her tail, revealing bones, and then nothing but the dark. Her own domain has defeated her, because of The One. I'm now free, but freedom never felt like such a thorough defeat.

Is a pyrrhic victory truly a win? Soon I will find out, and the Titans will help me.

# 30

# Titan Uprising

My bones ache as though they've been turned to powder, and a resultant pain seeps through whatever must still make up my body. I hover over the floor and drift closer to the entrance the medusa-woman created by smashing through the wall.

I can somehow see. The dust and crumbled stone, the monsters' corpses, and Ian's lifeless body litter the hallway. When I slide into the room, I can hear grumbling as if one Titan has lost a bet with another.

When I exhale, I can hear nothing, though a faint rasping emanates from somewhere within.

"Mortal," the patient one says. The vibration of his voice combines with its echo and somehow makes sense to me.

*"I'll get you out,"* I say. No sound escapes, so I try to add more volume. "*I have your word; you will help me find the Six."*

"He's a Shade," Justice comments. "Did you defeat Echidna?"

*It has a name?*

If I had a head I would nod, but instead, the cloud that composes me drifts forward and back to mimic agreement.

"Speak," an unfamiliar voice commands.

"I..." I can speak. My voice seems ephemeral, but for the moment, I'm making vibrations the prisoners can hear. "Who are you?"

"I am Coeus," he replies in an even voice through the bars on his cell door. "Titan of intelligence and learning."

I float among the ruins in the hall, my gaze fixed on the first door where Patience resides. "I think introductions are in order."

No one speaks for over ten seconds, and growing bored with the silence, I pipe up. "I am Kerry, and that is my son, Ian. I am a descendant of the Six Cretan Titans."

"And how do you know that?" Patience says.

My cloud wavers. "Ran into a few people, notably Persephone."

"You saw her?"

Hesitating, I move to clarify. "Not really. She spoke to me."

"And why would she seek you out?" Cronos asks me.

"Because she recognized me."

"Forgive Cronos," Justice says.

"The ruler of the Cosmos," Cronos adds.

Justice speaks again. Her voice seems to solidify as she introduces herself, to exhibit an authoritative stance. Speaking slowly lends her voice clarity and power. "I'm Theia."

"Hyperion," another voice says. "Embodiment of the Sun."

"Crius," yet another introduces himself.

"He doesn't even have a job," Cronos mocks.

A sleeker feminine voice sounds next. Her distinctive European accent makes it hard to decipher what she's saying. "Rhea, mother of the gods. Cronus is my brother."

Themis, Tethys, and Phoebe introduce themselves as titanesses next, followed by Oceanus and Iapetus.

The fiery voice growls behind his door. "You know who I am."

Prometheus, the Titan of fire.

"Twelve of you," I repeat. "You *will* help me find the Six."

"Who are you to command us?" Cronus asks without raising his voice.

My voice wavers as my soul fluctuates in midair before drifting to the cell where Iapetus introduced himself. Logic seems to dictate that I release him first, because as the father of the Titans, he will hold more sway with the others. "I command no one. I have been directed to set you free, but I have my own terms."

"Directed by whom?" Theia asks.

"The One ... True God of Darkness, Erebus. You know, Prometheus. One of your minions made me swear to serve him."

He roars with chattering, maniacal laughter. "They are not minions."

"Give me your word," I say, raising my voice.

"Our word is as good as our deeds," Theia says. "You must know what we've done to honor our promise."

"Cronos, you said you betrayed your father."

"We made war with the Olympians," Rhea admits. "Accused of betrayal, but we were the betrayed. For that, we were condemned to Tartarus forever."

"Then why does Erebus want you freed?"

Prometheus lets his laughter subside and croaks a stoic reply: "Revenge."

"Forget it," I rasp, backing away from Iapetus's door. "I'm not setting you free so you can destroy the universe."

"The One has a condition, does he not?" Theia asks.

"I'm not telling you about that."

"How, then, do you expect us to trust you?"

Rage spikes within me and my darkness casts a deeper shadow at his questioning. "Because I swore my service. Without that condition, I wouldn't have done it, the hell with death."

"Death," Rhea says, "seems to have found you anyway."

"Just a scratch," I joke, certain none of them will find it humorous. "What is your promise? No, give me your condition first."

"Once we find your ancestors," Cronus laments, "we'll be vulnerable. If they seek to do battle, you must not join them."

"They're defenders."

"Or so you've been led to believe."

A puff of wind emanates from me and then rotates around to rejoin me. "Fine. It's a deal."

"You must set me free first," Cronus says. "Or else the universe may collapse. A curse reigns over us because of our war with the Olympians, and I know how my father thinks."

I consider his plea and waver in place. While Iapetus promises to have logic behind him, I can't dismiss what Cronos claims. His father ruled over the cosmos before he took over, and if Uranus is as dangerous as Cronos is hinting at, then disaster could strike, and I might never see the Six because of an intractable war.

Their conditions wouldn't be acceptable if I give away my truest wish, without which I would not have agreed to free them in the first place. Keeping that a secret, at least for the time being, gives me substantial bargaining power and I'm not about to relinquish it.

They can trust me because only I know the true extent of my personality. Commitment has never been a question; when my heart yearns for something, I will stop at nothing to get it, and a commitment is honor.

So I won't join the Six in any battle with the Titans. If they want war, I'll just wait for the Titans to break their end of the bargain first. A history of betrayal indicates future incidents, no matter how much one wishes to change—and Tartarus isn't in the business of changing anyone. Instead, it makes them suffer the consequences of their actions and strips them of the ability to commit further wrongs. What dwells in the heart still lingers there; if not, punishment would be meaningless.

They are itching to be freed. I could have demanded anything, and they would have relented, because while they are trying to mask their inner desires, I can see them for what they are. They will seek revenge upon the Olympians, but that doesn't involve me. It doesn't destroy my contract with The One, and it doesn't break my bond with Becky. Nothing can, because I have the power of eternity in my corner. The welded washers mean everything to me because of her, and neither gods, Titans, nor the underworld itself can ever undo that weld.

No trust. If they stay true to their word, I won't have a reason to complain. But even if they don't, I have another play still. I'm not about to expect anything, but making contingency plans promises the best logical sense.

"You shall free me first," Cronos pleads.

Honoring his request might be a double-edged sword, but I decide to take the chance. I slide away from the monsters' hulking corpses toward the hall's left wall, aiming for Cronos's door. I don't need magic or godly powers to free him, because I'm a Shade. For now at least.

I can hear Cronos growing restless behind the bars in his window. His heavy chain drags across the floor and his breathing becomes softer and deeper. Entering his cell is as easy as pushing through the door. My cloud erases it atom by atom as I press against it. When I hover next to him, a subtle sense of awe hits me. His once muscular build has given way to malnourishment, causing his skin to sag and his rigid shoulder blades to underline a gaunt face. It might take him years to regain his former strength, which gives me yet another advantage.

Even with age and an improper diet, he stands at least six inches taller than me. Somehow, without a physical body, I can still sense my own height. If a Shade can perceive the same things as a living human being, then it should be just as frail.

I understand that weakness better than anyone. It has resided in me from the beginning, an indelible feature of my personality, and has guided me through peril and victory. Regardless of frailty, I know my course of action.

Cronus sighs as I dissolve the chain link that anchors the bindings leading up to the heavy iron gauntlets on his wrists. Rust has stained them orange over the centuries, yet that patina does not weaken the metal. The rust flakes away first, stains my cloud with swirls of orange and gray, and then dissolves into me. As I guide my cloud closer to his wrists, the link binding the chains to his gauntlet gives way. Lowering myself to where the inch-thick metal links attach to his ankles, I busy myself with freeing him from bondage.

Evaporating them is easy. When he's free from his bonds, he flexes his arms, stretches his back, and lets out a long, painful sigh.

I waste no time before punching holes in every door, absorbing the chains, and saying nothing. The less they know about me and my son, the better.

Ian might be a weak spot of mine, but I'm in no mood to let it damage me. As I free them one by one, I maintain caution not to look at him. If he's still alive, he'll leave with us, yet a creeping dread gnaws at my insides like corrosive acid.

Ten minutes later, I emerge from the last cell and wait for all twelve of them to join me. They survey the damage I've done as if to savor it; it's amazing how one minor change of viewpoint can reshape one's outlook.

Together the twelve Titans stand proud, their powers united in a common goal. Where moments ago, hope might have been fleeting, determination reigns supreme. With their shackles off, nothing can stop them. Had I not transformed into a Shade to defeat Echidna, they would have remained in bondage forever. Now they can accomplish their ultimate goal, no matter the stakes.

Not knowing or caring how their plans for revenge might play out, or the inherent consequences of their freedom, I allow that cloud of black sorrow to sink lower within me. I can't comprehend what this might do to me, but I must find the Six so they can lead me to Becky. After that, I'll figure out The One on my own.

Nothing will stop me from at least finding her; even if it means being stuck in the underworld for an eternity, it will all be worth it if I can feel her tender arms around me, witness the warm glow of her smile and the simple passion that ignites her spirit. In the literal sense, Becky might not be a goddess, but only I know she's more than that. She's everything; losing her would devour me forever, and with that darkness haunting my soul as I roam the hinterlands of the underworld, I would cease to be human and become a Shade forever. A fate worse than death.

"You're a fighter," Prometheus growls. He runs his hands over one another to birth a dancing flame in his palm, wrapping it again in his fingers and churning it into a ball of molten steel. The ball levitates for a moment as he lets go of it, and as it pushes into my cloud, the energy contained within rips the entropy apart, igniting my cells with enough purpose for me to become human again.

The miracle takes several moments to complete, and as the black cloud thins, my arms and legs emerge intact, scars and all. Pain once again rips through my limbs. Where the monsters have left their marks, the injuries still sting, but instead of defeating me they now strengthen me, as though forged into something stabler via the magic of fire.

Prometheus looks at me and grins, baring a row of badly-decayed teeth. Black splotches have spread around his palms and face, yet instead of looking livid, he approaches me with a simple note of thanks. I can feel it without him saying anything. When he nods, he lays his intentions bare, if only for a moment.

"I will always fight for what I know to be right," I say.

"Fighting takes spirit, my friend," Theia says, appearing next to me. "Peace takes something else entirely."

"Meekness," I say, knowing that I'm echoing the words of a pastor Becky and I used to listen to years and years ago. "Without it, there is only discord."

I have always approached the idea of meekness with disapproval. Society, especially among men, views meekness as feeble. Failing to fit into societal norms could make me a victim of both my own insecurities and social expectations of masculinity.

But I've learned the hard way that meekness takes more strength than argument. A lesson my brain has always been eager to forget, it still forges the anchor of my relationship with Becky. I let down my guard when I met her, and for that, she rewarded me.

"Not meekness," she replies. "Justice does not depend on that. It can only flourish when we construct and defend impartiality so that no flaws remain. It must apply to all equally, or it can apply to none."

"Justice can be cruel," I argue.

"It is blind. The cruelty is only in how your own bias interprets it."

If I had time, I'd love to sit down and debate justice with her over cocktails and appetizers, but we both have bigger plans. Her ideas speak to me in a logical sense, but those ideas are as susceptible to corruption as anything else. Two thousand years in chains may have warped her ideas beyond the way most would describe justice, but then again, the idea itself is only as good as the people who control and affect it.

"Are you ready to rise, Mortal?" Cronos says, holding out his hand to shake. When I grasp it, warmth surges through me. He leads me out through the front door and gazes up into the black. With a simple tug, he surges upward, and the rock walls of the abyss speed by, allowing no form to become visible. The other eleven rise behind us, and when we land on solid ground, the winged monster with a hundred red eyes greets us.

It glowers at us but seems to realize it stands no chance against all twelve Titans. Instead of fighting, it stands aside, emitting a mushroom of smoke from its serrated jaw and bowing. Prometheus rewards it with a flickering ember snack as thanks.

When we levitate again, Cronos carries me beyond the rim of the crater, arcs us high over the river of fire, and lands on the adjacent marshland. I feel that something is about to happen, yet instead of reacting to it, I allow darkness to fester within me. Ian is down there alone, and I've abandoned him. I'll have to run headlong into a brick wall to punish myself when I get the chance, but then again, all actions and choices have consequences, some more dire than others. Even I am not immune. How would the gods judge me for what I've just done?

Dwelling on it would be a waste of time that I don't have. The Titans are going to lead me to the Six as they've promised, and once I'm in their company, I can come to terms with how I have altered my reality.

# 31

# Revenge

Low-lying fog swirls like stew around my knees as I sink into the muddy bog up to my ankles. Although small, the marsh will prevent me from making much progress in decent time. I stand just under six feet tall, and even the female Titans rival my height. The men range anywhere from an inch to six inches taller by comparison, and their larger feet don't sink into the muck like mine.

I curse under my breath as the men leave me behind, advancing up to a hundred yards ahead of me.

"Wait up," I shout.

Most of them ignore me. Only Theia glances back my way, and when she does, a curious hunch in her shoulders suggests she's not the one calling the shots but must keep up with the rest of them.

So that's how they're going to play it.

"Should have let you rot down there." The darkness of my growl matches my expression, but they don't seem to slow down.

By the time I've reached the banks of the marsh, they look like tiny plastic army men in the distance. They have organized into a loose formation as if preparing for battle.

Three of them shuffle into a wide v-pattern at the company's rear, while the middle six form a pair of rows three abreast. The leaders of the group, who might be Prometheus, Cronos, and Rhea, march side by side about fifty feet ahead.

"You bastards," I moan to myself. There's no way they can hear me now.

To make up ground, I coax my muscles into a jog, but the pain spreading through my entire body only slows me further. How is it that these malnourished prisoners are suddenly so fit?

It doesn't matter to me, but the anger inside me only grows with every step. They don't care about me, my pledge, or my conditions. They seek only their own ends, and they've been clear about their motives. If I can't keep them in line, they're going to wreak such havoc that the world itself would only be collateral.

Why has The One been so adamant about setting them free? They work for themselves, giving no concern to his ambition. The One True God of Darkness has legions of servants, most of them dead.

*Do not question me. The twelve Titans were wrongly incarcerated. They gave too much power to the Olympians, and the Olympians betrayed them.*

Since when does he care about justice?

*Come to my lair, my servant, and I shall reward you.*

I have bigger things to worry about, such as finding the Six Cretan Titans, discovering my place in the universe, and bringing Becky home to the dimension where she belongs. When I'm done with that, Erebus can hang all the medals he wants over my neck.

Then again, the reward he dangles may not be Becky or any physical recompense. I gulp when I imagine meeting him.

*You shall.*

Darkness crowds my mind. I left Ian in the dungeon, and for that, I deserve any punishment The One might enact.

"I shall," I relent, sighing.

"Titans! I order you to stop!"

They didn't respond to my polite request, and they reacted as I would have expected in the prison when I tried to claim authority. After all, a mere mortal trying to command the progenitors of the gods? Blasphemy.

They might kill me for trying to dispense orders, but that would force them to heed my demands.

"Order!" Prometheus roars.

“Yeah, that’s who I think I am,” I mutter. They’re so far ahead that it doesn’t matter. My voice can only reach them if I scream at the top of my lungs.

“I know where you’re going, you cowards! The daemons will rip out your innards and eat you for lunch!” By now, making vain threats can’t do anything but further enrage them. I hope they do come to kill me.

The leaders of the group cease their march and the twelve break ranks to gather in a circle, obviously to discuss the matter of a mortal trying to boss them around. Good, discuss it long and hard. I still have my weapons.

Steeling my nerves lets me walk faster, although with the limp and the pain, my strides are so short I can only be wasting energy. I haven’t eaten in so long that the thought of food can’t even make me salivate, and without sustenance, energy is in short supply.

Agony saps what remains of my will to survive, but I’m gaining ground with every step. They stand huddled like a football team in their circle for over ten minutes, discussing Xs and Os the way any team must. A sudden realization that they’re making plans to carry on without me hammers through my chest, forcing me to rasp torturously. If that’s the case, I don’t care about their conditions. I’d rather talk the Six into hunting them down and sending them right back to Tartarus, where they belong.

*You shouldn’t call them names.*

I call lots of people names and I don’t care if they deserve it, because I consider it an exercise in catharsis. If it can make me feel better, I’ll do it and worry about the real consequences later. Anger hasn’t always served me well, but here in the underworld, I can use no other tool.

When they break their huddle and reform their ranks, they begin to float above the underbrush on the slopes of the hills. As if to survey the ground farther ahead, they gaze on in that direction, point at something, and fall back onto their feet.

Their gait increases when they touch the ground, and risking everything, I break out into a run to catch up with them. The thorns tear at my ankles as sharp, jutting rocks bruise my feet through my heavy, muddy shoes. With every step, pain attacks me from all sides.

Together, the twelve of them ascend the slope to the same ridgeline I’d followed on my way to the river of fire. That highland extends for a little over a mile, if my memory is correct, and then it dips into the valley where the daemons attacked us.

With their trajectory following the steps of my earlier journey, I glance at the ground every couple of moments to watch for my own footprints. By the time I've reached the ridgeline, I have closed to within two hundred yards. They might hear my gasping and groans of agony from there, but again, they seem to have slowed.

They huddle for a moment, fly above the hilltops, and survey the narrow valley from a bird's-eye view. I almost cough when I see something flying toward them, which they take as a threat. Their formation breaks, and four of them streak in a different direction to follow the interloping bird. The rest of them scatter; some settle back to the ground while others fly farther ahead. A strategy sound enough to deal with the daemons seems to be taking shape.

I watch them assemble into groups as I run.

Before I make it ten steps, the bird explodes in a fireball the size of an asteroid. Sparks rain from above to ignite the grasses, and once the grass is ablaze, I have few means of escape.

Prometheus pelts the remnants of the bird with a pair of red-hot snowballs, which only seems to add to its ire. The mushroom of fire extinguishes itself into smoke when Oceanus douses it with a wave he's pulled from nothing, and as the rapidly cooling orb falls with a heavy thud, I decide to wander in that direction.

Since Oceanus has summoned water, much of it will form a puddle I can use to get my weapons back. If he'd weighed that risk beforehand, I might consider it impressive, yet my real motive is discovering what they've just killed.

No, they didn't kill it; it writhes on the ground as though overcome with tremors of suffering. Its feathers appear out of the orb and its wings flutter as it attempts to take flight. The bird achieves no height and gives up. I assume the fall has broken one or both of its wings. I cannot help it, but why did it attack?

It didn't—the Titans were the aggressors. They're ransacking the landscape of the underworld. A place that has delivered so much pain might deserve to burn, but their non-existent regard for everything I might have considered holy burrows into my heart.

The several Titans that have taken flight now form a tight v-pattern while they glide aloft. They don't look down at me. Instead of trying to help the poor injured fowl, I fall to my knees in the grass, slosh around in the water, and gather handfuls of it to drink.

Once I've taken my fill, I pull the two pieces of amber from my pocket, dip them into the water, and watch them transform into nymphs. I cannot fly to catch up to the Titans, but my glowing swords may catch their attention.

The water trickles through a six-inch deep canyon descending the hillside between tuffets of brush and grass. A hundred yards further along the rim of the valley, the fire scorches an increasing area of underbrush. Without winds to fan the blaze and no firefighters to corral it, the flames will burn freely until they encounter a batch of fuel too wet to consume. In that case, the fire will slow its advance by the time it reaches the bottom of the hillside, since it will have spent all its dry fuel and will run out of energy to sufficiently dry enough moister vegetation.

When I peer down to the valley, I see what they're getting into a moment before it happens.

Creatures of all sizes and shapes pour into the valley out of nowhere. Oceanus rains down a hurricane from above while Prometheus launches fireballs at them. The daemons scatter and multiply from the anger the Titans have created. They stack atop one another in advancing waves, and, with the Titans occupied, I decide to follow the rim of the valley away from the fire and closer to the river. This landscape may or may not offer improved safety in that direction, but I'm in no hurry to battle the daemons again.

My strategy might only last ten minutes before they overwhelm me, but buying time might help me form a contingency plan should the Titans abandon me.

The flying Titans form a wall and bury the landscape below them with buckets of water, glowing balls of fire, and a thunderous rain of stones from the heavens. Instead of panicking, the daemons try to shield one another from the onslaught.

Hundreds of bodies crawl every which way. Half of them may be alive. Their eyes grow dimmer, and their motions suggest a heaviness that might cost them precision. Sharp fangs jut from their sagging lips, reflecting the flames and making them look like fire demons.

Without knowing the full torture they could unleash, I try to stay calm and watch them while I fade away from the vicious battle ensuing below.

Another rain of fireballs and meteoroids crashes to the ground like flaming hail as Oceanus's tempest fills the valley with enough water to cause a flash flood. Indeed, the torrent grows stronger and the rapids fiercer.

My plan will not work. The storm will wash the daemons downstream, and because the hills grow shallower and less pronounced the closer to the river I go, the flood will subside all the faster, allowing the daemons to get back on their feet and crush any living soul with waves of pain so deep they might as well have killed.

Then again, the torture-creatures aren't the only ones lurking here. I can see the eyes locking onto me as I stop dead on an overhanging rock. The waters rise and carry leaves, small plants, and rocks, rushing downstream to join the river.

With them come more of the daemons. Fiery eyes dart out from the undergrowth on the hill's slopes. I'm in it for myself; the Titans might wish to devour the entire landscape and drive away the daemons, but I bet they will leave me to face them alone.

Can I even *use the dark* now?

I attempt to gather all the blackness of emotion I can muster, wrap it into myself, and hope to turn back into a Shade—but even that is of no use. Defending against the onslaught will require the swords.

They scale the hillsides as dozens more climb out of the flowing stream, which is eroding enough soil to create a delta that fans out toward the river. I pull myself in to a crouch and let them climb towards me. Further upstream, the twelve Titans are raining hellfire on the hundreds or thousands of monsters that seek to slow their progressive march through the brush.

Howls emanate all around me as shouting voices command the daemons to step aside. More howls and screams come from upstream. In that direction, I see red being flung in every direction, like ribbons of blood splattering onto the plants' leaves.

They are unleashing hell, but the daemons don't retreat. They have built their armies to outlast the ranks of any advancing party that trespasses their lands. Perhaps millions of them crawl out of the brush to meet their foes in battle, and they are holding their own. Before long, they will overwhelm me. Instead of facing them head on, I choose to follow a rivulet of clay dirt back to the crest of the hill.

If they must burn energy to get at me, I will make them do it.

Before long, those hundreds of evil spirits spread out around me, encircle me, and close in. I narrow my eyes and hack at them with my swords as they pour out of the darkness upon me. Slicing off limbs and severing heads as I go, I manage to dismember a dozen of them before they dogpile on me. The ravenous creatures claw at my stomach, yank my hair, and gnaw at my arms and legs.

Torture swallows me as I cleave one of the smaller creatures in half. In response, it splits into two smaller monsters, grows new arms and legs, and joins the throngs pouncing on me from all sides. I can handle one beast; I electrocuted hundreds earlier, but now that the light within me has been extinguished, I have no mass weapon to ward them off by the thousands.

Despite their exceptional abilities, the Titans are so far failing to stop the daemons from multiplying. The screams and shrieks grow louder as an additional threat emerges on the far hillsides overlooking the valley.

A thousand sinister faces form a line, looking down at the relentless battle. Fire and rocks rain down from the heavens while Theia unleashes torturous judgment on the throngs of attackers. When the new enemy has locked itself into formation, the thousands of attacking creatures below form their own line to fight the army.

Two enormous forces are about to clash. If the new army is here to protect me from harm, I'd consider it a victory, but the way they leer at me suggests they're eager to defeat the daemons before they carry me to my doom.

When the flood waters wash higher, I sense that the new army has no interest in attacking the Titans, and now I know whom they fight for.

They advance down the hillside in legions, devouring the brush as they go. Thousands of dead and living warriors flood into the valley, swim up to the daemons, and attack.

The bodies froth like foam on a boiling cup of soup as they clash. The screams grow louder and more anguished with every second that passes.

With a new ally, the Titans begin to mow down the hordes of creatures still popping out of the vegetation. One titanic fireball incinerates dozens of them behind the lines, and then a meteor that must weigh a couple of tons crushes a dozen more.

The armies are proving efficient at devouring one another. This battle might last forever if majorities on both sides are already dead, but now that I know that the army of the dead is fighting on behalf of the Titans, I can assume they might be on my side. After all, The One has sent them to collect me.

I'll have to battle all of them myself and I might still not survive. Luckily, I know one thing the Titans don't: the legions of the dead fear the river. I'd seen them in action when the gigantic monster carried Ian and me across. They avoided the water.

The problem is that I'm not strong enough to swim upstream, either. Tactically, it might be worth it to admit defeat, but emotionally speaking I cannot.

The darkness that rages within me has a powerful match if I can exploit them both. Persephone, after all, insinuated that I can harness both light and dark, two perpetual enemies that vie for space across the cosmos.

Although light takes energy to create, darkness has a way of absorbing it, and once expended, the dark always wins by outlasting the onslaught.

I furrow my brows, clink my swords together above my head, and join the fray.

A hundred daemons pounce on me as I slash through them with ease; bodies and severed pieces fly in every direction. Ahead, a troop of daemons is dismantling a lobe of the attacking front. A thousand faces with no eyes bare their teeth by letting their skin sag.

When the daemons peel off the skin of their enemies, the enraged force of the dead fights on as skeletons. A million ribcages pile into the battle as the Titans scurry off to who knows where. Now that they have abandoned me, the army of the dead begins to fall back with them. If I can hitch a ride on one of their backs, I might make it out of the fray.

They seek to rob me of the pleasure as the dead forces recede. I jump on the back of a stronger, still-intact corpse and fling my blades in a circle as the dead man climbs the hillside, battling hordes of the daemons as it goes. I cut them down by the hundreds as I ride to the hilltop.

Before I do, the daemons begin to disappear back into the brush from which they'd emerged. Victorious, I dismount from my fleeing ride and fall face-first into a pile of sandy dust.

A white bird lands next to me in the dirt, offers a peaceful nod, and spreads its wings toward me. I'm in the mood to kick at it, but I stare instead as it tries to communicate using a strange avian language I'll never understand.

"Thank you," I say, my gravelly voice wavering.

Its wings flutter.

"I hope you're happy now. I'll have to let Harley know when I see him."

Memory. Although my trials have erased it more than once, it still prevails in unexpected ways. How? When I have a moment to ponder, I might try to devise a few theories on how it works, but I have more pressing matters at hand.

The Titans and the army of the dead scour away and trample the grass as they retreat. They've betrayed me, of course. My condition means nothing to them, and since I have already held up my end of the agreement, they are under no obligation to honor theirs.

I'm alone now, condemned to wander the underworld forever in search of the Six.

Before long, I see Rhea leave the group. She hangs back as if waiting for me to approach. As the pain digs deeper into every part of my body, the swords vanish into a glowing soup of fog that further dissipates as I go.

"You're all cowards!" I shout.

Her gray and white dress flutters as she stands taller.

I scream at her: "Get out of my way or I'll kill you!"

I don't mean it. Even if I wanted to, she has enough power in her pinky to swat me away like a flea. Her gaze doesn't break for the longest time.

Spitting on her toes does nothing. Instead, only a spark of annoyance passes through her voice.

"Find the Six," she advises in a soft tone, "by following the Styx back to its confluence with the Lethe. Cross the Styx, but don't dip your feet into the Lethe. A woman waits there to guide you."

I growl, "You're lying."

"They simply outvoted me," she says.

"How do I know you won't double-cross me again?"

She considers the question as though she doesn't know what to say, then allows a dark frown to cover her expression. Her body language suggests that she already knows the rest of them have made plans to conquer the underworld, and they'll tear the place apart to get their wish. If that's the case, time is everything, and it might take me days to reach the spot Rhea has described.

"You may yet see us again," she admits, "but not as enemies, unless you betray your commitment to Erebus."

"I don't give a damn about Erebus," I roar. "The hell with all of you! I'll gather the Six and we'll beat you all the way back to Tartarus!"

"Do what you will, Kerry, but I'm not your enemy."

"Sure as hell not a friend."

"Perhaps not. I hope you find what you seek—you are a liberator. And a fine one at that."

My jaw hangs open for a split second before I lash at her with all the venom my soul can muster. "What's that supposed to mean?"

She turns away, and as her dress flutters near the ground, her plaited hair waves behind her.

"You'll die screaming! I don't care if Zeus himself destroys you! I'll have popcorn waiting!"

*Zeus is her son, you fool.*

The voice, the Titans, the monsters, and every other evil that lurks here are too much for me to bear, but without the Six I cannot escape. If The One knows about my plan to find them, he doesn't seem all that concerned. Is this part of his plan, too?

Exhausted, I collapse to my knees and sob into the dirt where Rhea was standing. There's nothing left of me but darkness; if I can't find the light, the dark will win, and I'll be stuck in this limbo for an eternity.

And I'll deserve it.

# 32

# Euclidean Sorrow

Distance has never prevented me from doing the things I want or need, yet now that everything I seek lies so far away, I must confront the terrifying reality that I'm alone in this wilderness with no way out. Traveling without food or water, running into whatever creatures await, and dealing with my greatest nightmare stack up to something I cannot overcome.

My failure piles enough weight on my heart that only the darkness can lift it. Now, even that power seems untouchable. How had it proven so easy to tap into in Tartarus? And if nothing has changed within me, why can I not use the darkness now?

When you're a father, the recurring nightmares of losing a child squeeze out tears even when you cannot weep, and ignite fears buried deep within. Waking from them is a hell where you're not sure what is or isn't real, but you can't bear another moment of the resulting dread.

Living without that fear is something no father can do, and even should he successfully suppress the anguish, it shines through in many of his decisions.

My son is trapped in Tartarus as my own victim. His decision before we met will contribute to his fate. Still, going on without him causes tremors of agony to roll through me. I should have seen it coming and acted to prevent that explosion of lightning, but would I have been able to control it without hurting Ian?

This is my reality now; the pain binds itself to me. It can tear me asunder if I let it, and even the prospect of finding Becky and bringing her home cannot lighten the load. Now that the Titans have abandoned me, I must seek the Six on my own.

Rhea has probably sent me on an errand I cannot hope to complete, yet should her information prove correct, enough light is stirring within me somewhere I cannot find that I might yet achieve my goals.

When and if I find the Six, we're going to destroy the other Titans. But if I do that, Erebus might revoke the one promise that has guided me through this hell. Dreaming up ways to stop him from doing that can only lead to failure.

*Come to me.*

He has promised me a reward. Before I can take another step, a plan forms in my mind. I've done what he commanded, and it took everything I had to make it work; he'll reward me, and then I'll double-cross him by confronting the Titans one last time.

A solid plan, but not one that Erebus won't have prepared for. After all, he can both read and control my mind, and my heart dwells in his domain. Like it or not, I'll have to stick with him until I can illuminate the dark.

Where is his lair? I don't know where to look.

"I shall come find you," I stammer, my voice wavering on the edge of tears. "Show me the way."

*Ride the storm.*

A black thundercloud billows over the steppe-covered hills, far away from the river. A single flash of lightning flares, revealing its exponential growth, and within moments it towers so high that it scrapes at the stars.

It slides toward me over the hills faster than I've ever seen a thunderstorm advance. Its wind will lash at me before it reaches me, so I keep my head down to shield my face from the blowing dust as I continue on the path to the poplar trees.

My heart hammers in my chest as I feel it growing nearer, and now I remember what The One had called it.

The Elder Shade. The biggest, most destructive monster ever. And Erebus controls it.

It could take me to see him, but won't it erase me before doing so? The storm's mechanics compare to my own capabilities as a Shade, yet scaled up to mighty proportions with one or two added assets.

Lighting is one of its most powerful tricks. If Erebus can control something so huge that can emit light, his domain of darkness might take on similar qualities.

When the enormous storm cloud sweeps closer, it morphs into a face as it chews up every atom between itself and me. It can consume matter, and experimenting with how it works will have to wait. According to Einstein, all matter has mass, and total energy is proportional to mass. For a moment, I allow my mind to wander. If the gods are free to violate the laws of physics, maybe nothing can stop them—and Erebus is a god, even though he seems to oppose the Olympians.

Finally, the storm sweeps close enough to pelt me with sand, tiny stones, broken pieces of trees and shrubs that swirl in its fierce winds. It hurls them at me like shards of glass shot from a cannon. A small branch whips through the air and slaps my arm, while heavier grains of sand barrel into my skin like tiny spears. Instead of running from it, I stand waiting.

Before long it absorbs me, pulling me thousands of feet up to the thin, stretched anvil top shaped by the prevailing winds. My eyes sting with the sand as my body succumbs to its power. When lightning flashes within, fear sparks in my heart. My body is being eroded piece by piece, taken into the black. It wracks every square inch of my form with immutable pain.

I scream with a raspy chug as icy tears squeeze out of my eyes and then vaporize on contact with the soot cloud.

"Please, don't let it end this way," I scream. "Not now."

Consciousness sways in and out of my perception as the storm cloud whisks me away across the river. When I'm floating high above it, I can somehow see its sparkling waters. This must be possible because I am part of the Elder Shade.

A sensation of falling jars me awake, what feels like hours later. Panic swells within me as I drop, grasping for anything I might cling to, and then I slam onto a hard stone floor with enough force to crack my knees.

For a moment nothing greets me, and then a skeleton standing five stories tall lumbers toward me. I gasp as it reaches down to trap me in its phalanges made of fused human bones.

It picks me up and carries me deeper into the lair, a chamber dark enough to obscure the walls and ceiling in shadow.

A gigantic firepit carves a circular hole in the bedrock somewhere near the chamber's center, and a vat of smoking red coals scatters orange and red light that still can't reach the walls.

"My servant," he growls, taking the form of a man in the darkness. "You have freed the Titans."

"Yeah, thanks for almost killing me. Really appreciate it."

As if the comment has passed him without igniting the intended fury, he continues: "You must be wondering what task you must undertake next."

"You made me a promise."

"A promise indeed. By now, you must know the twelve Titans cannot be stopped; the Olympians erred when they condemned them to Tartarus, but they aren't completely blameless, for they were the ones that spawned the terrorists.

"Yes, I called them terrorists. They believe their awesome powers give them free rein to justify any punishment, no matter the consequences. You've probably heard the epic tales describing their compassion. It's all propaganda meant to deceive the mortals and their slaves.

"See, if they can hold such incredible power, they are unconstrained by the ideals of remorse. Such an excellent design. The best gods are those that don't control everything; they let humans have free will, experience joy, pain, happiness, you name it. But the Olympians are bent on control—they only care about the illusion of freedom.

"The Titans will make them rethink that notion."

"They stabbed me in the back," I protest. "We had a deal. No one down here has any integrity, including you. I won't participate in this war."

"Then you shall watch your world be destroyed."

"The hell I will. *My* world already has been—because of you. You brought me out of my home. It's all you. Don't give me any lessons about justice; with justice, I'd still be a loving husband and father, but now I have nothing because you took it all away!"

"SILENCE!"

"Tell me what you want, now! Tell me I get to bring her home."

"All choices you must make on your own," he argues. "If you want to. That is your reward for freeing the Titans. Your next task is to topple the tower of Hades; the Six will help you do it."

"Because you want control of the underworld."

"Because the underworld is unsustainable with Hades in charge. It will collapse, and all the souls within will cease to exist. All their loved ones left behind, their memories extinguished. And when memory evaporates, the world will collapse into anarchy. Millions will die."

"I don't believe you."

"You know the power they possess."

"So I go blow up the tower, and just like that, I'm free?"

He pauses. "Do you truly desire freedom?"

What kind of question is that? I glower at the suggestion that I'm in search of something I don't even recognize within myself. For an all-powerful god, The One doesn't seem to grasp concrete ideals. That will be his undoing.

"Then you'll give me transport to the Six."

"If you know where to find them," he agrees. "The Elder Shade will guide you there."

"And I'll live to tell the tale?"

He shakes his head and casts his darkened eyes into the shadows. "Live, yes. But you can tell no tales. The architect of Hades has mastered the power of memory."

I allow myself a moment to mull it over ... if I do it for him, he might exert power over me forever despite his promise of freedom. Deceit is an easy feat for the god of darkness. Then again, will he risk the chance that I might deceive *him*?

If I don't do it, he'll destroy the world, after which I'll never see Becky again. But at least I'll be able to watch the destruction unfold with the woman I love.

In such a scenario, what will happen to Ian? Compressing that thought into action will prove difficult. Instead, it only darkens my spirit and extinguishes the spark. Either way, someone is going to die. Millions, perhaps. And could I live with myself if I've condemned the naïve masses to an untimely death? I know myself, and even though The One thinks he does, he ignores the deepest, most intimate part of me. Darkness or none, that trait still shapes my every move.

I'm going to fight him, but I cannot let myself even think about it now. There is no other way.

Instead of striking back with a witty retort, I kneel before him, bow my head, and accept his assignment without words.

I'll worry about the specifics later.

"Good," he croaks, holding out his bony hand to help me up.

In an instant, I'm being pulled away from him, the fire pit, and the cavern itself. Darkness spirals around me and only one thing can keep me going.

As promised, the journey to the Six proves easier than I'd imagined. The Elder Shade draws me into the stratosphere and along the river for what feels like hours. When I arrive at my destination, only one person awaits me. She stands on a solitary rock overlooking the river as if in penitent reflection.

The Elder Shade drops me on the grass next to her, and without turning her head, she speaks to me in a gentle tone: "We've long wondered whether you'd come, Kerry. We need your help."

# 33

# Titan vs Titan

As if a solemn sunrise is about to illuminate the barren landscape with hues of yellow and orange, a warm light scatters on the horizon like an omen of darkness. My bones and muscles ache in every part of my body as the darkness billows within me.

"You ... you need *my* help?"

She nods as her thin silver hair flows down her back in a sheath and terminates in a simple curl between her shoulder blades.

Expecting further explanation, I hunch my shoulders and let my chin droop. This position makes her look taller and statelier, yet still charming. So many questions fill my head that I can voice none of them. Instead, I raise my eyebrows and express suspicious meekness. She will have to earn my trust, and I know how to provoke it.

"I can see in your eyes that you have many questions, Kerry. Please come inside."

Trying not to be too obvious, I scan our surroundings for any structure that might constitute a home. No buildings are visible, and only a single divot depression pocks the surface of the steppe land that stretches toward the sunrise. She holds out her hand as if to guide me toward it, and I allow myself to gulp.

In a slow and cautious gait, she steps off the rock and navigates through a twisted maze of sage-like shrubs that are bathed in an eerie blue. The extremities of their branches support a crop of tiny, bitter red berries that look delicious. If they're not poisonous, they could provide a source of sustenance.

Placing her spindly hand on my shoulder, she guides me into a gentle funnel-shaped valley that drains into a jagged pile of volcanic rock. The lower we go, the thicker the vegetation becomes. With more shade, some ecosystems contain microclimates better suited to sustaining diverse walks of life, and this terrain may qualify.

"You do not speak," she says as she rests a white-slippered foot on the jagged rock. "A remarkable achievement for a man who's gone through so much."

Still, my voice cannot make out the words I wish to say. An untold comfort meanders through her company, allowing me to reflect on myself in a more somber manner. The dark still swells down there in the fathomless pit of my heart, yet like the horizon, it leaks a mote of light.

When she places her foot on a peculiar, smoothed outcrop of the lava, the land trembles beneath my feet. A dusty opening emerges amidst the rock and the light illuminates a series of stairs that lead down into the darkness. She clutches my arm as we descend, and once we're bathed in the murk, I can see a faint glow emanating from around a corner ten feet down.

The ache still torches my bones and muscles, and when combined with the cold, subtly intensifies as the cartilage and muscles contract. The woman's dress grazes my thighs like sandpaper against denim as we descend. A lone mop leans against the bedrock wall near the foot of the stairs to mitigate the risk of slippage from any moisture that may drain into the cave or condense from the humid air.

"We have a visitor," she warns her roommates. "The one we've all been hoping to meet."

Arm in arm, she leads me around the corner into a broad chamber subdivided into rows of cubicles via bamboo shoots lashed together into partitions eight feet high. In the larger front room, a series of cuboid boulders forms a semicircle around a firepit ringed with cinder paving stones. Instead of ashes, the pit contains a bed of shiny resin heat stones, which normally indicate a natural gas connection. In the center of the pit rests a single lantern that casts diffuse yellow-orange light throughout the room and angular, opaque shadows behind the partitions.

The remaining five look up at me as though my presence does not surprise them, but instead of making me feel unwelcome, their faces express a dark charm as their cheeks droop.

"We have a stone saved for you," my escort says, motioning me to one of the granite cubes. Eight cubes stand concentric to the circular fire pit five feet away, spaced at four-foot intervals. I choose a seat in the center of the semicircle and rest my painful rump on the rugged surface. The stones carry rough edges, because of possible cutting mistakes; exfoliated sections have sheared off, leaving a rough surface.

The six of them take seats around me. A tall, slender woman takes up my right flank, while a short-haired, muscular man with a manicured beard rests at my other shoulder.

"You know who we are, Kerry," my escort says. "Perhaps we should introduce ourselves."

Introductions are a painful necessity of any first meeting; on jobsites, they take on a bleak formality where amiable personalities blossom, leaving you worrying about how to describe yourself. To save yourself the trauma and embarrassment of sharing anything too personal, you offer specifics only, somehow making yourself appear boring, at least in your perception. Then again, they already know my name, so I doubt I'll need to introduce myself.

"Remos," a man at the end of the semicircle says. "Titan of air and electricity."

"I'm sorry," I interrupt, grimacing. "You were all born on Crete, I presume. Which means you're familiar with King Minos."

"We are," my escort says. "We do not descend from the twelve original Titans, yet we come from a period two hundred years after their reign, when it became imperative to establish an order on Crete."

"I met him," I say, as vivid memories of Vanessa vanishing into the veil occupy my mind. "And the Minotaur."

She nods. "His daughter Ariadne gave you a special gift. She wouldn't do that for just anyone; she knew you were special. One of us."

"Persephone told me I'm of both light and shadow. Like she could read the deepest parts of me."

"Her gift was energy and light," she explains, "to complement your inner dark."

"Which has become weaponized somehow," I add.

"I am Ichthus," a man introduces himself to cut off my introduction. "Summoner of avians and harpies."

"My brother," my escort says. "I am Sherina. Titaness of water and desire."

"And I'm Alisha, the embodiment of virtue and grace," the woman on the end says, her timbre echoing a simple air of nobility.

"They call me Maximus the elevator of souls," the next man intones. His long, sleek hair is gathered into a loose ponytail near the nape of his neck. He wears a somber expression and looks upon me as if with mistrust.

Next to him, a radiant woman about my height with opalescent eyes and flaring hips speaks out. "I am a sister of Phaethon, one of the Heliades. You carry the tears of my sisters with you."

"You're Merope," I say, my mouth agape. "Lady of the Six."

"And you are a descendant of mine. It is time we formally induct you into the group as a Titan, Kerry, conveyor of light and shade."

"You got some kind of sacred chant?"

"It is done," she says. "You are the seventh Titan of Crete."

"Great," I say, not wanting to appear too eager. Staying and enjoying conversation with them might be polite, but I have a mountain of tasks I must complete, and the sooner I carry them out the better. "So what do you need my help with?"

"The original Titans," Merope says, "are free. You don't know the powers they possess. We must stop them before they conquer the entire universe."

"Actually, I do know what powers they possess. I'm sorta the one that set them free—sorry, but not sorry."

"*You* did it?" A faint air of incredulousness graces Maximus's voice.

"I'm sure you guys have a big problem with the Titans. I'm here for another reason, and I need help with two things."

"What do you need?"

"First, we need to destroy the tower of Hades. Then I must find a woman named Rebecca, who is my wife."

"We will not destroy the tower of Hades," she says. "It is a beacon."

"It makes the underworld unstable," I argue, the darkness permeating my spirit. "It must fall, or all of humanity will suffer."

"Where did you learn of this, Kerry?"

"The other thing you should know about me, for now at least," I begin, "is that I serve The One True God of Darkness. I made a deal with him. I'll never see Becky again unless I carry out the tasks he assigns—that is why I released the Titans."

"We expected you to help us to defeat them!" Ichthus shouts.

"After we destroy the tower, I'll consider that."

The six of them say nothing and pair off to peer into each other's eyes. This continues for at least ten precarious minutes, which makes it seem like they are performing telepathy.

When finished, they looked at me one by one and let their gazes stretch.

"Very well," Merope says. "If we help you with that, you will help us corral the Originals. After that, we will make you immortal."

I gulp. "I don't want to be immortal. No offense, but that idea sucks."

Not expecting them to understand modern American slang, I gaze at them as they seem to question my choice of words.

"Plus, if my wife is mortal, then I will be mortal. I am committed to her for eternity. I assume there's room for that in your—*our*—culture."

"Few accept the idea of eternity," Merope ponders. "Especially those subscribing to modern religion. But most religions build it in."

"Look, we don't have any time to lose," I interrupt her. "The twelve won't wait around to start a war with the Olympians."

Together, they rise from their stone cubes, disappear into their cubicles, and dress for battle. I wait for them for no more than ten minutes.

The men emerge first, clad in detailed stripes of warpaint highlighting their shoulder blades, eyebrows, and jaws. They wear a kind of half-tunic that is hemmed in frayed edges near their knees.

A few moments later, the women enter the main room, having donned tank tops and knee-length skirts. They have collected their hair into tight buns pinned to the backs of their heads via hooked sticks that look like modified knitting instruments.

"Ready to go to war," Merope says. "For the future of humanity."

They ascend the steps in single file, retrieve their weapons from an obscure cabinet I missed on the way down into their hideout, and gather in a huddle within the depression.

Time ticks away as they approach the river, pull a handmade raft from the underbrush, and board it. The vessel is large enough to hold the seven of us while allowing water to slosh on the surface as our collective weight displaces more water than the craft supports.

They row us to the opposite shore, where the tower stands in the distance.

The journey takes us several hours, during which the six of them regale me with stories from centuries past. I take it all in as a rapt student, even as my heart rate pushes into overdrive.

Once we make it close enough to the tower to admire its details, I realize we are not alone. The tower occupies a widening plain flanked by jagged mountain ranges so far in the distance that they only make black silhouettes under the dark sky. The sunrise still beckons far behind us, making me think it is permanent.

A group of warriors has assembled to defend the tower, while twelve figures are conferencing a quarter of a mile away. We'll need a strategy if we wish to prevail. The Lady of the Six, the tactician of the group, goes over the specifics while I admire the building that stands over a thousand feet tall.

A series of tiers twenty to thirty feet high comprise the tower's face, and atop each tier, turrets and battlements ring its rough-edged perimeter. The spires supporting each section are molded into stalagmites that create a honeycomb of caverns within each tier of the structure. These supports flank notches in the otherwise sheer walls where fires burn, and as each successive tier culminates in a flat top, the fires glow brighter, illuminating a staircase with no rails that spirals up the tiers, dodging the stalagmite supports as it ascends.

The tip of the tower burns with a blue and yellow flame that dances like a beacon for travelers that might journey within twenty miles of it.

The warriors, knowing they enjoy a numerical advantage, form squared-off regiments to confront the dueling threats. In this scenario, we must ally with the twelve original Titans, who have made it their duty to topple the tower and take the reins of the underworld. To do that, they must defeat Hades himself.

My specific directive is to destroy the tower; The One said nothing about defeating Hades, and I will follow his instructions to the letter.

"They're forming defenses," Merope says, glancing toward the groups of soldiers. "We'll split them into smaller groups. Ichthus, you will take the right flank, Alisha and Sherina, you will break off about a hundred soldiers each, and leave plenty of distance between you so that the groups can't reform as one. Maximus, you will go left, and I will take a hundred in the middle. That should leave Kerry enough room to make his attack on the tower. Any questions?"

"Just one," I say. "I don't have any idea how to break down the tower. I have these powers, great, but I don't know how to focus them."

"A slight problem," she says, "but not altogether unexpected. You will need to reach out with both of them."

"It's like my emotions have something to do with it, but right now the shadow dominates over me."

"Think about your most powerful emotions," she says. "Reach out. Let their threads tangle with your soul and spirit."

"Theoretically, I have enough energy to crush all their forces. And it's not like the original twelve won't help."

*USE THEM!*

Suddenly, I know what I must do.

Merope directs her forces to carry out her orders to the letter, and when they depart to take on the forces of Hades, I stand back to marvel at the tower's edifice.

Prometheus strikes first with one huge fireball that shoots out a tail of red flame as it flies toward the enemy. To join in the assault, Cronos summons a bombardment of space rocks that tumble into the scattered forces, crushing a dozen of them.

Oceanus and Sherina combine to create a tidal wave out of nothing. It speeds toward the unprepared troops, but not before they launch a salvo of flaming boulders from trebuchets mounted high on the lower tiers of the tower. The rocks fling outward in every direction like volcanic bombs but are too few to inflict any real damage.

Having failed to gain the upper hand in this way, the archers unleash waves of arrows, which Remos deflects by causing what seems to be a ripple of pressure in the air that radiates outward like an explosion's shockwave. The arrows fall harmlessly to the ground while the tsunami washes away hundreds of soldiers at the foot of the tower.

I can see Mnemosyne attempting to confuse them with her power of memory, while Theia and Tethys roll boulders together that erect themselves into gargantuan constructs. The boulder creatures lumber toward the tower; they are tall enough to snatch the trebuchets from the ramparts on the bottom tier, and when they do, they smash at the structure with the raw power of their weight.

The Titans unleash huge attacks that scatter the forces of Hades, while Remos flashes arcs of lightning at the fleeing forces.

Abandoning my plan to harness the light, I dig deep into the darkness, conjuring up memories of the beasts I've slain, the blackened, haunting memory of Ian's defeated body, and every heartbreak I've ever endured.

Seeing the welded washers next to Becky's bony, outstretched hand ignites me with an explosion of dark energy. And as Remos attacks the soldiers with lightning and pressure waves in the air, an idea clarifies.

Instead of using the power of the twelve original Titans, I must harness the electricity by drawing it in, and, like a slingshot of energy, redirect it at the tower itself.

The result is eye-popping.

Remos's lighting punctures my abdomen as my heart draws it in, darkens it, and concocts a destructive pressure wave powerful enough to demolish the tower. When he sends out a second pressure wave, it synchronizes with my outburst, and a Dyson-sphere ball of lighting rolls over the surface, electrocuting the remainder of the enemy forces and then smashing into the side of the tower.

As the pressure batters it, the tower begins to lean, and one by one the stalagmite supports crumble with the onslaught. The tower teeters even as Cronos hurls ever larger space rocks at it. I fall to the ground as the energy drains out of me. The Six rush out, away from the leaning tower, and hurl themselves to the ground as they watch the spectacle unfold. Falling into earthy boulders, the giant rock monsters tumble as the structure deteriorates.

The fires flare as the building gives way. Once the bottom tier has failed, the second crumbles, and then the third, and so on to the very tip of the pinnacle. The vertex fire bursts into a smoky explosion as the battling forces close in from all sides.

With a thunderous roar that rolls across the plain, I watch the shambles as the ramparts fall into a pile of debris a hundred feet high.

The Titans look pleased with themselves. They laugh and celebrate their victory, even as hundreds of Spartans converge on them. Avoiding the Six because of their sheer edge in numbers, the Spartan army marches into battle with the twelve.

Analyzing their behavior, I deduce that they will first attack the larger threat before turning their weapons on us.

The Six join in the fray by launching volleys of arrows, lightning attacks, and pressure waves their way.

When I'm ready, I feel the energy in my heart begin to crest.

"ATTACK THE TITANS!" I scream.

A million birds flock in from a cloud of blackness in the distance, and that legion of flying warriors responds to the birdlike vocal outbursts of their hybrid commanders, a group of muscular men and women blessed with huge wings that allow them to soar. Harpies.

When Mnemosyne and Tethys combine their powers to focus on the heavens, the birds break ranks. Remos, as though attempting to shield the birds, refrains from propelling pressure waves through the air, but the Titans will make handy grounding mechanisms for the lighting.

Prometheus seems to have expected this and sends up a mushroom of fire to divert our attack. The smoke absorbs the lightning and scatters it, preserving the birds.

The avians bombard the Spartans with rocks while their Harpy commanders loose poison-tipped arrows.

Cronus has gone power-mad and hurls asteroids and other space debris at the birds, who dodge the detritus, allowing the rocks to smash down on the advancing Spartan forces. I attempt to gather energy in my soul along with the darkness, but when Remos readies another shot of lighting, I falter.

A shard of flame rips through Sherina like she isn't there, and she collapses into a puff of steam and lies still. Prometheus roars with laughter and unloads another series of fireballs their way.

Theia and Oceanus combine to bring justice to Alisha and Maximus. The wave misses Alisha, but hits Maximus square in the chest as he leaps to avoid it. Blood pours from a fresh wound as the attack hammers Maximus directly. A moment later, he falls face-first into the grass.

The twelve original Titans are ripping through us, and we don't stand a chance. Oceanus unleashes a wave that means to knock out the rest of us, which Merope manages to deflect at the last second by creating what seems to be a flashing force field.

The remaining four Cretans try to reform their ranks while Cronus destroys all the birds with a supermassive asteroid he's pulled from the sky. The thud creates a light thunder when it hits the ground, sending a shockwave of super-heated dust in every direction. Still lying on the ground, unable to move, I avoid the worst of it, but Alisha mistimes it and it rips her apart and consumes her in fire.

Merope gathers more energy to stop the attack and creates another force field to protect Ichthus and Remos.

Ichthus creates a surge of wind to counteract the advance of the crater debris, and joined with Merope's force field, succeeds at stopping it.

But when Prometheus sets the debris alight, the fire spreads as though propelled by jet fuel. The inferno grows higher and hotter the longer he holds it, and when Ichthus lets go, the fire burns him to cinders.

With only Merope and Remos left, we cannot hope to match their firepower. I scrape myself up off the ground and begin to gather dark energy. All I need is Remos to provide one spark.

As he does so, Oceanus and Tethys launch a blindsiding wall of water and smoke at us. The lightning shoots out of his fingers as the water swirls him into a vortex that swallows him whole. The lighting boils the water, vaults skyward, and burrows into my heart, where my spirit darkens it.

It only takes one simple arrow from the last Spartan to defeat Merope—the arrow pierces her heart as she looks to me, the last Cretan Titan. And when the power within me explodes into an advancing cloud of coal dust, lighting, and rage, I fall to my knees in defeat.

Victorious at last, the twelve Titans scatter in the distance to make way for their next conquest.

Scraping myself across the matted grass to meet Merope, I gaze into her soulful eyes as the fire vanishes from her gaze.

"You are ... the last of us," she says, squeezing out a single tear. "Carry on the legacy, Kerry, Titan ... Titan of light and shade."

She passes away, and the darkness invades my heart. I have carried out Erebus's orders, and suffered defeat to the Titans, but I live on as the seventh and final Titan of Crete.

A gentle understanding prods at my soul and I gaze into the distance, beyond where the tower once stood. The verdant green is inviting to me, and suddenly I know how to find her.

# 34

# Elysian Fields

Of all the pain a human being can experience, perhaps the cruelest is that of grief. Like a vat of acid, it bores holes into your heart and removes parts of your soul you never realized you had. When that trauma unfolds, it leaves you breathless and praying for a release you already know will never come.

I know pain. Even reducing my life to the past several weeks, I've endured more than I can take.

Limping across the now-deserted wasteland to that verdant realm that holds promise and light, I let the agony warp my sense of self. There isn't a part of me that doesn't hurt. I'm dragging myself away from the battle scene; when rage joins in the torture, catharsis promises relief but rarely ever helps.

Because of the pain, I make slower progress than I'd like to. Each time I peel my eyes from the grassland, the green lingers on the horizon, but stays at arm's length. As a child, I remember relaxing in the backseat during a long journey and following the moon with my eyes. No matter which direction I'd turn or how fast we traveled, it was always there to taunt me, and I could never catch it. The green kingdom seems to work the same way.

Ignoring all else, even the betrayal of the Titans, I press on. As I grow nearer, the brush thickens. Where a grass prairie dominated the terrain in the valley, now a low-lying steppe wasteland replaces it. The ageless underbrush grazes at my knees as I navigate the clearest path. Closer in still, the brush is tinted green, as though the only water afforded it lies in the green world and the communal fungus and root systems under the soil distribute it outward like alms for the poor.

What amounts to hours later, I gaze into the distance. At the foot of a shallow hill, a wrought-iron fence plated in pure gold marks the boundary between the worlds. I trudge onward until I've descended the slope.

As if that next world has its own sun and climate, daylight drives the greens deeper. Forests thicker than those in rural Pennsylvania stud a grassland, and meandering through it runs a road paved in cobblestone.

For me, the stone presents a tripping hazard, if I can make it past the fence without sustaining further injury. When I reach it, I stroke the cool, golden, vertical bars with my fingers and yearning fills my soul.

A series of twisted square vertical uprights spaced a few inches apart make up the fence. Stretching as far as I can see, a plain square footer spans behind the bars, paralleled by a mid-member and a header. The spear-tipped bars point skyward in exaltation.

The centerpiece of the fence, at what appears to be an opening behind which the road begins, features an ornate gilded carving of leaves and twigs beneath a golden sun, whose graphic waves spread in all directions. A face appears within the sun, depicting the sun god Helios.

As I work my way toward the welcome gate, I see no one to greet me. Yet, when I attempt to push it open, someone does meet me. He grows a long crop of curled, silvery hair as he materializes out of the canopy. A matching beard ruffles his chin and frames an empathetic jaw. Scanning me, his expression morphs into one of pity.

"I can see you've endured much, traveler. What brings you to our sanctuary?"

An obvious question without an obvious answer. I hesitate; souls worthy of this estate probably enjoy their own gate beyond the veil, where Minos and the other judges whisk souls to their final destinations.

"I'm looking to—I *need* to see Rebecca. My wife."

"I cannot let you in," he says slowly. "The blood of Tartarus stains you."

I suppress a groan. "I traveled through there and pulled off an escape no one ever has. I've battled a million creatures meant to destroy me, and now you're telling me that the last leg of my journey is one I can't make? And I thought you guys were all about justice."

He offers me a patient gaze. "What is your wife's full name? I shall see if she is on the record."

"Susanne Rebecca Gearhardt, nee Freeman. Becky."

He hesitates and turns away from me.

"Would it help if I show you this?"

He turns back and watches as I pull the tiny rings of welded steel out of my pocket and rest them in my palm.

"I made it for her. The two rings represent two eternal souls. Together, they form the infinity symbol through a bond that can never be broken."

"You've brought a material possession into the underworld? That shouldn't be possible."

"Maybe it's different when it really means something to you, like this does."

"Well..."

"Please, let me see her. Just once, even for a moment."

Stroking his beard, he lets his voice's pitch go higher. "When you passed away—"

"I never did."

"But she did, did she not?"

"Does it matter? We're made for each other. There's no paradise if that kingdom of promise rips away the things that matter most to us in the name of purity."

"You're questioning the very nature—"

"Let me pass."

"And without revealing your true intentions—"

"Please."

He seems to grow weary of my begging. For a long time, he stands behind the gate, searching the vacuum for something he might never find. When he tilts his head to the right and strokes his beard, I can tell he's going to relent.

After a long sigh, he pulls open the gate, takes me by the hand, and leads me into the green. "Don't make me regret this," he says. "I'm breaking the rules."

"Are there a lot of rules in the freest place in the universe?"

He chuckles. "You might say we're the freest place *because* of those rules. Everyone respects them. Break too many rules, and you won't even find the gate."

"I guess that means," I say, playing along, "that despite my adventures in Tartarus, I've been good enough."

"Good enough doesn't get you here, Mr. Gearhardt. *Great* does."

While a sideways complement would usually make me feel dizzy and sheepish, I choose to let it go this time.

This man wants to riff on the meaning of life, death, and all things eternal in between. I only manage a few nods and "yeahs" along the way, interspersed with one or two vocal agreements.

After a while, his voice turns into a high-pitched droning, and I'm able to zone it out.

The road turns through stands of dense deciduous trees, draped with fuzzy tapestries of moss. Peering up into the canopy does little to shield me from the sun. Instead, the light pokes through in rough hexagonal shapes, where, despite the close quarters, the trees have agreed to not invade one another's growing space. The dark-green, large-leaved underlayer stretches through it like a carpet, to catch the scant light in a more efficient manner. After about a mile of forest, the trees thin out, revealing a bona fide city.

Many small, large, and medium-sized houses, constructed from local materials, tell their own tales, and no two of them are identical. The cobblestone streets, worn flat to allow for smoother travel, zigzag through the dense houses in a maze unlike any I've ever seen, and where they intersect, local merchants have set up trading stalls where the city people gather to socialize and trade goods.

I watch as a thousand smiling faces grace each other with kind greetings, passionate conversation, and good-natured jokes.

The city streets grow lush green grasses through the cracks and at the shoulders, while a few of the houses sport tall trees at the front windows for shade. A pair of laughing children chase one another along a wide avenue, and an old man shouts at them from a second-story window.

Marveling at it all makes my heart hurt. Such an energetic and kind-hearted city, filled with thousands of wonderful people, deserves all the upkeep it can get, and as if its greatness is a product of the people, removing the greatest one of all might have a negative effect. Will Becky even want to leave it behind for one more chance with me?

A young woman with a thin cloth binding her hair and wearing a colorful dress greets my escort, telling him good morning and offering him a giant fruit, which he declines.

After a while, I gain the courage to ask where he's taking me, and when we reach a taller building flanked with expansive grass and playgrounds, he releases my hand and points at the structure.

"Goodfield School," he introduces it. "One of the finest there is, home of the best and brightest."

"You have schools? I would think everyone here knows everything already."

"A common misconception," he counters. "When a person dies, he or she only knows what they learned in life. And since a lifelong pursuit of learning and knowledge is a passion more than a chore, of course we have schools. From infants to graduates, virtually everyone participates."

"What happens if the subject you wish to study contradicts peace, tranquility, or glorifies violence? Say, if I'm interested in how nuclear bombs work..."

"Are you?"

"Well..."

"One can learn the how and why without ever wishing to use that awful power. It's one of the greatest aspects of wisdom. I believe your wife is a teacher here."

"She.... Oh my God, thank you!"

I shake his hand and jog toward the building. When a bell rings, students pour out of a backdoor and stream toward the playgrounds. When I see a woman standing next to the door with her hair pulled into a plaited ponytail, my heart flutters in my chest.

It's her.

Breaking into a run, I sidestep a child sprinting to a merry-go-round, hurry through a chalk-outlined hopscotch, and barrel toward the decorative stone steps.

She glowers at me from afar and raises her voice to warn me to stop running. But when she recognizes my face, scarred and dirty as it is, her heart seems to melt. I fling myself into her arms as tears stream down my cheeks. Reunited at last, all the accumulated pain fades away. I'm complete and whole.

She kisses me, rests her head on my shoulders, cries, and laughs all at the same time.

"Kerry, it's you. It's really you."

"Got a few stories I can tell, but maybe later. Now we have to go home."

She sobs and holds me, clasping her fingers together behind my back. "Kerry, we *are* home."

"I mean Harrisburg," I say, wiping the tears from my eyes.

"Ker?"

"We're going back home so we can be together forever."

She sniffs, as though her heart has broken all over again. "Why ... why can't you stay here?"

I frown, a reflexive reaction I can't control. I hope it will take the edge away from what I'm going to explain to her. "Because I don't belong here. I'm ... I'm alive. And—oh God. I left him. I left Ian. In Tartarus."

"Kerry? Ian's still alive."

"What?"

"Don't you understand? He was entering college when I set out to find you. And that's when—I don't remember how it all happened. Philadelphia was so different, it was like anarchy. I heard you were there. And I wanted to give you—"

"This," I say, holding out the washers.

Tears pour down her cheeks. "You found it. And that means you found ... me."

"Now I'm here to save you."

"I've already been saved, Ker. I want to be with you here, not in Harrisburg."

"But I ... I can't stay. Come with me, please."

My heart sputters as the tears soak my face. She pulls me in tighter and whispers into my ear: "Just promise me you'll never leave again."

“I … I didn’t leave. I got pulled away. Ian, he said I remembered something earlier that night. I dismissed it as his artistic style, even though he insisted it was real.”

“I remember that,” she says. “A week or so after you … you were pulled away…. He was talking about it. Says he thinks you went back to battle the monsters. You know him.”

“I’m afraid it’s true—all of it. Even the monsters. The problem is that … I shouldn’t tell you the rest. It’s too horrible.”

“Tell me.”

“No,” I sniff. “We have to get you home before anything else happens. After that, I can come back and find him. So we can all be together.”

Emitting a warm sigh, she pulls me closer, hugging me so tight that I may faint. Now I know where to begin; my heart melts as I give in to the sweet sense of peace that permeates the city of Elysium.

And I begin to glow from her warmth.

# 35

# Gaia's Earth

From the edge of the schoolyard, two hundred yards away, the gatekeeper watches us with furrowed eyebrows. I expected him to leave after having reunited us, but his continuing presence gives me an anxiety that I'm not prepared for.

No doubt another rule that everyone respects, his next task might cause me more trauma than I know how to deal with.

The pain in my legs having evaporated, I descend the concrete steps while leading Becky by the hand. Her blue and white chevron dress gathers the sunlight and reflects it in every direction, making her appear to glow. When I remember the last time I saw her in this dress, I choke up. The day I met her at that party all those years ago, and when she approached me I considered her the most gorgeous woman on the planet. Later on, dating her felt as though I'd stolen something, from an unnamed someone whose sole quest would be to get her back. I was either the luckiest man alive or some kind of criminal.

And now, accomplishing my goal might feel the same way.

Hand in hand, we stroll back to the gatekeeper, who has taken a keen interest in two children climbing on the playground. When one of them glances his way, he reflects a warm, genuine smile and then retrains his gaze on us. Farther away, the canopy of the trees hosts a rich tapestry of wildlife.

The upper branches are awash with the song of birds of various species, and what even sounds like monkeys. The way the city blends in with the forest is something I've only ever seen in those AI images of future cities in China where the architecturally interesting towers grow their own forests.

Each building carries a distinctive style, and although most seem to be residential buildings, a few business high-rises poke up into the canopy in the distance.

"Hello, Mr. Coromas." Becky greets the gatekeeper with a comfortable smile parting her lips. She wipes away some of the tears on instinct, and somehow it makes her glow brighter.

"How are the children today?"

She utters a laugh. "A little unruly, but nothing out of the ordinary."

Unruly? Everyone here is so perfect, and children can be unruly? The *rules* in this city make no sense, but everything is glorious. I won't be able to describe this place with enough words to make it sound realistic in the future, no matter how complete my memory.

"We've got to get going," I interrupt them.

"Get going where?"

Mr. Coromas looks somewhat agitated, though he masks it with a curious little grin. Does unspoken deceit not violate the rules?

"I'm taking her home," I say.

"She lives not far away," he agrees. "Shall I escort you?"

"No. Go back and guard the gate. You do a great job, and the rules will be offended if you're not there to catch anyone trying to break in."

He laughs. "No one can break in."

"If someone wants to bad enough," I say, "they'll find a way to penetrate the fence."

"You don't quite understand," he argues. "I'm a greeter. The fence cannot be penetrated. We have set many defenses in place, so anyone not deserving to visit here will ever find it. And if they get here accidentally, like I assumed you did, the border deters that person by altering his or her emotions."

"Wow, thanks for the compliment. Becky and I have some catching up to do and we'd prefer privacy."

He nods and grins. "I see. Thank you for the gesture, Mr. Gearhardt. Susanne, always a pleasure."

He turns to stroll away and approaches a woman loading a wheeled cart with vegetables.

"Susanne? He thinks he's on a first name basis, when he doesn't use your real first name."

"Susanne is my real first name. You know that."

"But every acquaintance of yours I've ever met calls you Becky."

She grasps my hand tighter. "Does it matter what they call me anymore? Maybe I found it odd too, but everyone here is so peaceful. I don't think I'm ready to leave it all behind."

Blindsided by her honesty, I grip her hand tighter and react to her movement along the cobblestone street fronting the school. It doglegs left into a dense neighborhood, where the houses abut the street with only a two-foot-wide strip of grass separating the building veneers from the stone avenue. An English Tudor-style home borders a typical German residence across the street from a two-story ranch style home with stucco arches, red mission roof tiles, and within its walls, a courtyard grows two tall fan palms.

My steps become shorter and more labored as I glance down at the smoothed stone beneath my feet. She's so good at deciphering body language that she'll already know what I'm thinking before I ascribe words to it.

"I battled monsters, daemons, and Titans to find you. At several points, I even forgot what I was doing, but there was always something that guided me. Now I know. No matter what, I was going to bring you home. Because I've always known that our dimensions are intertwined."

She lists sideways and tries to perch a false smile on her lips. One of her tells when confused, and I've learned to impart understanding with only a few words.

"We've done this before. Interdimensional time travel has a few laws governing how it works, and one of them stipulates that any dimension you travel to is yours alone. Unless they become intertwined, which always happens when two people share a complex relationship."

"I see."

"You don't believe me? Even here?"

She smiles and pulls me into her hip. "I've always believed you. Even when you're being *you*, I know the *real* you."

Ouch. Half the world's men might run for the exit when confronted with a riddle like that, and although I may be the only man who understands what she means, it still hurts.

Trying not to show indignation, I playfully shove her away from me, pull her back by her hand, and plant a passionate kiss on her lips.

"Monsters? What kind?"

"The kind from your worst nightmares, including four-foot spiders, a twenty-foot-tall medusa-woman who can turn you to stone, and my favorite, the loving bride of Typhon. I'd love to tell you all about it, but first let's get you to Harrisburg."

"I'm not sure about that," she says, lowering her voice. "Don't get me wrong; there was always some anger at you leaving, and it took me years to properly cope with it. But Ian helped me a lot."

Her mentioning him pings my heart like a poisoned needle sewing up a gaping hole.

"A big problem with that," I say. "I'll tell you about it when we get there. I need you. There's nothing else I need in the entire universe. Please."

She smiles. "You're trying to lather me up."

"Always have been good at it."

"Stop," she giggles.

"But this time, I mean it deep down, on an atomic level."

"Still reading about physics, I see."

I summon the courage to smile, which pushes the desperation aside, if only for a few minutes. "Harley's fault."

"Hmm.... Such an interesting man, and you've always spoken highly of him. I'd like to meet him some day."

Laughing somehow feels so natural to me. As though the human within me latches onto the outside world, I choose to let it invigorate me. Some people seek to hide from it, to remain untarnished by the evils it allows, but once you see the humanity in people you can't help but withhold judgement just long enough to understand what makes them tick. And once you realize you share the same world and some of the same experiences, you begin to find common ground where you never believed you could.

"You might feel different after the fact," I joke.

"No one's *that* interesting."

She leads me to a cottage-style home with a comfortable ambiance and surprising curb appeal. The grass grows longer in tufts where the river-rock veneer obscures the concrete foundation. Inset into the front wall behind a half-arch craftsman column, the front door rests in the shadow of a loft overhang with a dormitory window overlooking the street. A young, slender tree provides shade in the minimal yard, where a two-foot-wide cobblestone path meanders toward the stoop. She turns the key in the lock, pushes open the door, and reveals an intimate living space with a nook kitchen, set aside from a spacious living room adorned with shelves featuring various knickknacks. There is a voluminous collection of books, two of which rest on an antique coffee table with ornate carved legs.

"This is the real you," I marvel. "I hope there's room for me, and our son, in the future."

"You could still stay." She seems to be testing me.

"I still have to go back and get Ian, after I bring you home. Then, when we're really done with life, we'll live here forever as a family."

"I have a lot of reservations about that, Ker. What if I'm not ready to challenge God for what he means to happen?"

"You still believe that?"

I step toward her sofa, positioned at the edge of a decorative mosaic-pattern throw rug with tasseled corners resting atop the polished hardwood floor.

"That everything happens for a reason, instead of God letting random things happen to people because of that freedom of choice he gave us all?"

"Freedom of choice is part of the reason," she argues.

"And natural disasters?"

"God allows them, to test the people who live there. And those who watch from afar, in how they give love and support, or a lack thereof."

What's weird to me is how her unquestioning loyalty towards the only religion she's ever known seems contrary to everything I've experienced, yet it all fits in with the broader perspective. If the Greek religion meshes so well with Christianity, then how might Christianity offer similar perspectives to other major world religions? Could every religion be true in equal measure, at least in terms of the specifics?

She looks into my eyes for a long time, presses her body against mine, and closes her eyes. One kiss will do. My heart beats a million miles an hour as she grips the back of my head and lets her tongue pass mine.

Before I know what is happening, she is pulling up my shirt, and when I'm bare-chested, I pull her tight and lead her to the bedroom.

We never make it. Halfway down the hallway, the house twists into a spiral, and as we tumble through the heavens, I whisper her name.

The streets of downtown Philadelphia glitter with the glass of the sleek towers overhead. We stand on a concrete sidewalk next to a small independent bookshop dealing with new and gently used volumes. Once I get a feel for my bearings, I lead her along the sidewalk toward a hotel building near the central business district.

My heart seems to pull me in that direction as we battle the traffic and dodge hurried pedestrians.

She clings to my hand the whole time, and when we enter the lobby and approach the elevator, her posture changes to one suggesting relaxation. Pressing the round light-up button feels so automatic that I only glance at my surroundings. To the left, a cozy restaurant juts off from the main lobby through a well-lit and decorated hallway.

The lobby gives off a sleek, modern charm with simply upholstered furniture interspersed with a diverse array of potted plants, which along with the soft, mosaic carpet and chrome accents lends it a cosmopolitan yet homely appeal.

When the elevator doors open, a couple exits and turns toward the restaurant. Becky inhales with a sleek whisper as we enter, and when the elevator lurches into motion, the intimate confines swirl into space. We are whisked through the stars and emerge in our own hallway.

The house feels so comfortable and serene. When I glance toward the kitchen and living room, her hand pulses in mine. She gives me a tender kiss that I could enjoy forever, but the moment our surroundings materialized, my memory vanished. It's been forever since I occupied this room, and now that I'm here, I recall very little from my long absence.

Just as I remember it, the plush gray sofa sits centered between twin end tables with matching lamps. The coffee table bears about a month's worth of dust, along with a tissue dispenser, a book, the TV remote, and one or two toys.

Why does Becky own toys when we've never had children?

A hand-drawn, colored picture rests behind glass in a frame on the wall, and a pair of marble track segments lie nestled at the tucked edge of the soft carpet. Behind the living room sofa, a half-drunk glass of milk leaves a condensation ring on the polished laminate surface.

Something is wrong. I let go of Becky's hand and extract the washers from my pocket. Opening her palm, I place them on her fingers and gaze deep into her eyes while I lean in to kiss her.

"Stay with me," she whispers. "Please."

"I—"

I can't even finish my reply.

The same whirlwind takes me through space and time, back to the hotel elevator, and no matter how many buttons I press I cannot make it send me back to my dimension.

Gripping the wooden wheelchair railings to relieve my muscles of the tension cannot stop the torment of emotions from overwhelming me. My body shakes as the light-up numbers on the screen count upward as it ascends.

Tears spring to my eyes, and when the elevator finally opens, a maid pushes her cleaning cart into the elevator and nods at me with curious eyes. My heart explodes in a panic as the reality that I may never find home sets in.

I'm in limbo, and somewhere, sometime, love waits for me at the end of a tunnel I cannot traverse.

# Glossary

**Algea**—Daemons, personifications of sorrow; daughters of Eris, the goddess of strife.

**Aphelion**—The point farthest from the Sun in a celestial body's orbit. It is derived from Greek words *apo helio,* meaning away from the Sun

**Arachne**—a skilled weaver who challenged Athena to a weaving contest. She depicted the gods in their amorous adventures in her tapestry, angering Athena. As a result, Athena destroyed her work and transformed her into a spider

**Ariadne**—A Cretan princess, the daughter of King Minos, known for her role in helping Prince Theseus navigate the Labyrinth and defeat the Minotaur

**Asphodel Meadows**—The plain in the underworld where ordinary souls were sent to live after death, inspired by the herbaceous plant Asphodelus

**Circe**—An enchantress and minor goddess. In most accounts, she is described as the daughter of Helios and the ocean nymph Perse

**Danaïdes**—The fifty daughters of Danaus. They were forced to marry the fifty sons of Danaus' twin brother Aegyptus, a mythical king of Egypt. All but one of them killed their husbands on their wedding night. After being sent to Tartarus, they seek to wash away their sins by bathing in a basin that leaks

**Daemons**—Supernatural beings between mortals and gods. They can be either good or malevolent

**Eidolon**—A spirit image of a living or dead person; a Shade or a phantom look-alike in human form

**Elysian Fields**—Also known as Elysium, the paradise where gods and nobles spent an eternity in the afterlife

**The elm from which false dreams cling**—A tree in the underworld near the crossing of the Acheron

**Euclid**—An ancient Greek mathematician, known as the father of geometry

**Hecatoncheires**—"Hundred handed ones," monstrous giants with fifty heads and a hundred arms each, born of the primordial deities Gaia and Uranus

**Heliades**—The seven nymph daughters of the Sun god Helios; sisters of Phaethon. When Phaethon was struck from the sky, they were transformed into poplars to help them cope with their grief

**Lethe**—A daemon, the goddess of forgetfulness, often associated with the river Lethe, one of the five rivers of the underworld, known as the river of forgetfulness

**Orpheus**—A musician, poet, and prophet said to have traveled to the underworld to rescue his lover, Eurydice.

**Ouroboros**—An ancient Greek symbol depicting a serpent eating its own tail representing the eternal cycle of life, death, and rebirth

**Paradox**—Derived from Greek, meaning "contrary" or "beyond belief"

**Phlegethon**—An underworld river of fire encircling Tartarus

**Ptolemy II Philadelphus**—The namesake for Philadelphia; the Greek ruler of Egypt and the son of Cleopatra and Mark Antony

**Sirens**—Creatures with alluring voices that lured sailors to their destruction

**Strix**—A bird of ill omen, often depicted as an owl or bat, that fed on human flesh and blood

**Tartarus**—The underworld abyss; a dungeon of torment and suffering for the wicked

# Acknowledgements

Believe it or not, the bones of this sequel materialized soon after I completed the first draft of Revelation. I had many ideas for digging deeper into the Greek myths, although a few of them didn't make it into Reflection. From the start of this book, I foresaw only two books, but after plotting the final ten chapters, ideas for a third book began to surface. A keen reader will pick up on the bits of foreshadowing what might happen in Book 3, but I can promise that it will be an exciting conclusion.

If you enjoy fantasy, more will be coming, and if you like crime thrillers, you will be excited to learn that a fifth installment to the non-sequential Thousand Branches series is in the works.

For Reflection, more meticulous detail went into researching many of the characters and monsters mentioned. For this reason, I needed to do more research. I have a few sources that I would like to mention. For basics, I searched Wikipedia and cross-referenced sources such as Greekledgendsandmyths.com, Greekmythology.com, and Greekgodsandgoddesses.net to ensure I have done the myths justice. Any conflicts that occurred between sources I bridged by taking bits of both to round out those characters. For example, one source referenced Merope as one of Phaethon's sisters, while another source tells a different story. One source mentions that Cygnus was Phaethon's lover, while others described them as close friends.

As with Revelation, I used creative license for some other characters. You will remember mentions of The Six from Revelation. These characters are my own invention. I needed to give them diverse powers in comparison to those the original twelve Titans possess. I also knew early on that Kerry would descend from them.

I would like to thank all who aided in the creation, editorial, and production of this work. First, the professionals at Atticus.io have been an amazing resource. Their formatting software is second to none, and the beautiful layout you see in this book is a result. All users need specific guidance and troubleshooting tips, and the support staff at Atticus offer prompt and accurate service.

Several beta readers offered indispensable advice, for which I'd like to thank them. Author Bernard K. Finnigan. Audrey Coulombe, Ashley Kolvek, and Nathan Hance have dependable eyes and ears.

Jeanine Henning, who has created all my covers, did an unbelievable job capturing the style of Revelation while introducing fresh ideas. If you are a writer looking for a designer or illustrator, I recommend contacting her.

Tarryn Thomas, who provided editorial service for Revelation, also helped with Reflection. She has a deft ear for voice while seeing many issues that the author cannot. Thank you, Tarryn, for taming the present tense beast!

For the past year, I have had the pleasure of communicating with the staff at many local bookstores. I would like to thank the kind personnel at the Idaho Falls, Idaho, and Boise, Idaho Barnes & Noble locations for hosting events for me. Also, I want to give a shout-out to Winnie and Mo's Bookshop in Idaho Falls, Green Avenue Books in Meridian, Idaho, and Kuna's Book Habit in Kuna, Idaho. Fellow author Brian McBee owns and operates Kuna's Book Habit, and it has been a joy speaking with him.

Last year, the Boise Public Library organized an event for local authors. It was a lot of fun meeting so many readers and writers there. Thank you to the kind staff for organizing that event, and also for placing a beautiful copy of Revelation on your shelves!

Thank you to my family, who have always believed in me, including my daughters for your support.

Finally, I will never forget to mention all you loyal and new readers for embarking on this journey with me. I appreciate your support.

-bm

# About the Author

Brad Mathews bends genre rules by creating dynamic, unorthodox characters thrust into criminal investigations.

He is known to use abstract imagery to construct striking realities that build into suspenseful mystery tales.

Mathews is Certified in Plumbing design, and his extensive Building Information Modeling experience gives him a unique ability to detail mechanical and industrial settings in his novels.

Mathews resides in Boise, Idaho with his family.